DAN
SUGRALINOV

RE-START

*May every new day
in your life
become a Level Up day!*

Dan Sugralinov

LEVEL UP + 1

MAGIC DOME BOOKS

Re-Start
Level Up, Book One
Copyright © Dan Sugralinov 2018
Cover Art © Vladimir Manyukhin 2018
English Translation Copyright ©
Irene and Neil P. Woodhead 2018
Published by Magic Dome Books, 2018
All Rights Reserved
ISBN: 978-80-88295-75-4

ALL BOOKS BY DAN SUGRALINOV:

Level Up LitRPG Series:
Re-Start
Hero
The Final Trial
The Knockout (with Max Lagno)
The Knockout: Update (with Max Lagno)

Disgardium LitRPG series:
Class-A Threat
Apostle of the Sleeping Gods
The Destroying Plague

World 99 LitRPG Series:
Blood of Fate

TABLE OF CONTENTS:

CHAPTER ONE

THE MORNING
IT ALL STARTED

*"Please, there's gotta be something else
I can do. Like mow your lawn every
week for two weeks. I can't do it next
week."*

Homer Simpson, *The Simpsons*

AT FIRST, THE GAME HAD BECOME MY LIFE. And later,
life itself had become a game.

I'd failed at life. By my thirty-plus I had a wife, a
string of one-off freelance gigs, a state-of-the-art
computer, a level 110 rogue character in a popular RPG
game and a beer gut.

I also wrote books. A book, rather. I hadn't
finished it yet.

1

Before, I used to feel flattered whenever someone called me a writer. But over the years, I'd finally forced myself to face the uncomfortable truth: I wasn't a writer at all. The only reason they called me so was because I had no other social tag to describe me by.

So who was I, then? A failed albeit once-promising sales rep who'd been fired from a dozen workplaces? Big deal. These days, everyone and their dog called themselves online marketing gurus.

Me, I couldn't sell anything. In order to promote a product, I had to believe in it. I just couldn't do it knowing the customer had no more need for it than for a garbage can.

I used to sell extra-powerful vacuum cleaners to gullible senior citizens; I'd hawked the latest water filters to big-city geeks who lived on rehydrated foods; I marketed premade websites to wannabe startups who'd mortgaged their homes to open their first businesses. I'd sold online advertisement, package tours, weight loss supplements and vermifuge pills.

I couldn't sell jack. I kept losing job after job after job. I also used to run a blog in my spare time (and admittedly during my work hours as well) where I published short stories to entertain whatever meager readership I could garner. That gave me enough ground to consider myself a decent Internet marketer.

Eventually, I'd even found a job with a company looking for someone to run their online store. Still, my very first meeting with their director had exposed my utter incompetence. He demanded to see their conversion rates, average order value, customer engagement levels, bounce rate, LTV and all the paraphernalia of stats I'd been supposed to present him with.

Apparently, running an online business had more to it than just keeping a witty blog peppered with comments and likes. Did you say trial period? They'd fired me before it had even run out.

Offended to the quick, I decided to finally learn the ropes. I downloaded a whole pile of courses, textbooks and video tutorials and even signed up for a few webinars.

I lasted exactly a week. For the first five days or so, I thoroughly enjoyed my new status. This wasn't going to take long, after all. With my enthusiasm and application, I was going to grasp the science of online marketing in no time.

I already pictured myself as a popular expert with a customers' list to match, someone who could charge top dollar for their knowledge of the market. I would finally buy myself a house and a decent car; I would take frequent vacations and enjoy all the perks of the four-hour workweek lifestyle.

Although admittedly euphoric, I wasn't in a hurry to actually hit the books. Over the course of those five days, my enthusiasm had finally worn thin, leaving me in the same place as before. When finally I forced myself to sit down and actually study, I quickly felt sad and bored. By the end of the second day, I realized I wasn't cut out for this sort of thing.

I spent the next year scraping by on my meager blog advertising income and doing occasional freelance jobs. Yanna, my wife, still had faith in me and my supposed potential — but her patience was already dwindling. Eight years my junior, she was at an age when all her friends were discussing the best shopping and vacation destinations while the best she could do was accompany her blogger husband to an occasional closed movie preview. Anyone can lose faith under these circumstances.

Then again, take Gabriel Garcia Marquez, for instance. His wife had supported him and their children for many a long year while he technically did nothing but eat, make children and write *One Hundred Years of Solitude*. Had her faith in him worn out? Not that I know of.

Now Yanna, she was different. She was younger and child free. Which was probably why these days her voice rang with sarcasm whenever I mentioned my book.

In actual fact, as the months went by, her respect for me seemed to be fading. It showed in lots of little things I'd never paid any attention to at first.

And as far as my book was concerned... you see, there had been a moment when I realized that I would turn thirty pretty soon, with nothing to show for it really. My life was reaching its zenith; very soon it would begin its decline.

I still remember that moment very well. I awoke after the mother of all parties and decided to write a bestseller. With my talent, nothing could have been easier, I thought.

Funnily enough, writing proved rather hard.

Either I'd overestimated the extent of my talent or maybe — just maybe — I hadn't had the said talent to begin with. My brain struggled to produce words which my hands then duly deleted.

It had taken me three months to write the first page, all the while reporting my excellent writing progress in my blog according to which, I was already working on Chapter Twelve. My friends kept offering their services as beta readers. Still, I was pretty sure that even if I'd had something to show them, they wouldn't have stuck with it. The fact remained, I had nothing to show them so I didn't, explaining my decision by my unwillingness to make an unfinished draft public.

When finally I'd completed Chapter Three, I couldn't resist the temptation any longer. I uploaded the whole thing to my blog, looking forward to a dose of comments, likes and other people's opinions.

But before doing so, I asked Yanna to take a look. She refused.

"I want you to finish it first," she said. "Then I'll read it in its entirety. I don't like works in progress, be it a book or a film."

Much later, she would read the completed part of the novel, anyway. By then, she probably didn't believe I'd ever finish the wretched thing.

I didn't post the chapters in my blog though. Instead, I uploaded them to a popular writers' portal under an assumed name.

That night, I went to bed excited. This was similar to how I used to feel as a child the night before going on a fishing trip with Dad, looking forward to a day of happiness, joy and eventual success. I imagined myself getting up in the morning, taking an unhurried shower, shaving and brushing my teeth, making myself a cup of extra strong coffee, lighting a cigarette and finally, opening the page with my first chapter, bursting with the readers' praise and demands to post the rest of the book.

I awoke about lunchtime and hurried to open the computer before even brushing my teeth.

Two page reads. No likes. One comment:

I couldn't finish this, sorry. I don't think writing is for you.

At that particular moment, I decided I was going to finish the damn thing, even if only to piss that person off. I smoked half a packet of cigarettes, then began working on the next chapter.

Only I couldn't. Neither that day nor the next. If the truth were known, I haven't written a single line ever since.

It wasn't just because I couldn't think of anything to write about. I simply couldn't concentrate. I was constantly being distracted by social media notifications, chatroom messages, our cat Boris (more about her later), the cold draft in the room, Yanna, the flies, the boiling kettle, my empty coffee mug, the articles and blog posts I needed to read, feeling sleepy, my favorite TV series coming on in five minutes' time, feeling hungry, a craving for a cigarette, and the uncomfortable stool which I then replaced with an equally uncomfortable easy chair I'd gotten on a sale... You name it, it distracted me from writing.

And that's not even mentioning the Game.

That's right: the Game with a capital G. Because by then, it had long become my life.

It was in the Game that I'd met Yanna. It was there that I'd booked the biggest successes of my life (that's not a joke LOL. I really think so.)

Our clan had even made it to #2 in the rankings. We were literally snowed under with new applications. We could have taken our pick of new players — and that was exactly what we did. We didn't accept all and sundry.

As the clan leader's deputy, I was responsible for lots of things — which put a considerable strain on my time. We used to offer all sorts of in-game services to loaded players, securing a small trickle of income both for the clan and its leadership. Still, if you converted those amounts to real-world money, it was laughable.

Last night, we'd been busy exploring the new updates — which had turned into a non-stop frag fest of wipes and resurrections as we tried to complete the new dungeon. Its boss just didn't want to die. The air in the voice chat was blue with our cussing. We kept wiping time and time again with no progress to show for it — but still we stood our ground and kept trying. Not that it helped us a lot.

For many of us, this *was* life. We were your typical hardcore nerd gamers who did all their socializing, living and achieving in VR.

In the game, your every action is immediately measured and rewarded — or not rewarded, as the case may be — with quite tangible payoffs such as XP points, gold, new achievements, Reputation, and quest awards. That makes your relationship with the game world perfectly square and correct.

Which was probably why I'd eventually become ambitious and motivated in the game but not IRL.

Which was also why we had to complete the new instance that same night before other clans got wind of it.

Only we hadn't.

By the time we'd finally called it a day and disbanded, it was already early morning. I'd only just dosed off clutching the unfinished beer when Yanna got out of bed.

I used to know this guy who liked to point out the difference between the sympathy levels of the early birds and the night owls. The latter seem to be much more tactful with their early-riser friends, tucking them in and asking everyone to keep their voices down after 9 p.m.. The early birds didn't seem to possess the same finesse of character. They loved nothing more than to drag a peacefully sleeping night owl out of bed before midday! Yanna was no exception.

"Hey, time to wake up! Breakfast's ready! You've been playing all night again, haven't you?"

She turned the TV on, opened the windows and began rattling with something in the kitchen.

"Phil Panfilov, damn you! Get up now! I'll be late for work!"

Having breakfast together was one of our rituals. It'd started at a time when we'd spent long sleepless nights together — either playing or making love. When Yanna had finally graduated and found a job, our daily schedules had become pretty incompatible. But still we always had breakfast together.

My mind struggled to blank out the annoying cheerful yapping of a washing powder commercial. I needed to mute the wretched thing before it blew up my brain.

Without opening my eyes, I groped for the remote and put the sound down. I staggered toward the bathroom, turned the tap on, scalded myself, swore, turned the cold tap on, splashed some water on my face, brushed my teeth and looked up in the mirror.

A rather worse-for-wear cross between a goblin and an orc which must have respawned one time too many stared back at me.

I really needed a shave. Maybe. One of these days.

We sat down to breakfast, facing each other at our tiny dining table in the corner. I unenthusiastically munched on my omelet. Yanna drank her coffee while expertly applying her makeup.

I remembered how I'd first met her. I'd been waiting for a raid to begin. Bored, I'd decided to let my phoenix mount stretch its wings for a while. We were flying over Kalimdor when I heard some low-level priestess begging for help in the local chat. Her name was Healiann. Apparently, she was being hurt by some nasty Tartar ganker. Naturally, I had to stop and teach him a lesson. She added me to her friend list. For a couple more months, I used to help her level up. Eventually we got talking in the voice chat. That's when we'd found out we lived in the same city. I invited her to join our clan. It was during one of our clan's drunken IRL meetups that we'd finally met face to face.

"Do you like blondes so much?" Yanna's voice broke the silence.

What was I supposed to say to that? I did like blondes, true. Still, I also liked girls with dark hair as well as redheads and brunettes. Back in college I used to be in love with this girl who'd dyed her hair blue. Later, she'd shaved her head — but it didn't make me love her less.

Yanna was a natural brunette going through a raven-black stage.

"Hair color doesn't really matter to me," I said. "Nor do other girls. You're the only woman I've been in love with for the last, er, four years."

Pretty stilted, I know.

"Yeah, right," Yanna chuckled, apparently not too convinced. "Who's that blonde in your book, then? At least you seem to remember how long we've been together."

I choked on my ham and cheese sandwich. She was right. The main character in my book indeed fell in love with a blonde girl. But he wasn't me, dammit!

I swallowed and cleared my throat. "*I* don't like blondes. The guy in the book does. My main character."

She squinted at me. "What's so main about him?"

Her yet-unmascaraed eye reminded me of Gotham City Two-Face. She rocked her leg nervously until her fluffy slipper went flying across the room. That's just a habit she had.

"Nothing," I said. "He's just a book character. It's just that the book is written in the first-person POV. I find it easier to write this way."

"Liar. You think I can't see it? You're blushing. Look at your hand, it's shaking."

The reason my hand was shaking was because I'd had too many beers the night before. Still, she had a point. I *was* lying.

"Very well, *author*," she invested all her sarcasm into the word, "I must be off now."

The heavy trail of her perfume hit me, arousing and sickly sweet. She gave me a peck on the lips and walked out.

The front door slammed.

I stared at the sandwich in my hand. I wasn't hungry at all. I was sleepy.

I laid my head on my arms and studied the meager expanse of our kitchenette. The place reeked of frugal misery. The tiles above the sink were crumbling. The monotonous sound of the dripping tap was killing me. The broken oven door didn't close anymore. The stove top was caked brown. The low ceiling, rusty gray from all the tobacco smoke, hung gloomily overhead.

The sight made me want to walk out onto the crumpled balcony of our one-bedroom apartment, climb its flaking wooden railings and just sit there dangling my feet in the air. Then just push myself off and jump down.

I got up, leaving the dirty plates on the kitchen table, and walked out onto the balcony.

The bright sunlight hurt my eyes. I squinted and stretched my stiff body, then reached into my pocket for some cigarettes.

The pack was empty. I swore and heaved a sigh. I was past caring. Must have been the nicotine withdrawal that did it to me.

I leant over the railing and stared at the eight-story drop. A deep puddle of rainwater glistened below, its steely surface reflecting a hasty procession of white fluffy clouds above.

The clouds parted momentarily, releasing a bright beam of sunshine.

It blinded me. I felt almost electrocuted.

The view swam before my eyes. My vision failed, then came back — sort of. It was now crowded with lots of little floating specks that looked suspiciously like some kinds of symbols and numbers.

I slumped onto a shaky old stool and wiped my eyes, trying to blink the illusion out of them.

Enough. Time to go and get some cigarettes. And coffee. And once I was back, I really needed to sit down and finish that wretched book.

I kept getting this nagging feeling that once that was out of the way, my problems would be over.

All I needed to do was finish the damn book.

CHAPTER TWO

WTF?

"We can't stop here, this is bat country!"

Hunter S. Thompson, *Fear and Loathing in Las Vegas*

I WALKED GINGERLY, LEAPING OVER THE RAINWATER puddles that lay in my way. My left sneaker was falling apart but I didn't feel like fixing it. I couldn't afford to have it fixed, either. A new pair would have to wait. We had too many bills to pay. The rent, the utilities, the Internet. We had groceries to buy. Me, I'd have bought new sneakers first — but luckily, Yanna had her hands firmly on our purse strings.

Our backyard didn't differ much from the others in our district. A classic Russian disaster of dirt, mud and chipped curbs; a paraphernalia of mismatched windows and glazed flaky balconies; discarded plastic bags caught on tree branches and washing lines;

---

garbage spilling out of industrial-size bins. A couple of winters ago, the council had had to do some emergency repairs on the burst waterworks (another Russian classic) so they'd bored through the frozen tarmac, fixed the leak, then covered everything with a layer of earth which now turned into a swamp every time it rained. Nothing to rest one's eye on, really; the first dainty green of the budding trees was the area's only redeeming feature, holding the long-forgotten schooltime promise of approaching summer vacations.

The dilapidated playground at the center had long become a meeting place for the local drunks. Some of them were my age, their development apparently arrested while still teenagers. Others were youngsters running their errands. They were presided over by Yagoza, a sinewy man of indeterminate age, his skin blue with prison tattoos, wearing shapeless track bottoms and a green Che Gevara T-shirt the size of a tent. He was some sort of a criminal authority around here.

Yagoza was smoking a cigarette and sipping beer from a can.

They looked bored and down on their luck. Even from where I stood, I could see they were desperate for something stronger than beer. Beer was like water to them.

One of them was hanging on the kids' monkey bars, apparently imagining himself a gymnast. Seeing me, he jumped down and rubbed his hands together. "Phil? Hi, man."

The others looked up at me, then returned to

their beers, disinterested.

Not good. I'd had problems with the guy before. Known under the moniker of Alik, he'd once followed me on my way back from the corner shop. At the time, I'd been in a good mood. I'd just received a nice check from a client so I'd done some grocery shopping to celebrate. Alik and I got talking. I gave him a beer. Once I got home, I promptly forgot everything about our encounter.

He hadn't. From then on, every time he saw me he tried to give me a bear hug and cadge a smoke or a beer.

"Hi, man," I replied unenthusiastically.

He walked over to me and shook my hand while lacing his other arm around my shoulders and slapping my back. His hand brushed my jeans' back pockets as if searching me.

My vision blurred again. I peered at his face but it appeared sort of out of focus.

"Jesus. You alright?" he asked matter-of-factly without a trace of compassion.

"Not really. Wait a sec," I eased him away and rubbed my eyes, peering hard at him.

His face came back into focus. His eyes were framed with the thickest, longest eyelashes I'd ever seen. I'd never noticed them before. He must have been a very pretty child before life had had its way with him.

A pockmarked face with oily skin. A broken lopsided nose. Nicotine-yellow teeth. Greasy hair...

And what the hell was that?

I peered at him harder, rubbed my eyes and

peered some more.

Alik startled and looked around him. "Wassup, man? You alright? Tell me! What the f-"

"No, wait," I raised my hand and ran it above his head.

I couldn't feel anything. Still, I could see it!

My breath seized. I couldn't take my eyes off a big inscription in clear green letters hovering over his head.

Romuald "Alik" Zhukov
Age: 28

Romuald? His parents had some sick sense of humor. Had my name been Romuald, I'd have probably turned to the bottle too.

"Is your name Romuald?" I asked.

He startled again. "'xcuse me?"

"Your real name, it's Romuald, right?"

"Well... Yeah but... wait. How do *you* know?"

I didn't reply. My thoughts were racing like a herd of wild horses, trampling everything in sight.

This wasn't real. Couldn't be. A hungover hallucination, maybe. Drinking too much. Playing too much, sleeping too little.

I focused on the inscription which obligingly unraveled like a parchment scroll.

Romuald "Alik" Zhukov
Age: 28
Current status: Unemployed

Social status level: 4
Unclassified
Unmarried
Criminal record: yes

The last line flashed red. I focused on it, hoping to unravel it as well. Didn't work.

"Phil! Wake up, man! Hello!"

The message folded back in, its lone top line still glowing in the air.

"Sorry," I said. "Surprised me, that's all. Romuald is a real rare name, isn't it?"

He shrugged. "Dad's idea. His grandfather was apparently Romuald. Why?"

"Just wondered. Never heard anything like it before."

"I don't think you have," he agreed with a suspicious ease. "Listen... I've got things to do. I'll see you around."

"Sure."

"Spare a smoke?"

"I've run out, man."

He heaved a sigh, then swung round and began to walk back.

"Alik, wait!"

He turned and stuck out a quizzical chin, "What now?"

"How old are you, twenty-eight?"

He nodded and walked off. The inscription continued to hover over his head, growing smaller in size as he moved away until it disappeared completely.

I didn't risk following him even though I was dying to find out whether it might work with the others too. I could kill for a smoke. I crossed the backyard and walked out onto the street.

As I headed for the shop, I kept peering at everything in my way: shop windows, traffic signs, cars and occasional passersby.

Nothing happened.

I'd been working too hard lately, that's all.

But what about his name? I couldn't possibly have known that! Nor his age! I didn't even know the guy!

Still deep in thought, I entered the shop, walked over to the cash register and offered a handful of loose change to the woman, "A packet of Marlboros."

The middle-aged saleswoman — a mutton dressed as lamb — was busy talking on her phone, cradling it between her ear and her shoulder. Without interrupting her conversation, she took my money, counted it, fished for some change and laid it next to the pack on the counter, momentarily locking her gaze with mine.

Holy mama mia! Yes!

With a shaking hand I scooped up the change and the smokes, shoved them in my pocket and barged out.

The moment she'd looked me in the eye, a system message had appeared over her head,

Valentina "Valya" Gashkina
Age: 38

Back in the street, I cussed. That had been really stupid of me. I walked back in and offered her some more money,

"Sorry, Valentina. I forgot to buy a lighter."

"I'll call you back," the woman said into her phone. She peered at me, uncomprehending.

Then she visibly relaxed and reached for a lighter off the shelf. She probably decided that I was one of the local drunks who was on first-name terms with all the liquor vendors.

As she turned her back to me, I scrolled down the message,

Valentina "Valya" Gashkina
Age: 38
Current status: Salesperson
Social status level: 9
Class: Vendor. Level: 3
Widow
Children: Igor, son
Age: 18
Ivan, son
Age: 11
Criminal record: yes

Let's try it again, then. "How are things, Valya? How's Igor and little Ivan?"

At this point it must have dawned on her. She stared at me, lighter still in hand, apparently trying to remember where she might have met me. Unwilling to admit she couldn't remember someone who seemed to know her, she finally replied,

"Igor's fine, thanks. He's finishing his second year at uni. Ivan is nothing like him. He doesn't want to study at all. Igor does his best to knock some sense into him but Ivan just won't listen. He's not been the same since his father died..."

She fell silent, apparently surprised at her own indiscretion. Heaving a sigh, she handed me the lighter. "If you don't mind me asking, how do you know me?"

"We met at some friends once," I mumbled, accepting the lighter, then walked out.

I headed for a small boulevard, unwrapping the cigarettes as I walked. I lobbed the crumpled plastic wrapper into a bin and lit up, drawing in a lungful of smoke.

What kind of criminal record might she have? Dipping into the till, maybe?

I finally reached the first bench and slumped down on it, sprawling my aching legs. I could sense the nicotine course my arteries, reaching my brain.

Something flickered in the corner of my eye. As I squinted at it, a message appeared, growing in size. This time it was about me.

Warning! You've received a minor dose of toxins!
Your Vitality has dropped 0,00018%.
Current Vitality: 69,31882%.

What did they mean, vitality? Was it supposed to be the same as hp?

I finished my cigarette, all the while imagining myself losing 0,00003% vitality with every draw. I didn't enjoy it at all. My ingrained gaming habit had warned me against any behavior that could be classified as DOT or a debuff. I kept smoking purely out of principle.

Wait a sec. How much life did I actually have?

A red bar appeared in the lower left corner of my field of vision. It was 69% full.

Excuse me? Where were my remaining 30-plus percent vitality?

Had I just lost 30% health just by smoking a cigarette? Or was this supposed to be some kind of cumulative effect? What could I have possibly done to-

I knew very well what I'd done. That was all those sleepless nights, junk food, drinking, smoking, not to mention all the environmental problems. A no-brainer, really.

This I could understand.

What I couldn't understand was, WTF was going on?!

CHAPTER THREE

THE FIRST QUEST

"Who are you and why should I care?"

Futurama

CAREFUL AS I'D BEEN, I MUST HAVE GOT A FEW sneakerfuls of rainwater as I'd walked. No system messages this time: apparently, I risked no hypothermia-related debuffs no matter how wet and miserable I felt.

My head swam with thoughts. Was I going mad? Could this be a brain tumor? Or some personality disorder? Should I see a doctor?

Sucking on my third cigarette, I tried to think of an appropriate clinic. Finally I gave up, Googled a list of local practitioners and made an appointment.

That felt a bit better. Having said that... how sure was I that the world around me *was* real? Crazy, I know. But what if there was nothing wrong with me?

Could it be reality itself that was glitching?

The cigarette smoke, the group of drunks hanging around the kids' playground, my own wet feet and a tiny ant crawling up my arm — everything around me was screaming its absolute authenticity.

But how about Amra and Mahan? Those were two of my favorite LitRPG heroes. Didn't they feel the same when they'd found themselves transported — one to the Boundless Realm, the other to Barliona? At first, neither of them had even realized they were in VR, so real was everything around them. So my idea made sense, really.

I could in fact have been abducted by aliens — or some mysterious powerful corporation as the case might be — who must have placed my waning body into a VR capsule and sent me here. Why? No idea. I'd never considered myself special, even when I'd been elected class monitor back in grade school.

Still, I could try and test it, couldn't I? I'd played enough games in my lifetime to be able to tell fact from fiction.

With my right hand, I reached into my pocket for the lighter while holding my left hand in front of me. I placed the lighter under my hand and clicked it a couple of times, casting Fire. Ouch, that hurt!

I lasted only a few seconds. I'd never been one of those masochistic types capable of self-mortification.

A system message appeared out of nowhere, then faded just like some 3D movie picture,

Damage taken: 1 (Fire)

I blew on my scorched hand. Pain was a perfect proof of this world's reality. So was my burned skin. But the system message... it glaringly contradicted both.

Also, what was it supposed to mean? *Damage taken, 1* — one of what? How much hp did I have? Where could I see my stats? What skills did I have? What was my social status? Was it the same as a player's level? And how was I supposed to earn XP here?

I rolled my eyes this way and that, searching for an interface but found none. I couldn't see any icons, buttons or status bars. The health bar was the only thing still hovering in view.

I blinked. The health bar slid up and disappeared.

Wait a sec. I blinked again. Immediately the bar was back, as large as life and twice as ugly, sporting the number 69,31792%. Aha.

I focused on the number. Nothing happened.

I blinked again. Same result.

The number annoyed me. If only I could see the actual amount of my vitality points!

The figure promptly disappeared, replaced by a new stat:

6,238/9,000

What, just like that? All I had to do was think about it?

Never mind. I really needed to look into all of

this. Skills, stats, that sort of thing. But first I needed to work out all those nasty debuffs I apparently had. How was I supposed to bring my life back to the required 9,000?

Then again, that too could wait. Life, XP, all that sort of stuff. First I needed to determine whether this was real life or not.

The moment I thought this, a shadow lay on the tarmac by my feet.

"Excuse me?"

I looked up. An old man in funny-looking clothes and a fedora hat stood before me, staring down at the ground.

My good manners got the better of me. I jumped to my feet. "How can I help you? Would you like to sit down?"

As I spoke I looked over the boulevard. There were plenty of empty benches around as most people were still at work.

"Thank you," the old man uttered in a weak, lispy voice. "That's very kind of you. The reason I would like to speak to you is this. I have trouble walking. Still, I'm supposed to do some walking every day. So I come to this boulevard and I keep trotting up and down the lanes, up and down. Then I'm forced to sit down and read a paper. Because reading fresh newspapers is very benefici-"

He had a very funny, stilted way of speaking. Almost like a book character. I kept nodding my understanding, all the while trying to meet his gaze but he kept averting it, staring at the ground at my feet.

He was wearing light summer loafers, a shabby business jacket patched at the elbows and an enormous pair of baggy jeans reaching to his armpits and secured by a belt with a shiny steel buckle saying *Jamiroquai*, of all things. Which looked suspiciously like an Easter egg courtesy of the mysterious designers of this snazzy NPC character.

I suppressed a giggle. The old gentleman stopped and looked me right in the eye in surprise.

> *Mr. Samuel "The Rat" Panikoff*
> *Age: 83*

ROTFLOL! The *Rat?* I peered closely at him, triggering another dose of information,

> *Current status: Retired*
> *Social status level: 27*
> *Class: Office Worker. Level: 8*
> *Widower.*
> *Children: Natalia, daughter*
> *Age: 54*
> *Grandchildren: Max, grandson*
> *Age: 31*
> *Criminal record: yes*

"Mr. Panikoff? If you don't mind me asking..."

The old man averted his gaze and lisped, "You're lucky this isn't the year 1936, young man. At the time, when strange young men addressed you by name on the street, it could only mean one thing. Which promised nothing good. I was only a small child at the time, of course, but I heard my fair share of all those covert arrest stories. I, in my turn, apologize I can't return your courtesy. I'm absolutely sure I don't know you. I may be old but I have an excellent memory for both names and faces."

Definitely a bot. They had absolute memory, didn't they? Then again, an NPC would have never expressed surprise at my addressing him by name. But this one had. In fact, he appeared clearly uncomfortable.

"Mind if I take a seat?" he asked.

"I'm Philip," I muttered. "But you can call me Phil."

"Very well, Phil," the old gentleman sat down, removed his hat and smoothed out his thinning hair. "So how do you know me? Wait a sec... I had the honor of teaching a course in Marxism in — when was it now? — nineteen... nineteen sixty-"

"Please, sir," I interrupted him. "You really don't know me. It's just that I met Max — he's your grandson, isn't he? His mother Natalia told me a lot about you. I have a lot of respect for you and your achievements."

I meant it. Compared to the alcoholic Alik with his measly level 4 and the presumably thieving saleswoman with her level 9, the old man was level 27! How awesome was that? He must have done some quality leveling in his lifetime.

I'd have loved to have known my own level too. But how was I supposed to do that?

The old man visibly relaxed, apparently happy with my explanation. "Oh, that's nothing. I served my country, that's all. We all did at the time. Not like the young people of today who'd love nothing better than to go and live abroad. My Max too thinks of emigrating! And when I was his age-"

"I agree entirely," I shuffled my feet on the tarmac, lighting up a new cigarette. I needed to use the bathroom really badly. "I'm terribly sorry but I think I need to go now."

"Of course... Phil. Absolutely," he faltered, undecided, then continued. "The reason I approached you is because I have trouble walking. Still, I'm supposed to do some walking every day. So I come to this boulevard and I keep trotting up and down the lanes, up and down..."

Dammit. He *was* an NPC, after all. Even chat bots had more natural speech patterns. I needed to check it.

"Excuse me, sir," I interrupted him. I knew it wasn't polite but if this *was* VR, politeness would have to wait. I needed to work this out. "Who was President of the Soviet Union in 1941?"

He shook his head so hard that I was worried his scrawny neck might snap. "There was no President in 1941 in the USSR! The person who was in control of the country was Comrade Joseph Stalin, General Secretary of the Central Committee of the Communist Party!"

Definitely a bot. And a very primitive one at that. Any other questions I could ask him?

I didn't have the time to conduct a proper Turing test so I decided to adlib. "Mind if I ask you something else?"

"I'm not in a hurry, my dear Phil."

"Is it brandy of vodka?"

"Water. And before that, I only used to drink the best brandy I could get."

"Arsenal or Real Madrid?"

"What nonsense! The best soccer team this side of the Atlantic is Zenith! The finest club in Leningrad — or as you call it these days, St. Petersburg," he enunciated the city's name clearly, then burst into a happy childish laughter.

"Bingo," I muttered.

He *was* real. No NPC was capable of such a quirky train of thought.

The old man stared at me. "Pardon me?"

I beamed back at him. This world was real, after all. Even more, I seemed to be the only one here in possession of a rare and useful ability. I really should help him. "It's all right. I'm sorry I kept interrupting you. What was it you wanted me to do?"

"Just as I said, I have trouble walking. Still, I'm supposed to do some walking every day. So I come to this boulevard and I keep trotting up and down the lanes, up and down..."

What was that now? He'd said this twice already! He was repeating the same lines over and over again, just like a stuck record... or a glitchy script.

"Sorry I'm rambling," he suddenly stopped himself. "I think I told you that already. To cut a long story short, sometimes I get tired so I'm forced to sit down and read a paper. Because reading fresh newspapers is very beneficial for one's mind. Without them, I'd feel dead. What kind of life do you expect an old man like me to have? I read newspapers in order to stay on top of what's going on in the world. I find sports events especially fascinating. Unfortunately, today of all days I forgot to buy the latest issue of *Sports Express* which I always do on my way here. Which also means that I can only buy it on my way back home because I don't think I'll be able to walk all the way to the newspaper stand and back here again. Which means-"

"Which means that you don't have anything to read right now."

"You're quite insightful. So I'd really appreciate it if you could get me the latest issue of *Sports Express*. I'll pay you back, of course."

Immediately, a large system message blasted into my field of view, blocking out half the scene.

A quest!

Sport Brings the World Together
Mr. Samuel Panikoff, retired, is asking you to get him the latest issue of Sports Express so he could enjoy it during his solitary walk.

Time required, 30 min
Rewards:
XP, 10 pt.
Reputation with Mr. Panikoff, 5 pt.
Current Reputation: Indifference (0/30).

How was I supposed to accept it? Where was the wretched button? I looked all around the message but saw nothing.

So I just said, "No problem, sir. I'll get it for you. You stay here."

"I'm not going anywhere," he replied with a mysterious smile.

The message faded away.

Quest accepted, a voice clicked in my head.

An exclamation mark began flashing somewhere in the periphery за my view. I focused on it. A quest list opened, containing only one quest — the one I'd just accepted.

I saluted the old man, turned round and hurried to get him his paper.

For the first time in years I felt in my element in the real world.

Chapter Four

The Alliance and Its Great Victory

"I may have somethin' for ya."

Warcraft III

I SKIPPED AND HOPPED ALL THE WAY TO THE newsstand. What was the name of that game where I'd learned to move that way? Hopping and skipping made it harder for your enemy to sight in on you. That had been followed by Morrowind where you could level Acrobatics, so that finally I'd gotten into the habit of hopping, leaping and skipping everywhere I went in VR. And seeing as this *was* a game for me now — I could adopt this manner of walking IRL, why not? Provided this *was* IRL, of course. Provided I hadn't lost my marbles.

    I popped into a fast food joint on my way, used

their restroom, received +2% to Satisfaction, then continued on my quest.

As I trotted along, threading my way past billboards and the preoccupied passersby crowding the sidewalk, I kept thinking. I could get 10 pt. XP for completing this quest. Which meant that in theory, I could level up too. I still couldn't work out the correlation between real-world levels and statuses. Mr. Panikoff, this old-age pensioner, was much more advanced than the unemployed Alik — but by the same token, Alik was physically much stronger than the old man. Then again, I could be wrong and the social status could have had nothing to do with characters' levels.

Did I just say "characters"? Sorry. I meant human beings, of course.

Halfway to the newsstand, reality dealt me a cruel and unexpected blow: I got out of breath. Gasping, I pressed on, hoping to eventually level up both stamina and athletics.

After two more minutes of a forced trot, my head began to ring. My teeth started aching; I had a burning sensation in my legs. I panted, struggling to catch my breath but unable to get enough air down my lungs.

This was madness. What the hell was I doing? Why did I have to run? This was real life, for crissakes! What was I talking about? There were no quests nor levels here! I was losing it...

I stopped, my lungs erupting in a bout of sickening viscous coughing. I leaned over a trash can. As I spat into it, my gaze alighted on its unsavory contents. I retched, leaving my entire breakfast — omelet, sandwich and all — in the can.

I glared furiously at a new system message which appeared before my eyes. Apparently, my Vigor had dropped to zero and I needed to get some rest!

The message was too appropriate to be a coincidence. Too well-timed to be a mere hallucination. Dammit.

Ignoring all doubt, my mind gladly embraced the familiar world of gaming stats and characteristics.

My Stamina numbers must have been truly laughable — probably, worse than those of my new friend Mr. Panikoff. I might need to level up a bit, but how? Should I go jogging in the mornings? Oh no. Anything but that. I might just concentrate on leveling Intellect.

Having caught my breath and spat out the remains of my breakfast, I lit up a cigarette. Another system message promptly informed me of a toxic debuff I'd just received, illustrated by the slowly growing damage counter.

I didn't care. I just needed to get rid of that sickening taste in my mouth.

I continued on my way, walking unhurriedly this time.

As soon as I'd bought the newspaper, a new message loomed into view about my receiving the quest item. I looked all through the paper but found nothing special about it. It was a good job he'd only asked me to get him one and not a dozen like NPC quest givers usually do.

I smirked as I thought about it. *Mr. Panikoff would like you to bring him ten wisdom teeth from the local street thugs.* Now that would be a quest!

I thanked the level-5 newsstand vendor (*Mrs. Zinaida Nikolaeva, Age: 60*), and returned to my old gentleman.

Mr. Panikoff was still there. He was sitting in the same pose as I'd left him, offering his squinting eyes to the sun and humming something. A small flock of cooing pigeons bustled nearby.

"Mr. Panikoff..."

"Ah! Phil, my friend!" the old man accepted the paper, brought it to his face and drew in a deep breath.

Shifting my feet, I patiently waited for the quest to close.

"I love the smell of fresh newspapers," the old man explained. "There's something *enchanting* about it. Here's your money, thank you very much. I really appreciate your help!" he offered me the handful of small change he must have prepared as he'd waited for me.

I accepted the money and waited for the quest message. Nothing happened. I looked at the money in my hand, then at the old man with the paper. Nothing.

He opened the paper. "Holy Jesus! I just can't believe it! Manchester City is full of surprises!"

"Why, what have they done?" I asked mechanically.

The absence of the quest message worried me a little. Could this be a glitch? I focused on the exclamation mark which obligingly opened, offering me an empty drop-down menu.

What was that now? The quest had been closed, hadn't it? In which case, where were my XP points? Where was my hard-earned Reputation?

"What have they done?" he repeated. "They've just become English champions, that's what they've done! That's exactly what I said to Valiadis the other day! I told him Man City was a power to be reckoned with! Guardiola is a real brain. A tough cookie. I wouldn't trifle with him. He's commanding this parade!"

He pried himself away from his paper and cast me an expectant look. That triggered his name tag back into view, hovering over his head.

Yes!

Mr. Samuel "The Rat" Panikoff
Age: 83
Current status: Retired
Social status level: 27
Class: Office Worker. Level: 8
Widower.
Children: Natalia, daughter
Age: 54
Grandchildren: Max, grandson
Age: 31
Criminal record: yes
Reputation: Indifference 5/30

It worked! Our glorious Alliance had won another great battle!

If I'd received Rep points, it meant I must have had the XP too, stashed away somewhere. I really needed to find it and work out how to monitor it somehow.

I nodded to the man, "Absolutely, sir."

"Actually, my friend," the old man's voice grew stronger. He didn't lisp anymore. "I suggest you remember the name. *Valiadis*. He's a real brain. One day you might be happy you did."

I nodded again, not quite understanding what he was going on about. A new message which I hadn't noticed before had become clearer in my mind's view.

Your Reputation with Mr. Samuel "Rat" Panikoff has improved!
Current Reputation: Indifference 5/30

Aha. It looked like this gaming system followed the usual rules. Which meant that someone's attitude to me could be calibrated on a scale from hatred to adoration. In this particular case, once I earned 30 Rep points, my relationship with Panikoff would change from Indifference to Amicability, followed by Respect, Reverence and Adoration. Each of those would have their own scales from zero to whatever points were necessary to make the next level. The higher the Reputation, the more points I'd need to earn in order to move on to the next one.

And if, by some chance, my Reputation with Panikoff somehow dropped below zero, it would turn negative, from Dislike to Animosity to Hatred.

Having said that, the gaming scale missed such real-world notions as Love and Friendship. Did they have calibrated bars of their own too?

Very well, Provided this wasn't a hallucination born of my overwrought brain, I might have plenty of time to find that out.

I wanted to say goodbye to the old man but he was deaf to the world around him, consumed by the latest sports news. Never mind. I said goodbye to him anyway, then hurried back home.

I should have asked him about his moniker, really. The Rat! A prison nickname? Why not? He'd very possibly served time during Stalin's post-war purges.

Once back home, I peeled off my soaked sneakers, the socks and even the pants which were wet to the knee. I shoved the clothes into the washing machine and set the sneakers out onto the balcony to dry in the sun.

There, I slumped onto a wobbly stool and lit another cigarette. I had this tendency to chain-smoke whenever I felt nervous or excited. That always made me feel totally sick the day after, giving me a strong incentive to quit smoking... which might even last a couple of days. Then, once my body got rid of all the nasty substances I'd inhaled the day before, the urge would inevitably come back.

I took a good tug on my cigarette, staring at my feet.

If this were indeed a game... what kind of stats would my sneakers have?

It would probably go like this,

A Scandalous Pair of Shabby Sneakers of Misfortune
    -9 to Attractiveness
    -6 to Agility
    Durability: 3/60

How stupid was that? Spending ten to twelve hours in the game just to upgrade a piece of virtual gear while having no desire to replace a very physical pair of shoes IRL!

I yawned. It was almost midday already. I really should clean the place and cook dinner by the time Yanna came back from work. Then I could rejoin the raid and finally complete the dungeon with a clear conscience.

I put out the cigarette, set the alarm clock to 4 p.m. and went to bed.

As I was falling asleep, I realized I wasn't that interested in the raid, after all. I wasn't in the mood for playing for some reason. I seemed to be developing munchkin tendencies IRL.

When the alarm awoke me, I was bathed in sweat. My whole body was aching. The taste in my mouth reminded me of a latrine in Orgrimmar. Boris the cat was pawing my chest, reminding me of her meal time.

I'd found Boris on the street during the era when the world's top guilds were only beginning to tackle Illidan. I hadn't even looked at him — her — properly. At the time, it was just a soggy ball of red hair. I'd brought it home, rolled it out on the kitchen floor and offered it a saucerful of milk. The kitten immediately stuck his little head in it. While he was feeding, I'd come up with a name for him: Boris.

After some time, a friend of mine kindly informed me that my Boris wasn't a Boris at all.

"Hey, it's a she!" he announced.

I still have no idea why he'd had to check its rear end. Did he have a cat fetish?

After all, what difference could a cat's gender possibly make?

God was I wrong.

The next spring our Boris had gone mad. She screamed in a nasty screechy voice, demanding a partner, while moving around the apartment with her backside stuck high in the air. I'd had to have her fixed ASAP.

And once I'd met Yanna, the ultimate dog person, Boris' life took a steep turn for the worse. Because Yanna had a Chihuahua. His name was Boy. Boy took an instant dislike to Boris — and the feeling was more than mutual.

For a long time, Yanna had been trying to talk me into getting rid of Boris. If you listened to her, cats were useless creatures. They shed, they cost you money in food and litter filler, and they didn't even bother to catch mice these days, meaning they had no place in the house. When, in response, I dared question Boy's potentially useful qualities — pointing out that in this day and age it was pretty unusual to expect pets to earn their keep — Yanna really took offense. That had been one of our first big arguments.

The problem had sorted itself out naturally. One day we went out, leaving both animals at home. Boris' litter box was on the balcony, so we left the balcony door open.

No idea how it happened — but somehow the little Chihuahua managed to kill himself by falling to his death from our eighth floor. We found his broken body on the ground under the balcony. Yanna was heartbroken. I borrowed a toy shovel from some kids next door and buried Boy on an empty lot behind the row of communal garages.

Since then, Yanna hated Boris with abandon, refusing to do anything for her. Feeding and cleaning up after her was entirely my responsibility.

The cat must have noticed I was awake. She meowed, demanding attention. I climbed out of bed and stretched. My joints screeched their protest. Every muscle in my body hurt after my morning paper run.

The memory of the weird morning kicked back in. I struggled, unable to tell reality from the dream I'd just had.

I picked up Boris and stared hard into her feline eyes.

Yes!

Boris. A female cat
Age: 9
Current status: pet
Owner: Philip Panfilov

Wait a sec, what about her level? And social

status? That didn't make sense.

I tried to focus harder, expecting the message to unravel, but Boris struggled free from my grip, gave a hearty shake and began grooming herself, casting offended glances in my direction.

Finally, something must have clicked in the mysterious game system, adding another line to my pet's stats,

Relationship: Adoration 10/10

Adoration? No way!

My lips stretched in a happy grin. I jumped off the bed. "Boris, I love you too!"

It hadn't been a dream, after all. My Reputation with Boris was all maxed-out. How awesome was that?

I turned the TV on and switched it to a music channel, then picked up Boris and waltzed my way into the kitchen.

I measured out a generous helping of her dinner and went into the bathroom to make myself presentable. This wasn't a game, Mr. Panfilov. People actually washed here.

I took a shower, brushed my teeth, had a shave, wiped myself dry, put some clean underwear on, then walked back into the kitchen.

I opened the fridge and studied its contents. I needed to decide what to make for dinner. We still had one raw chicken drumstick left, a few potatoes and a bunch of other veg. I might make some chicken soup. That way there'd be some left for tomorrow, as well.

Time to do some shopping, really.

I put the chicken in a pot, added some water and set it on the stove just as the kettle began to boil. I spooned a generous dose of instant coffee into a mug, added some sugar, stirred it, then walked out onto the balcony.

By then, Boris had already finished her dinner and decided to keep me company.

I drank my coffee, smoking and thinking. The familiar system message informed me of the nicotine damage received. Still, my Vitality numbers seemed to have improved somewhat. It must have had something to do with getting a bit more sleep and the fact that my body must have gotten rid of some of the last day's alcohol. And still my Vitality bar wasn't full but hovering at 73%.

What was happening to me? Why? I really needed to find out what was going on. I had to work this crazy system out.

I came up with several theories but none seemed convincing enough. Undecided, I spent some time experimenting, trying to locate my own stats. That would have given me some starting point.

Finally I noticed a tiny little icon almost out of view, in the top right corner of my field of vision. Risking to dislocate my eyeballs, I somehow reached for it, locking it with my screwed gaze.

It worked. Another icon appeared promptly next to it.

The first one seemed to list my buffs. Or debuffs, rather. It depicted a large red letter N enveloped in clouds of smoke.

A countdown above the first icon kept clocking down the seconds,

116:31... 116:30... 116:29...

A prompt hovered into view,

Nicotine Saturation
Your body is saturated with nicotine. Your metabolism is accelerated 15%.
Warning! Your blood contains high levels of carbon monoxide!
+3 to Satisfaction
+2% to Vigor
-1 to Stamina
-1 to Intellect
-1 to Perception

The second icon depicted a black letter C. It reported a caffeine buff received. It offered +2 to Satisfaction and +10 to Metabolism while slightly improving Vigor, Focus and Reaction Times.

The problem was, I had nothing to compare those numbers with. How much Stamina did I have in total? Because if it was 100, then -1 pt. wasn't a big deal. But if it was 10, then my smoking habit did a lot of damage to my stats!

I returned to the kitchen deep in thought and began peeling some potatoes while the chicken was still cooking. I must have been mad all those years. Who in their sane mind would deliberately inflict a permanent debuff on themselves? Because that's what I was doing with all that smoking.

I peeled the potatoes, finished my coffee and began cleaning the place.

It would probably be better not to tell Yanna anything... at least for the time being.

Chapter Five

SIGNS OF LIFE

"Life always bursts the boundaries of formulas. Defeat may prove to have been the only path to resurrection, despite its ugliness."

Antoine de Saint-Exupéry, *Flight to Arras*

I STILL HAD SOME TIME BEFORE YANNA CAME HOME. The soup had been made. I'd cleaned the place, taken out the trash and started a load of washing. House chores out of the way, I could finally do some work.

Provided I had some.

A housemaker earning a pittance and sponging off a wife eight years his junior... it felt uncomfortable. It wasn't as if it had never bothered me before — but before, I'd somehow managed to suppress the voice of my conscience. I was an artist — a writer. Our clan was

#2 on the server! And even if you did compare my and Yanna's earnings, you'd see that I'd always managed to earn slightly more than she did. Not much but still.

For some reason, today it failed to reassure me. What was I like? Threadbare jeans, faded T-shirts, my only pair of sneakers falling apart... How was Yanna supposed to feel, having chosen to spend the best years of her life with *me*?

I sat down to check my computer. My game client was bursting with messages from my clanmates. Still, I had more important things to do.

I checked my inbox, silently praying for new job offers. I scrolled through a hundred-plus letters which had accumulated over the last two days, deleting any potential spam without reading. Nothing I could use. Shame.

That was weird. Only a few hours ago, the absence of job offers would have been good news: it meant I could log back into the game with a clear conscience. And now I felt disappointed for some reason.

I decided to check a few freelance websites for any private messages. Nothing. No one seemed to be tempted by my wide range of services including "the writing of concise and eloquent website articles, press releases, speeches, reports and promotional materials". Might they have been put off by my rather high rates?

I chuckled. I was an idiot, really. I used to justify my high rates by the fact that I was an accomplished author: not a college student but someone with a life's wealth of experience behind him. While in fact I'd simply been unwilling to do the work, too wary of putting in the actual effort. Because accepting a job would mean I might have to work hard, writing, rewriting and editing my hard-gained words time and time again.

Which was admittedly boring. Also, I had the game to play. Still, today I somehow wished I hadn't.

I picked up my cell phone and scrolled through the contacts. One of those people just might have an assignment for me to do.

I finally dialed Ivan. He worked in an advertising company which sometimes hired me to write a blog post or something. Faking cheerfulness, I asked him if they had anything for me, by any chance.

"I don't think so," he replied unenthusiastically. "We don't have any clients ourselves at the moment. Wretched recession. We'll keep you posted. Thanks for staying in touch."

Sure. In recession times, everyone had to cut corners. And the likes of me were the first to get the boot.

The air in the room was still rife with my badly-digested ambitions which had appeared so alluring ten years ago. By now though they'd almost completed their full circle through my rich psyche and were about to reveal themselves to the world as a perfect pile of complete garbage.

And Yanna would be the first to witness its arrival.

I'd scrolled through the entire contacts list

without calling anyone. I simply hadn't dared. I was too scared of more rejections. Also, I hated making other people feel uncomfortable by having to say "no" to me.

I spent the next hour updating my job profiles. I chose some of my best work and uploaded it to my portfolios making sure it looked attractive. The only things I now mentioned in my profile were experience and my ability to work under pressure to meet urgent deadlines. You get this sort of skill by doing hardcore raids.

That got me thinking. Freelancing was all well and good — but should I be thinking of getting a regular job, maybe? I could try living a normal life for a change. Waking up at the same time as Yanna, having breakfast together, then leaving the house, driving to work in some office or other, then heading back home in the evening with a clear conscience...

A regular paycheck might help me get back on my feet and earn some self-respect. I might even become friends with my workmates. So basically, why not?

I rummaged through a junk heap of ancient files until I unearthed my old CV. I updated it a bit, adding a new mug shot and a fresh portfolio, then Googled an employment website and signed up.

I could give the game a miss for a while. Raids could wait. Real-life leveling was admittedly fun.

With that out of the way, I walked out onto the balcony and lit another cigarette, habitually closing a new debuff message.

My lips stretched in a smile. I was more than

pleased with myself and my decision.

The setting sun had colored the horizon purple. The yard below echoed with children's voices and the booming sounds of a 1992 disco hit from someone's window. A flock of pigeons fussed below.

The sound of breaking glass and Yagoza's furious cussing disrupted the bucolic atmosphere. One of his subordinates had just dropped a bagful of booze on the tarmac.

I heard the key turn in the door. Yanna was back. I put out the unfinished cigarette and went back in to greet her.

She walked through the front door loaded down with shopping bags. She must have done the shopping on her way home from work.

How embarrassing. I took the bags from her and gave her a hearty kiss. She answered it unenthusiastically.

"Hi," I said.

"Hi there. What's up? What's with the shaving? Why aren't you-" she cut herself short.

I knew what she meant. Normally, whenever she came home, I was either asleep or sitting behind my computer wearing a pair of headphones.

I shrugged. "It's just that... I missed you."

I took the bags into the kitchen and began putting the shopping away. I couldn't stop thinking of what I'd just read on the name tag hovering above her head,

Yannina "Yanna" Orlova

Age: 24
Current status: lawyer
Social status level: 8
Class: Office Worker. Level: 3
Married.
Husband: Philip Panfilov
Children: none
Reputation: Amicability 5/60

Only Amicability? And only 5 points?

Never mind. This weird game system probably didn't even list Love on its Reputation scale. But still...

Engrossed in these thoughts, I began laying the table. How funny. Yanna was the first person today who didn't seem to have a criminal record.

She'd already changed out of her office clothes and slumped onto the kitchen stool. "How was your day, then?"

"Fine. I've cleaned the house, spent some time looking for a proper job and uploaded my CV to Headhunter.com."

"Poor you! You've cleaned the house! *And* uploaded your CV! You must be exhausted!"

I stared at a new system message.

I just didn't understand it.

Your Reputation with Yannina "Yanna" Orlova has decreased!
Current reputation: Dislike 25/30

I seemed to have been right: this *was* a standard

gaming Reputation system. But at the moment, I couldn't care less.

Dislike, why? What had I done?

I felt a surge of blood flush my face. My ears burned.

I gulped, trying to take it all in, then looked up at her. Yanna's unfriendly stare was boring a hole in me. There was no love in her eyes.

I spoke slowly, weighing every word and trying to sound calm,

"I know how you must feel. I'm sorry. You work hard while I stay home sleeping, then spend nights playing. You have to lug all that shopping around... I know. I've made up my mind. No more playing. No more raids. I'm getting a proper job."

"You don't mean it!" she exclaimed, faking amazement. "Just about goddamn time!"

"I'm serious. I've also dropped my freelance rates today. This way I might get more job offers while I'm looking for work."

"You're full of surprises, you! Did you also write your book?"

"No, I didn't. I didn't have the time. Actually... it's possible I might not-"

I faltered but strangely enough, I felt relieved. For the first time in my life, I'd spoken my mind instead of just offering excuses.

Yanna raised an eyebrow. "Anything happen?"

Oh yes. It most definitely had. Still, I wasn't going to tell her. She wouldn't believe me. She'd just think she'd been living with a nutcase all these years.

"Everything's fine," I said. "Tuck in."

She chuckled.

We ate in silence, each thinking our own thoughts. No idea what she was contemplating. Me, I was pondering over the fact that I'd just received a numerical confirmation of Yanna's alienation which she'd expressed on a few occasions before.

After dinner, she retired to our bedroom while I did the dishes and had another smoke break. Then I joined her and sat on the bed next to her. We really needed to talk. We needed to get this out of our respective systems.

She was lying in bed as if I wasn't even there, listening to the music in her earphones and scrolling through her Instagram feed.

I peered at the message hovering over her head,

Yannina "Yanna" Orlova
Age: 24
Reputation: Dislike 25/30

Then a new message popped up,

Your Relationship with Yannina "Yanna" Orlova has decreased!

Current Reputation: Dislike 20/30

I reached out to touch her, wishing to say something.

A new message appeared above the first one,

*Your Relationship with Yannina "Yanna" Orlova
has decreased!
Current Reputation: Dislike 15/30*

I sprang off the bed and shot out of the room before my own wife aggroed me.

She couldn't even bear being next to me!

For the next couple of hours, I circled the rest of the apartment like a caged animal, smoking, drinking coffee, then smoking some more, then making more coffee, occasionally trying to Google instances of spontaneous virtual-reality disorders (which I apparently had) or scrolling through pages of marital advice.

Should I go on that raid? Or make a appointment with a doctor? I logged into the game but kept checking my email every couple of minutes, hoping for new job offers.

Basically, I was just going mad. My brain was in overload. I was losing Yanna.

My PM box was bursting with messages. I could understand my clanmates. The raid had already started, they could see I was logged in but still I wouldn't join them. My avatar was standing frozen like an idiot in the middle of the game's capital city.

I didn't notice Yanna walk out of the bedroom, standing behind my back and watching me sitting at my computer staring at the game interface.

I did notice the new system message, though.

Your Relationship with Yannina "Yanna" Orlova

has decreased!
   Current Reputation: Animosity 20/30

"Didn't you just say *'No more playing'*?" she asked behind my back. "*'No more raids'*, yeah right! You're a jerk, that's what you are. I think I've had enough."

I didn't turn. Pointless. When your relationship dropped to Animosity, it meant no one would even talk to you. I could only make matters worse.

She slammed the bedroom door. I sat there, listening to her pack her stuff and talk to someone on the phone. Her voice sounded so sweet — flirty even — and ringing with happiness. You wouldn't think it was the same person who'd just hissed and vented her fury at me.

I put on my Shabby Sneakers of Misfortune, scooped up my cell phone, the cigarettes, the lighter, the wallet and the apartment keys, dumped it all into a backpack and walked out of the house as I was, in a pair of shorts and a faded T-shirt (-1 to Charisma, Durability: 2/20).

For some reason, I headed for the ramshackle pavilion in the center of the playground and sat there, staring at the flickering light above the front door. Everything went out of focus.

Had it not been for the wretched Reputation message, I might have tried to go back and apologize like I'd done many times before. I might have tried to explain and beg her forgiveness. We might have dissolved into one of our night-long shouting matches when I'd be trying to put my arms around her while she'd scratch me, telling me to keep my filthy hands to myself. Then, when the sun finally showed up and our janitor, a Tadzhik migrant who could barely speak any Russian, started swishing his broom outside, we'd finally make up. We had this agreement never to go to bed angry.

So any other day we might have finally kissed and made up, then indulged in some angry, desperate, mind-boggling lovemaking when all you could feel was that the two of you had become one, united in your passion.

This time, however, I knew: this was the end of the line.

It hadn't happened overnight. Whatever feelings she'd had for me — whether love, friendship, respect or adoration — they had been fading, dropping a point each day, every day, until today their count had finally arrived at zero. She'd run out of love and friendship; she didn't have any respect left for me and as for adoration... just forget it.

A Jeep pulled up at some distance from the house. A young guy climbed out, took Yanna's suitcase from her and put it in the trunk. They exchanged a hug and a kiss (on the cheek!). He opened the passenger door for her. Yanna got in, and the car drove off.

A figure appeared out of the shadows. "Fancy a drink?"

I looked up sharply. It was Alik.

He must have taken my staring back at him as a yes because he offered me a beer can.

I downed half of it. A new system message appeared promptly, informing me of a drop in both agility and perception and a slight rise in confidence and charisma.

He offered me a light, then lit his own cigarette. "Easy, man! Wassup?" he nodded at the front door.

"Nothing," I drew deeply on my cigarette, then added against my better judgement as I exhaled, "My wife's just left me."

Your Reputation with Romuald "Alik" Zhukov has improved!
Current Reputation: Amicability 5/60

I started to laugh, louder and louder, until I dissolved in a bout of hysterics.

Amicability! With a local bum! Was it because I'd been honest with him? Or because of the beer and smokes we'd shared?

Whatever. It was hilarious, anyway. Only a few hours ago, my wife, the love of my life who'd been with me through thick and thin, had the same reputation reading with me as this street thug with whom I'd barely exchanged a few words.

Had this been a game, I might have thought I had some kind of stat booster or a premium account which offered fast-track Reputation leveling. And had this indeed been the case...

Alik gave me a hearty slap on the shoulder, ignoring my bout of hysteria. "Happens. So she left you, big deal. You can get her back if you really want to.

Take it easy, man."

"Yeah, I suppose so," I replied absent-mindedly as another thought struck me.

A stat booster. Why not? Because if it were so, then...

My head boomed, replaying a single song snippet over and over again,

"...how can I describe
The TV shows running through this brain box of mine

World, I'm back,
You'd better watch your back
You wanted my head
Too bad
I'm showing you signs of life"[1]

I could get Yanna back.

Enough wallowing in self-pity. Enough wasting my time.

"Thanks for the beer, man," I shook Alik's hand. "And for the advice. I'm gonna go for a walk. I need some fresh air."

Your Reputation with Romuald "Alik" Zhukov has improved!
Current Reputation: Amicability 10/60

"I can go with you if you want," he offered.

---

[1] An excerpt from the song *Signs of Life* by a leading Russian rapper Oxxxymiron

Was it the alcohol? Or the stat booster? I really needed to find that out. Time was an issue.

"Next time, man," I handed him the unfinished beer and left the pavilion.

I walked out onto the street and hurried along while reaching for my earbuds and connecting them to my phone. I put some music on and started jogging, breathing in the springtime night air infused with the aromas of early blossoms, budding leaves and exhaust fumes.

I threaded my way among the passersby, leaping over pools of rainwater, past parked cars and apartment buildings, block after block, stopping occasionally to catch my breath.

It started raining. I kept jogging, catching raindrops with my open mouth and wiping my forehead with my sleeve as I ran.

I only stopped when I reached the city limits. My sneakers were soaking wet. My lungs were on fire. My legs were giving way under me.

No idea how long I'd been running. The rain had long stopped. The sky was getting lighter. I could hear dogs barking in nearby cottages.

And me? Well, I was grinning!

Your Stamina has improved!
+1 to Stamina
Current Stamina, 4

I set my backpack on the curb and slumped down on it, then reached for the soggy pack of cigarettes. I took my time lighting up and smoking it, then lit up a new cigarette with the first one.

Cleansed by my run through the nighttime city, my lungs and blood greedily soaked up the new dose of nicotine. It went to my head. My legs felt weak. New debuff messages kept flooding in. Still I kept smoking, trying to remember exactly how it felt. The foul taste, the slackened muscles...

I scrambled back to my feet and staggered over to a trash can, crumpling the remaining cigarettes in my hand. I shoved them in the trash, then did the same to the lighter.

CHAPTER SIX

NEW LEVEL

"You could claim that anything's real if the only basis for believing in it is that nobody's proved it doesn't exist!"

J. K. Rowling, *Harry Potter and the Deathly Hallows*

LATER, I COULD BARELY REMEMBER HOW I'D GOTTEN back home after my night run. I'd walked along the city streets, then hitched a ride with some early-morning gypsy cab. I must have fallen asleep; I remember rummaging through my pockets for any loose change as I hadn't had enough to pay him. I remember peeling off my soggy clothes and dropping them on the bedroom floor. I then collapsed onto the bed and pressed my face to Yanna's pillow.

Just before falling asleep, I somehow remembered to set the alarm for 9.30 the next morning.

I had a doctor's appointment at 11 a.m.

When the alarm awoke me, I was about to hit snooze, then remembered the appointment and shot out of bed. "Shot out" was probably a bit of an overstatement. I'd indeed sprung out of bed, then promptly collapsed on top of it. Diagnosis: an acute case of Phil-itosis.

My whole body hurt as if some vicious warlock had cast several DOTs on me, flattened me repeatedly under a press, then thrown me into the path of a herd of Siberian mammoths.

Trying to move slowly, I somehow made it to the bathroom. I took a shower, gingerly touching my smarting body which felt completely dead after last-night's marathon. After an equally careful shave and a cautious tickle of the toothbrush, I felt marginally better.

My chest groaned with the sense of loss. I missed Yanna something rotten. I missed her voice and her "Breakfast's ready!" My hands kept reaching for the phone, desperate to dial her number.

Still, I forced myself to stay calm. I wasn't ready yet. Nor was she. By calling her now, I could ruin everything.

To get my mind off it, I decided to do a bit of Strength leveling. A few sit-ups and pushups might do just fine.

God was I ever wrong. I managed a few half-hearted sit-ups, but the pain in my legs was just too much. My creaking knees were killing me.

And as for pushups... the moment I tried to bend

my arms, they gave under me and I collapsed to the floor. Luckily, my belly acted as a shock absorber.

I made myself some coffee and walked out onto the balcony. Mechanically my hand reached for my cigarettes but found none.

Unlike all my previous attempts to quit, this time I wasn't upset by their absence. If anything, I felt relieved. I stood on the balcony, breathing in lungfuls of fresh air and washing it down with hot, strong coffee.

Having received my coffee buff, I put on some clean clothes and hurried to my doctor's appointment. I still had some money on my bank card — enough for his fee and also hopefully for any tests the Doc deemed necessary.

She did. The doctor turned out to be a pretty young blonde who didn't bat an eyelid at my rambling story. She asked me a long list of questions, then sent me to have an MRI of the brain which cost an arm and a leg.

"Once you're done, come back to my office with the images," she said. "The way you describe it, it could be anything. I can't diagnose you based on your symptoms alone."

"Thanks," I said, peering at the system message hovering over her head. "Thank you, Olga. Am I to come back to see you once I have the images?"

"Absolutely."

"Very well. Oh, and one more thing. You're very pretty."

Suppressing an embarrassed smile, she pointed at the door.

Yeah right! She could point at the door all she wanted but the system knew better!

I smiled back and walked out. The smile still hovered on my face as I contemplated the system message I'd just received,

Your Reputation with Olga "Lola" Shvedova has improved!
Current Reputation: Indifference 5/30

This system didn't mess about. Five more compliments, and we might become friends.

I was lucky: the clinic had its own MRI equipment which saved me a trip downtown. I had to wait for my turn but I didn't mind that. I could use a pause. I needed to have a good think and decide what to do next.

I used the chance to check my health points. They seemed to have grown a bit. The bar now read 73,17102% and kept creeping up. This was the best anti-smoking ad I'd ever seen.

It looked like in order to get Yanna back, I might need to first win her love — and her respect. This wasn't a question of whether I wanted to be with her or not. I needed her. Even though my initial feelings for her had somewhat faded over these four years, my love for her had only grown stronger.

And as for winning her respect... I was no expert in women but I had this nagging feeling that this time mere promises and declarations of love wouldn't be enough. I could find out where she lived now, of course.

I could send her flowers at work. I could bombard her with texts, stalk her on social media, keep calling her number, shower her with rose petals and beg her forgiveness on a reality TV show.

Wouldn't work. It might have, once. But not now.

Had she had some feelings left for me — yes, maybe. But this mysterious game system didn't lie. What Yanna felt for me was animosity. Which must have had something to do with my being a total jerk, passive, disinterested and perfectly happy with the current state of affairs.

"You're such a loser really," she used to tell me only half-jokingly. "At your age, you still don't have a job. You don't have a car. You don't even have a place of your own! You're thirty years old and you still sponge off your wife, playing games all night long..."

So she hadn't been joking, then. That should have been the first clue. If only I'd realized it then! But no — the only thing that had worried me at the time was whether I could become the server's top rogue, beating some guy called Nurro to the title.

The answer was "no" to both. I hadn't become the top rogue nor had I managed to keep Yanna.

"Panfilov? Come in, please," a voice called from the MRI room.

The fifteen minutes spent motionless in the cramped confines of an MRI capsule echoing with spooky sounds is every claustrophobic's biggest nightmare. Then I had to wait another half-hour for my results. Finally, they handed me an envelope containing images of my gray matter from every possible angle.

Envelope in hand, I returned to the doctor's office.

I reached for the door handle, about to walk in, when a male voice protested from behind me,

"Where do you think you're going? How about waiting your turn?"

My hand still in mid-air, I turned around. A burly man, bald-headed with a wrestler's neck, sat on one of the chairs lining the opposite wall.

A few other patients next to him voiced their indignation,

"What a cheek!" an old lady in a bright-colored headscarf shook a disapproving head.

"You hear what he said? Come and take your place in line," a gum-chewing woman next to her advised rather threateningly. Her plump high-cheekboned face was plastered with a thick layer of makeup.

"I'm not here to see the doctor!" I tried to explain. "I only need to give this to her! I have an appointment!"

"So do we," a frail old man with a goatee protested in a passionate whisper.

"Don't you get fresh with us!" the plump lady raised her voice.

"Right," the burly man stood up. "You heard it. Come and take your place in line. Don't make me lose it with you."

I could understand them. Still, I wasn't going to wait in line twice for the same appointment. All I needed to do was give her the envelope. The appointment times were all screwed up, anyway. I'd had to wait an hour for mine even though I'd arrived on time.

A chain of new system messages flooded my field of vision.

Oh, no.

Your Reputation with Anatoly Magaradze has decreased!
Current Reputation: Animosity 20/30

Your Reputation with Aigul Ramadanova has decreased!
Current Reputation: Animosity 20/30

Your Reputation with Violette Ryzhova has decreased!
Current Reputation: Animosity 20/30

Your Reputation with Mark Zalessky has decreased!
Current Reputation: Animosity 20/30

I needed a break. Obediently I stepped away from the door and took my place in line after the frail old man. All the chairs were already taken, so I just leaned against the wall next to him.

I met the burly man's gaze. Aha.

Anatoly Magaradze

Age: 44
Current status: truck driver
Social status level: 9
Class: long-haul truck driver. Level: 7
Married
Wife: Irina Magaradze
Children: none
Criminal record: yes

I spent some time focusing on each of the patients, retrieving the information I needed and planning my next move. It would be terribly unfair to waste my time waiting in line, especially if the images proved there was nothing wrong with me. In which case, I'd have to finally work out the mysterious game's interface, retrieve my stats and come up with a new leveling strategy. One that would allow me to get Yanna back.

Still, I knew very well what I needed to do in order to get her back. I had to find a job and earn my own living. Pretty obvious, I know. Still, that would be the most meaningful sign of my being on the mend. I needed to lose some weight, anyway. The beer diet and sedentary lifestyle had done my waistline — or the absence thereof — no favors.

So what did I know about crowd control? First, you had to surprise them. After that, you had to shock them. Then they'd be eating out of your hand, compliant and perfectly malleable.

And this wasn't even a crowd but only a group of four people united by one goal: to see the doctor in their due time without letting an aggressive intruder jump the line.

The fact that they'd acted so unanimously against me gave me some hope that my idea just might work.

I grabbed at my head. My knees slackened. Slowly I slid to the floor, making unintelligible sounds to attract their attention.

"Is he all right?" asked the gum-chewing lady, a.k.a. Mrs. Aigul Ramadanova.

"Yeah yeah," the burly Mr. Magaradze laughed. "Pull the other one!"

"*Mmmmhooomhooo,*" I enunciated, trying to sound forlorn and desperate.

"God save us," the old Mrs. Violette Ryzhova made the sign of the cross. "Lord Jesus Christ, Son of God, have mercy on me!"

"*Ishnu'alaaaaahhhh,*" I groaned, switching to the Darnassian language of Night Elves.

"He's a demon!" the old Violette pointed her gnarly finger at me. "I assure you! Lord Jesus..."

"Will you please stop your nonsense?" the truck driver interrupted her. "Hey you! Are you okay?"

I didn't reply. Slowly I rose, sliding my back up the wall.

My knee caps crunched clearly in the silence.

I raised my right hand and pointed at the old woman,

"You! Violette Ryzhova! You're a faithful servant of God! Hearken unto me!"

The woman kept crossing herself and

whispering prayers, unable to take her eyes off me. She looked almost crippled with fear.

I turned and pointed at the other woman. "You! Aigul Ramadanova! Hearken unto me!"

I turned again. "You!" my index finger very nearly poked the truck driver's forehead. "Anatoly Magaradze, listen to me!"

"And you!" I turned my attention to the frail old man. "Mark Zalessky, sir! I want you to pay attention!"

Ramadanova's mouth opened. The gum dropped to the floor.

The old woman's hand froze mid-air in an unfinished sign of the cross.

The old gentleman seemed to be dangerously close to a stroke.

The burly Magaradze was the only one who hadn't bought it. "What's that for a circus show?"

"Aren't you fed up with trucking?" I asked him in my normal voice. "Your wife Irina must miss you something awful."

I must have touched on a tender spot. He didn't say anything, just clenched his teeth.

"I'm very sorry," I said, clutching my head with both hands. "I have this problem... I can see right through all of you! I don't think my head can take it... Will you please let me see the doctor? Please?"

"I don't mind," Mrs. Ramadanova hurried to agree before I could reveal any more sensitive information about *her*.

"Let him see the doctor," the old lady echoed.

The burly Magaradze didn't say anything, just

nodded at the door.

"Thanks," I whispered voicelessly, taking a place by the door.

"Listen..." Magaradze touched my shoulder. "I don't know your name-"

"It's Phil."

"Listen, Phil... Did you say Irina misses me?"

I stared into his slightly bulging eyes surrounded by a fine net of wrinkles. They were the eyes of a person who'd been around the block a few times.

I paused. "She does. A lot."

He gave me a bear hug. "Thank you! I owe you!"

Without saying goodbye to anyone, he turned round and hurried down the clinic corridor toward the front door.

Your Reputation with Anatoly Magaradze has improved!

Current Reputation: Reverence 10/210

Oh wow. I hadn't done anything special, really. Just told him something he'd probably already known. But what a leap in Reputation, from animosity to reverence!

The doctor's door opened, letting out a patient followed by Olga herself.

"What's with all the noise?" she asked.

No one replied.

She saw me. "Aha. Have you got your images? Come in, I'll take a look."

As I closed the door, I heard Aigul and the old lady Violette embarking on a heated discussion.

I took a seat, waiting for the doctor's verdict. I was shaking, my hands clenched into fists. She studied the images against the light, lowering her head this way and that. Finally, she heaved a sigh and started writing.

So what was wrong with me, then? Was I nuts? Or just hallucinating? Did I have a brain tumor?

"And?" I finally managed with a dry throat.

"You're perfectly fine," she gave me a studying look. "Relatively speaking. You're overweight. Marginally obese, to be frank. So you need to take better care of yourself. You need to eat less and exercise more. At your age, you shouldn't let it get out of hand."

She kept going on about the obesity-related dangers of an early stroke and heart disease. Finally I interrupted her,

"I'm sorry! I promise I'll watch my diet and start a healthy lifestyle. I already went for a run yesterday. And I quit smoking. But please tell me," I pointed at my temple, "am I all right... there?"

"Oh, absolutely fine. No problems at all. I can't see any abnormalities. Your blood pressure is a bit on the high side but nothing you should worry about."

"Thank you so much! You're an angel!"

On impulse I grabbed her hand and kissed the tips of her fingers. Her cheeks flushed.

Your Reputation with Olga "Lola" Shvedova has improved!

Current Reputation: Indifference 10/30

"All right, all right, that's enough," she said, smiling. "You can go now."

Without taking my eyes off her, I rose, trying to imbue my gaze with all the joy I felt and all the happiness at the fact that nothing was wrong with me after all. She didn't avert her gaze, as if teasing and encouraging me.

Your Reputation with Olga "Lola" Shvedova has improved!
Current Reputation: Indifference 15/30

Oh wow. I tried to pull myself together and headed for the door.

As I opened it, I turned back to her. "Thanks a lot, Lola."

Her dropped jaw made a funny sound. I walked out.

A small crowd heaved by the door outside: the same familiar patients plus several more who must have just arrived.

"There he is!" Aigul shouted.

"Saint Phil, glory be to thee!" the old lady enthused.

"Phil! Phil!" the crowd cried out, reaching out to grab my hands, touch my shoulders or stroke my face.

It looked like I'd made a big mistake. You couldn't play with people's feelings the way I'd just done. Especially not with sick or old people — and they were all either sick or old here.

I raised my hands in the air. The crowd parted.

"You, Aigul!" I said in the surrounding silence. And you, Violette! And you," I peered into the crowd, calling out their names one by one. "Listen to me, all of you! Hearken unto me!"

I could hear Olga strain her voice behind her office door, calling the next patient.

"You! All of you! You're all going to be happy! Yes! Happiness for everybody, free! No one will go away unsatisfied!"[2]

Having thus prophesized, I promptly left the building.

Enough playing tricks on unsuspecting citizens. I was worse than a child, really.

As I walked back home, the system kept showering me with Reputation reports from Aigul, Mark, Violette and lots of other people I didn't even know. And then...

And then I received a new level!

Congratulations! You've received a new level!
Your current social status level: 6
Characteristic points available: 1
Skill points available: 1

It was time I finally sorted out the interface.

---

[2] *"Happiness for everybody, free! No one will go away unsatisfied!"* — Phil borrows a suitable line from *The Roadside Picnic*, the benchmark first-contact novel by the two leading Russian science fiction authors Arkady and Boris Strugatsky

Chapter Seven

Questions Without Answers

"It makes me think of my life, my nonexistent accomplishments and my overall abilities in incompetence."

Markus Zusak, *I am the Messenger*

ONLY LEVEL 6!

Never before had I felt so utterly worthless.

Only earlier that morning, I'd had the same social status as Alik, that drunken lowlife!

Me, Philip Panfilov, the next great Russian author (sarcasm intended) — and Alik! He and I shared the same place in the world's food chain!

While my Yanna (provided she was still mine) was already level 8.

I kept walking blindly until I very nearly bumped

into a moving car. Followed by the driver's cussing, I hurried across the street. My head was teeming with exclamation marks. Too many shocks for one day. My sensitive psyche of gamer-turned-blogger just couldn't take it any longer.

As I walked, I kept screwing my eyes trying to locate something in my internal view that might allow me to open that wretched stats window and distribute the points I had available. No such luck. The only thing I found was an inconspicuous debuff icon.

Nicotine Withdrawal
Duration: 14 days
Your body is deprived of nicotine!
Nicotine takes part in your body's metabolism. -5% to Metabolism
Warning! High probability of a spontaneous Enrage!
Warning! Your aggro radius has increased!
-3% to Satisfaction every 12 hours

I chuckled. My previous attempts to quit had never come with a deadline. Only two weeks? Before, the sheer thought of having to struggle with nicotine dependency for the rest of my life had made me panic.

I might actually counter the debuff. I could drink more coffee and do more exercise. I might also try to raise my Satisfaction numbers with some nice tasty food. Having said that, wouldn't my favorite books and movies have the same effect?

So basically, it was a no-brainer. I knew I could

do it.

I still couldn't find any character stats. Or my stats, rather. So I stopped scaring the passersby with my wild eye movements. Pointless. I might give it another try later at home when no one could see me.

As I walked along the boulevard, I noticed my first quest giver, Mr. Samuel Panikoff, busy reading a fresh copy of his newspaper. The old man was oblivious to my presence so I decided not to disturb him.

I popped into a nearby KFC restaurant and got myself a bucket of chicken wings to go.

I don't like eating in public. I much prefer doing it in the comfort of my own home, hunched over a favorite book. My Dad gave me this habit. I know it's not good for you but it's my top guilty pleasure and I'm not giving it up for the world.

As I waited in line, I checked my smartphone notifications. My inboxes were groaning with missed calls and messages, mainly from fellow clan members. A couple of calls were from numbers I didn't know. They could be job offers. I called back but no one picked up.

Never mind. I'd have to check my emails once I got home.

A new system message came up,

Hunger
You're experiencing food deprivation!
-10% to Metabolism
Warning! Your body lacks glucose!
Warning! Your body lacks amino acids!

Warning! Danger of muscle mass decreasing!
Debuff received: Weakness
-1 to Stamina every 24 hrs.
-1 to Agility every 24 hrs.
-1 to Perception every 24 hrs.
-1 to Intellect every 24 hrs.
-1 to Strength every 24 hrs.
-2% to Satisfaction every 2 hrs.
-3% to Vigor every 2 hrs.

That was nothing to sniff at. Even though I couldn't quite work out its mechanism, my knees felt weak as if I had indeed received a debuff.

The bucketful of wings smelled awesome. I had to really exercise my willpower not to scoff the whole lot on my way home. No wonder: last time I'd had something to eat was dinner with Yanna last night, and now it was already past midday.

Yanna. My chest groaned stronger than before, pushing the euphoria of my earlier clinic visit to the background of my mind. All the joy of what was happening, including the new level I'd just received, had faded into insignificance.

I can't tell you what had prompted my next step. It could have been the desperation of losing her. Or it could have been the hunger debuff affecting my judgment. In any case, instead of going home and trying to work out the mysterious game's interface as I'd planned, I turned round and headed for Yanna's workplace. Her company office was only a few blocks away.

Clutching the KFC bucket under one arm and the MRI envelope under the other, I hurried over there, ignoring the passersby's surprised looks.

How many movies had I seen where the hormone-driven hero, instead of saving the world or going about his own business, hurried to reunite with his loved one instead. How many books had I read which described exactly the same scenario. And how angry had I been with the author or screenwriter, how passionately had I hurled the book across the room when the said hormone-driven hero would reject a good job, a lump sum of money or even the offer of superpowers simply to keep the woman he loved.

"You idiot!" I'd yell at the hero. "What do you think you're doing? Go put a knot in it and do something useful!"

Now as I walked, I said the same things to myself. It didn't help though. My legs kept carrying me to her.

I only stopped by the entrance to their posh business center. I needed to catch my breath. I was sweating like a pig. I wiped my face with my sleeve, dropping the MRI envelope into a puddle of rainwater in the process. I bent down to pick it up and sensed her gaze on my back.

I must have looked a sight: soaked and disheveled, standing in the middle of a filthy puddle fumbling for my envelope in the water. Plus that damned KFC bucket in my other hand.

I'd been here a few times before to pick her up, and every time she'd asked me to wait for her outside.

Did I embarrass her? Had I been so dumb not to realize it?

She'd never invited me to their office parties, either. "It's okay, you can stay at home and play with your computer if you wish, we're not obliged to bring a spouse."

And I'd so readily agreed every time she'd said it...

Bracing myself, I picked up the envelope, shook the water off it and turned round.

I'd been mistaken. The person who stared at me wasn't Yanna at all. It was their security guard — a bundle of muscle wrapped in a cheap black suit — who mumbled something into his radio as he gave me a hooded look.

Max "Boss" Bosiara
Age: 29
Current status: security guard
Social status level: 3
Class: wrestler. Level: 4
Unmarried
Relationship: Dislike 15/30

Only level 3? Poor bastard! Even Alik had a better social status. And he was already disliking me? He didn't even know me.

I was so pissed with this "Boss" as if it was his own fault that Yanna had left me. What had the system message said about "spontaneous Enrage"? This must have been it.

The thought had calmed me down a bit. Still I couldn't resist getting even with him.

Copying his body language, I produced my cell phone and spoke into it, holding it close to my mouth,

"One, two, three, do you read me? Over..."

He gave up first, averting his gaze, then turned his back to me.

Stupid, I know. Still, it distracted me for a bit. My fixation with Yanna seemed to have subsided a little.

I walked home hung with debuffs like a Christmas tree. I was too tired to jog.

Once home, I peeled off my sodden clothes and shoved them in the washer, then headed for the shower to remove all trace of today's legwork. I'd been rushing around like a headless chicken all day — but my Stamina hadn't even budged.

I had lunch listening to the monotonous dripping of the leaky tap. I couldn't even taste my food. Having finished, I made myself a cup of hot black tea. That was better. The Weakness debuff was already gone. Later, I might also have some strong coffee to give my Metabolism a boost.

Once I cleaned up after myself, I received an optimistic message,

You've consumed 378 calories.
Warning! The food you've eaten contains chemicals which may be detrimental to your health!
Warning! +0,00039% to your risk of developing cancer!

-0,071345% to Vigor
-2% to Metabolism. Duration: 12 hrs.

Ooh. Life is a bitch. I'd basically swapped one debuff for another. These days whatever you picked up from a supermarket shelf was bound to contain some "detrimental chemicals". Thanks a bunch, mister game designer. You can warn me all you want but I'm not giving up fast food even if you keep dishing me up debuff after debuff!

I slumped into my decrepit leather chair. It groaned under my weight, creaking, then succumbed to its fate. I took a big swig of coffee, closed my eyes and tried to concentrate.

As always after a meal, I was dying for a smoke. I was too used to having a cigarette in my mouth whenever I needed to think. Still, I ignored the urge and took a few deep breaths, then focused on the task at hand. I needed to see the game's interface.

My field of vision filled with blurred flashes of iridescent light. I noticed a dark shape moving in a row of amorphous spots. It was rather small, diamond-shaped, but most interestingly, it appeared to shimmer.

When I concentrated on it, the spot began to come into focus. Now I could see it clearly: a black diamond bearing the sign of a red exclamation mark.

I opened my eyes. The sign hadn't disappeared. It hovered in mid-air in front of me like a 3D movie effect.

I reached out to touch it. Predictably, my hand

went right through it. I tried to mentally "click" it.

It worked! A dialog window opened,

You've received a new social status level!
Current social status level: 6
You've unblocked a new skill: Insight I
Skill type: Passive
Now you can connect to the universal information field in order to see your data and that of the world around you, within the limits of your skill level.
Skill points available: 1

Accept/Decline

"Yes please! Accept!" I shouted.

Nothing happened.

I focused on the *Accept* button, mentally "clicking" it.

The world imploded onto me.

* * *

WHEN I FINALLY CAME AROUND, I WAS LYING on the floor in the fetal position. I must have fallen from the chair.

The room was dark. I could see the night sky through the window.

I tried to scramble to my feet but my arms gave under me, sending me face first back onto the floor. I very nearly fainted again. I rolled onto my back and waited for my numb body to wake up.

My eyes were itchy as if I had sand in them. My whole body was stiff. I was drooling from the corner of my mouth. Still, my mind was crystal clear as if I'd just had my brain formatted and a new OS installed.

I rubbed my eyes until finally I realized: those were no grains of sand.

They were icons and status bars.

I had my interface opened!

Unlike a traditional game interface, this one didn't have any of the pretty bells and whistles. The edge of my vision was lined with several gray icons covered in black symbols. They were positioned along the top border which made them look a bit like eyelashes.

In order to "control" them, I had to roll my eyes. Then an icon would grow and come into focus, becoming clickable.

I glanced over the symbols without opening anything yet. A human silhouette; a book; a globe; an exclamation mark, and a question mark.

Not much. So where was my one-size-fits-all non-dimensional inventory bag?

I tried to move the icons around. It worked. I positioned them at some distance from myself. Now they looked like road signs hovering in the air a few feet away from me.

The status bars were located in the lower part of my field of vision. The already-familiar Vitality bar (or health bar, I suppose) was red, about three-quarters full. The one next to it was yellow, only half-full. I focused on it. This was Satisfaction.

Finally, in the lower right corner of my vision was a blue bar, full to the brim.

That just had to be mana.

All 100% of it.

Mana. *Magic.*

I was already envisioning myself hurling fireballs as I single-handedly battled a whole army (provided there was a war on) or stealthing into the bank vaults of some get-rich-quick scammers in order to retrieve their bankrupt old-age victims' savings, or confronting a bunch of mafia toughs and bringing them to justice...

Bummer!

This was a fail to end all fails.

The blue bar meant Vigor. Vigor, of all things.

Well, what could you expect from someone who'd designed a *red* (not green!) health bar?

Actually, whose idea was this?

Who had come up with all the system messages? Normally, game makers hired special people to write them. But this wasn't a game, was it? This was real life. I wasn't dreaming. My brain was perfectly healthy, so no chance of hallucinating, either.

Where did it all come from? All these gaming terms and the system itself? Who calculated my social status or my Satisfaction points?

If you took that guy, the security guard — "Boss", wasn't it? If I asked him about his purpose in life, what would he say to me? Would he say he was a level-4 wrestler? I don't think so. He might say he's a security guard, or a human being, or a bodybuilder, an

85

athlete, an avid angler, or her mother's son — take your pick. His answer would depend on the timing and the asker's identity. Still, according to the system he was a wrestler, period.

And how about Yanna? A level-3 office worker? Yeah yeah.

In any case, why was it happening to me of all people?

Just think of the mayhem that would have ensued in the social media if something like this would have become known! A RealRPG! This wasn't some viral video of a cute cat or a celebrity wardrobe malfunction. The Internet would have exploded!

Still, there was no sign of any such breaking news anywhere. I'd spent the last forty-eight hours scouring all the newsfeeds and tabloid sites; I'd even posted a few questions on various forums with provocative titles like "What would you do if..." In those posts, I'd described my own case as a gamer's fantasy. Admittedly, my posts had garnered a wealth of replies — but none of the commenters seemed to have taken my question seriously. Some dude called Igor_Bogeyman even wrote that he would have "leveled up soccer" and "finally brought Russian soccer under the spotlight". His comment was seconded by several more guys — probably enough to make Russia's new soccer team in time for the World Cup.

I tried to remember everything that had happened to me prior to this weird glitch in my perception. Still, I couldn't think of anything. I might have overdone on WoW, that's for sure. But that wasn't how it was supposed to happen, was it? If you think of it, Bruce Banner had had to suffer a blast of gamma radiation in order to become Hulk. Peter Parker became Spider-Man after he'd been bitten by a radioactive spider. Tony Spark had built a powered suit of armor which turned him into Iron Man. Virtually all superheroes had a very clear transition from "before" to "after". While in my case...

Having said that, my ability to divine other people's attitude to me was a superpower, wasn't it? In which case I too had a "before" and an "after".

One thing I couldn't yet work out was what had actually happened in the period between the two.

I'd read a book once where the MC was ported to a world that worked similarly to an RPG game. His surprise lasted for, like, half a paragraph. He looked around himself and immediately started leveling up. As in, *Look at me! I've got a level-1 Observation skill! Cool! I should be leveling it!* Because while you sleep, your opponents are leveling up. He then spent hours "observing" while lifting some weights and prancing around in order to improve his Strength and Agility too.

What a lot of BS.

Admittedly, I too had acted stupidly at first. Just think of me hopping and skipping all the way to the newsagent's to get the old man's paper! But that was understandable. I'd still been in shock. In moments like those, your brain goes into auto pilot. Which in my case meant switching to familiar patterns of game behavior.

And as for my going on a jogging marathon after

Yanna had left me — well, that was an experiment of sorts. An important one, too, which had allowed me to finally work out the logic of this new game world...

No, not a game world, of course. Just the world the way I saw it now. How else did you expect me to do it? It wasn't as if there were any guides or manuals available.

Let's take XP, for instance. How were you supposed to earn it? Where were you going to find mobs and how were you supposed to smoke them? How about quests? I hadn't received any XP for the sole quest I'd completed, fetching the paper for Panikoff. Since then, I hadn't come across anything that even marginally resembled a quest.

And what was this social status thing, for crissakes? Was it the same as Popularity? Or Fame? Hardly. Could it mean your contribution to society?

My head was about to explode with all the questions. Never mind. As my Granddad used to say, *you should do it one step at a time.*

I needed to study the interface and the stats, everything that the few available icons had to offer. I had to work out their leveling scenario — but that might take some trial and error. I'd almost run out of money; new bills were coming soon; my fridge was empty. I needed to find a job. I also had to contact my clanmates, explain the situation and take a hiatus from the game. Then there was Yanna...

So basically, I had myself and my problems to sort out, relationships to mend and a life to fix. Once that done, I could finally afford to look into all this and decide whether it was a gift or a curse, then try to locate the person who'd bestowed it on me and why. Following that, I could always save the world if necessary.

I focused on the icon depicting a human silhouette and pressed it.

Chapter Eight

A NOOB TO END ALL NOOBS

"The meeting with ourselves belongs to the more unpleasant things."

Carl Gustav Jung

AGILITY HAD ALWAYS been my characteristic of choice, even in the old text-based browser games. It was probably because in real life I was anything but agile even if you pointed a crossbow at me. Klutz was my middle name. Or could it be my inner shrink telling me that I simply loved frequent crits and high dodge numbers? Whatever the reason, I'd never for one moment hesitated over my character choice. A Rogue. A thief. All stealth-stun-combo-vanish, rinse and repeat. And if by some chance my enemy had survived, I'd dart for my dear life.

No wonder nobody likes the rogue. It's a mean class who likes playing dirty, its trickster nature far removed from the noble chivalry of the paladin or the dignified integrity of the warrior.

I opened the character window. Uh oh. So much for my playing a rogue in *this* game.

The window's modest layout matched the austere design of the rest of the interface. I couldn't see my picture anywhere. The 3D figure of my character was missing, as were the gear slots.

All I could see were a few lines of text against a translucent gray background,

Philip "Phil" Panfilov
Age: 32
Current status: gamer
Social status level: 6
Class: Unclassified
Married
Wife: Yannina "Yanna" Orlova
Children: none

Main Characteristics:
Strength: 6
Agility: 4
Intellect: 18
Stamina: 4
Perception: 7
Charisma: 12
Luck: 6

Secondary Characteristics:
Vitality: 74%
Satisfaction: 48%
Vigor: 97%
Metabolism: 83%

In order to access more data, you need to level up Insight.

Unclassified? Status, *gamer?*

My already plummeting megalomania took a further dive. Judging by my stats, I'd been leveling as a wizard, clumsy and charismatic.

Big mistake. This world didn't have any magic, did it?

I tried to click on the stats to see the meaning of each of them and hopefully work out how they were supposed to interact.

Nothing. Either the interface designers were some cack-handed hack artists or the interface owner — the game's *user?* — was supposed to know it all.

At 18, my Intellect wasn't that bad, at least compared to all the other stats. Then again, it could be average — or low even — compared to other people. I was no Nobel prize winner, that's for sure, but I can't have been that dumb, either. So if we assumed that my Intellect reading was a tad above average, then all the other characteristics should have been in the 12 to 15 range.

Which meant that they were way below par.

Then again, what did I expect? Was I fit? Hardly. So these stats seemed to reflect the current state of affairs.

What was their effect on my life? This, too, was pretty self-explanatory. If the elevator in our apartment block broke down, I'd never be able to climb the stairs all the way to my apartment on the tenth floor. Could I swim a few laps? Yeah right, I just might drown halfway. And if I tried to perform a little juggling act, I might just get killed in the process.

I was quite surprised at my high Charisma reading. Then again, it might only mean that I didn't make other people puke on seeing me.

I spent some more time staring at the stats window before finally closing it.

No idea what I did wrong. Maybe I sent a wrong mental command or just blinked unintentionally, but the window simply disappeared. If I'd expected it to disintegrate into a gazillion glittering fragments, or fold into a swirling vortex and be sucked back into the icon, I'd been wrong. No pretty animation, no visual effects. It was just gone.

"Miaow!" a demanding howl disrupted the silence.

It was Boris, apparently suffering from nighttime munchies. She rubbed against my leg expectantly. I heaved a sigh, rose, gave her a pat on the neck and headed for the kitchen. As I poured a generous helping of cat food into her bowl, she purred like a tractor, polishing my legs with her fluffy flank.

I left her in the kitchen and returned to the room. This time I sat on the couch, just in case I zoned out again.

I clicked on the icon with the book.

A huge field of text opened up before me.

It was a complete list of everything I'd learned in my lifetime since day one: from learning to walk to my recently-acquired dart-playing skill.

Skills:

Playing World of Warcraft: 8
Russian speaking skills: 7
Russian reading skills: 7
PC skills: 7
Russian writing skills: 6
Empathy: 6
Online search: 5
MS Word: 5
MS Excel: 4
Vending: 4
Social skills: 4
Intuition: 4
Deception: 3
Creative writing: 3
Manners: 3
Photography: 3
Decision-making: 3
Learning new skills: 3

English: 3
Seduction: 3
Cooking: 3
Self-discipline: 3
Driving: 2
Self-control: 2
Plan-making: 2
Marketing: 2
Leadership: 2
Perseverance: 2
Pushbike riding: 2
Public speaking: 2
Map reading: 2
Walking: 2
<...>
DIY skills: 1
First aid skills: 1
Singing: 1
Insight: 1

I spent some quality time going through the list which unfolded in the best-to-worst order. I had so many skills still at level 1! I kept scrolling through them but the list seemed interminable.

It looked like the system took meticulous stock of everything I'd ever tried in my life. For instance, I even had a "knife handling" skill. That must have had something to do with our childhood games of throwing knives at the shed wall. Couldn't be anything else: the only thing I'd ever used a knife for was to cut myself a slice of bread.

I also had a level-1 Agriculture skill. Of course. Hadn't I helped my parents with their cottage garden? I used to weed it and dig it up, I'd even planted some potatoes for them at some point.

Running, swimming, skiing, skating... all level 1. Plus playing soccer, poker and chess, and dozens of half-forgotten computer games which I used to passionately play in the past. Most likely, a skill's level dropped when it fell out of use.

I even had level 1 in Poetry — I had indeed dabbled in it once — and Sewing (probably from my college attempts to fix a hole in a T-shirt). Also, Wrestling. Back at school, my father had signed me up for a judo class where I'd lasted all of two months.

That wasn't what pissed me off. According to the list, the area of my biggest expertise was game playing! Logical, of course. I'd spent at least a hundred and fifty thousand hours mastering the wretched thing. No wonder its level was comparatively so high.

So that's who I was, then. I wasn't an author at all. I was a deceptive WoW user with decent Googling skills and a good working knowledge of Microsoft Word.

In everything else in life, I was a total noob. A useless noob who could only get through life by trailing in Yanna's powerful slipstream.

My reading and writing skills were worse than my game playing. That was all you needed to know about my life over the past twelve years. Twelve years! I only had another thirty left till my retirement![3]

How very nice of you, Blizzard guys, thanks a bunch.

Oh. My vision blurred again. I felt weak.

A new debuff message appeared before me,

Apathy
Duration: 18 hours
You're emotionally drained. Your central nervous system needs some rest. We recommend that you get some quality sleep, a balanced diet and some exercise.
Warning! The state of Apathy can easily escalate to Depression!
-5% to Satisfaction every 6 hrs.
-1% to Vitality every 5 hrs.
-6% to Vigor every 6 hrs.
-2% to Metabolism every 6 hrs.
-5% to Confidence every 6 hrs.
-2% to Willpower every 6 hrs.

What a nasty debuff. As if the nicotine withdrawal wasn't enough. This way, I might not live to see the weekend. I'd just drop on my back on the floor like a beetle and expire.

Which was something I couldn't do. My old parents needed help. My sister was a single mother

---

[3] The official retirement age for Russian men was 60 at the time of writing

who could use my support too. I had to fight to win Yanna back, dammit! Plus I had so many projects.

Apathy, they said? I didn't give a damn.

What did they want me to do? I couldn't get quality sleep at the moment, not until I was finished with that wretched interface. A healthy diet? The only healthy foods I had in the house were an onion and a box of green tea. The remaining half-bucket of KFC wings hardly counted as a balanced meal, let alone a healthy one.

That left exercise.

I cast a doubtful glance at the clock. It was past two in the morning. Chuckling, I peeled myself off the couch, started my favorite playlist and began warming up like they'd taught us to in that long-forgotten judo class. All the bending, stretching and rotating: wrists, arms, knees and hips... Now ten sit-ups.

My head went round. I had to stop to catch my breath, then did ten more. I was lightheaded again. I walked into the kitchen and put the kettle on. Should I do another ten?

My legs were rubbery, my knees weak. My hands were shaking. My teeth began to ache.

I poured some boiling water over a teabag, leaned against a stool and did five... six... come on, just one more... seven pushups.

I hurried to peel and slice the remaining onion and made myself a quick cheese and onion sandwich with some dry rye bread. I left it on the table next to my tea and walked out onto the balcony to catch my breath. Then I returned, dropped to the floor, hooked my feet under the edge of the couch and tried to do a few crunches.

These proved to be the trickiest. I couldn't do a single one. In the end, I just lifted my feet off the floor and tried to keep my legs up for as long as I could.

Which wasn't for very long. I tried again. And again. My abs were killing me. I was sweating buckets.

Enough. Shower time.

I lingered under its hot-and-cold jets, getting rid of all the sweat and grime. Finally, I received a new buff: my Metabolism was on the rise, both Vigor and Satisfaction were in the black.

A new message arrived, informing me that my Apathy debuff had been reduced to 12 hrs.

Excellent. I ate my sandwich, making sure I chewed properly, washed it down with some tea, then returned to the couch and continued my research.

Strange that my creative writing skills were so high though. 3 points! Could it have been all the countless blog posts I'd written?

Wait a sec. Where was my Finance? I'd spent five years in college studying that. I had a degree, for crissakes! And it wasn't even level 2? I'd studied hard enough; I'd taken all the exams and had very decent grades throughout. Admittedly, my professional experience had been limited to a one-month internship at a major engineering plant where I'd registered the incoming email and helped the bookkeeper girls replace printer cartridges and create user profiles at various dating sites. That had been the extent of it. Whatever experience I'd had afterward was limited to online buying and selling. No wonder my Vending skills were so high. If you applied RPG rules to real life, I was entitled to a 15% discount everywhere I went.

What a shame this wasn't virtual reality.

My high Empathy levels weren't a surprise to me though. I'd always had this ability to divine what other people were feeling. The moment Yanna walked through the front door, I knew what kind of day she'd had. I could tell my Dad's mood just by the way he was breathing and knew what Mom was feeling just by looking into her eyes. I didn't even need to see the person: show me a text message, and I'll tell you what the person was feeling while writing it. Most of the time, anyway. The emoji culture has a lot to answer for.

The fact that the mysterious game system so effortlessly listed the names of certain programs — like MS Word and Excel, for instance — made me think that the generation of those system messages actually took place in the user's head. It was as if someone had scanned my character's brain — *my* brain, — then analyzed and classified its entire database.

I yawned. I needed some sleep. I clicked through some of the skills without much effect, then closed the window and went back into the kitchen to get some coffee. As the kettle was boiling, I opened the next icon: the one with the globe.

A map opened.

It was surprisingly clear, too. No dark spots; no unavailable areas concealed in the "mist of war". It looked rather like an aerial view taken from a satellite or something.

A golden dot shimmered at its center. That just had to be me. I recognized my apartment block and the area around it.

I zoomed in on the scene. Now I was looking at our courtyard from a height of about a hundred feet. I could even make out a few human figures still lounging about in the playground.

Heh! Fancy seeing you here, guys!

This was crazy. I could even tell precisely who they were thanks to the name tags which hovered over their heads. Yagoza, my friend Alik, and all the others: Sprat, Vasily, Fatso... Alik was marked with a green dot and all the others, with yellow ones.

I zoomed out to see the entire city. It was flooded with hundreds of shimmering dots: red, green, orange, emerald, blue and turquoise. Some of them were bigger than the rest, others considerably smaller.

I focused on two especially large blue dots.

A prompt popped up,

Mom and Dad

Aha. So the system indeed used my brain as

a starting point. I was the only person in the world who referred to my Dad as "Dad". To all the others, he was either Oleg Igorevich Panfilov, or simply Oleg.

Wow, just wow. How's that for an app? Compared to this, the Marauder's Map was child's play. Harry Potter, eat your heart out!

I scanned all the other dots. These weren't just my friends and acquaintances — no, they were actually all the people I'd ever come into contact with. That amber dot over there was Lola — or should I say Dr. Shvedova — whom I'd consulted at the clinic earlier today. And one of the red ones turned out to be Kostya, my ex co-trainee at an advertising agency a few years back. He used to hate me with a vengeance; you could cut the office air with a knife.

And that orange dot over there...

That was Yanna.

I zoomed in. She was at her parents'.

Relief flooded over me. Only now had I realized how much tension, bred from jealousy and the feeling of loss, I'd suffered over the last twenty-four hours. No matter how hard I'd been trying to blank them out, these thoughts kept growing like cancer cells, multiplying and assaulting my brain with vivid pictures of Yanna's supposed infidelity.

I zoomed out again until the map shrank back to the size of a globe. I was now looking at a view of planet Earth from space, with me still at its center. The continents' outlines were dimmed as it was nighttime in our hemisphere.

I could see more dots scattered all over the planet's surface. I discovered one of my school dates, the popular Maya Abramovich, in Australia, no less. Another dot shimmered in the South of Africa, and this one was my sixth-grade pal Pashka Pashkovsky. I was surprised I still remembered his name. We used to go to the chess class together.

Memories flooded over me. My school friends, fellow college students, my ex co-workers... What a shame I couldn't access any more information about them, only their names, and some of the names didn't even say anything to me anymore. It looked like I certainly needed the Insight skill in order to do that.

I began to experiment. I turned the virtual globe around, trying various commands. Finally, I managed to sort the dots by their Reputation with me, removing all those whose status was below Amicability.

I kept fiddling with the globe until I could find certain locations — countries, cities or objects — by merely willing to see them. Had the real Earth been able to rotate that fast, it would have long shaken everything off its surface, trees included.

I kept traveling across the map. London, Hollywood, the legendary Lake Baikal, the Kremlin, my primary-school love Veronica, the Camp Nou stadium in Barcelona, Phuket Island, the Niagara Falls, Beijing, my parents, Yanna, the President of the United States...

Warning! The current level of your Insight skill is insufficient to access the information you've requested!

Okay, so Mr. Trump was off limits for me, then. Never mind. Did that mean that once I'd leveled up Insight, I could find any person on planet Earth? Anyone at all?

My breathing seized. The possibilities it opened were mind-boggling. I could search for missing people. I could locate terrorists. I could track down every movement of every millionaire and top politician I wanted. *Ready or not, here I come, you can't hide!*

And what if I could locate objects, as well? All the secret stashes, the hidden treasures, the Aztec gold...

Cool down, man. Get a grip.

I closed the map and walked out onto the balcony for a breath of fresh air.

I stared into the night sky. Somewhere up there coursed the super powerful satellite built by whoever had created my new abilities. The satellite which could rush to any location at my slightest whim just to show it to me.

But what if the satellite didn't even exist? What if I'd been accessing the information from — what was it called now — the *universal information field?*

I gulped in the fresh air of May, unable to get enough of it.

Leaning against the railing, I opened my interface and clicked the icon with the exclamation mark.

Just as I expected, it was a quest list. But contrary to my expectations, it wasn't empty.

Tasks available:

- make up with Yanna and move back in with her;
- master the augmented reality control interface;
- work out how to level up skills and other stats and come up with a leveling strategy;
- find a stable job;
- check emails;
- check the freelance sites for any new jobs and apply for them;
- call parents and ask if they need anything;
- update the blog;
- apologize to clanmates for my silence;
- buy groceries;
- give Boris a brush

They had to be kidding me. These were all snippets of various to-do lists which I'd occasionally made on either my phone or computer. Nothing was clickable. I couldn't open the tasks to read their descriptions or see the rewards.

Then again, what kinds of rewards did I expect? *Quest name: Find a stable job. Reward: A regular paycheck.*

Yeah right. *Quest name: Update the blog. Reward: A new blog post.*

How stupid was that?

Having said that... admittedly, it was quite convenient. This was every time-management freak's dream: an automated logging in and prioritizing system.

Wait a sec. What was that now?

The window I was looking at was entitled *Tasks available.* I hadn't even noticed that it indeed had another empty tab, marked *Quests.*

And? How was I supposed to get them? Was I supposed to walk around town looking for any quest givers?

Never mind. That could wait. I'd deal with it some other time.

The only remaining icon was the one with the question mark. I had a funny feeling this was some kind of Wiki.

I was right.

Dawn was breaking.

It didn't look as if I was going to get any sleep tonight.

Chapter Nine

THE CRAZIER THE EXPLANATION, THE CLOSER THE TRUTH

"You aren't a failure until you start blaming others for your mistakes."

John Wooden

EVERY RPG PLAYER IS USED TO THE CONVENTIONS OF online games. If you take such a basic thing as a health bar which is a prerequisite in most of them, it allows players to always know their own health levels. Quite often they might also know those of certain other players, too. This is so normal that a player takes it for granted. Logical, really: if your char's DPS is a meager couple of thousand, you'd think twice before attacking a monster whose hp is measured in millions.

Now let's imagine that this characteristic

becomes available IRL. Just think how many deaths from terminal diseases that could prevent. Think of a person who's going happily about his or her life, considering themselves perfectly healthy while their health numbers are slowly dwindling... and once they see that, they go to the doctor for a check. And indeed, this turns out to be the early stages of cancer which are perfectly treatable and have a very favorable prognosis.

How's that for a good life?

This also means that any magicless level-1 newb in possession of a non-dimensional inventory, a built-in map and a number of status bars could automatically become the next Forbes sensation in the real world. All he'd have to do was open a medical diagnostics center. And even if medicine wasn't his vocation, he could always use his inventory to make a living pinching vodka in supermarkets. The possibilities were legion.

Those were the kinds of ideas I was contemplating while studying my interface.

The built-in Wiki had given me answers to quite a few questions. I still didn't understand what had prevented the game's mysterious creators from uploading all the data directly to my head. That could have been a simple solution for someone that powerful. Then again, it could have been technically (or biologically?) impossible. Probably, the information had to be acquired organically, via normal channels such as eyesight and hearing.

The tab contained a standard brief menu,

- *About the program*
- *Wiki*
- *Settings*
- *Available updates*
- *Technical support*

I can't even tell you how relieved I felt staring at these lines which looked so familiar to me from the countless other pieces of software I'd used before. Even though the first three entries were rather nondescript, the last two spoke for themselves: I'd somehow ended up with a computer program installed in my brain. Which meant that someone must have built it.

Do you know what I did first thing? Checked the available updates, of course.

Impossible to establish connection with the updates server

It might be unavailable

Check your universal information field connection settings

The same thing happened when I tried to contact Support.

Ignoring the *Wiki* and *Settings* buttons, I opened *About the Program.*

My jaw dropped to the floor.

Augmented Reality! 7.2 Home Edition
Copyright © First Martian Company, Ltd. 2101-2118

I don't know how long I spent just sitting there staring at the copyright line.

When I'd been a kid, I'd read my fair share of time travel books where a humble student like myself somehow ended up in the future. How many times had I wished it had been me! I'd have loved to have seen our planet's future and hopefully even travel to Mars. At the time, I'd have given anything for a peek at the awesome world of the future.

As I grew up, I'd switched to dystopias and post apoc. Add to this all the zombie apocalypse blockbusters and my infatuation with Fallout games, and you'll understand why I wasn't so eager to see the future anymore. Still, even then I wouldn't have said no to *Gray's Sports Almanac 2000-2050* or some such artifact.

And now it looked like my pipe dream had finally come true. I'd just received a big tangible kick in the butt compliments of the twenty-second century.

I crawled back in bed and lay there buried under the sheets like a snail trying to retreat into its shell. The super ability freebie I'd just received weighed heavy on me. It felt very much like stumbling across a briefcase containing a million bucks in a dark alley. On one hand, it made you deliriously happy; on the other, a find like that bode nothing good. No one was stupid enough to leave a million bucks in a dark alley which meant someone was already looking for it.

The expiration date did nothing to improve my plummeting mood, either. What was going to happen to me and my brain once the license expired? Would they just unplug me? Or offer an extension? In which case, how did they expect me to pay?

If, at some later date, I decided to write a book describing these events, I would have to omit this moment of weakness entirely. I'd begin the book with me working hard. I'd sign up for all kinds of courses and classes and start leveling everything from archery to cooking to online marketing.

Reality wasn't as simple as that.

Unable to sleep, I stayed in bed till midday making all kinds of plans, then envisioning their sinister consequences. This fabulous gift from the future definitely came with strings attached. As a result, I received two mutually exclusive debuffs: Insomnia *(duration: 12 hrs.)* and Lack of Sleep. Between themselves, they'd decimated my Vigor, Satisfaction, Perception, Intellect, Agility and all the other stats for good measure.

Whatever. I didn't care anymore. All I wanted to do was continue researching this game system.

I actually discovered that all that eye-rolling wasn't really necessary. I could very easily control the interface by sending mental commands.

I opened *Settings*.

It allowed me to set up my system message preferences, play with colors and the interface layout by moving around bars and buttons, add a clock and a mini map, set up an alarm and change the task logging parameters. I could also enable the auto accept quest option (whatever that was supposed to mean), and activate some thingy which blasted an alarm whenever a certain person came within direct line of sight. Etc., etc.

I could deal with all of that later. Now I had the best course of this digital feast staring me in the face:

Wiki.

Someone else might have opened it first, ignoring all the other tabs. It's just like kindergarten kids who eat their dessert first, then move to the more boring dishes. Me, I'd always left the dessert for last. It was the only thing that could motivate me to finish my carrots and gulp down the sickening milk soup which Russian nutrition authorities believed beneficial for children's growing bodies.

The Wiki turned out to be very helpful. It was a proper virtual assistant: the moment I thought of something it offered me a page with answers, then read its contents to me out loud. Eventually, that became a problem because I kept thinking of new things as I read, which prompted an avalanche of new windows overlapping each other. Every time I thought of something, my virtual assistant would stop mid-word and switch to my new inquiry, which in the end became admittedly chaotic.

At first, the assistant's voice was devoid of emotion and even gender: it was too high for a man and too low for a woman. It spoke Russian with just a hint of an accent. Not that I paid any attention to it: I was too busy learning how stats were calculated.

They actually turned out to be quite simple. I'd been right: the system adapted to the user's understanding. Had I been some clueless newb without any gaming experience I might have received the following system message,

Congratulations! Even though you're not that strong (2), you're very smart (14) and have enviable intuition (16). You're quite observant but unfortunately, not too enduring (4). To make up for it, you're agile and supple (11). And you have tons of luck (15)!

Mind you, this was only my conjecture. Numbers would be no use to a clueless newb. He or she wouldn't know what to do with them.

One thing I'd managed to work out was that the stats numbers were in keeping with some average values — probably, shared by all human beings. How the mysterious game creators accessed those numbers was a different question entirely. Most likely, they extracted them from that universal information field they'd already mentioned. An average human being's stats seemed to hover around level 10.

In any case, what exactly did the system mean by Strength, Perception or Agility? How were they supposed to work and what were they supposed to affect?

Strength stood for a user's brute physical force. Using weightlifters' language, it was the number of weights a person could lift using any given muscle group. The system summed up the numbers of all human beings on planet Earth in order to work out an average, which was then divided by 10 to calculate the value of one point.

Which meant I was 40% weaker than an average Terran. Sigh. The good news was, Strength was one of the easiest stats for a newb to level thanks to the so-called "beginner's effect".

Agility, according to Wiki, was "the ability to learn complex coordinated movements and use these acquired skills continuously in constantly changing environments". Unlike Strength, it was calculated using some arcane chart of complex movements and their performance times.

I had a funny feeling that the chart listed cartwheels and leg splits which I'd never mastered at school. Otherwise, why would I only have 4 pt. Agility? Luckily, it too could be leveled up with various exercises and gym practice.

As for Intellect, it wasn't as simple as one's IQ reading. In fact, the game had its own IQ test which also calculated the person's creativity and their ability to think out of the box. There were other contributing factors, too. Like Erudition which was calculated as the percentage of the user's knowledge of the planet's entire information database. Or the ability to generate new knowledge which figured heavily in the IQ calculation formula. There were also Life Experience, Problem Solving and other such factors.

I indeed proved to have high Intellect numbers. Finally something I could be proud of. I could level it up even higher by studying, through learning the existing knowledge and generating new data — for instance, via my writing.

Now, Stamina. Here the Wiki flooded me with data about my lung volume, respiratory metabolism and ventilation rates. I stared at columns of digits depicting my CO_2 rates and metabolic heat production, trying to come up with questions which could explain it in layman's language. Finally, I worked out that all those numbers could be improved upon by performing extended periods of certain types of physical activity such as jogging, swimming, uphill walking, jumping, making love, or pull-ups.

Getting the right answers from my virtual assistant was a job and a half. I showered it with questions, trying to work my way through lists of scientific terms and make my questions as straightforward as possible:

"Does sex count?"

"Yes. The time spent in the active position can be used as a variable which would allow you to calculate the average..." the assistant would go on and on until I interrupted it with my next question.

Perception was another complex characteristic which included Eyesight, Hearing, Taste, Smell, Intuition, Rapid Memory, Attention to Detail and Foresight. Even though I hadn't quite managed to work out their calculation principle, I could see they were all interrelated. As for leveling it, I decided to leave it till later.

Charisma included Attractiveness, Credibility and Charm. No idea how the system was supposed to calculate the latter. Apparently, it had performed a virtual simulation of each and every legally capable human being on Earth in order to see how many other people he or she could attract and influence.

Finally, the calculation of Luck. That's where I thought I must have been losing it.

"We have analyzed every day of every person's life from the moment of his or her conception, taking into consideration all key life events which have affected his or her existence," the assistant said matter-of-factly. "Then we used the 'good-to-bad life choices' ratio in order to produce the average Luck reading."

"How? How did you access the data?"

"It was provided by a particular local segment of the universal information field."

God bless their information field. And its local segment, whatever that was supposed to mean.

In order to level up Luck, you had to make correct life-changing choices. One thing I couldn't work out was the effect it was supposed to have on your life.

"This parameter is involved in all processes," the assistant replied evasively.

"What, all of them?"

"Oh yes. Luck affects all stats. It has a decisive influence on a user's life."

The assistant dissolved in a wordy explanation. According to it, even the probability of a lethal blood clot entering my bloodstream was determined by Luck.

Having studied all the characteristics, I moved over to skills. Their number wasn't limited. Their levels depended on the number of hours spent practicing them. Each consequent skill point required more hours (or reps) than the one before it. Sometimes loads more. If you took gaming, I'd apparently spent over 15,000 hours playing online — but I was still only level 8.

This system was actually quite predictable and not that different from the one used in gaming. In any given game, you could make level 1 in a matter of hours. Then you sometimes had to spend hundreds of hours just to reach level 2. To give you some idea, bringing one's skill to level 5 required about 10,000 hours of practice.

And anything beyond level 10 was considered Top Expertise which required a minimum of 21,000 hours of training and practice.

Still, those were only the basic numbers which didn't take into consideration the cumulative effect of other skills. Which was indeed a problem. The time required to make the next level of any given skill depended on the combined value of all the others. You just couldn't become a munchkin by leveling everything in sight. The explanation of this phenomenon lay in our brain's capacity. Logical, really: once you've used up some brain space by leveling, say, chess skills, there'll be less space left to learn cooking.

Having said that... today's scientists seemed to

question this theory. Then again, what did I know? The experts of the future seemed to have studied this problem extensively.

Was there any way I could delete useless skills from my memory? Why would I need all those early Mortal Kombat tricks, like remembering the correct button order for each combo and memorizing all the fatalities as well as each warrior's special abilities? All those "back, back, forward, press X"? That was a veritable mine of useless information which encroached on my brain space.

Some skills required Spirit points, too. I hadn't yet worked out what exactly they were. Apparently, they required a higher level of Insight which could only be leveled through constant use. All I managed to work out was that it too directly depended on stat readings.

That made sense. My Agility was admittedly low which meant that I couldn't succeed in leveling any agility-heavy athletic skill, no matter how hard I practiced. By the same token, practicing a skill could improve its respective characteristics.

The good news was, my improved Insight meant that now I didn't need to make eye contact with other people in order to see their stats.

When I'd finally finished going through the charts, I heard a melodious jingle followed by a new system message,

Task Status: Master the augmented reality control interface
Task completed!

XP received: 5 pt.
+1% to Satisfaction

That was nice of them. Shame I couldn't see the XP bar. I might need to ask the assistant about it.

I spent some more time in the *Settings*. I temporarily disabled the mental command function, changed the assistant's voice to female and called her Martha.

Martha spoke in a husky old-Hollywood kind of voice,

"Welcome to Augmented Reality System!"

"Hi, Martha."

"How do you do, Mr. Panfilov?"

"Oh please. Call me Phil."

"Request accepted."

"Who are you?"

"I'm your virtual assistant for the Home Edition of Augmented Reality!7.2."

"Who made this game?"

"First Martian Company, Ltd."

"Which is where?"

"Please be more specific."

"What's the company's office address?"

"The offices of First Martian Company, Ltd are located in Georgetown, Schiaparelli, Mars."

Were they really? Did that mean that we'd colonize Mars, after all? When would that have happened? Was its atmosphere OK? What other planets would we've colonized?

It was a good job I'd disabled the mental

command option. The answers to all those questions would be no good to me at the moment.

So I posed another question, which admittedly had strings attached,

"Who was the company founder?"

"The company was started by Zoran Savich."

"Is he a human being? What planet is he from?"

"He is originally from Earth, born in the Eurasian Union in 2058."

I committed the name to memory. If I lived to see him, it might not be a bad idea to stock up on his company shares.

"And what year is it now, Martha?"

"It is two thousand eighteen by the Gregorian calendar. This is your default chronology option, based on the results of your brain scan."

"In that case, can you explain to me how on earth could it have happened?"

"Please be more specific."

"When exactly was the game's current version released?"

"In twenty-one hundred eighteen by the Gregorian calendar. This is your default chronology option, based on the results of your-"

"Okay, okay. Can you just tell me how on earth did it end up a hundred years earlier?"

"Sending request to server. Please wait," Martha temporarily zoned out. "Server connection timeout. Impossible to establish connection with the server."

"Ah, forget it."

"Please be more specific."

"I mean you can cancel the server query."

"Request accepted."

"Where is the server, anyway?"

"The server is located along the Lagrangian points within the Solar system."

"You have any idea why you can't connect to it?"

"Sending request to server. Please wait. Server connection timeout. Impossible to establish connection with the server."

"That's because there's no flippin' server in those wretched Lagrangian points at the moment!" I snapped. "Never mind. But if the server's not available, can you tell me how come I can still access other people's data?"

"The data is extracted from the local segment of the universal information field."

"The local segment? What exactly is it?"

"The local segment of this sector of the Galaxy contains all the information on the human race as well as one other sentient species."

"Which sentient species?"

"Unauthorized query. Your access level is insufficient. Your license is limited to your personal use only."

"And this universal information field, what exactly is it?"

"It is the sum total of all knowledge accrued by all sentient species in the Universe."

"How many sentient species are there in the Universe? We aren't alone, are we?"

"Apart from you, this location contains a

creature belonging to the species of *Felis domesticus* which is a small, typically furry, carnivorous mammal. Would you like me to mark the creature's location on your mini map?"

"She's not a 'creature'! Her name is Boris!"

"Information surplus to requirements. Your brain scan data contains the creature's name."

I did a mental facepalm. "Martha?"

"Yes, Phil?"

"How many sentient species are there in the Universe?"

"Unauthorized query. Your access level is insufficient. Your license is limited to your personal use only."

"I thought I had a premium account!"

"This is class AAA+ access level. This kind of privileged information is not covered by premium accounts."

"What kinds of privileges do they cover, then?"

"The only privilege the premium account offers is a triple bonus after having calculated your levels and stats such as characteristics, skills, XP points, Reputation and social level."

I knew it!

This was a leveling booster!

How cool was that? I'd hit the jackpot! This was every paying player's wet dream!

I did a quick mental calculation. If I decided to become the next soccer star like, say, Lionel Messi (at thirty-two years old, yeah right), I'd have to practice for twelve hours a day, every day. I'd need 21,000 hours to reach the Top Expert level. Without the booster, it would have taken me about five years. But now it was going to take me just over a year and a half.

Which still wasn't too good, really. My license expired in a year. Which meant I wasn't likely to achieve anything spectacular.

It also meant that my initial idea to level up every stat I had wasn't really viable. I had to come up with a good leveling plan. And I had to think fast because every day mattered now.

"Martha, how do I get the access level I need?"

"Please be more specific."

"How do I get the access level required in order to find out how many sentient species there are in the universe?"

"You need to purchase *Augmented Reality! Professional Edition.* Would you like to place an order?"

"Absolutely."

"Sending request to server. Please wait. Server connection timeout. Impossible to establish connection with the server."

"I see. Mind telling me how much the professional version costs?"

"Please specify purchase currency."

"Russian rubles."

"Unfortunately, we only accept Martian credits, Eurasian yuans or Federate dollars."

"Okay. Martian credits."

"Your upgrade will cost 199,900 Martian credits. Would you like to proceed to the checkout?"

"Yes please."

"Error. Insufficient funds on your account balance."

"Can I see my account?"

"Your account balance is negative. You have minus 49,000 Martian credits on your account. Allow me to remind you that your financial commitments should be honored. Failure to fulfill financial obligations is a basis for initiating court proceedings which might seize your property and make you compensate damages by doing hard labor."

"Okay. One last question. 49,000 Martian credits, how much would that be in rubles?"

I expected another server connection timeout message. Still, this time Martha replied promptly,

"Based on the evaluation of the planet's strategic energy resources in 2018 as compared to those of the Solar system in 2118, the going rate is 22,730 rubles. At the 2018 conversion rate, 49,000 Martian credits equals 1,113,770,000,00 Russian rubles."

How much?

I stared blindly at the number Martha had just read out to me. Did I really owe one billion rubles? To whom? What for? Was it the price of the game license I was currently using?

Without saying a word, I closed the interface. By then, I was yawning non-stop. I couldn't keep my eyes open. Between the Apathy and Lack of Sleep debuffs, both my Vigor and Metabolism were already in the red. The system kept showering me with alert messages, warning me against the dangers of lack of sleep.

And this last bit of news had completely put me

off any further conversation with her.

Still, masochist that I was, I couldn't resist the temptation of summoning Martha one last time,

"You mentioned damage compensation. What exactly did you mean?"

"Any incurred damages are compensated by doing hard labor, namely mining uranium on one of Jupiter's moons. There's a 83,71% chance of the said moon being Io."

I smiled sadly. In this case, I had every chance of becoming the first man on Io.

"Martha?"

"Yes, Phil."

"How much time do I have to pay for my license?"

"Your license has been paid in full. It is valid for one year from activation. The license expires on May 16 2019."

"You know who paid for it?"

"Sending request to server. Please wait. Server connection timeout. Impossible to establish connection with the server."

"Oh great," I muttered before passing out.

I slept through the rest of Friday and the following night.

I AWOKE WITH A JOLT. BEFORE EVEN OPENING MY EYES, I could see a new system message hovering in my mental view.

Good morning, Phil!

You wanted to wake up at 7.00. It is 6.42 a.m. now, which is the best awakening time based upon your sleep cycle.

That's right. Hadn't I set the system alarm for 7 a.m.? I couldn't find the alarm tone options at the time, wondering how on earth it was supposed to wake me up. And it just had! I simply woke up in the best of moods, feeling refreshed and energized.

Don't get me wrong: I could still remember every word of my last night's conversation with Martha. Still, I looked at it all differently now for some reason. Hard labor? Uranium mines? They didn't even exist yet. Not for another hundred years or so.

Without getting out of bed, I summoned Martha.

"Good morning, Phil."

"Morning! Remember you told me something about my duty to honor my financial commitments? When exactly is the deadline?"

"The deadline for honoring your payments to First Martian Company, Ltd. is December 31 2118."

"Thanks, sweetheart," I said, suppressing a triumphant scream. "Thanks a bunch. You be a good girl. I'll be back soon and then we can talk some more. This time we're going to discuss the leveling options of that so-called social status of yours."

I spent half the day straightening the place up. Now that both the Lack of Sleep and Apathy debuffs had expired, I'd finally seen our apartment in a truly unadulterated light. I didn't like it. The sight gave me a desperate desire to scrub the place clean.

So I had to walk the talk. I scooped out all the junk from all the drawers and cupboards, shined the fridge inside out, fixed that wretched kitchen tap, washed the windows, then sorted through my wardrobe, discarding everything I'd never had the heart to part with before.

In all these tasks, I was greatly assisted by the Object Identification skill courtesy of my Insight.

Like a child who'd just learned to read and now scrutinized everything she set her eyes on, I studied the stats of all of our household items. Even though I couldn't see much with my current level — not even the brand's name — the program identified all the items correctly, adding a brief description. For instance,

An LCD television set, 32". A long-distance device allowing for the reception and display of visual and audio signals.

A table fork, stainless steel. Part of a set.

A T-shirt, white, 100% cotton. An item of clothing.

The simpler the item, the shorter the description was. Some displayed their Durability numbers, others didn't. All items with Durability below 20% went straight in the trash.

Interestingly, some of the items of clothing had stat bonuses. Quite impressive ones sometimes. For instance, my reading glasses gave my Perception a

---

considerable boost. Or maybe it was just me with my admittedly ruined eyesight? My only pair of good shoes offered +1 to Charisma while my old track bottoms did exactly the opposite.

Armed with this knowledge, I unhesitantly discarded my torn sneakers with -1 to Charisma, replacing them with a pair of black Derbies I'd unearthed in the depths of the wardrobe.

Those were actually my wedding shoes. The only time I'd worn them was when I'd married Yanna.

How did I know they were Derbies? Simple. Their tag had told me as much,

Black Derby shoes
Material: leather
All-purpose open-laced footwear, worn with both
casual and special-occasion outfits
+1 to Charisma
Durability: 17/20

I'd had them for ages without actually knowing what they were. I just loved my new abilities.

Having finished cleaning, I booted up the computer. First of all, I wrote back to my clanmates. Just think of all the sleepless hours we'd spent together; all the days and nights — years even. We'd been playing together since vanilla.

I let them all know I was leaving the game. I thanked them for the great time and wished them luck on Argus. Just a down-to-earth message devoid of sentimental crap. I'd met quite a few of them IRL, anyway, which meant we weren't parting ways for good.

Task status: apologize to clanmates for my silence
Task completed!
XP received: 5 pt.
+3% to Satisfaction

I donated all my gear and resources to the clan bank. I sifted through all my legendaries one last time, thinking how much time and effort each of them had cost me. I gave the empty Stormwind one last check, then took the Deeprun Tram to Ironforge. There, nostalgia got the better of me. I took a screenshot of my rogue char, exited the game and deleted him together with all the alts. I didn't even consider selling him. It just didn't feel right.

I uninstalled the game and heaved a sigh.

Fare thee well, Azeroth.

Task status: Stop playing WoW
Task completed!
XP received: 50
+10% to Satisfaction

Stop playing WoW? I didn't remember seeing this task on the list. It must have added by itself when I'd made that decision.

Still, its results were impressive. I could use more of the same. The jump in Satisfaction gave me a feeling of incredible relief — the kind of sensation you get when you remove uncomfortable shoes after a day spent walking.

The number of XP points was also considerably higher. Martha had been right saying that the system awarded them depending on a task's difficulty for a particular user.

True: it hadn't been easy for me to erase almost twelve years of my life.

I didn't stop there. I deleted Steam and all the remaining games, followed by gigabytes of guides, TV series, graphic novels, meme collections and other such junk. I sorted through my work files, cleared the computer desktop and checked the email.

Apart from spam, it also contained two very welcome letters. The first one was an appointment for a job interview from some packaging factory in need of a sales rep. They said they'd phoned me earlier but I hadn't picked up.

The interview was for Monday morning. I'd have to spend some time preparing for it.

The other letter was from some Siberian pine nut distribution company. They'd contacted me via a freelance portal asking if I'd be interested in writing content for their corporate web site.

I immediately replied. Despite the weekend, one of their workers answered almost instantly. After we'd agreed on fees and deadlines, I set to work straight away.

Task status: Check the email
Task completed!

XP received: 1
+1% to Satisfaction

The more time I spent closing the unfinished tasks, the more I liked it. It wasn't even about all the system buffs. It was more about my newly-acquired feeling of accomplishment. I wasn't wasting my time playing or watching TV series: instead, I was being useful.

I was so hyped up that I used the short breaks from pine-nut content writing to finalize some other tasks. I gave Boris a good brush, did a quick grocery shopping, wrote a blog post about me quitting the Game and called my parents.

I spent the rest of Sunday finishing the content assignment and preparing for the next day's interview. I went to bed early. As I was falling asleep, I realized I'd completely forgotten to look into my social status which I'd already begun leveling. I even had an available stat point to show for it.

I really needed to invest it into something useful.

131

CHAPTER TEN

AN UNDOCUMENTED FEATURE

"If at first you don't succeed, failure may be your style."

Quentin Crisp

"HI, MY NAME'S PHIL PANFILOV. I'VE GOT A JOB interview at nine-thirty."

The pretty receptionist ignored me entirely, too busy scrolling through an Instagram page. She yawned, covering her mouth with her smartphone, then finally looked up at me. Her fake eyelashes were so long she could probably fan herself on a hot day just by fluttering them.

"Sorry, what is it?" she yawned again. She must have had one hell of a weekend.

Monday mornings in an office inevitably

resemble a disturbed anthill. But this particular company gave me the impression of an ant revolution in progress, with furious worker ants rushing around, about to dethrone the queen. Telephones rang non-stop. The air was blue with cussing. Printers rattled; doors slammed; the coffee machine gurgled.

"Martynov! Get off your ass and mail the proposal to Butchers Market! They're begging to be closed!"

"Which one?"

"To the Armenians, you dimwit!"

"Who's taken my coffee?!"

"Which part of 'cash before delivery' don't you understand?"

"Who's got the Virgil file?"

"Cyril, do you mind? This is my spoon! Kindly put it back once you're finished with it!"

"No, we don't do cash after delivery. Only before. Which means we need their money first!"

"Max, the accountant girls are looking for you everywhere! Their printer is down! They can't process the invoices!"

"How do you do, sir? Yes, I can most surely mark it down..."

"They're out of printer ink, that's all!"

Normal. Business as usual.

I looked around me. The spacious office was heaped high with boxes and product samples; the desks groaned under tons of paperwork. The management area looked like an island of tranquility in a raging sea of sales reps who occasionally tried to breach its calm waters.

"Excuse me," I squinted at the girl's name tag hovering over her head, "Darya, isn't it? I have a job interview at-"

"Down that corridor, last door to the right. It's marked HR."

"Thank you.... Darya."

With a nod, she turned her attention back to her phone.

I found the HR department. The corridor in front of it was quite crowded. It looked like I would be there for quite a while.

"Hi," I said. "Are you all interviewing for the job?"

"We are indeed," a small and lively young guy grinned at me. "Don't tell me you too have a nine-thirty appointment! You're interviewing for sales rep, aren't you? Well, you're late, man! It's nine-forty now."

He squinted his bright blue eyes at me, chatting non-stop. "Only joking. We all have the same time. What's your name? I'm Greg. I used to sell windows. That bastard of a boss of ours stopped paying our bonuses. And my wife's pregnant so I need the money real bad. I haven't quit my current job yet though. I told them I had a meeting with a customer. Clever, eh? And you? What did you do?"

"A bit of everything," I shook his proffered hand. "I'm Phil."

The guy was a born sales rep. Talk about skill! He could sell windows for a submarine if he really had to.

He was also a born bullshitter. He wasn't

married at all. I could see his stats, couldn't I?

Gregory "Bullshit Artist" Boyko
Age: 25
Current status: sales rep
Social status level: 7
Class: Vendor. Level: 5
Unmarried. No children
Criminal record: yes
Current Reputation: Indifference 0/30

Then again, so what if he wasn't married? He might have a live-in girlfriend.

Losing all interest in me, Greg B.S. returned his attention to a quiet girl standing next to him, resuming the conversation apparently disrupted by my arrival. Her age and clothes betrayed her as a college student. Was I right?

I most surely was,

Marina Tischenko
Age: 19
Current status: college student

I peered at all the others. Almost all of the job applicants were younger than me. All of them were wearing office clothes and even ties.

I'd very nearly done the same. I too had a business suit gathering dust in the back of the wardrobe. Still, reality proved quite harsh. No matter how hard I tried to tuck my stomach in, I just couldn't button up the trousers. So in the end, I'd had to make do with a pair of jeans and the suit jacket worn over a clean white T-shirt.

I curiously studied their product samples which littered the office, peering at their stats. Rolls and rolls of cling film, thermoforming film, anti-corrosion film, water-soluble film, shrink film and air bubble film...

Air bubble film, yes! I just loved popping it. Who doesn't?

My Insight skill could identify anything within direct line of sight, saving me the trouble of actually approaching or handling any of the items.

"Phil? What do *you* think?" Greg demanded.

I stared blankly at him.

"What's the easiest product to sell?" he repeated.

Everyone's eyes turned to me. Apparently, Greg had been the heart of the unfolding discussion.

I didn't have to think hard. "The easiest product to sell is the one your customer needs. You don't even need to sell it to him. He'll buy it anyway."

"Exactly! He's right!" the others chimed.

My Reputation with some of them, including the Marina girl, had grown a little. Now it was Indifference, 5/30.

So easy? They didn't mean it!

"Aha! You see?" Marina grinned victoriously at Greg. "So much for your windows!"

She wasn't as timid as I initially thought. In fact, she was very much like Yanna used to be at her age.

I took another look. She was quite pretty, actually. A delicate face with rather thick eyebrows under which sparkled a pair of emerald eyes amazing in their purity.

She met my gaze and gave me a wink. Embarrassed, I looked away, suppressing a smile.

"I don't think so!" Greg insisted. "How do you know what your customer needs? And you don't need just one! You need loads of them! And they don't give a damn that you have a quota to meet! They don't care if you lose your bonuses! Or if your product is out of season! And this," he pointed at the rolls of packaging film, "who needs these things? Shops? Supermarkets? Farmer's markets? Cling film suppliers are one big mafia, man..." he nodded at the office seething with workers.

I froze. He had a point.

I opened the map and sent a mental search request.

Nothing happened. I tried to reword my query several times until finally I had every shop and market in town marked on the map.

Fingers crossed.

I told the system to sort the shops, leaving only those in need of a packaging supplier.

"So windows are big, trust me!" Greg concluded. "They're something everybody needs!"

The current level of your Insight skill is insufficient to access the information you've requested!

Bummer!

The HR door opened, letting out a disheveled job

---

applicant. Frowning, he looked over at us, then left.

"Next please," a male voice called from behind the door.

They spent no more than five minutes with each applicant. The company's turnover must have been huge, forcing them to hire everyone who'd agree to work for a minimum wage with a prospect of bonuses.

Finally, Greg walked in. He stayed in the room longer than everybody else and walked out grinning from ear to ear, utterly pleased with himself.

"I'm good! And I don't care. If they don't hire me, it's their loss. See ya, guys! I've got windows to sell!"

He shook hands with everyone, gave Marina a wink and left.

Marina walked through the HR door. I was next.

After a while, she walked out with an embarrassed smile. "I think they've hired me," she whispered.

I walked in.

"Good luck," she said behind my back.

Thanks, girl.

* * *

I LEFT THE PACKAGING OFFICE FEELING GOOD. I HAD A funny feeling I'd made it. They said they'd call me — same thing as they'd said to everyone else, I suppose. In any case, the day was so good, the air filled with the bountiful aromas of summer blossoms. The sun touched my face, heating my shoulders. I removed the jacket and slung it over my back.

I turned my head this way and that, identifying everything in sight just to level up a little.

I was curious, too. A concrete trash can; a *Porphiry Govorov, age: 12, middle grade student*; a curb, a car, a *Lyudmila Voronina, age: 72, retired*; a LED streetlamp, a *Vita Balashova, age: 24, a fortune teller...*

Wait a sec. *Age, 24?* The person looked like an old woman!

I took another look. A street beggar, most likely a Roma judging by her traditional Gypsy garb: several frilly floral skirts worn on top of each other and a matching flounced blouse peeking from under a filthy woolen cardigan. A torn knitted shawl was wrapped over her shoulders for a bit of extra warmth. She indeed appeared ancient.

The likes of her — whether begging, selling counterfeited goods or simply offering to tell your fortune — were a common sight on Russian streets. I couldn't see her face from under the black headscarf. Still, her hands betrayed her: filthy but smooth, definitely not the hands of an old woman.

I knew of course that not all of them were genuine Roma. Many of them were rip-off merchants of any nationality, making good money on people's sympathy to the underprivileged.

But posing as an old woman? What an actress!

A skeletal dog lay on the soiled tarmac next to her, resting his filthy head on his paws. A dirty washing line was tied to the collar constricting his neck.

Richie. A German Shepherd.
Age: 6
Current status: pet
Owner: Svetlana "Sveta" Messerschmitt

I stopped next to them. Without raising her eyes, the fake "Gypsy" mumbled monotonously,

"Cross my palm with a few coins, dearie! Just for a crust of bread for me but mostly for the dog, he needs feeding... Cross my palm with a few coins, dearie! Just for a crust of bread..."

"Excuse me," I said, not knowing how to begin.

She kept mumbling, ignoring me.

"Excuse me, is this your dog?"

"Of course it is. Spare a few coins for the dog, dearie, he needs feeding..."

I chuckled. Her dog, yeah right. "Richie? Richie my boy!"

The dog raised his ear. He opened his eyes and lifted his head, looking at me curiously with his intelligent eyes. He was a handsome dog with an off-white patch on his chest.

"Richie, good boy! Come!" I slapped my leg.

The dog scrambled to his feet, intending to walk over to me. His short leash pulled tight.

The fake "Gypsy" tugged at it sharply. Whimpering in pain, the dog dropped to his side.

Panting heavily, he kept staring at me. His tearful eyes were caked in some filthy goo.

That was the last drop. I loved all cats and dogs indiscriminately (Yanna's departed Chihuahua being the only honorable exception). I couldn't watch them being hurt.

"Stop torturing the dog *now*," I said. "This isn't your dog. I know who it belongs to. I'm calling the police," I pulled out the phone, pretending I was dialing the number.

The fake Gypsy exploded into some desperate screaming.

Heavy footsteps resounded behind me. A godawful whack on the head sent me to the ground.

Damage taken: 93 (a punch)
Current vitality: 77,64501%

The edges of the system message turned crimson. A new warning appeared,

You've received a Bleed debuff!
Duration: 30 min

-0,01151% to Vitality per sec
Current vitality: 77,53350%.

The fake Gypsy stopped screaming. I clutched at my head. My fingers touched something wet and sticky. My attacker must have had a signet ring or something on his hand.

I tried to scramble back to my feet. Immediately I received an almighty kick in the ribs which knocked the wind out of me. My throat seized with an agonizing pain.

Damage taken: 126 (a kick)
Current vitality: 76,17388%.

Holding my stomach, I rolled onto my side to see my attacker. The "Gypsy" was busy dragging the struggling dog away, followed by a man in track pants and a leather jacket[4].

Georgy Balashov. Age: 29
Current status: Unemployed

I submitted this data to memory.

Gradually, the pain began to release me. My Vitality began to rise. That was good news, meaning I hadn't received any internal damage.

What a bastard! He'd stripped me of nearly 2.5% health with just two hits!

Staggering, I climbed to my feet and brushed the dirt off my jeans and my good jacket. The street was quite busy — but no one had approached me, offering help. That was all right. How many times had I ignored people lying unconscious in the past, thinking it must have been some useless homeless drunk? Oh well, welcome to the club.

Wonder if it had something to do with my low social status? Some sort of karma effect? And how many times had I myself attacked people from behind in the game, shamelessly raising my Honor (or should I say Dishonor) point count?

---

[4] Track pants and a leather jacket: a typical attire of a low-class Russian gangster

What a shame I'd lost the dog, though. To pay my attacker back in kind would have been nice too. But it looked like their wrongs would never be avenged.

Still, there was something I could do.

I opened the map and submitted a query.

Immediately I saw all three of them: the dog, the fake Gypsy and her back-stabbing sidekick. They seemed to be back at the farmer's market which is usually the center of petty criminal activity in most Russian towns.

What a shame I didn't have a single combat skill on my list. Just to get even with him, you understand. Having said that, he wouldn't be alone. And I just wasn't good enough to singlehandedly take on an entire gang.

Which is why I used the map to lay the route to the nearest urgent care center. It was only half a mile away, so I walked there.

I didn't skip and hop around anymore. This was real life, after all. The human body was very different from a digital cartoon. Here, stat-building required some dedicated training and the proverbial second wind.

The urgent care doctor studied my head wound as if it was the most normal thing in the world. He administered first aid by applying some medication to the wound and dressing it properly.

His actions removed the Bleed debuff entirely. Finally, he wrote a statement for the police and sent me on my way.

The station was just next door. Desk Sergeant

Kravetz listened to my complaint with a skeptical look on his face. Another cold case was the last thing they needed.

So I embellished it a little, telling him the dog was mine and that it had been missing for a while. And today I came across it in the street accompanying a street beggar.

"You sure it was your dog? How did you know?"

"It's my dog. His name's Richie, a German Shepherd, six years old. He has an off-white patch on his chest. There aren't many dogs like that around."

"Maybe there aren't but I've seen a few," the Sergeant replied, hesitating.

"I called him, and he reacted to his name."

"I see. And then what happened?"

"I wanted to take him from her when someone attacked me from behind. They hit me on the head, then kicked me in the ribs. Here's a statement from the first-aid place. Here's my bandaged head. And here's the bruise under my ribs."

I attempted to describe the fake old woman and my attacker. On second thoughts, I also mentioned a young girl who was allegedly with them (in case the fake Gypsy had already shed her old-woman disguise).

Finally, I told him I knew their current location. "They're at the north entrance to the farmer's market."

"How do you know?"

"I followed them," I inconspicuously checked the map. "I think they're still there."

"Yeah right. Why didn't you tell me at once? They must be miles away by now."

144

The sergeant sent a patrol to the market, armed with the descriptions of all four: the dog, the goon and the two women, one old, the other young. Then he returned to his desk and motioned me to a bench along the wall.

I wasn't born yesterday. I doubted very much they could help me. Had it happened before my involvement with the game, I'd have just turned round and walked back home to nurse both my wounds and my injured pride.

I'd never filed a complaint with the authorities before, ever. I'd been in a scuffle or two in my lifetime. I'd had my nose broken in a bar brawl. Another time, a couple of large individuals who hadn't liked the way I'd looked at them decided to punch my lights out. I'd also had my phone taken from me by a gang of local kids.

Still, I'd never reported any of this to the police. I'd just suffered in silence, refusing to believe they could actually do anything about it. Criminals and lowlifes always get their own way in life, don't they?

As I waited, I switched to my mental interface and summoned Martha. "Hi."

"Greetings, Phil," her voice echoed in my head, seemingly reverberating through the room. "I need to inform you that you need to have some bedrest ASAP. Go home and spend at least several-"

"Sorry, I can't," I interrupted her. "If you don't mind me asking, do you have any visualization options? Talking to a voice in my head isn't very healthy, is it?"

"Yes, I do have the option you require. Please

specify the details."

"The details, well... A female, 18 to 35 years old. Dark-haired."

A shapeless blob comprised of various colors filled my interface. "Martha, what's that?"

"There're 482,352,941 matches. Would you like to narrow your search?"

That was half a billion pixels. Talk about too much of a good thing. "I don't think I'm physically able to check them all. I need your help."

"I can create an image which will have a 97% probability of matching your personal taste in ladies."

"Yeah right. You just want to show off your knowledge of my brain scan results. Go ahead, then. Do it!"

Holy Jesus! I jumped, suppressing a much stronger word.

"Keep quiet, you," Sergeant Kravetz grumbled.

It was easy for him to say! A stunningly beautiful young lady stood but a couple paces away from me. Almost six foot tall, she was wearing some ripped denim shorts, a pair of Converse sneakers and a white T-shirt hugging her bronze body. Her gorgeous dark hair flowed down her back. Not a trace of makeup.

The girl was chewing gum, grinning at me. Her eyes sparkled with mischief.

She gave me a wink. "Hi. You okay?"

I realized I was still sitting. I hurried to stand up to answer her greeting. "Are you Martha?"

"Good! You're not hopeless, after all!"

Was she teasing me? Even her voice was

different, melodious and cheerful. But still...

"What's wrong with you?" Sergeant Kravetz snapped. "Are you hearing things? Sit down and stop your nonsense!"

Martha brought a finger to her lips. "Be quiet."

"Got it," I replied mentally. "But you... you're so different!"

"I'm sorry. I did indeed study your brain scan results. According to them, a girl's appearance wasn't the only thing that mattered. I had to build a new person with her own character, voice and behavioral patterns. I had to analyze your dreams as well as your favorite books and video games in order to isolate the most common objects of self-gratification..."

I jumped to my feet. "*What?!!*"

"Enough!" Sergeant Kravetz snapped. "Out, you! Go and wait outside!"

"Fap fap fap," Martha mouthed teasingly.

I knew better than to argue with a police officer. I headed for the door. Martha hooked her arm through mine and followed. I could feel her touch. I could smell her — a fresh, briny scent of some vaguely familiar perfume. I tried to remember what it was called but couldn't.

How was that for a full immersion experience? This was better than Dolby Atmos in 3D!

Once outside, I pulled out the phone, turned the camera on and tried to take a picture of the two of us.

Predictably, I was alone on the screen.

"Phil, give it a break, man. I'm in your head! Do what Sergeant Kravetz just told you and stop your nonsense."

"But... How did you do it?"

"How do you think you can see the interface and all the messages?" her voice betrayed some emotion. "Do you remember what the program is called?"

"Augmented Reality 7.2. Home Edition, wasn't it?"

"Exactly. *Augmented* being the operative word."

"Are you now going to stay like this?"

"Phil, use your brain. You wanted an embodied assistant and that's exactly what you got. You still can summon or unsummon me at your convenience."

Oh yes, she was embodied all right. I thought she'd be some sort of cartoon head in the corner of my interface window, a bit like the MS Office talking paperclip. A 3D animation, maybe. But this... this was mind-boggling. It wasn't just the fact that she was so beautiful — no, I did like her cheekiness, her sarcasm, her girl-next-door friendliness.

I might need to ask her to replace this avatar with something less provocative, otherwise I might never look at a human woman again. Not even Yanna.

A patrol van pulled up by the station. I sent Martha a mental command to disappear. She popped a gum bubble and dematerialized, licking the bits of gum from her lips.

The patrol officer called me, then opened the back door of his van. "Your dog? You need to get him to the vet. He's in a bad way."

Richie was lying in the back with his tongue stuck out, panting heavily.

Come on boy, don't let me down.

"Richie!" I was just so happy they'd found him. "Richie, come!"

Reluctantly wagging his tail, the dog rose and sniffed my proffered hand. I used my other hand to stroke the scruff of his neck and scratch behind his ears, all the while telling him he was such a good boy, that we were back together now and that everything was going to be all right...

"Good!" the officer said. "Take him. We don't have all day."

"How about the Gypsy woman and the other one?"

"They were gone. We searched the market but didn't see them anywhere. We found the dog lying by the market fence. He answered the description so we took him. You should be grateful."

"I am. Thanks a lot!"

"Thanks don't pay bills," he said pointedly.

I pulled out my wallet, opened it and showed it to him. "I'm broke, sir."

He heaved a sigh. "Shame. How about some cigarettes?"

"I don't smoke," I turned to go.

"Wait," he said, averting his gaze. "The Sergeant wants to see you."

I took the dog and walked back inside.

"Happy?" Kravetz said. "Good. It would be better if you revoke your complaint now."

"Why?"

"You've got the dog, haven't you? And we'll never

be able to locate those two. And we have quotas to meet. You understand that, don't you?"

Oh yes, I did. They'd already gotten their baksheesh from the two crooks who must have paid the patrol officers off, given them the dog and disappeared. He was right: it was pointless looking for them now. My complaint was only going to add to their cold-case statistics.

Justice as usual.

"Not a problem," I said, then left the station.

Richie staggered along on his shaking legs.

We stopped in a small park under an old maple tree. I fed him a bread roll and gave him some water from a plastic cap I'd bought from a street vendor on our way there. Richie lapped the water greedily, splashing it around and grazing my fingers with his rough tongue.

Having finished, I opened Facebook. The search wasn't long: we had only one fourteen-year-old Svetlana Messerschmitt in our town. I left her a message saying that if she'd lost her dog lately, I might have found it. I gave her my cell number and decided to wait a little.

If she didn't reply soon, I might need to take Richie to the vet myself. What little money I had should be enough for some first aid. And by then, I should have received the payment for my last-night content writing gig. Provided the customer didn't request any edits.

I summoned Martha. I needed to sort out a few things. Might as well do it now.

"Hi, Martha."

"We've seen each other today, haven't we?"

"True. Mind telling me how the social status thing works? Also, how do you gain XP points? How many of them do I need to make the next level?"

Martha spat her gum into the trash can and turned serious. "The social status basically shows a person's value to society. The higher the level, the more important their voice is in global decision making. Think of things like elections, passing new laws or the abolition of the death penalty. Any person below level 10 has no say in such matters. The higher one's social status level, the more privileges they receive. Their lives are more valuable in terms of human civilization. In your historical period-"

"What did you say?" I interrupted her. "Do you see now?"

"Phil, I'm not stupid."

I just didn't understand anything anymore. This was surreal. She couldn't be an AI!

I jumped off the bench. Richie raised his head warily.

"Martha, only two days ago you kept trying to connect to a non-existent server!"

"Phil, please sit down. No good getting so upset."

"Okay. Come and sit next to me," I made an inviting gesture. "Now tell me."

"That wasn't me. That was a bot. Highly sophisticated but still a bot. When you decided to summon me, you authorized the system to allocate bigger resources on your assistant. That allowed me to activate the dialogue function. It's an undocumented feature, very useful. Had I been back in our time, the system would have contacted the server and engaged an available AI. But seeing as there's no server in your time, I made the decision to initiate myself."

Her mention of resources was what worried me the most. What kind of resources? Did she mean my brain? "What are the resources required for the system to work?"

"Sorry. That's classified information."

"Come on, give me a hint."

"You've no idea how far technology will go by the 22nd century. Human beings are capable of working wonders you can't even imagine. That's all I can tell you. If you want to find out more, you'll have to level up Insight."

"Never mind. Just forget it. Now, XP points. How do you earn them?"

"Phil, Phil. The only reason I created a gamelike interface was because that was what you were used to seeing in games. But this is real life. This isn't computer simulation. The social status level has nothing to do with cartoon avatars and their stats. You can't level up here just by farming XP and smoking mob packs! Yes, sure, you could go to war — provided there *is* a war — and become a hero by killing thousands of enemy soldiers. But even in that case, you might become a hero in your own country but not for the whole of humanity. Every word and action which is beneficial for the human race will cause your XP to grow."

My phone rang. Martha tactfully fell silent.
I picked up the phone. A girl's voice asked,
"Did you find Richie?"

Chapter Eleven

Cat and Dog

"In fact, no relationship should be taken for granted. They are what life is about, the whole point."

Gary Vaynerchuck, *The Thank-You Economy.*

KIRA WAS MY BIG SISTER. I WOULDN'T EXACTLY CALL our relationship cordial. We normally only saw each other during family reunions. She used to boss me around a lot when we were little. As long as I remembered myself, I'd always been the object of her petty criticisms. She'd been nine years old when I was born, so she took the brunt of the childcare in our parents' absence.

Looking back now, I realized it can't have been easy for her. She'd had to babysit me while all her friends were out having fun; she also had to do the bulk of housework. Dad rotated on and off an oil rig while Mom worked as a hospital nurse on a twenty-four-hour shift basis.

Kira'd done a good job though, even if I say so myself. I'd never hurt myself, counting the only time I fell from the window — but luckily, I was already six years old and the window was only a few feet from the ground.

Still, she must have been thoroughly fed up with the experience. So much so that she hadn't even gotten married until she was nearly forty. Instead, she'd concentrated on her banking career. Then she met some sleazy pickup artist ten years her younger who treated her to a couple of mind-boggling dates — and that had put the lid on her professional life. A wedding, a pregnancy, a baby, a house, a family, a spoilt and abusive husband and two years of constant fighting, crying, cheating and making up. Finally, a divorce.

Kira had never been known for her tact and consideration. Knowing her, the decision to terminate her marriage must have been entirely her initiative. But when it had finally happened, both me and our parents had finally heaved a sigh of relief. Leo, her husband, was a classic gigolo with ambitions bigger than his stomach. All of us could see it straight away — all but Kira, that is.

Now she was back at the banking helm, raising the five-year old Cyril and finding the time to take care of our parents. She'd always considered me a failure, an irresponsible loser who'd wasted the best years of his life on useless things.

And she didn't even know about Yanna dumping me yet!

So when I heard her voice on the phone, I tensed inside, readying myself to withstand a new flood of accusations peppered with a liberal dose of f-words.

I pressed the *Reply* button.

"Oh, hi there!" I said into the phone, faking cheerfulness. "So great to hear your voice! How is it going?"

"Phily? Are you flippin' mad? You've had it this time, haven't you? What happened between you and Yanna?"

Phily! That was another problem I had with her. No matter how many times I'd begged, I'd always be Phily to her. What was wrong with my parents, couldn't they've given me a normal name? Something safe like Sergei or Alexander? I'd even agree to Afanasy! Anything's better than being called Phily in front of everyone!

Her shrill voice seemed to slice through all of my sore spots like a laser. I brought the phone away from my ear. I almost envied her ex-husband at this point. For him, the torture was already over.

"You really are going to drive our parents into an early grave, aren't you? As if my divorce wasn't enough for them! Now it's you and your nonsense! You flippin' idiot! They've been waiting all this time for you to finally get your a*s in gear! They hoped you'd get a job and a family — a proper family! They want grandchildren, for crissakes! And you..."

"Eh, Kira, listen-"

"No, *you* listen! Her parents have just called me. They said she means it this time. She's filing for divorce. And what they don't understand is why you're sitting on your fat a*s doing nothing! She's just walked out on you, for Christ's sake! And you haven't even called her! You didn't even try to make up with her! Have you been drinking or something? Or are you so engrossed in your computer games you haven't even noticed she's been gone?"

"Okay. Which question am I supposed to answer first?"

"Don't you get fresh with me! Where are you now?"

"I'm at home. I was just going to go to bed."

"I'm coming now. I want you to wait for me. And none of that game nonsense! No *raids* or whatever you call them!"

She slammed the phone down.

I gave the room one last check. It looked clean and tidy. Except for a big scraggy dog, black as the devil, lying on the floor by the couch staring at me with his tongue hanging out.

My Reputation with Richie had already grown to Amicability. His owner Sveta Messerschmitt had resorted to sobbing when I'd sent her the dog's picture: a grinning head with a moist black nose taking up half the screen. That way she couldn't see how gaunt he really was. I'd made sure his wounds weren't visible, either.

As it had turned out, she was away on vacation with her parents, due to return in two weeks' time. As soon as we'd finished talking, Richie and I shuffled off to the nearest vet. He might have to stay with me for a while.

The vet had given Richie a thorough wash with flea shampoo, treated and dressed his wounds, cleaned up his eyes, given him a few injections and fed him a vermifuge pill. I paid unhesitantly, using up most of whatever was left on my card and spending the rest of it on some meat scraps from the market butcher's. I also bought a packet of spaghetti for myself. It was a good job I'd quit smoking, otherwise I might have bought some cigarettes instead. I just hoped that the Siberian pine nut producers had already transferred their payment to my bank account.

Boris the she-cat had greeted the canine newcomer from the strategic height of the back of the couch. The sound she'd made upon our arrival resembled the hissing of a boiling kettle rising to the wailing of a Banshee. She hadn't yet realized that a fully grown German Shepherd was a far cry from a Chihuahua.

At first, Richie watched her curiously, tilting his head to one side. Then he sneezed and stood up, resting his front legs on the couch. Reaching out, he attempted to sniff the cat.

Boris gave him a hearty slap on the muzzle, then clung to the couch, her ears lowered, her tail swishing around. She was making weird guttural sounds reminiscent of the growling of the walking dead.

The dog opened his jaws and gingerly grabbed Boris by the scruff of her neck. Tilting his head high, he carried the cat toward the front door. Boris hung in his grasp obediently like a newborn kitten.

"Richie, *no!*" I snapped.

Richie spat the cat out and looked at me inquiringly.

Covered in the dog's saliva, Boris darted off, climbed up the curtains and jumped onto the wardrobe. From its relative safety, she warily watched the new enemy's movements while zealously licking herself clean. She stayed there for the rest of the day and even ignored her dinner.

I spent the afternoon contemplating my leveling strategy. I had to stop in the evening to take Richie out.

The dog had turned out to be remarkably smart. He knew all the commands. As I had neither a leash nor a muzzle for him to wear, I had to walk next to him holding onto his collar until we reached the park. There I took a look around to make sure there was nobody nearby and set the impatient, whimpering dog free to do his business.

I bet he received +100% to Satisfaction for his patience!

As for my leveling, I decided to concentrate on my urgent needs for the time being. I needed to earn some quick money in order to pay the bills and decide what I was going to do about Yanna.

Yes, you heard it right. In the last few days, I seemed to have calmed down a bit. My heart still clenched with the memory of the loss but... how sure was I that I really needed all this? Were we happy? I mean, *really* happy? Or was it just the convenience of having a female attendant in my life?

So far, I didn't have the answers to that. The news about her planning to divorce me hadn't changed much. We'd still have to sit down and talk. Even if we parted ways, we needed to do it properly, to make sure we didn't have to turn away every time we ran across each other on the street.

You couldn't really call this a leveling plan. Honestly, I hadn't yet decided which stats I should concentrate on. Logically, it would be a good idea to start with physical characteristics, if only to bring them up to average. That would positively affect lots of things: my health as well as appearance and probably even self-confidence. As for improving such arcane characteristics as Intellect and Perception, I still had no idea what benefits it might garner.

The job of a sales rep required Charisma, Perception and Empathy, as well as Vending skills. You have to be able to *feel* your client. Question was whether I still wanted to do it. Not at the moment, but as a career choice.

I didn't have the answer to that, either.

As for Luck, I had no idea how to level it up. I remember reading some LitRPG book where the MC had managed to level up Luck by betting recklessly in a casino. Unfortunately, the lamentable state of my wallet prevented me from trying that out. Which was a good thing, probably. My common sense — or should I say my inner greedy pig? — prevented me from going down that route.

Should I go out and start collecting quests from

all and sundry? Firstly, I still had no idea how I was supposed to receive them. And secondly, what would it give me? It could probably improve my social networking skills — or even help build a few "connections" by raising my Reputation with a large number of useful or influential people. Beggars can't be choosers, can they? Still, the idea gave me a bad taste in my mouth. It was a bit like helping an old lady across the street simply to impress the girl you're with.

I may be a smarmy bastard but all my smarm resulted from the several years spent trying to sell junk. And you can't sell junk to people without sacrificing your integrity. But you still have to do it in order to put food on the table. You need to pay for modern-day luxuries which make the base of our consumer pyramid, such as quality food, fast Internet connection and flat-rate gaming plans. In my case at least.

So this was the outcome of my hectic day: my leveling plan for the next month, a dog sleeping on the floor by my bed and Boris howling her fury from the safety of the wardrobe.

Early next morning, I received a small but urgent job offer to edit a graduation thesis. The offered fee of two thousand rubles was enough to last us a couple of days. I agreed unhesitantly and spent until lunch working on it. The client paid straight away, followed by an online transfer from my Siberian pine nut customers. Time for the beggars to party!

Richie and I went to the pet shop and bought him a new leash and a muzzle, which consumed most of the thesis payment. Then we popped into the nearest budget supermarket and got ourselves some groceries.

I also bought a pair of the cheapest Chinese sneakers I could find. They stank but at least they added 1 point to Agility and were much more comfortable to jog in than the wretched Derby shoes.

Later that night, Richie and I walked out into the back yard for a bit of practice. I had Strength and Agility to level. I tied Richie next to the kids' monkey bars and, much to the excited encouragement of our local gutter intellectuals in the face of Yagoza, Sprat and Alik, performed a free routine of parallel bars, wall bars and pull-ups.

I must have looked pathetic. Squirming and swaying, I performed zero pull-ups, zero bar dips and another zero leg raises. Yagoza was laughing so hard he fell off the bench.

That wouldn't have been so bad but Richie immediately decided that the old jailbird was trying to aggro us and critted him with a dose of Stun Bark. Our audience was suitably impressed and tried to tone down its excitement.

Afterward, Richie and I headed for the park. I left him to do his business and went for a run. I ran till my teeth started to ache and only left when the evening air began swarming with mosquitoes.

I needed to buy a gym membership with my first available earnings, as well as some gym clothes and a pair of running shoes. I had a funny feeling that running was going to seriously improve Agility, Stamina and Sprint speed and probably also relieve my constant knee pain caused by having to lug around tons of excess weight. My Vigor might stop plummeting every five minutes, too.

When we came home, Boris habitually trotted out to greet me but barged right into Richie's Aura of Fear. With a panicky howl, the cat scrambled back to the safety of the wardrobe where she stayed, watchfully eyeing the demonic hellhound.

Before going to bed, I decided to check out the latest heavily hyped flick. It turned out to be pure trash. My Satisfaction dropped to 3% halfway through it, forcing me to switch it off.

Then Kira rang.

* * *

AS I WAITED FOR HER TO ARRIVE, I STARTED READING A marketing tutorial. I was curious to see if it could have any effect on my stats. I'd made my way through a couple of chapters when Kira rang.

I answered the door, then promptly jumped out of her way as she barged in like a furious harpy. (Is there even such a thing as a harpy that's *not* furious?)

Bang! she gave me a hearty slap across the head.

"*Ghrrrr*," said Richie.

"Doggie!" Kira's five-year-old son Cyril hurried to give Richie a bear hug.

Richie froze in bewilderment, drooling nervously but suffering my nephew's familiarity in silence.

"Rich, *no!*" I exclaimed, worried about the boy.

"Cyril, *no!*" Kira screamed.

Boris glared at the scene from the heights of the wardrobe top.

I scooped Cyril up in my arms; Richie retired into a corner to recuperate from the penny damage he'd received. Kira rushed around the apartment like a hurricane searching for evidence — any evidence! — of my moral degradation: stacks of empty vodka bottles, overflowing ashtrays, bagfuls of dope, traces of lipstick on coffee cups, a call girl in my bed, a dead body in the closet...

She'd found nothing. Apart from a gaunt scruffy dog, that is.

"I shouldn't have called you, should I?" she finally said. "I can see you got rid of the bottles."

"Sure. Thanks for the tip-off," I replied, peering at her name tag.

Kira Panfilova
Age: 42
Current status: Bank manager
Social status level: 21
Class: Financial expert. Level: 13
Divorced. Ex-husband: Leo Zosimov
Children: Cyril, son. Age: 5
Reputation: Love 1/1

I froze open-mouthed, refusing to believe my eyes. Kira's social and professional levels were indeed impressive. But Reputation?

I reread the lines several times. *Reputation, Love.*

One out of one.

Kira loved me? This Kira here? She who'd never once commended me or shown her affection to me? Kira the sourpuss who'd never had any compassion for my childhood tears or complaints?

"Phily, what's with this looney look on your face?" she kept nitpicking. "Mind shutting your mouth? That's it. Much better!"

"Let me go, Uncle Phily!" little Cyril demanded.

I lowered him onto the floor.

"Go to the bathroom," Kira told him, "and wash your hands with antiseptic. What a terrible dog! Where did you get him from?"

I told her Richie's story, reassuring her that the dog was here only temporarily.

"Thank God for that! You can't look after yourself, let alone a big dog like that! This isn't the kind of dog you keep in a city apartment, anyway. Are you even sure his owners want him back?"

Finally, we sat down. Or rather, Cyril and I did. Kira fussed around the kitchen laying the table. She expertly kicked the broken oven door shut as she rushed about, all the while showering me with questions. She wanted to know whether I was okay on my own. She demanded to hear my plans for the future. She asked matter-of-factly whether I was considering getting a job and a family.

I could see she wasn't in a hurry to bring the issue to a head. This was our family tradition: no problems discussed at the dining table.

I looked at her affectionately. Stern and rigid,

often too blunt for her own good — but she did love me, idiot that I was, with all the force of her sisterly love.

Love, 1/1. It meant that this feeling couldn't be leveled. You either loved or you didn't. The kind of love didn't matter: it could be your husband, your parents or your sibling.

Unable to hold it in any longer, I rose from the table and gave her a hug.

"Are you nuts?" she demanded without rejecting my embrace.

"Thank you."

"What for?"

"For raising me. For supporting me. For always being there for me. I wish I understood that at the time."

She didn't say anything.

"I want to see the doggie!" Cyril announced.

Kira didn't reply. Her shoulders shook. She was crying.

We spent a long time just standing there locked in a hug. She was a good head below me, my tiny Sis, who was nevertheless so brave and ballsy. I didn't need a better role model.

When she finally calmed down, she sat us all down to a quick dinner she'd cooked with whatever groceries she'd brought along. Cyril had finished his food first, so I found some kiddy channel on YouTube for him. With him thus immobilized, at least temporarily, we had tea in silence.

Finally, Kira sighed. "Tomorrow morning she'll come around to get her stuff. She'll probably have someone with her. She didn't want to call you so she asked her mother to give you a ring. Apparently, her mother wasn't too keen on talking with you, either, so she called me instead and put me in the picture. There's one thing I wanna ask you. Please don't start another argument with her. Be a man. Try and talk it over. Ask her to come back and give you another chance. Tell her you're a different man now. Tell her you're looking for a job. And if she doesn't-"

"She won't."

"In that case, just let her go. Give her some time. You might try again after a while. And if it still doesn't work... well, then it just wasn't meant to happen."

"Very well. I won't pick another argument, I promise. I'll talk to her."

By then, she'd already cleaned the table and done the washing up.

Cyril was fast asleep in front of the computer. Gingerly I scooped him up in my arms and carried him to the car. We said our goodbyes and gave each other one last hug.

The car left.

I paused outside, enjoying the fresh air.

Alik's drunken voice disrupted the silence,

"Phil! Dude! I can see you found yourself a new one? A single mother!"

"What? That was my *sister*!"

"Oops," he said, visibly embarrassed. "Sorry, dude. Spare a smoke?"

"I quit."

Back home I climbed into bed and read a couple

more chapters of the marketing tutorial. Finally I closed my eyes but sleep wouldn't come. I couldn't stop thinking about Yanna coming the next morning. Who was she going to come with? How was I supposed to talk to her? What if she continued to ignore me?

I was almost asleep when the familiar small diamond-shaped black icon appeared in my fading mental view.

I opened it.

You have 1 characteristic point available!
In order to add it to a characteristic of your choice, open your profile window.

That was the point I'd received for making a new level. I'd forgotten all about it.

I opened my profile but saw nowhere to add it to. How were you supposed to invest it? Having said that...

I mentally focused on Luck. Immediately a new window popped up,

Accept / Decline

My mind raced. *Luck affects all stats*, Martha had said. Logically, it should be the one to invest into. In any case, there was no other way of leveling Luck, apart from making the right life choices. Then again, how were you supposed to know whether you'd made the right choice? Some people lived their entire lives without knowing how their life would have come out had they made a different choice. They were simply unable to think several moves ahead.

Then again, leveling Luck might improve decision-making too. And crits! Crits were essential, weren't they? They were a must!

Very well, then. Let's invest it in Luck.

Half-asleep, I felt my wobbly upper arm and the hollow chest. Didn't they say that Lady Luck favored the strong?

I deselected Luck and chose Strength.

Just as I zonked out, a red system warning popped up.

CHAPTER TWELVE

OPTIMIZATION

"Her gaze was begging, mournful, wet, hateful, defeated, anxious, disappointed, naïve, proud, contemptuous — but still it stayed blue."

Frédéric Beigbeder, *Love Lasts Three Years*

I AWOKE IN THE DEAD OF NIGHT, DRIVEN BY INHUMAN hunger. I needed to find some food. This seemed to be the sole driving force behind my existence, my body's single quest and purpose.

My field of vision was littered with alerts and debuff messages,

Extreme Hunger!
You're starving!
-30% to Metabolism

Warning! Your glucose reading is critically low!

Warning! Your amino acids reading is critically low!

Warning! Critical threat of losing muscle mass!

Debuff received: Weakness II
-2 to Stamina every 24 hrs.
-2 to Agility every 24 hrs.
-2 to Perception every 24 hrs.
-2 to Intellect every 24 hrs.
-2 to Strength every 24 hrs.
-5% to Satisfaction every 2 hrs.
-5% to Vigor every 2 hrs.
-1% to Vitality every 4 hrs.

Extreme Thirst!
You're parched!
-20% to Metabolism
Warning! Your body fluids reading is critically low!

Debuff received: Weakness III
-3 to Stamina every 24 hrs.
-3 to Agility every 24 hrs.
-3 to Perception every 24 hrs.
-3 to Intellect every 24 hrs.
-3 to Strength every 24 hrs.
-10% to Satisfaction every 2 hrs.
-5% to Vigor every 2 hrs.

-2% to Vitality every 4 hrs.

My mouth was so dry that my tongue grated against my palate. My throat rasped. It took me a good ten minutes to literally crawl the forty feet to the kitchen, taking frequent breaks.

Richie pranced around me in concern, dropping to his front legs and looking me in the eye as if asking, 'You okay, boss?' Even Boris left the wardrobe and rubbed against my dragging legs, pushing them forward with her large forehead.

Scrambling back to my feet in order to reach for the sink tap proved to be the difficult bit. Leaning against a stool, I finally did it. I opened the tap and took a long, luxurious drink, enjoying every mouthful. I must have drunk at least a couple of quarts. I'd never been so thirsty in my life.

Finally, the Thirst debuff disappeared. I could move around again.

I opened the fridge and wolfed down everything that was left from Kira's cooking. I then grabbed the large chunk of cheese she'd brought last night and gobbled it like an apple.

And then I found her oatmeal cookies.

I boiled some water, made myself a large mug of tea and attacked the cookies. *Ooh Kira, they're so good, thank you so much!*

What was wrong with me? I'd never liked cookies. Especially not oatmeal ones.

After about twenty minutes, the Weakness debuff was finally gone. Now I was sleepy. As I finished the tea, I noticed the familiar black diamond icon with a red exclamation mark.

Wasn't it the same one I'd glimpsed before falling asleep?

The black icon expanded into a message,

Warning! We've detected an abnormal increase in your Strength characteristic: +1 pt.

Your body will be restructured in keeping with the new reading (7) to comply with your new metabolism and chronotropy values.

Changes required: development of new muscle tissue and the strengthening of sinews, ligaments and tendons.

It went on and on, telling me about the changes made to my glycogen and intramuscular phosphocreatine levels, intramuscular and intermuscular coordination, etc., etc. But it all paled into insignificance next to a small notice at the end. It was written in big fat letters and framed in red. Which, in my opinion, they should have shown me even before offering me the *Accept/Decline* button!

Warning!
The restructuring of your body functions requires a considerable amount of nutrients. In order to avoid danger to your life, you're strongly encouraged to consume a minimum of 10 oz. animal protein, 3 lbs. of carbohydrates and 3 oz. of animal fats. A shortage of nutrients may result in body function failure.

Warning!
*Artificial characteristic boosting of more that 1 pt.
at a time is strictly forbidden! Strong chance of fatality!*

Oh, great. Just what I wanted to hear. And what if I'd left it till next level when I'd have two points to distribute? Would I have just dropped dead on the spot? With no hope of ever being rezzed?

The mere thought of this outcome made me break out in a cold sweat. I was desperate for a smoke, so much so that I very nearly made a dash for a nearby 24/7. The only thing that stopped me was the Nicotine Withdrawal debuff still hovering in my mental view. I had only eight days of it left. I could do it.

Instead, I summoned Martha, greeting her with a liberal amount of f-words. She replied that she'd have had no authority to intervene even if she'd been activated. I unsummoned the useless wench and went back to bed.

Before falling asleep, I did check my stats. I had indeed grown stronger, judging by my *Strength, 7* reading. My arm muscles, too, felt slightly harder. My chest seemed to be bulging just a tad more. But that was the extent of it.

I awoke from Richie's desperate barking. The doorbell was about to shake itself loose.

I glanced at the phone: half past seven. Who the heck could that be so early?

I stumbled to my feet, threw some clothes on and hurried for the door. Someone was already banging on it, kicking it impatiently.

They shouldn't, really. I hated this kind of aggressive behavior. There were three things I couldn't stand: road ragers honking at me, a phone that won't stop ringing when you can't pick it up, and someone kicking the door before you can even answer it.

"Open the door, *now!*" Yanna's voice came from outside.

"Coming," I snapped over Richie's barking.

I locked him in the bathroom so he didn't scare her. The banging stopped. I could hear her whispering something to somebody she'd apparently brought along.

I opened the door. Ignoring me, my mother-in-law barged into the apartment, loaded with empty bags.

"Hi," I said to her back.

Yanna stood in the doorway, looking good and dressed in a neat business suit with a white shirt, a light blazer and a skirt which ended just above her knees. She was wearing a gold watch and a matching bangle I'd never seen before. The heavy, seductive scent of an expensive perfume hung around her.

"Hi Yanna," I said as calmly as I could, trying to level my heartbeat.

She didn't reply. For a split second, she lingered in the doorway, then walked directly into the bedroom, looking appraisingly around.

"I can see you've got a dog now," she said without turning. "I thought you didn't like them?"

"It's not my dog," I said. "I'm taking care of it for a while."

She wasn't listening. She walked into the bedroom and locked the door behind her.

I seethed. She couldn't have shown her lack of respect for me any clearer. This used to be our home. Our love nest. And I'd cleaned it — the least she could do was wipe her feet by the door.

I suppressed the desire to barge into the bedroom and tell them everything I thought about them. Then I reconsidered. Yanna was her mommy's little girl. Between the two of them, they'd make quick work of me.

So I walked into the bathroom instead and began brushing my teeth. Let them do their packing in peace. I had no desire to speak to Yanna in her mother's presence.

I brushed my teeth angrily, realizing I'd never been comfortable around the older woman.

Although outwardly supportive of her daughter's choice, in reality her mother had always been against it. I could sense it in her constant sarcasms and in the contemptuous way Yanna treated me whenever she'd come back from visiting them. The old lady seemed to despise me with abandon, barely deigning to notice me.

When Yanna and I had still been dating, every time I'd come round with a bunch of flowers, my future mother-in-law would answer the door and shout, "Yanna, it's what's-his-name! He's got some twigs with him this time!" She never called me by my name. She'd chuck the "twigs" nonchalantly onto the shoe rack without ever inviting me in. I had to wait for Yanna on the landing every time, until we finally got married.

The wedding had been rather modest. We didn't even have a honeymoon. I was pretty sure that her mother (or even Yanna herself, maybe) blamed this on me too.

I was ravenous again. My body was probably still restructuring itself.

"Wait here," I told Richie, then walked out of the bathroom.

Both Yanna and her mother were already busy in the kitchen packing stuff. They rummaged through the cupboards, scooping out pots, skillets, mugs and plates.

"Look, this is the kettle I gave you as a wedding gift!" the older woman held a running commentary. "It's still new! And a packet of buckwheat. Is it expired? — no. Excellent. Take it!"

I didn't know what to say. I suppressed my desire to shower them with sarcasms about their petty greed. Let them take whatever they wanted.

Just as I was thinking about it, Yanna's mother opened the fridge and pulled out some meatballs and a carton of eggs Kira had brought me yesterday. She brought the box up to her eyes, squinting at the expiry date.

"Excuse me!" I raised my voice. "These meatballs are mine!"

I immediately regretted saying anything because Yanna felt obliged to chime in, "You've never had any balls, you. Stop kidding yourself."

"We're only taking what's ours," her mother said magnanimously, hurling the box back into the fridge.

"Thank you very much," I said. "You're most kind."

I focused on her stats, just to keep my mind off the scene.

Natalia Sergeevna Orlova.
Age: 49
Current status: housewife
Social status level: 13
Class: office worker. Level: 7
Married
Husband: Sergei Orlov
Children: Yannina, daughter. Age: 24
Reputation: Animosity 15/30

I picked up an old pot she'd discarded as not having passed her quality control. "Do you mind?"

She ignored my question. I filled the pot with water, placed six eggs into it and put it on the burner.

Mrs. Orlova scooped up the blender and the toaster and hurled them into one of the bags. Her appraising gaze alighted on the microwave. "Is it ours?"

"No, it's not," Yanna said. "It came with the flat."

"Very well, then," losing all interest, Mrs. Orlova staggered out of the kitchen into the lounge, dragging the heavy bags behind her.

"Mom, wait!" Yanna called, holding a bottle of dishwashing liquid. "I bought this."

Her mother's face brightened. "Come on, chuck it in. It's always useful."

By then, I was beyond flabbergasted. I knew

Yanna was the frugal type — stingy even — but this was a bit too much.

My phone vibrated in my pocket. I answered it. "Yes? Yes, it's me. How can I help you?"

I could sense them freeze in the lounge, pricking up their ears.

"Phil? Phil, it's Darya," a girl's voice rattled off in the receiver. "You saw me during the interview you had with our company, Ultrapak, the other day. I'm very happy to tell you that you've been accepted for a trial period. You think you could start tomorrow?"

"Hey!" Yanna shouted from the lounge. "Mind getting your mutt out of the bathroom? We need to check it out!"

"Or, absolutely," I replied into the phone, then covered it with my hand and shouted to Yanna, "Coming!"

"Very well," Darya's voice said. "You know the address, don't you? We start at eight a.m. We'd like you to bring-"

Mrs. Orlova barged into the kitchen, "Take the dog out *now!* We don't have all day!"

I gestured for her to wait till I'd finished. Stepping back, I very nearly stumbled over a hungry Boris rubbing against my feet as in, 'whassup boss, it's breakfast time, where's my chow?'

I rummaged through the cupboards for the cat food but couldn't locate it in the mess. Never mind. I grabbed a carton of milk and poured some into his bowl. That one was sorted.

Mrs. Orlova opened her mouth to speak. I

hurried to switch off the phone's microphone.

"Phil, are you there?" Darya's voice asked.

I cussed and switched the mic back on. "Yes, sure. What do you want me to bring?"

"Get the dog out now!" Mrs. Orlova growled.

"Oh, just a recent photo of yourself... sorry, what did you say?"

"Er... no, nothing."

"Yes, a photo for your name tag. A digital one will do. And-"

"Hey!" Yanna's voice rang with hysterical notes so familiar to me.

Mrs. Orlova stood hands on hips in the doorway, boring me with her impatient stare. I clenched my teeth and went to the bathroom.

Richie dashed out and went for the older woman who scrambled to safety just in time. I grabbed at his collar and led him out onto the balcony, "Heel! Richie, heel!"

He was straining on the collar, wheezing and pulling me along, his paws slipping on the lino.

"Off!" I shouted to him.

"What a monster!" Mrs. Orlova sobbed. She was dripping with cold sweat.

"Please make sure you take your paperwork to the HP department before you start working," Darya finished, nonplussed.

"Yes, absolutely! See you tomorrow! Thanks a lot," I cradled the phone on my shoulder in order to lock the balcony door.

"See you tomorrow, Phil. We're looking forward

to working with you."

I switched the phone off.

I had a job! A tidal wave of relief and pleasure flooded over me.

Task Status: Find a stable job
Task completed!
XP received: 50 pt.
+10% to Satisfaction

I dropped onto the couch, savoring the moment. It felt so good I might even get used to it. So this was the feeling which turned people into workaholics and time management freaks?

I needed to see my XP bar really badly. I just hoped it would sooner or later appear in my interface.

A Godawful crashing noise came from the bathroom, followed by a torrent of f-words courtesy of Mrs. Orlova. Richie outside leaned his front paws against the balcony door, whimpering. I hurried to the bathroom to assess the damage.

"Mom, are you crazy?" Yanna fussed around her. "You could have hurt yourself!"

"It's all right," the older woman said, rubbing her forehead. "That's what happens when you don't have a handyman in the house! Things are held together with spit and a prayer!"

The bathroom cabinet lay shattered on the floor, its contents spilled all over the place. Shower gels, shampoos, my shaving foam, our two razors, toothbrushes and toothpaste, as well as a broken tumbler. It looked like my mother-in-law had at some point leaned her 200 pound-plus weight against the cabinet which had collapsed, unable to sustain the extra pressure.

Mrs. Orlova scooped everything into a plastic bag, only leaving me my toothbrush.

"Hey, that's my razor," I attempted to protest. "You don't need the shaving foam either, do you?"

"I bought it with my money," Yanna announced. "I use both, anyway. You can buy your own. You don't even need them, do you? It's not as if you shave very often!"

I smiled. Their attempts to provoke me were truly pathetic. This final quip had actually become the last straw: now I didn't feel anything. They could take what they wanted, I didn't care. All I needed was my computer and the mattress to sleep on, so they were very welcome to take the bedframe if they wanted, too. They could strip the whole house bare, be my guest!

What did hurt was this petty attempt at revenge from a woman I used to love so much right until this morning. Her hatred was so blatantly obvious that I really didn't feel like talking to her, let alone try to kiss and make up. Actually, I was happy it had happened now and not after a lifetime of living together. It was a good job we didn't have children. I knew it wasn't a good thing to say but that's the way it was. First, she'd been too busy graduating, then we'd had to settle down and wait for me to start earning... until at some point we'd simply stopped thinking about kids. At least I had.

Yanna seemed to be reading my mind. "Oh, and

by the way," she said matter-of-factly. "We need to go to the registry office and file for divorce. I can't do it this week. I have too much work. So it's gonna be next Tuesday. I'll text you when."

"Please do," I said. "I'll have to take time off work."

She raised a quizzical eyebrow but refused to comment.

Finally, Mrs. Orlova was done plundering. Yanna dialed her phone,

"Vlad? You can come up now. We're finished. What did you say? It's okay, we can wait."

"It's all right," I said. "I can help you."

Showing no reaction, they picked up a bag each and walked out of the flat. I lifted all the remaining bags and staggered out of the apartment.

I actually did feel stronger. The bags were still heavy but at least my fingers didn't slacken on the handles as they would have before.

As I walked out onto the landing, I remembered the eggs, cussed, trotted back in and turned off the gas. Then I carried the bags downstairs, not bothering to wait for the elevator.

Strangely enough, I didn't give a damn about Vlad, whoever he was. They could do what they wanted. Even though formally Yanna and I were still married, I didn't feel any pangs of jealousy or whatever a male ape was supposed to feel having lost his female to a stronger opponent.

I just didn't care.

I immediately recognized the Jeep which had

picked up Yanna the night she'd left. Vlad stood next to it: a tall fit guy with short slicked-back hair. I sort of remembered him: he was Yanna's workmate. He was wearing a hugging blue shirt and a fancy belt in his dark pants. His polished shoes reflected the sunshine.

He didn't seem to be in a hurry to help them with the bags though. He just stood there staring at the two women staggering under the weight of their ill-gotten gains. He simply opened the trunk and turned away, talking into his phone.

Grunting like a weightlifter, Mrs. Orlova hauled the bags into the trunk. She never stopped panting and complaining how tired she really was. I put the remaining bags in too. Still, one last plastic bag didn't fit in the trunk.

"D'you want it in the car?" I asked Yanna.

She shrugged, then took the passenger seat in front.

I was getting a bit fed up with all this. I swung the back door open and sat the bag onto the seat.

"Are you nuts? What do you think you're doing?" came from behind as I was brushing my hands. "Get your crap out now! This is *leather*, you dimwit!"

"You mean it's not shark skin? That would suit you better," I slammed the Jeep's door shut and walked back to the house.

"Hey you!" Vlad raved behind me. "Come back here *now*! I tell you!"

I'd had enough. I couldn't control myself any longer. I swung round and walked back, all the while studying his profile.

Vladimir Korolev
Age: 30
Current status: Manager
Social status level: 13
Class: Administrator. Level: 6
Not married
Children: Radomir, son. Age: 2
Reputation: Indifference 0/30

I walked over to him, so close I'd very nearly stepped on his polished shoes, and locked my gaze with his. Admittedly, I had to tilt my head up to do that.

"What's your problem, dude?" I asked, investing all my anger into the question.

He wasn't impressed. "This isn't an Internet chat, *dude*. You'd better behave yourself."

He grinned, enjoying Yanna's attention. He was clearly winding me up. "Take your junk out, get a protection cover from the trunk, spread it on the seat, then put the stuff back in."

"Really?" I faked surprise. "WTF? If you're Yanna's new-"

"Leave him, Vlad," Mrs. Orlova intervened. "Just go!"

"What do you mean, 'just go'? This is leather! I really don't want him to-"

"Hi Phil," Alik's unmannered voice resounded next to us. "Problems?"

He stood behind Vlad in a relaxed, slightly stooping pose, hands in his sweatpants pockets, cigarette hanging from the corner of his mouth, his eyes squinting predatorily, his lower lip slightly bulging. He looked like the epitome of a street thug if ever I'd seen one.

Your Reputation with Vladimir Korolev has decreased!
Current Reputation: Dislike, 15/30

Vlad cast a nervous glance around him. "Get in the car," he snapped at Yanna's mother. He jumped into the driver's seat, slammed the door and stepped on the gas.

Yanna leaned out of the open window, "Tonight Dad will come to collect the TV! Make sure you're at home!"

"Tell him to call me first," I began. "I might be out-" I fell silent, realizing no one was listening to me.

"Is she gone?" Alik asked. "Like, *gone* gone?"

I nodded.

He offered me a packet of cigarettes. "Have a smoke."

I took one and turned it over in my fingers for a while, then gave it back to him. "No, thanks. I haven't smoked for a week. I want to keep it that way."

"Nice job," he said. "Wish I could quit too. Costs me an arm and a leg..."

"It does, doesn't it?" I agreed. "Thanks for helping me out. It would have been a shame to have had my lights punched out by my ex's new acquisition."

I paused. "If you don't mind me asking... you're not following me, are you? It's just that every time I come out into the courtyard you're always around."

Alik's face darkened. He took a deep drag on his cigarette and chuckled, chewing his lips. He heaved a sigh and prepared to speak.

A yellow exclamation mark appeared above his head.

He was a quest giver!

"You could say that," he admitted. "I don't have a place to stay, do I? So I just take it one day at a time. Sometimes I sleep in the basement. Or at one of the guys'. And when it's warm like this I just sleep on a bench in the yard."

"No way? I thought you had a home?"

"I did," he faltered. "Basically, my Dad took out a payday loan. Just to celebrate his fiftieth birthday in style, if you know what I mean. He kept up with his payments at first. And then he got fired. And we still had to pay off the loan. So we're subletting our flat to some migrant workers. My parents have moved to their allotment shed in the country. We have a garden allotment, you know, so they live there now. Mother is really sick now. Worse than before. And Dad just drinks all day. I have to handle the bailiffs..."

"Why don't you find a job? Or just move in with them? You could help them with the garden..."

"There isn't much to help, man. Also, it's a shed as I told you. Normally we keep garden tools in it. And as for finding a job, nobody wants me. I worked at a building site for a while but their foreman, the bastard, fired me for being on the bottle. He never paid me," he turned away.

We stood there for a while, each thinking his own thoughts.

The yard was getting busy with people leaving for work. The sounds of starting motors filled the air as cars began pulling out of their parking spaces. The day was slipping into gear. I had lots of things to do.

"Is there any way I can help you?" I asked Alik point blank.

"I don't think so. I know you're broke. Crashing out at your place isn't an option, either. But if you hear of a job..."

Help Alik Find a Job!
Your neighbor Romuald "Alik" Zhukov is in bad need of regular employment.
Rewards:
XP: 400 pt.
Reputation with Romuald "Alik" Zhukov: 30 pt.
Current Reputation: Amicability 10/60

No *Accept/Decline* buttons anywhere, just like it had been the last time with old Mr. Panikoff and his sports newspaper quest. Apparently, the only way to accept the quest was by saying it out loud.

"I'll see what I can do, man." I said.

The quest window disappeared.

"Thanks," Alik proffered me his hand. "It means a lot to me."

I went back home, had breakfast and began cleaning up. Having finished, I picked up the full trash bag and took Richie for a walk. We headed for the park so I could put in a bit of jogging too.

As I jogged, Sveta Messerschmitt called me. "Hi, Phil. How's Richie?"

"Like a dog with two tails," I replied, panting. "He's actually running next to me. Richie, speak!"

"Oh sorry, I didn't mean to disturb you."

"That's all right. You don't need to worry about him."

"Thank you. Dad wanted me to tell you that he'll make sure you get the reward for finding him."

That was good. I could use some monetary reinforcement. Having said that...

No. It just felt wrong.

"Sorry, Sveta," I stopped to catch my breath. "I didn't do it for the reward. Just promise me that when he fathers some puppies I can buy one."

"You can have one! Of course!"

"Deal," I suppressed an involuntary smile. "I'll be off, then."

"Thank you so much! Can you please send me some more pictures of him?"

"Absolutely. Bye!"

I took a few more pics of Richie, sent them to her and resumed my jogging.

My Vitality bar caught my eye. I knew for sure it used to be red — but now it was yellow. *Yellow.*

I focused on it. I had 80,00173% Vitality. Did that mean that anything below 80% was in the red?

In which case, everything over 90% was probably green. Oh well. That was something to work towards.

Having finished my run, I dropped onto a bench. I really needed to check my stats. It had been exactly a week since I'd discovered the interface.

I opened the stats window,

Philip "Phil" Panfilov
Age: 32
Current status: unemployed
Social status level: 6
Unclassified
Married
Wife: Yannina "Yanna" Orlova
Children: none

Main Characteristics:
Strength: 7
Agility: 4 (+1 bonus from the Stinky Chinese Sneakers of Nimbleness)
Intellect: 18
Stamina: 4
Perception: 7
Charisma: 12
Luck: 6

Secondary Characteristics:
Vitality: 80%
Satisfaction: 78%
Vigor: 47%
Metabolism: 103%

In order to access more data, you need to level up

Insight

Aha. My "gamer" status was gone, replaced by "unemployed". Hopefully, not for long. The sneakers' bonus to Agility was quite impressive. I just loved their name-generating engine! Luckily, it didn't seem to have any negative readings. Otherwise I wouldn't be surprised if the word "stinky" detracted 1 pt. from Charisma, and the word "Chinese", from Durability.

The rest was more or less clear. I'd brought up Strength by investing the available point I'd had. As for Stamina, I'd leveled it up by running non-stop the night Yanna had walked out on me.

That was the extent of my last week's accomplishments. Never mind. I'd spent a lot of time working out the interface. Now I had to concentrate on Insight as well as social status, all the while improving the main levelable stats and whatever skills could make a difference in real life.

Just out of curiosity, I checked my skill list. It would be a good idea to copy them all to an Excel file and ponder over them.

I scrolled through the list until I came to a weird line at the very bottom written in pale gray ink,

Optimization: 0

What was that? Some yet unblocked skill the system had bestowed on me?

I tried to open it. Pointless. A message popped up,

In order to access more data, you need to level up Insight

I summoned Martha. This time she was glitchy as hell, answering all my questions in a grave tone,

"In order to access more data, you need to level up Insight!"

This Insight seemed to be increasingly important. Almost as important as the new debuff I then received on my way back home,

Sexual frustration!

You're suffering from lack of sex! It negatively affects your general health. Continuous sexual frustration and arousal may lead to prostate problems and neurotic disorders.

Warning! High probability of spontaneous erections!

Warning! Your aggro radius has increased!

Warning! High probability of receiving a Depression debuff!

Warning! The Sexual Frustration debuff cannot be disabled by self-gratification!

-5% to Satisfaction every 12 hrs

As if to please, the street seemed to be packed with girls in skimpy summer clothes. Trying to blank them out, I hurried to my front door. Just as I crossed the doorway, I got the mother of all spontaneous erections.

CHAPTER THIRTEEN

A BOX OF CHOCOLATES

"Of course I don't believe the lucky horseshoe superstition. But I understand it works whether you believe in it or not."
Niels Bohr

"Charisma is something you're born into."
Victor Chernomyrdin[5]

PEOPLE HAVE A HABIT OF STARTING A NEW LIFE NOW AND again. The only difference is in how they do it. You can turn a new leaf by quitting smoking and drinking on a

---

[5] Victor Chernomyrdin: a prominent 1990s Russian politician notorious for his inappropriate and ungrammatical statements

New Year's Eve. Or you could buy a gym membership starting next Monday. You could even get a new lease of life on your favorite Internet forum by registering a new account.

You could delete your old game char and create a new one from scratch, then level it up using the knowledge and experience you already have.

You could do it in real life too, by changing your job, your appearance, your habits and even your lifestyle.

The older we get, the stronger our desire to rewrite our lives, deleting all our failed relationships, expired contacts and stupid actions. It's probably why readers love the stories of characters going back to their youth and reliving their old lives by taking a different, mistake-free route.

Today was the perfect chance for me to turn a new leaf. Everything seemed to fall into this pattern: my final decision to break up with Yanna, my first day at work and the mysterious gift from the future whose boosting mechanism allowed me to compensate for some of the wasted time.

As soon as I walked back in through the door, I gave Kira a call and told her about Yanna and her mother's visit.

"I'm afraid it's the end," I said. "Next Tuesday we're meeting up to file for divorce."

My sister heaved a sigh. "I see. Never mind. Just one of those things. Keep your chin up, li'l bro. It's not the end of the world, is it?"

"It's not. I'm starting a new job tomorrow. In

sales. I got a funny feeling they're gonna give me a run for my money. I just won't have the time to be depressed."

"Did they hire you? No way! Excellent, well done! Listen, what if we all have dinner at our parents? Would you like that?"

"Good idea. How about Friday?"

"Okay. I need to go now. See you on Friday!"

I smiled. My heart felt strangely warm.

While still inspired, I concentrated and made a new task list. This was how it looked like now,

Tasks available:

- visit parents;
- level up Insight;
- get accepted for the Ultrapak job;
- finance my new start in life;
- downsize;
- finish reading the marketing book;
- buy some decent work clothes;
- buy some workout clothes and gear;
- buy a gym membership;
- return Richie to his owner Ms. Svetlana "Sveta" Messerschmitt;
- remove the Sexual Frustration debuff;
- meet up with Yanna and file for divorce

The old task *Make up with Yanna and move back in with her* had disappeared from the list, replaced by exactly the opposite. Interestingly, the program had classified the divorce application task as the least important, giving top priority to my upcoming family dinner. The thing that worried me the most, however, was how to get some money without having to borrow it, least of all from those close to me. Still, subconsciously I must have missed my parents a lot, realizing the importance of some quality family time.

I also needed to move into a smaller apartment. Another important step in my quest for a new life which required more cash injections.

Unhesitantly I put my state-of-the-art gaming computer up for sale, widescreen monitor and all. I priced it at 25% less than its analogs: I needed the money pronto.

By my estimation, it should fetch me enough to rent a studio, buy some clothes and guarantee a month or two of Spartan life, including gym membership. I had some ideas about starting to level up combat skills and even signing up for various classes and seminars that might improve my professional skills — but that would depend on my first sales results. Ultrapak's earnings were bonus-oriented so I had to work hard to earn a decent wage.

I called my landlady to tell her I'd move out as soon as the rent ran out. She wasn't pleased. I listened to her anxious objections about me not having warned them a month in advance as the contract required. Still, I explained the situation to her and managed to solve the problem in my favor. People like it when you're honest with them, and the mention of a divorce invariably stirs up their sympathies. It's almost as if they project your situation onto themselves, feeling sorry for you and empathizing with yet another broken dream.

Immediately afterward I received a phone call from some stuttering guy asking about my computer. When I told him that yes, it was still available, and yes, it was indeed the latest mega-machine good enough to launch shuttles into space, he wanted to come straight away to take a look and possibly to buy it on the spot.

I started copying all my personal files onto an external disk, preparing the computer for sale. It took quite a while — long enough for me to rustle up a proper pasta meal.

Just as I was about to sit down to lunch, the potential buyer finally arrived. It was a puny guy wearing a pair of shorts and a hugging T-shirt one size too small. He looked a bit jumpy and restless.

He spent about ten minutes checking the computer's characteristics, ran some sort of performance test, then reached for the money and started thumbing through it without even trying to haggle over the price.

What, just like that? "Wait a sec," I said, trying to keep up appearances. "It's been a while since I cleaned it. I won't be long."

"Doesn't matter," he interrupted me. "I can do it later."

He was so impatient to get away and start using the machine he even forgot to stutter.

"Mind if I format it?" I asked.

He heaved a doomed sigh. "I took time off from

work to come over here."

"Just a quick one," I said, "to delete all the data and restore it to factory settings."

He nodded and started pacing the room, casting impatient glances at the formatting progress bar and giving Richie a wide berth. What a fidgety individual.

I checked out his stats. *Maxim Travkin, age 24, social status level 3, criminal record: yes.* Just out of curiosity, I looked him up on social media. By the time I scrolled through his feed, the computer had almost finished formatting.

I took the money and counted it, focusing on each note. The mysterious game system obligingly identified them,

5,000 rubles
A bank note issued by the Bank of Russia
Nominal value: 5,000 rubles
Issue date: 1997
Last modified: 2010.

I thumbed through the wad until I came to a note whose stats were different,

A piece of paper covered in artistic design
Size: 6.1811" by 2.71654"

Excuse me? A *fake*?

I felt it in my fingers, then peered at it against the light. It seemed to be perfectly genuine, watermarks and all.

Only apparently it wasn't.

I set it aside for the time being. "You wouldn't tell the difference, would you?" I said matter-of-factly to my buyer.

He got even more fidgety.

I turned to the dog. "Richie, watch him!"

"Eh, I... you know..." he began, stuttering.

"You know what?"

"I must be on my way. I need to get back to work... they've just called me," he showed me his phone making sure not to expose the screen, then rose and reached for the money.

"It's almost finished!" I insisted. "It's 97% done, look!"

"Sorry, I really got to go," he squeaked. "I'm off now."

"Wait a sec," I said, investing all the 12 pt. Charisma into my voice. Had I had my Derby shoes on, it would have been 13 pt.

"Could you tell you dog to keep away, please? I'm a bit scared of dogs."

He didn't lie this time. I could hear it in his voice. Well, so much the better.

"He's not aggressive, don't worry," I said. "If you don't make any sudden movements, he won't attack you."

Leaving him with the dog, I walked over to the front door and locked it. Having returned, I studied the remaining notes. I found three more identified as *"pieces of paper covered in artistic design"*.

"Now, Maxim," I said. "Here's what we're going

to do."

His eyes widened. He hadn't told me his name, had he?

I plucked up whatever courage I had — whatever Yanna might think of my non-existent *cojones* — and continued to speak in a level voice,

"Four of these five-thousand notes are fakes," I said. "That's a rip-off of twenty thousand rubles[6]. Even though I'm already selling it at thirty thousand below its market price. Do you agree with me?"

"I didn't know..." he began.

"Of course you didn't. So you won't mind if I call the police."

"Please... please don't!"

That's when I knew for sure he'd known about the fakes all along. An honest person would have been surprised at my discovery, probably upset but hardly scared of the police. Still, I already knew from his profile that he was a petty crook. Apparently, even the likes of him enjoyed a good gaming computer.

"In that case," I said, "We'll make an agreement. You're buying the computer for the price we agreed upon-"

"Yes, of course!"

"And that's not all," I took in a big gulp of air, braced myself and tried to add some weight to my words. "You're going to compensate me for my emotional suffering induced by your little scheme for the same money as you tried to rip me off."

---

[6] 20,000 Russian rubles is about $350 at the time of writing

He zoned out, making some mental calculations. "It's a lot of money for me," he finally said. "How about we scrap compensation? I have two little girls, Tania and Masha. My wife is nursing the third..."

He wasn't stuttering anymore, was he? Did he feel safe already? Never mind. I knew how to make him nervous.

"You're not married," I said. "You don't have children, either. All right, I've had enough of this. I'm calling the police."

"I don't have so much money on me! I can go and fetch it if you-"

"I don't think so. I even think you've got enough money on you. You just want to get out of here, don't you? In which case I just might tell you what I know about you. Your name is Max Travkin, twenty-four, and you have a serious gambling problem. You bet on sports, don't you? You're also a convicted felon."

Trrrrrr! Trrrrrr! That was Boris who'd unsheathed her long-untrimmed claws and began clawing the couch with a dreadful ripping sound.

No idea whether it was her claws, Richie's fangs or my high Charisma figures but Max dialed a number on his phone and spoke to someone, asking them to bring the money.

I looked out the window. A young guy got out of a car parked next to the playground and headed for my house. I paused, weighing up the risks, then decided to play it safe.

"Alik!" I called out of the window. "Alik!"

Hearing my voice, Alik woke up and sprang from

his bench in the pavilion, looking around himself. Finally he saw me.

"Mind coming up for a second?" I shouted. "I'm at number 204! Eighth floor!"

"I'm on my way!" he shouted back.

Soon I heard the sound of the elevator doors opening on the landing outside. The doorbell rang.

I motioned Max to follow me and went to answer the door. The guy from the car stood outside. Alik hovered behind his back, scratching his belly under his wife beater vest.

"Whassup, Phil?" he asked. "Problems?"

"Nah. Come in. Need to talk."

The guy from the car (*Rustam Abdullaev, age 19, social status: student*) looked around anxiously. Alik shouldered him out of his way and walked in.

I turned to the student. "So, Rustam? You've got the money?"

The student looked askance at Max who nodded his affirmation.

"Here," he handed me the bank notes.

"Excellent. To the left!" I slammed the door in his face and counted the money. "That's right. Forty grand as agreed. The computer is yours. Alik, come to the kitchen, man, let's have lunch together. You like pasta Navy style?[7]"

Alik perked up. "I like pasta in any shape or form. Especially Navy style."

---

[7] Pasta Navy style: a simple pasta dish with ground beef and onions which used to be a staple in the Soviet Navy

I helped Max collect the cables and pack them into a plastic bag, adding the headset, the Kargath Bladefist mouse pad and the multi-button gaming mouse for good measure.

"Chin up, man," I said, opening the door. "You'll still get a good profit on it. See you."

Max handed the heavy 50-pound desktop tower to his student partner. The student staggered toward the elevator with Max in his wake lugging the monitor and the plastic bag.

They climbed into the cabin. The elevator doors closed.

How strange. I wasn't at all sorry to see the last of my trusty old PC. When I'd bought it a year and a half ago, I was happy as the proverbial pig. Its out-of-this-world settings turned any game into a breeze even with maxed-out graphics. No more slide shows on a raid! I remembered an old PC I used to have, when I'd force myself to look down at the floor whenever the graphics card lagged, trying to visualize all the colorful paraphernalia of VFX emitted by a couple of dozen wizards, warlocks, shamans, paladins, priests and other such spell-casting folk.

And now I wasn't even upset. Later I might buy myself a laptop. In the meantime it wouldn't do me any harm to stay computer free for a while.

Why would I even need it? I had cutting-edge twenty-second century wetware uploaded to my brain!

Also, it made the task of moving house much easier. I didn't have to lug a 50-pound monster around anymore.

I slid the wad of money into my pocket. Good riddance.

Immediately, a new message popped up.

Congratulations! You've received a new skill level!
Skill name: Vending
Current level: 5
XP received: 500

500 XP per level — was it a lot? I needed the XP status bar really badly now. I was desperate to find out how much I had left till next level.

Task Status: Finance my new start in life
Task completed!
XP received: 20 pt.
+5% to Satisfaction

I lingered, reveling in the moment. I wouldn't mind more of the same.

Actually, things had worked out really well. The prompt sale, the fact that I hadn't been ripped off, even my leveling of Vending just in time for my first day working as a sales rep... was I really sure I'd invested the extra point into Strength and not Luck?

Finally, I awoke from my reverie. I had Alik to take care of. I walked into the kitchen.

He'd already poured the pasta and the sauce into the large heavy skillet my mother-in-law had rejected, and was busy warming it up.

We ate in silence. Alik shoveled mouthfuls of pasta into his mouth with one hand using the other to soak up oil from the skillet with a piece of bread. After a while, he leaned against the back of his chair and emitted a contented sigh. "Phew..."

"Have you had enough?"

He pricked up his ears. "Why? Have you got something else?"

"Only tea and cookies."

"Why didn't you say so! Cookies and tea, far out! You don't have any milk, by any chance?"

"Why, do you like milk with your tea?"

"Of course!" Alik sprang back to his feet, eager to put the kettle on, but I forced him back down.

"You're my guest," I said. "I'll make the tea now. Only I don't have any milk. Sorry about that."

We drank our tea to the accompaniment of his army stories and tales of his failed wedding. In the end, I laid four bank notes of five grand each on the table in front of him — the "compensation" I'd received from sneaky Max.

"It's twenty grand," I said. "Take it. You pay it back when you can. If you can."

I didn't count on him paying it back to me. Easy come, easy go. But to him it could make all the difference.

He stared at the money in disbelief, afraid of even touching it. "Are you serious?"

"Of course. I can't help you find a job so I thought I'd do this instead. And now I'm really sorry but I have things to do..."

"He's sorry!" Alik roared, springing to his feet and giving me a crushing hug.

Your Reputation with Romuald "Alik" Zhukov has improved!
Current Reputation: Respect 10/120

Another message followed the first one,

You've received +1 to Charisma!
Current Charisma: 13
You've received 1000 pt. XP for successfully leveling up a main characteristic!

Oh wow. I hadn't expected that at all.

How cool was that? I must have done something truly special today if the game system had decided to shower me with enough XP to make the next Charisma level.

My improved Reputation must have had something to do with it too. And the mysterious stat booster.

Strangely enough, I was happier now than I'd ever been playing the Game. Which was understandable. These stats would be with me for life. I wasn't going to lose them as a result of some stupid system update.

I saw Alik to the door. He shook my hand long and hard before leaving. Finally, I closed the door behind him.

And then, *bang.*

Hidden quest alert: A Friend in Need. Quest completed!
XP received: 300
+15% to Satisfaction

It felt so good I could barely stand on my feet. It only lasted a couple of seconds — but my brain had already processed this pleasure fix and was craving more of the same.

I really needed to capitalize on my lucky streak. Time to find myself a new home.

I started checking the classified ads, marking down those that sounded interesting and copying the owners' phone numbers. I wasn't in the mood to go and view them now. Not quite yet. I still had time to move out.

Today, I had work clothes to buy, workout gear to choose and a decent gym to locate. I still had to finish the book I'd been reading, give the TV to Yanna's father, walk Richie... how was I supposed to do all that in one day? If my workday started at 8 a.m., I'd have to get up at six — five even, if I wanted to fit some running in. Which meant I had to be in bed by 10 p.m.

I set some money aside, enough to rent a new place and last me until my first paycheck. "Boris, I leave you in charge!" I said, getting ready to go out to the mall. "Richie, you're the security guard tonight."

The two were already lying within a couple feet of each other, following me with their gazes. Apparently, they'd come to some sort of compromise.

Richie had gained quite a bit of weight. Very

soon his greedy chops wouldn't fit on my smartphone screen. All this time, he'd kept finishing off Boris' food and never stopped begging. Whenever I sat down to eat, he was there looking at me with those miserable eyes as if saying, "Please spare a scrap for a hungry old mutt..." Thanks to my generous offerings — but hopefully not only thanks to them — my Reputation with him had already risen to Reverence.

I took a minibus to the mall. As I rode, I tried to identify everything my gaze chanced upon: cars and passers-by, cats, birds and inanimate objects. It served two purposes, leveling Insight and adding to my people database. You never knew when it might come in handy.

I spent some quality time in boutiques, looking for clothes with decent stat bonuses. I lingered next to an expensive business suit by one of the famous makes. The full set gave you +6 to Charisma as well as considerable bonuses to Communication Skills, Vending, Seduction and Leadership.

The price tag was absolutely exorbitant. I could, in fact, go back home and use the money I'd set aside, but then what? What was I supposed to do afterward, seductive, charismatic and broke? Chat up single ladies in sleazy bars hoping to find a place to crash for the night?

In the perfume store, I couldn't help myself any longer. I bought some aftershave offering +1 to both Charisma and Seduction. Very befitting, considering my newly-acquired debuff. Having said that, the tasks I'd completed had more than made up for its downsides.

I finally bought a track suit and matching running shoes by a well-known brand name. The set gave +1 to all physical stats as well as Charisma. Okay, +1 to Agility or even Stamina I could understand, but Strength? How on earth would wearing this undoubtedly functional set of gear make me stronger? Apart from its cooling and self-ventilating properties, did it also affect my self-confidence or motivation? No idea.

I also bought two nice shirts for work, a pair of light summer pants and a belt. Their bonuses were negligible — same package of Charisma, Vending and Communication Skills — but combined with my own stats, even these crumbs began to add up.

I also took a chance to stock up on socks and underwear.

As I continued shopping around, I'd made a remarkable discovery. In the long run, there was no difference in stats between mass market items and expensive brand names. What did make a difference was how the item looked on me. The same shirt in two different sizes could either add or detract Charisma points. Which was logical, really. Could anyone look charismatic in a shirt three sizes too big? As a clown yeah, maybe. Then again, a clown was supposed to be funny. Or sad. Or cute. Was there even such a thing as a charismatic clown? Probably not. Unless your name was Vladimir Zhirinovsky[8].

Also, it went without saying that clothes stats had to match the wearer's identity. This wasn't a game. The bonuses coming with a mini skirt wouldn't do a male owner any favors.

Finally I left the mall. The system paused, making sure I was done with my purchases, then rewarded me with 10 XP and +2% to Satisfaction for completing the task.

I took a minibus home, once again trying to ID everything in sight. Yanna's dad had already called me asking when he could come to collect the proverbial Idiot Box. We agreed to meet up at my place a bit later. I still had to pop into the gym to buy a membership. I was itching to close the task and start leveling up as early as next morning.

The gym membership turned out to be more expensive than I'd thought. Still, it included a free trial and a consultation with a coach. Also, I could always pay on a pay-per-visit basis without having to shell out for a monthly plan. Which was probably a better option if I failed to find a new place in the same neighborhood.

Despite this minor hiccup, the system duly closed the task, rewarding me with 10 XP. No Satisfaction bonuses this time.

I came back home just in time. My father-in-law was already waiting in front of my apartment. Richie behind the door was barking in short weighty bursts,

---

[8] Vladimir Zhirinovsky: a Russian extreme right-wing politician notorious for his antics and controversial statements.

very believably impersonating Gandalf's *You... Shall... Not... Pass!*

Yanna's father was a regular hard-working guy, balding and on the brink of retirement. You could always count on him to join you for a drink and a heart-to-heart. Whenever Yanna and I had had a falling out, I sensed his silent support behind my back. As a fellow man, he understood me — but as a father, he was obliged to take his daughter's side. He just loved her too much and didn't seem to mind his wife's bossing ways. Also, he wanted grandchildren. Shame it hadn't quite worked out.

"Ah, Phil," he said, noticing me.

I shook his proffered hand. "Hi, Mr. Orlov."

"I'm sorry it came to this."

"So am I," I said, opening the door.

For a brief moment, I meant it. I was sorry it had had to come to this. Really.

I unplugged the TV from the cable, lifted it from its stand and helped Mr. Orlov to wrap it in a blanket and tie it up with a piece of string. He was a provident guy. I would never have thought of bringing that sort of thing along.

I helped him to carry the TV to the elevator and pressed the button.

Entering the elevator, he shrugged sort of apologetically. "Don't get mad at them. Women! I'll see you around."

I took Richie out for a quick walk, then cooked a humble bachelor's dinner of jacket potatoes and meatballs with some sliced cucumbers on the side.

Now the apartment looked completely empty. I only had the dog and the cat to keep me company. Both were with me now in the kitchen.

As I cooked the meatballs, I curiously studied the stats on each of them. What a shame I couldn't see their contents! Were they really *"beef, 50%, pork, 35%"* as the packaging claimed?

Just I'd finished cooking them, I was blinded with an abundance of new messages. *Bang! Bang! Bang!*

Congratulations! You've received a new skill level!
Skill name: Cooking
Current level: 3
XP received: 500

You've received a new system skill level!
Skill name: Insight
Current level: 2
XP received: 1000

You've unblocked new emotional characteristics!
Emotional characteristics available: Mood, Spirit, Willpower, Confidence

Task Status: Level up Insight
Task completed!
XP received: 200 pt.
+15% to Satisfaction
Would you like to see the skill's full details?

Just as I heaved a gasp of ecstasy, a new buff message appeared,

Happiness I
Your Satisfaction levels have exceeded 100%!
+50% to Vigor
+1 to all main characteristics
Duration: as long as Satisfaction levels exceed 100%

Now I began to understand what people felt when they said they could fly with joy. I'd never experienced anything like that — not after my first sex, not even when I'd attained my highest WoW achievements. Even when Yanna and I had begun dating, it hadn't felt like this despite me being madly and happily in love.

The excitement had completely put me off my food. I munched mechanically on my meatballs simply to avoid getting the Hunger debuff.

As I ate, I studied the detailed description for Insight II.

Insight II
Skill type: Passive

- Allows you to receive advanced information about your characteristics and skills, including XP, characteristic, and skill progress bars

- Allows you to register and enter the following

additional secondary characteristics: Mood, Spirit, Willpower, Confidence, and Self-Control

- Allows you to receive advanced item information, including their composition, production history and approximate monetary evaluation

- Allows you to receive advanced information about other people and living beings, including their main characteristics and primary skills

- When interacting with others, allows you to see their Mood and Interest levels

- Provides information on any available skills which are currently blocked

- Marks the location of people and other living beings on your map, provided your knowledge of them is equal or exceeds 5 KIDD points.

- Displays your heart rate, current date and time and a mini map

I temporarily zoned out, not knowing where to begin. I must have dropped a meatball from my fork, judging by the scuffle that ensued (which Richie predictably won). I was even oblivious of Boris' sneaky paw reaching for my plate. My subconscious must have duly registered my pets' insolent behavior but my brain was in overdrive.

I summoned Martha, hoping to receive an explanation of the mysterious KIDD points.

Martha leaned her lithe back on the wall pressing the sole of the foot against it. Exactly what I didn't need with my newly-acquired debuff. My body reacted to her presence without my consent.

"Martha, could you please change your avatar?"

"Request denied. Insufficient resource."

"Could you at least change into something more presentable?"

She immediately "changed" into a skimpy evening dress. Oh, great. This was getting worse.

"Never mind," I said. "Mind telling me what KIDD is?"

"KIDD is Key ID Data. One KIDD point contains one key property of an object which allows for its repeated successful identification."

"Could you give me an example, please?"

"For human beings, it can be a close-up photograph of a person's face, their full name or date of birth, their place of birth, place of current employment or any such information about their family members, among other things."

"How can knowing someone's place of birth help you to find them?"

Martha shook her head in silent amazement. "Phil, Phil. Compare the planet's entire population to that of even its biggest city."

"Okay, I got it. Now please get lost. I'm not in a good way. That wretched debuff!"

"Request accepted. Allow me to bring to your

attention that you are recommended to enter into a sexual inter-"

"Piss off!"

She disappeared. I opened the skill tab, scrolled it all the way to the end and focused on the yet-inactive Optimization.

AFTER A SHORT WHILE, I WALKED OUT ONTO THE balcony and looked up, gazing at the stars.

Today had just turned out to be the best day of my life.

In any known RPG, Optimization would be a perfectly legit skill. Well, almost.

But in real life... goodness me, this was a cheat to end all cheats! If you put it in a book, no one would believe such a Deus-ex-freakin-machina! But there I was, having it courtesy of the mysterious game system.

Optimization I

- Allows you to select primary and secondary skills.

The development of primary skills will take 50% less time than average. The development of secondary skills will take 50% longer than average.

- Allows you to convert secondary skill points to primary ones at a rate of 2 to 1, with the consequent deletion of the secondary skill.

Cooldown: 30 days

Warning! In order to activate the skill, an undisturbed 12-hour period of sleep is required. Please ensure your location is safe. You are recommended to adopt a prone position.

I desperately needed a skill point.
And to get it, I had to keep leveling.

CHAPTER FOURTEEN

THE DOG EAT DOG WORLD

"Accomplishing the impossible means only that the boss will add it to your regular duties."

Doug Larson

"THERE YOU GO," A PRETTY GYM RECEPTIONIST HANDED me a towel and a magnetic locker key on a bracelet. "Your personal coach is Alexander over there. Once you've changed, you need to go and speak to him. Enjoy your workout!"

"Thanks," I replied, suppressing a big yawn.

I'd gotten up before 5 a.m. Waking up hadn't been such a problem thanks to my smart internal alarm clock. Still, I couldn't fool my own body. I simply hadn't had enough sleep. At least I hadn't received the Lack of Sleep debuff this time. No matter how hard I'd tried to force myself asleep, I'd tossed and turned through the best part of the night deciding on what I should do next.

Two things that were virtually guaranteed to satisfy most of one's needs were money and power. Also, money could lead to power just as power could lead to money. Which meant that acquiring one of the two was probably enough to get the other — plus all the perks one could think of.

Would you like to make this world a better place? In this case, you should invest in science and medicine, help the poor and support non-profits. Or would you rather indulge in the most unthinkable debauchery? In which case, you were more than welcome to an unlimited list of pleasures delivered directly to your Presidential Suite. And if it was vanity you were after, why not buy a top soccer club, pack it chock full of stars and enjoy the world's standing ovations and TV appearances?

You could make your childhood dreams come true by becoming a space tourist or investing in space exploration; you could enjoy the privacy of a tropical island complete with white beaches and picturesque vistas; you could finance and lead a revolution in some remote banana republic; or you could shoot a blockbuster movie about dinosaurs and beautiful androids in skimpy bikinis... you could do lots of things. Your imagination and the size of your wallet were the limits.

As for power, that was something I'd never been interested in. But money... money didn't earn itself. I had less than a year left until my paid membership ran out. I'd have to make the most of this time.

This was the proverbial crossroads. I was thirty-two with nothing to show for it. What was normal for my peers — a stable income, a family, a place of their own, decent cars and frequent overseas vacations — was still out of reach for me. So whatever decision I made now would gradually, over months, take me further away from any alternative routes.

What should I invest my time and effort in? Should I pursue my writing career? Or become an advertising expert? Persevere with sales or start my own business while I gained enough experience?

This kind of choice was still academic — I was too busy trying to survive for the time being. But my other goal, to bring my main characteristics up to average, was pretty obvious. Whatever I decided to do, I couldn't afford to be worse than the average Joe — not when I had this premium augmented-reality account to help me.

This was my chance. If I used it right, then by the end of the year I'd be able to live a new life unassisted by the interface. I'd be strong, agile, intelligent, charismatic and lucky enough.

I really should have invested into Intellect, Luck or Perception. Had I known that these characteristics were more than just numbers! It looked like they really could affect your life with every level you gained. Crazy, I know, but would I have really become smarter had I invested in Intellect? How about Luck — would I have started making better decisions? I also had a funny feeling that an improved Perception might have restructured my vision.

Naturally, I had to concentrate on important stats, clearing my head from all the worthless extras. Optimization had a month's cooldown, after all. According to Martha, this wasn't just some arbitrary limitation. Apparently, the human brain couldn't be rebuilt overnight. The artificial rerouting of neural paths was a time-consuming and highly delicate procedure, especially if the skill required introducing new data to the brain.

I'd already made up my mind to get rid of my WoW skills. That would give me 4 extra points for level 1 of some other skill. But what was going to happen if I did that? Would I forget that the game even existed? Would I still be able to remember my guild and the names of my clan members?

According to Martha, I'd be able to remember all of it, only that the memory would become weak and blurred as if it were something that had happened decades ago. A bit like I remembered my childhood games in my grandparents' village. We had this game of throwing pocket knives at targets. I could vaguely recall us drawing some circles on the ground and dividing them into sectors depending on the number of players... but that was the extent of it. I couldn't remember the rules nor the faces of my playmates. I didn't even know anymore if I'd been any good at it. The knife we'd used — had it been a pocket or a kitchen knife? Had its handle been made of wood or held together with a length of tape? I just didn't remember...

I still didn't know how many skills I could select as primary for use with Optimization. Were there any restrictions? And which ones should I really level?

Unfortunately, system skills such as Insight could only be leveled up through repeated use. So if I thought strategically — not just about this year but about my life as a whole — I really had to improve Learning Skills which gave 10% to Learning Rate with its first level gained.

In this light, making the next social status level was becoming a priority. I needed this skill point in order to activate Optimization. Then by the time the license ran out, I would have converted ten or eleven worthless skills into something useful.

Leveling social status was also important for another reason. Even though I still didn't understand what exactly I gained from it, I now knew that each level gained gave me an extra system point to invest into characteristics and skills.

Now that I could finally see all the stat bars, my progress had ceased to be guesswork. Each new level required 1000 XP more than the one before it. Skill bars were calibrated in percent.

Currently, I was level 6. In order to make level 7, I had to amass 7,000 XP. At the moment, the XP bar was filled a little more than a half.

Current level: 6
XP gained: 3760/7000

Interestingly, I'd earned most of that XP last night — by leveling Charisma, Insight and Cooking, and by having helped Alik out. I already knew that I received no XP for any system leveling of my stats — but I did receive 1 pt. for each Reputation point as well as for each point earned for completing self-assigned tasks.

True, you couldn't earn much XP by setting your own tasks. The game could read my mind, so it knew which things were hard for me to do and which ones were easy peasy. At first, I'd had this idea of making a to-do list of a hundred entries for the next morning: get out of bed, walk into the bathroom, open the tap... yeah right. It hadn't worked, had it? The tasks hadn't even added to my 2do log.

I'd love to know how Mr Panikoff, my old-age pensioner, had managed to level his social status to level 27? That was over 300,000 XP! Hadn't he said he used to be a university lecturer? Could it have been all the Respect his students had for him? That could explain it. That way he could have earned one level a year easily, even without any boosters.

I could only imagine the numbers achieved by medical workers. Having said that, some so-called doctors could be mere quacks who didn't give a damn about their negative karma as long as they could line their pockets.

I smiled, remembering Olga, the cute shrink from the clinic. Should I visit her again, maybe?

I toyed with the idea for a bit until I realized it must have been my wretched sexual debuff putting thoughts into my head. No, I'd better give this one a miss.

I was curious to check out celebrities' levels, just to see if their fame affected their real Reputation. Questions, questions... The more answers I discovered, the more new questions I had.

Then there was money, of course. I had to become my own boss. I could already see that this new job in Ultrapak wasn't going to pay millions even if I owned the company itself which I didn't. I was a humble sales rep on a trial period. And in order to come up with any moneymaking ideas, I might need to experiment. I had to find out which KIDD points counted and which didn't.

I equipped my brand-new workout gear and walked out of the locker room. Considering this was still early morning, the place was heaving. I had no idea we had so many health freaks in our country.

My debuff-ridden gaze seemed to gravitate to all the shapely gym babes. In a way, this was actually motivational, encouraging me to lose weight, gain muscle and improve stamina. All of that might considerably improve my standing with the fairer sex.

I spent the next hour working out with my coach Alexander (*age: 28, married, social level 9*). He asked me about my objectives (strength and stamina) and began trying me on all sorts of machines. We started with a warmup on a treadmill, followed by sit-ups, bench presses, cable rows, hyperextensions and a few other exercises, all of them with the minimum weight.

"First we need to teach you technique," he

explained. "It might take us a couple of weeks. We'll be doing it nice and slow, gradually adding more weights."

As I worked out, I received several system warnings about my heart rate exceeding safe parameters. I was so out of shape my heart was pounding after every set — but I had to start a new one before I even had a chance to catch my breath.

I walked back to the locker room on rubbery legs, soaked in sweat. My towel was dripping wet.

Much to my surprise, my Strength numbers hadn't changed. It was still level 7, the progress bar frozen at 18% (I'd checked it on purpose before I'd started working out).

Alexander's last words seemed to shed some light on this mystery. "At the moment, it's better that you take a full day's rest between sessions," he said as he parted with me, with a suggestion I had a protein shake. "Muscle tissue requires a 48-hour recovery period in order to enter the supercompensation stage."

The effects of his training session manifested themselves in a totally different way. Once I got out of the shower, I received a message informing me of my increased Metabolism, Satisfaction and Vigor. My Mood, Spirit, Willpower and Confidence had also received a bit of a nudge. I couldn't complain, really. Benefit was apparent.

Seeing as my Happiness buff was about to expire, I went to the gym bar and had a delicious chocolate protein shake. Was this how people became addicted to exercise?

***

AS SOON AS I WALKED INTO THE ULTRAPAK OFFICE, I noticed a few familiar faces. Both Marina and Greg "Bullshit Artist" Boyko were there too — the guys I'd met at the job interview three days previously.

Only three days! So many things had happened since — mainly in my head, though — that it felt like an eternity.

We hung in the sales department, not knowing what to do with ourselves. There was nowhere to sit down, anyway. All six of us — myself, Greg, Marina and three other guys of various ages — stood in a tight group by the water cooler.

No one seemed to be paying any attention to us. Either they viewed us as competition or they'd already seen loads of hopeless wannabes like ourselves.

We spent a quarter of an hour shooting the breeze and listening to Greg's half-baked stories. Today he'd arrived dressed all in white. He admitted he hadn't had the guts to quit his old job. He'd just taken some time off without pay.

Finally the door opened, letting in the company's commercial director: a grim man of about thirty. I remembered him: he'd been present at my earlier interview.

He walked through the room, dishing out orders left and right while talking on his phone and drinking coffee. He motioned us to follow him.

We trotted in his wake through a maze of office corridors until finally we came to the conference room with a projector mounted on a large oval table. Still busy arguing with someone on his phone, he motioned us to sit down.

I checked his profile. Pavel Gorelov, 31 years old, corporate leader, a level-11 vendor. Married with three kids. Social status level: 18.

I remembered what Martha had earlier said about having children: apparently, children were considered society's future so raising them could positively affect one's social status too.

I checked his primary skills and main characteristics. Predictably, he had high levels of Sales Skills, Leadership — and Boxing, of all things. Oh wow. *Strength: 15, Agility: 14, Charisma: 16...* this was one hell of a dude!

And I was a year his senior...

The moment I thought this, I received a debuff message,

A Pang of Envy
You're experiencing jealousy of another person's success.
-5% to Confidence
-5% to Satisfaction
-10% to Self-Control
+5% to Willpower

There you go, Phil. You're a jealous bastard, aren't you?

Admittedly, I had every reason to be. My future boss cut a fine figure with his crewcut, his fit body, his expensive suit and megawatt smile. He projected confidence an wellbeing.

We took our seats, waiting for him to finish his conversation. Finally, he switched the phone off. Without sitting down, he leaned both hands against the back of a chair.

"Morning, everyone. We've met already. Still, for those who might have forgotten me, my name's Pavel and I'm the sales director here at Ultrapak. I can see there're six of you here even though I specifically told the HR that I only needed five people. One of you will be going home now. By the end of next week, there'll be only three of you left. And by the end of your trial period, only one person will join us as a new sales manager. If you're not sure you can do it, I suggest you don't waste my time — or your own. You'd better leave *now*."

His searching gaze lingered upon each of us as he studied our reactions. No volunteers.

"Very well. In which case, allow me to take my pick."

Then — I kid you not! — he began reciting a children's counting rhyme, pointing his finger at each of us in turn,

> "Tinker, Tailor, Soldier, Sailor,
> Wizard, Warrior, Rogue or Gambler,
> Dwarf or Druid, friend or foe,
> One of us will have to go!"

His finger alighted on my chest. "You. You're free

to go."

All eyes were upon me. One of the guys grinned triumphantly, not bothering to conceal his relief.

My ears were burning. My throat seized. I received a "high pulse rate" system message.

I stared at his groomed manicured finger poking my chest, then looked up at him.

"You can go now," he repeated.

I feverishly rummaged through all my available options. Finally, I braced myself and rose from my seat. "If I may-"

He raised a protesting hand. "Oh, no, no, please stop. Should I call security?"

He seemed to be losing his patience with me. This guy valued every minute of his time.

"Please don't," I said. "I'm going now. I just wanted to make a counteroffer. You won't be losing anything by accepting it."

"Make it quick."

"I'm gonna close a sale before the end of the working day. If I fail, you won't see me again. Do you need an extra sale?"

"Absolutely. You can sit down-" he faltered.

"I'm Phil," I helpfully offered.

"I know your name. You can sit down, Phil. And you," he turned to the guy with a smug grin, "you can go now."

Now I knew what it looked like when someone wiped a smile off your face. The guy turned crimson. Stuttering, he mumbled something in his defense which met with Pavel's cold, disdainful glare.

The guy beat a dignified retreat, slamming the door behind him.

A new quest message followed,

A One-Day Chance
You must close a sales deal for packaging products produced by Ultrapak, Ltd.
Deadline: end of the workday

Rewards:
A chance to win a sales rep's position with the company
XP: 1500 pt.
Reputation with the company's commercial director Pavel Gorelov: +10 pt.
Current Reputation: Indifference 0/30

Penalties:
Loss of your chance to work with Ultrapak, Ltd
Reputation with the company's commercial director Pavel Gorelov: -30 pt.
Current Reputation: Indifference 0/30

"Now, where were we?" the director continued. "Today I'm going to introduce you to our products and give you a quick guided tour of the company. Then I'll assign each of you to one of our managers so you can watch them sell..."

He turned to me. "That doesn't apply to you, Phil. I suggest you don't waste your time and start selling as soon as you acquaint yourself with the list of our products."

* * *

BIAXIALLY ORIENTED POLYSTYRENE, OR BOPS FOR short, stands for those clear plastic containers used by supermarkets, restaurants and fast food joints to sell salads, prepackaged foods, cream cakes and other goodies. It can't be reused which means that the demand for it is just as high as for the foods themselves.

This particular type of packaging had caught my attention — especially when I compared the price charged by Ultrapak with its real price which I could see in my mental interface. Its market price was 6 rubles apiece. Peanuts. Still, Ultrapak sold it at 324 rubles apiece.

What was the catch?

Once we'd finished familiarizing ourselves with the company's produce, Pavel sent me directly to the sales department where he found me a spare desk with a telephone. A dog-eared business phone directory sat on the desk next to it, covered with its previous owner's scribbles: "*Not to call*"; "*Speak to Svetlana the company buyer*", "*They're all idiots!!!*"

No one had shown me the client base. I could understand them. I was still a nobody here.

I spent the next hour copying the names of all of the city's markets and fast food chains, then walked around the room with the list to make sure I didn't call someone who was already a client. Other reps stared at me like I was some kind of idiot. Still, they didn't tell me as much. Instead, they glanced over my list, ticking off the names of their own clients.

One of the managers, the fat Cyril Cyrilenko, took me aside. Assaulting me with a strong tobacco breath, he told me to follow him into the smoking room.

I agreed unhesitantly. In my situation, any information was precious.

"You don't need to call Pesco Market," he said. "I work with them."

He drew hard on his cigarette, then wheezed, exhaling, "How did you manage to get a sale? Normally, he won't let trainees anywhere near sales for a week at least. How did you do it?"

"Dunno," I didn't feel like lying to a potential workmate. "He wanted to fire me straight away. He said we were one too many. So what he did, he..."

"He recited a counting rhyme," Cyril grinned and immediately exploded in a bout of coughing. "Isn't that typical. He always uses the same rhyme. Was it the one about wizards and rogues? I'll tell you something. He didn't like you from the start. He already knew how to recite the rhyme so that it ended with you."

"What was the point? They could simply fail my interview."

"Or no, they couldn't. If he fired someone now, the others would give up hope and become desperate. So how come he didn't give you the boot?"

"I promised him a sale. If I fail to close a deal by the end of the day, then he can fire me."

"You're not shy, are you?" he laughed, then

exploded in another bout of coughing.

I peered at his health numbers. 62,6%. Should I say something? Or ask about his health? He might think I was prying.

A new task message appeared in my view.

Ask about Mr. Cyrilenko's health and suggest he makes an appointment with the doctor.

I waited for his coughing bout to subside. "What do I have to lose? It's not as if I have another job," I said. "Maybe you could give me some advice? Tell me which places are best to avoid?"

"I shouldn't count too much on our advice, if I were you. Competition is tough here. Everyone has mouths to feed and mortgages to pay. Rents, children, vacations; wives and mistresses to support.." he paused. "If I can be brutally honest, you don't have a chance in hell. All the big clients are already taken — if not by us, then by other firms. And the small fry are just not worth it. You'll spend months trying to close them and haggling over the bottom line. They count every cent and won't just sign up because you're there."

"I see," I replied, wondering if I should ask him about the difference in market price. "If you don't mind me asking... what's with the high profit margin?"

His Interest bar began to shrink. I had to be more open and persuasive. I didn't lose anything by trying, anyway.

"Oh, come on," I said. "I just need this job real bad, you know. I haven't got a pot to piss in. My wife left me the other day. I don't need advice, just some information."

"Your wife left you? Oh... I've just got divorced myself. Not the best feeling, I have to admit," he heaved a sigh and lit another cigarette. "Just between you and me. We have our own production line, you know. And marginality is virtually non-existent. The bosses prefer to work by volume. We already sell at wholesale prices while all these shops just whack on the price of the packaging on top of their own product price. And thirdly, the kickbacks. All buyers charge them. They buy in bulk at deflated prices and split the difference. Pavel is quite scrupulous about it. He has respect for the market, even though we have to deal with this problem every month. The most we can do is invite a buyer to a good restaurant, or give him a nice birthday present, but that's the extent of it. You personally, what would you choose — a bottle of good brandy for your birthday or a few thousand dollars under the table every month?"

"But this is-"

"I know. That's why we do it like we do. Our price is the lowest on the market simply because it doesn't include kickbacks, black cash conversions and higher profits. Come on, let's go now."

"Thanks," I proffered him my hand.

Mechanically he shook it and walked out. I followed in his wake, mulling over what I'd just heard.

Back at my desk, I opened my phone and Googled the list of all the biggest supermarket chains. Then I spent some quality time studying each of them:

their logos, the brands they carried, the number of stores and their respective locations, stocks and the names of their top management.

Then I opened my own map and highlighted all their offices all over the country. I took a deep sigh, crossed my fingers and entered a new search filter:

Delete all those who are not Ultrapak's clients

A couple of dots disappeared from the map.
Bingo.
The rest was the database I could work with.
I ran a few more queries, narrowing my search by the type of packaging ordered, and excluding all those who bought our products for more than 50% over the wholesale price. A few more dots expired, leaving me with four chains out of the original ten.

I went back to Google and began looking up the companies' owners, shareholders and beneficiaries. I perused their biographies and interviews, and copied all the data into a fat agenda I'd bought the night before.

By lunchtime, I was done. It had taken me a while but now I had plenty of KIDD points to play with.

All my fellow trainees and their coaches had already left for lunch and a bit of a get-together with their mentors and future workmates. No one had bothered to invite me along.

I hurried out of the building and bought myself a quick shawarma in the nearest underground passage. Strangely enough, this prime example of street food so popular in Russia didn't result in any health alert messages. I wolfed my lunch down and returned to my desk.

As I walked into the room, I saw the stooping figure of a girl by the window. Seeing me, she turned away.

"Hi Marina," I said. "Everything's okay?"

"Everything's fine, thank you," she replied without turning.

Was it my imagination or had she been crying?

I checked her status. Her Mood was really low. Still, I decided to give her some space for a while. No good me trying to intrude on her feelings.

I took my place at the desk and sent a request to see the locations of my shortlisted candidates.

Much to my disappointment, all of them were either in a different town or abroad. My crazy initial idea of visiting them in person had failed miserably.

Or had it? As I zoomed in on the map, I saw that I'd been wrong. One of the markers must have overlapped with that of my own town which was why I hadn't noticed it at first. It belonged to a certain Nicholas Valiadis, the owner of one of the supermarket chains.

Valiadis? Wait a sec. Wasn't that the guy whom the old boy with the newspaper had mentioned? At the time, he'd suggested I remember the name. *"One day you might be happy you did."*

I sent another search request to see his current location. Valiadis was in the gym, of all places. Was it my Luck kicking in? Had he been at home or in the office, my crazy idea wouldn't have worked at all.

Very well. Let's go to the gym. It wasn't a humble budget affair like my own but a top fitness club where a year membership cost the price of a new car.

I gave them a call and booked a guest visit.

"I'm out to see a client," I told Marina and rushed out. Ignoring the elevator, I took the steps three at a time, calling Uber as I hurried out.

I had no idea how I was supposed to approach him, let alone talk to him. That was something I'd have to think about on my way there.

As I rode an Uber cab, I kept an eye on his map marker. According to it, he must have been in the swimming pool. Where else can you spend half an hour just moving to and fro? His path through the weight room would have been much more complex.

Which meant I needed some swim shorts.

Finally, we were there. I took a deep breath and walked inside. Immediately I saw a small shop selling all sorts of training gear. I bought myself a pair of swimming trunks which cost the same as a decent business suit — and that was with the club discount!

Several young receptionists smiled to me from their desk. I explained the purpose of my visit, showed them my ID, paid for the guest's three-session subscription and received a silicon guest bracelet, a pair of disposable slippers, a towel, a bathing cap and a bathrobe.

My crazy idea had already cost me much more than I could afford. All the money I'd set aside for the next two weeks was already gone. Never mind. I could always use a new pair of swim trunks. Ditto for the three-session ticket: that was in fact an excellent leveling opportunity. So I'd better relax and enjoy this educational foray into the life of the rich and beautiful.

The locker room was empty. Excellent. I undressed, took a quick shower and walked out into the pool.

The place was nice and clean. Soft upbeat music bubbled in the speakers. The walls were lined with deck chairs. Athletic life guards kept watch poolside. Bar servers froze by the walls, ready to take your order at your slightest sign. A group of pretty girls with legs which went on forever were chatting and laughing in the corner drinking their herbal teas.

Herbal? I wasn't even sure it was tea at all. Whatever.

Valiadis was still busy doing his laps. I couldn't see his bodyguards anywhere. Or could those life guards actually be his bodyguards? I'd hate to have to find that out. The more natural and "accidental" our conversation, the better.

I left the bathrobe, the slippers and the towel next to an available deck chair and entered the water. It wasn't cold but it wasn't very warm, either.

Trying not to splash, I swam slowly in the opposite direction. My swimming skills had always left a lot to be desired. My lung capacity was way below average. So after a couple of laps, I flipped onto my back and relaxed, watching Valiadis out of the corner of my eye.

Finally, I sensed it was now or never. He'd been

here for an hour already. I would only have two opportunities to talk to him: either in the locker room or in the sauna. The latter option was even better. In the locker room, he'd probably be already thinking about work while in the sauna he might relax and lower his guard.

I got out of the water, toweled myself dry, removed the cap and headed for the sauna.

That turned out to be another puzzle. They didn't just have one sauna. They also had a Russian steam bath and a Turkish hammam. Which one should I choose?

I finally decided on the sauna. Its glass door and the absence of steam offered an excellent view of the entire pool and the locker room door. If Valiadis headed there instead, I could catch up with him in no time.

I lasted the first ten minutes just fine, albeit sweating all over. Still, the longer I remained there, the more I wished I could run out and throw my overheated body into the welcoming freshness of the pool.

By the time Valiadis finally climbed out of the pool and headed for the Russian steam bath next door, the Thirst debuff was killing me. I rushed out of the sauna and headed for the cooler, gulping water down by the bucket. Once the debuff icon was gone, I toweled the sweat off and walked into the steam bath.

Valiadis was sitting there with his eyes closed, wearing a felt cap.

He pried his eyes open and nodded, greeting me. I did the same. He was in excellent shape, sinewy and fit with broad shoulders and a six-pack.

I took a seat some distance away from him, respecting his personal space. From where I could finally study his profile and stats.

Nicholas "The Duke" Valiadis
Age: 47
Current status: Tycoon
Social status level: 29
Class: Businessman. Level: 33
Married
Wife: Arina Valiadis. Age: 38
Children: Sergei, son. Age: 16. Paulina, daughter.
Age: 11
Criminal record: yes
Reputation: Indifference 0/30
Interest: 0%

I was quite happy that his Interest to me was at zero. I was afraid that by disturbing his privacy I might have alienated him.

"Mr. Valiadis?" I tried to strike up a conversation.

He tensed ever so slightly. His watchful stare sized me up. He must have decided I was no threat to him. "Have we met before?"

"I don't think so. Still, it would be strange if *I*," — I stressed the last word, "didn't know you."

"Why not?"

"Our company provides packaging materials for supermarket chains. So it's my job to know everyone who's anyone in our line of business."

He nodded, apparently satisfied with the answer. "I don't think you've come here by accident."

"I haven't," I admitted.

"One of the staff must have sold me, I suppose. Oh well. Shame about the pool, I liked it."

He removed the felt cap and used it to wipe the sweat from his forehead. "Are you the company owner?"

"Not at all. I'm not even their commercial director. If the truth were known, I'm just a trainee sales rep."

"Are you really? So what is it you want from me, Mr. Trainee Sales Rep?"

"I want nothing from you, Mr. Valiadis. On the contrary. I'd like to help you lower your packaging costs."

I paused, watching his Interest bar grow out of the red zone and stopping at 11% in the orange sector.

"Keep talking," he said.

"I don't know the conditions your suppliers offer, but I'm absolutely sure we can offer you 50% less."

That caught his interest. It soared, reaching 50%. The sight gave me wings.

"If we take BOPS, for instance, we can supply it to you for 3.24 rubles. I'm pretty sure you're now buying it for four-something. Or five even."

He gestured to me to stop, opened the door and shouted, "Misha!"

After the briefest of delays, his assistant appeared in the sauna. "Sir?"

"I want you to call Hermann and tell him to come

now. It's urgent."

Misha made himself scarce. Valiadis rose. "I suggest we move to the bar. They make good detox cocktails here-" he looked at me askance.

"I'm Phil, sir."

"Nice to meet you, Phil. Come on, then."

Your Reputation with Nicholas "the Duke" Valiadis has improved!
Current Reputation: Indifference 5/30

Soon, a certain Alex Hermann arrived at the club. He blushed, shifting from one foot to the other, as Valiadis showered him with insults, wrestling from him the admission that yes, their suppliers indeed charged them extra for packaging materials.

Valiadis turned to me. "You think you can supply our demand?"

"Absolutely," I replied, praying it was so.

"Very well," he glanced at his watch. "I need to be going. Alex and Phil, please exchange your details. Alex, I'm pretty sure the company CEO would like to see you personally, but I'd like you to speak with them in his presence," he nodded at me.

Our eyes met. "Mr. Valiadis, may I?" I asked, jumping at the opportunity.

He leaned toward me.

"I just wondered," I whispered, "if the name of Mr. Samuel Panikoff rings any bells?"

Valiadis startled ever so slightly. He gulped but didn't reply. As he stepped back, I noticed a barely discernible nod.

Finally, the big boss was gone, leaving me with Alex.

I could see he was pretty pissed off. He didn't like me. Still, you wouldn't be able to tell it by the way he spoke.

"Phil, here's my card. When can I meet your employers?"

I took a cab back to the office. As I rode, a new system message was bestowed on me,

Your Luck has improved!
Current Luck: 7
Experience points received for improving a main characteristic: 1000

Thanks to the message, I now felt I was moving in the right direction. I was bursting with confidence. The workday was nearly over. I absolutely had to see Pavel or the company's CEO before my deadline expired.

I was in luck. Pavel was still there.

"May I speak with you?" I asked.

He shook a dismissive head, preempting my possible excuses. "Please spare me the details. I won't give you one more chance. Nor another day."

"I don't need another day. I've just sold us to J-Mart. A long-term contract on our entire range. They want to meet up with you and the CEO now. They've just fired their previous supplier. They expect us to start deliveries tomorrow morning."

If you beach a shark, it'll be just as helpless as some humble small fry. It'll be squirming on the shore opening its toothy jaws and moving its gills but despite its predatory fame it'll still remain a fish out of water. I watched Pavel open and close his mouth, gulping for air. His Interest bar had soared to a full 100%.

Still, he recovered quickly. "Follow me," he rose, put on his business jacket and strode toward the CEO's office. I walked closely behind, followed by the workers and trainees' stares. Cyril gave me a wink. I winked back at him.

Pavel took me to the CEO's office and gave him a brief run-down of the situation. He finished by saying, "I think you should be the one talking to them. It's your level."

"With whom did you speak?" the fit, sinewy CEO asked me.

"I first spoke to Valiadis, who then introduced me to Hermann. I heard him tell Hermann to make out a contract with you."

"Just look at him!" Pavel enthused. "How on earth did you meet Valiadis?"

I shrugged. "Pure luck, I suppose."

Pavel tensed. "Are you sure? You're not making this up, are you?"

I gave him Hermann's business card.

New system messages promptly informed me of my improved Reputation with both. It was still Indifference but quite close to Amicability.

"Point taken," the CEO chuckled. "Well done. Should I give him a call, then?"

He picked up his phone, then gave me a long look.

"I could call them myself," I said, "but I think Hermann wanted to discuss all the details with you."

Squinting shortsightedly, the man (*name: Mr. Peter Ivanov, age: 48, current status: Chief Executive Officer at Ultrapak Ltd*) began dialing Hermann's number.

Then we went to meet Hermann and two more execs at the J-Mart HQ. There were three of us: Pavel, Mr. Ivanov and myself. An hour into the talks, the parties shook hands on the deal.

I very much doubted they normally closed new contracts with such speed. Or the fact that Hermann's presence would normally be required. He must have been there on personal orders from Valiadis.

I could almost see him ask Hermann at their meeting the next morning, "How was that thing with the packaging deal?" And Hermann would reply, "It's all done, sir. We've signed the contract and received the first delivery already. That'll give us a saving of hundreds of millions a year. Our security team is currently investigating the old buyers. Two-timing rats!"

Everybody was happy. With the exception of the bribe-taking buyers and their associates, of course.

Two teams of company lawyers worked on the contract until late at night. None of the workers and trainees dared leave before the top brass. I was starving. I wanted to pop out to grab something quick to eat but Pavel didn't let me. He wanted me to stay in the office. He probably wanted me to watch every stage of the contract making, learning from the pros.

It was already past 10 p.m. when Mr. Ivanov walked out of his office, holding two bottles of good single malt whisky.

Pavel joined him. "May I have your attention, please? Phil, will you come over here?"

Can't say I was pleased. I hate being the center of attention.

"Tonight we celebrate!" Pavel announced. "Let's have a quick drink and then we'll go to a restaurant for a nice meal. It's on the company. Mr. Ivanov, your turn to speak."

"Dear colleagues... and friends," the CEO paused and cleared his throat. "Our company has just arrived at a new level by getting an exclusive contract with J-Mart. I don't need to tell you what it means to us all. And what's even funnier, the person who closed it is our new trainee! It's his first day at work! Ladies and gentlemen, I give you Phil!"

I'd have loved to say that his last words were drowned out by a standing ovation. They weren't. A few unenthusiastic claps was all I received — and even that was probably because I'd earned them all a free dinner.

"Pavel, where are those bottles?" Mr. Ivanov concluded. Everybody sprang into action, lining up with plastic cups in their hands.

What worried me was that I hadn't yet received a "Quest completed!" message. According to the game, the One-Day Chance quest was still active. I asked Pavel if my trial period was over.

He faltered, then replied cheerfully, "Well, what do you think? Tomorrow we'll put you on the payroll."

Why tomorrow, I wondered. All the HR people were here, congratulating Mr. Ivanov and toasting their success.

Pavel left me. I stood whisky in hand, not knowing what to do with myself.

Finally, I saw Marina sulking in the far corner. I walked over to her.

"Hi," I said. "Why aren't you celebrating?"

"Ah, it's you," she mouthed. "Congratulations. Well done. Wish I could say the same."

"Why, whassup?"

She sighed, ignoring my question. Both her Mood and her Interest in the conversation were nearing zero.

I left her alone. I could see she would have loved to have gone home but felt obliged to stick with the crowd and keep the corporate spirit.

Greg left his group of sales reps and walked over to me.

"So how was your day?" I asked him.

"Congratulations," he said dryly, overcoming his jealousy. We clinked our plastic cups. I thanked him and he returned to his group.

His group? He hadn't even quit his old job yet! Selling those windows or whatever it was. And he was already friends with everybody else!

I caught their sideways glances and overheard a few whispers.

My boss' praise had done its job, alienating

everybody against me. I received a chain of warning messages, informing me of loss of Reputation with virtually all of my new workmates.

How were you supposed to work in a team whose every member envied and despised you?

And what bonuses could I expect from today's sale if I wasn't even officially hired?

"Hello!" Pavel called, attracting everybody's attention. "We're all going to the Tsar's Grill now. Dinner's on the firm!"

Everybody got their stuff and began leaving the office in small groups. I walked down the stairs with them and waited outside as they got into their cars and left.

Five minutes later, I was standing on the street alone.

CHAPTER FIFTEEN

ONLY HUMAN

"Late last night and the night before,
Tommyknockers, Tommyknockers
knocking at my door.
I want to go out, don't know if I can
'cuz I'm so afraid
of the Tommyknocker man."

Stephen King, *The Tommyknockers*

IN A GAME, A CHARACTER'S MAIN AND SECONDARY characteristics have a very discriminatory relationship. Intellect can affect one's magic and mana numbers; Strength can add to one's damage and load capacity while Agility improves your attack speed and dodging chances. But in a game, there's no way Strength can

249

affect Intellect, neither can Stamina improve Agility. You just can't do it.

Life is different. You don't need an interface to know that. In real life, a person's body and their personality have a much more intimate bond than a player's avatar and the actual person controlling it.

In life, good Perception Skills depend on one's health. Smoking prevents you from enjoying the entire plethora of tastes and smells that surround you. Good eyesight allows you to notice things unavailable to a bespectacled geek. You can't have good health if your stamina is low but here, stamina isn't just a number on the life bar. It's your heart and your blood vessels, strong and sufficiently leveled up. A healthy mind in a healthy body, indeed! Apart from several honorable exceptions, most inventions and works of art in human history have been created by healthy people between thirty and forty — that is to say, at the peak of their brain activity.

And now I could see it all in my own interface. A 100% full Self-Control bar allowed one to remain cool under pressure. Ditto for the Confidence bar: at 100%, you just didn't question your own actions and decisions.

Now, however, my Self-Control was deep in the yellow. What had just happened to me was so unfair.

Low Self-Control numbers logically resulted in low Confidence. So should I even go to that restaurant? What was the point? Could they have left me behind on purpose? Maybe they'd already lost all interest in me?

Funny, really: I had a piece of state-of-the-art

software uploaded to my head, with all the knowledge of and insight into people's actions and their attitude towards me. And still there I was, standing alone in the rain like some starved loser from an old movie while my workmates were stuffing their faces in the warmth of an expensive restaurant, celebrating *my* sale.

They weren't even my workmates, come to think about it. All the other trainees had already signed their work contracts, albeit for a trial period. Everyone but me.

I didn't *have* to join them, of course. I could always wallow in self-pity, feeling sorry for myself. Look at me: I'd done the impossible! Where was my well-deserved work contract and a seat in the CEO's limousine?

Oh no. Whining wouldn't get me anywhere. I should stop suspecting them of trying to rip me off. Pointless seeing enemies in my future co-workers. *'Life isn't fair,'* yeah right. Enough. As Martha would have said, this wasn't a productive tactic.

A productive tactic would be to switch my overworked imagination off and go to the restaurant. So they'd left me behind, big deal. They weren't obliged to chaperone me around. They'd been all pretty drunk already, anyway. I was invited. I knew the address. What was my problem, then? Joining them or not was entirely my choice.

I suppressed my uneasiness, feeling pretty foul as I did so. My wounded pride wouldn't get me anywhere.

I left the safety of the doorway and offered my

face to the rain. With my arms spread wide, I enjoyed the moment. I didn't give a damn about my workmates' jealousy. I couldn't care less about my bosses' lack of consideration. Right, so I hadn't made any friends today. But at least I'd done what I'd said I would. I'd made it. Never mind I hadn't closed the quest. And even if I lost today's bonus, what did that matter? If I'd done it today, I could do it again.

I smiled to the rain which at the moment epitomized the entire world to me — good and bad, kind and evil, ugly and beautiful. Suddenly I realized it wasn't me against the world. The world wasn't against me, either.

My confidence soared. My self-control hit the 100% mark.

I was alive. I was in good health. I was happy. Everything would work out just fine.

It wasn't as if I'd always made the right choices in the past. Often I'd selected my own selfish desires over what was really important. Like when Yanna had needed help cleaning the house and I'd had a raid to do. Or when my parents had invited us over for a meal and I was like, "sorry, some other time," because I'd had a raid to do. Or when I hadn't delivered a file to a client, "oh sorry, I'm in sick, you'll get it Monday!" because — no, I hadn't had a raid to do, I was just too lazy to do it. You didn't need an analyst to see where this strategy had taken me.

Unhesitantly I hailed a cab and went back home. I knew I was making the right decision. Because whenever you're faced with a tough choice, you should always choose family above everything else.

And I had Richie waiting for me back home, desperate for his walk.

In fact, it was a rational decision. I had loads of time. My workmates had to get to the restaurant first. Then they'd have to wait for their tables, pore over their menus and place their orders talking over each other... And then another long wait until they finally got their food. I had an hour at least — and seeing as my house wasn't very far and the streets were virtually empty by now, I could get back home, walk the dog, change into dry clothes and drive back to the restaurant.

I could hear Richie whine already in the elevator. The moment I unlocked the door, opening it a crack, he darted out like a black bolt of lightning, poked the flat of my hand with his moist nose and hurried toward the elevator.

"Hi there, Richie," I said, pressing the elevator button. "Time for walkies!"

Richie scratched the elevator door with an impatient paw. As we rode down, he very nearly climbed the walls in desperation but held it. Which is more than I can say about some of the human beings living in our apartment block.

It didn't take him long to do his business. Half an hour later, I was already sitting in a cab heading for the restaurant.

"Just look at this weather," the level-5 cab driver started the conversation. "The best thing to do in this weather is stay at home having a TV dinner. A nice hot bowl of borsch and cream, a slice of rye garlic bread and a healthy shot of vodka..."

My stomach rumbled its protest. The heating inside the cab was insufferable. I yawned but felt obliged to keep the conversation going. "Good idea. I haven't had anything to eat yet, either. Been running around like a headless chicken all day."

"That's something you should never do, son," the driver said. "You should never skip meals. Didn't they teach you that in the army?" he paused, then glanced at me in the mirror. "You did serve in the army, didn't you?"

I could see by his stats that he was getting angry with me.

"Or did you dodge the draft?" his voice tensed. "That's what you all do these days! It's okay shirking around — but when your country needs you, you're gone with the wind!" he gave me a long look in the mirror, waiting for me to answer his question.

What could I say? I had indeed dodged the draft. Still, neither his accusations nor his patronizing tone sat well with me.

I closed my eyes, unwilling to speak.

A phone call saved me from having to answer his question. The driver put the radio down — either to be tactful or just not to miss what I was about to say.

"Phil? Is that you?"

It was Pavel's voice.

"Yes, sir," I replied.

"Where are you?"

"I'm coming. I'll be there soon."

"Aha. Well, it's probably better that way. Mr.

Ivanov asked me to tell you that we won't be needing you, after all. You don't have to come. Best of luck elsewhere."

Best of luck? Were they out of their minds?

"No, wait a sec, man," I said, suppressing my fury.

"What now, *man?*" he mimicked my tone, then laughed. "Sorry, I don't have much time," he added, suddenly deadly serious. "They're serving the main course already."

"Just tell me what this is all about! Why? Okay, I thought your offer of a bonus was too good to be true but this? In less than six hours, I gave you your dream deal! Do you still think I can't do it?"

He didn't reply. I could hear him rise from the table and walk to a quieter corner, away from the cheerful clamor around the table.

"That's the problem. I still don't know," he finally replied. "Today you've been lucky. You met Valiadis purely by accident, you said so yourself. The rest was entirely due to Ivanov and myself. We closed the deal and signed the contract. What was your part in that? You just sat there doing nothing."

"You'd have closed jack had I not spoken to him first!"

"We don't even know if you spoke to him. You might have just found Hermann's card lying around. Sorry, I really don't have the time."

He hung up. I just sat there staring at the screen.

The phone rang again.

Mother.

I cleared my throat, trying to sound calm. "Hi, Mom."

"Where are you?" she demanded, her voice anxious and tense.

"I'm out on busi-."

"Kira's dead!" she interrupted. "Phil, my boy! Kira's been killed!" she sobbed.

"Mom?"

The news came down on me like a ton of bricks. My heart exploded in my chest. I became numb. The phone reverberated with Mom's sobbing.

"Phil, we're at the Municipal Hospital Three," Dad's toneless voice finally said. "Come now."

He forgot to hang up. I could hear him trying to calm Mom down. I listened to his clumsy attempts to comfort her as she went on sobbing. I felt like screaming.

"Sorry, chief, change of plans," I said to the driver. "We need to go to the hospital. My sister's just died."

"My condolences," he said.

He drove me there, taking shortcuts via some back lanes and dark alleys.

I closed my eyes, trying to take my loss in. I needed some time alone with it.

Then I realized I'd forgotten to give him the address.

Before I could do anything, a syringe needle pricked my neck.

I passed out.

WHEN I CAME ROUND I COULDN'T MOVE. MY HALF-SHUT eyelids let in a piercing light irradiating from an impossibly high ceiling. The top edge of my field of vision was lined with debuff icons. Intoxication, Paralysis, Dehydration, Starvation, Feebleness, Mind Suppression...

"The subject has regained consciousness," a dull emotionless voice said.

I tried to focus but I was numb. I tried to ask where I was but my tongue didn't obey me.

"Ilindi, remove the DoT."

I'd definitely heard this voice before but couldn't quite place it.

A silvery veil of mist enveloped me. Its weightless touch penetrated my every skin cell, then was promptly ejected back out, tinted with red and black.

My entire body itched like hell. I vomited violently. It was a good job I could move again: I leaned over the raised edge of my bed and puked all over the floor, disgorging some sort of slimy substance.

"Give him some water," the same voice said.

A flask appeared in my view, its cap unscrewed.

"Drink it."

I gulped the water down without even bothering to rinse my mouth first. It felt like such a shame wasting even a drop.

"Feeling better?"

"Can I have... some more..."

"Make him another one, Ilindi."

Someone handed me another flask. I downed it and felt slightly better.

I tried to focus again. My vision was still blurred. I could see some vague silhouettes which appeared human... but no, one of them wasn't. It was at least ten foot tall. I tried to ID it but couldn't.

"Don't bother. Your Perception is debuffed. And your Insight is too low to work with senior races."

"I'd like to sit up," I said.

"Please do."

Overcoming the pain in every muscle, I gingerly sat up. Now I could see Valiadis. A girl in a turquoise evening dress next to him must have been Ilindi. Her platinum blonde hair cascaded down her shoulders.

Valiadis stood half a head below her. His shimmering black armor reminded me of a high-level rogue set used in WoW. Black smoke billowed from under its pauldrons.

The room was large and well-lit. I couldn't locate the sources of the light: bright but not blindingly so, it seemed to be seeping from everywhere without creating shadows.

The unhuman being peered me in the eyes, processing my mind. I could feel him rummaging through my head as he sorted through my memories.

I looked aside, breaking eye contact. His intrusion into my mind stopped straight away.

"Mr. Valiadis?"

"Yes, Phil. I apologize for this intrusion. Sorry about the debuffs. This is an abduction requirement set by senior races for all new candidates."

"Senior races? Abduction requirement? How long have I been here? What's this place?"

"You will receive answers to your questions soon."

Then I remembered. "My sister's just been killed!" I leapt off the bed. "I need to go and see her!"

"We know. We're very sorry about your loss. Ilindi, cast Tranquility on him."

Another mist enveloped me. This time it was emerald green.

After a moment, I felt great. All my worries, even my panicky desperation — they were now gone.

Valiadis gave me a close look, making sure I wasn't trying to escape anymore. "I'd like you to meet Khphor. He acts as the official representative of the Vaalphor civilization. Or at least that's how it sounds to the human ear. The Vaalphors are one of the three most influential races in our Galaxy.

I shifted my gaze to the giant. My debuffed Perception didn't allow me to see him in every detail. Still, what I could glean was more than enough.

I was staring at a massive humanoid body clad in a seamless pressurized suit of armor streaming with the shimmering charges of a force field (or whatever it was). He had two arms, two legs and a helmeted head. He also had a pair of hooves and a tail. A demon if I'd ever seen one.

"Greetings, human," Khphor's voice echoed through my head.

"How do you do, sir. Sorry, I can't say it's nice to meet you though."

Ilindi emitted a stifled giggle.

Valiadis smiled. "It's okay. You don't need to pay

any attention to him. Khphor is here purely as an observer. Our conversation is a necessary vetting stage for you."

"Are you here vetting me? Why, what for?"

"Allow me to start from the beginning. The three eldest races of our Galaxy form the *Droh Ragg*, or the Council of Elders which adheres to the Principles of Common Good of the Commonwealth of Sentient Races. The Council of Elders never interferes with the development of the younger races but keeps an eye on them from the moment the new race leaves its first informational imprint. As soon as the new race is advanced enough to independently discover and enter the universal information field, the Council makes an official contact with it."

"Does it really?" I asked. "Because I don't remember anything on the news about it."

"It hasn't yet but it will. The human race will discover and enter the universal information field at the end of this century."

"Why?"

"Why what? Why would it do that?"

"No. Why me? What's that got to do with me if it hasn't even happened yet?"

"Ilindi, will you please renew his Tranquility? And make me some water. That's a good girl."

He took a few swigs from the flask which the girl had conjured out of thin air, then continued. "Phil, I'm going to answer your question in a moment. Please bear with me. When the human race discovered — sorry, discovers — the universal info field, that will allow them to instantly receive any kind of information, giving them access to absolute knowledge. It will allow us to colonize the Solar System and start the terraforming of planets and bigger asteroids, adapting them for human habitation. We'll be able to teleport between planets. Humanity will enter the heyday of its history. But by entering the universal info field, we will also expose ourselves to other civilizations. The fact that we're not alone in the Universe will deeply traumatize humanity because our civilization will prove to be the youngest and least developed of them all. In case of an invasion, we'd be helpless against some of the most incredible alien technologies. Only there'll be no invasion. We'll receive a greetings message from the Commonwealth of Sentient Races, complete with their invitation to submit ourselves to their standard diagnostics procedure which is to define humanity's place in our Galaxy's hierarchy of sentient beings."

"Not just its place," Khphor's voice echoed through my mind, "but also its readiness. Such diagnostics will show if humanity's ready to integrate into the Commonwealth."

"These diagnostics are actually a series of tests," Valiadis continued. "And if we fail them..."

"Then we'll annul your race," the voice in my head said. The visuals which accompanied his words showed a much more gruesome picture, though.

"...then we'll cease to exist," Valiadis finished.

I stared at the visuals unfolding in my mind. Deserted, crumbling cities long reclaimed by wildlife; the beginning of a new evolution; the change of landscape as natural disasters shifted continents and created new seas, new mountains and new animal species; and finally, a new sentient race entering the stage.

Telepathy was definitely the most efficient means of communication. The five words uttered by Khphor had unfolded into an instant movie in my head, revealing millions of years of the planet's humanless future.

"Keep going," I didn't recognize my own hoarse voice.

"We need to select thirty thousand of humanity's most worthy representatives. They will participate in the tests."

"Twenty-eight thousand five hundred and sixty-one persons," Khphor corrected him.

"We'll have to select them from the numbers of the candidates who pass the initial screening stage."

"So have I passed?" I asked, unsurprised. This was so surreal that I only spoke mechanically, keeping my end of the conversation going. "Why did you choose me, anyway?"

"You haven't passed the screening yet, no. Like all the other candidates, you've been selected by the Council."

I turned to the Vaalphor giant. "By you, then?"

"The best representatives of any race, or passionaries, are not qualified," he replied. "We've already had the sad experience of entering some of the contender race's choicest thinkers and activists into our diagnostics. As a result, the race's potential was sadly overestimated. And as further developments showed later, it had been a fatally wrong approach. The bulk of any race is not capable of ever reaching high levels of its top specimens."

"Which is why this time the Council has picked the most average and unexceptional candidates among those who've never been able to achieve anything," Valiadis concluded. "Starting with our time period. They didn't want to venture earlier in time — simply because before the advent of the Internet, the human mind wasn't yet ready to adopt the augmented reality interface. There was a high risk of its failure and consequent mental problems."

"But how did they do that? Did they arrive from the future?"

Once again, Khphor's voice echoed through my mind, "Time manipulation is one of the Council's most important achievements."

Unable to hear him, Valiadis replied in his turn, "This is still beyond our understanding, I'm afraid. I'm only a candidate like yourself, the only difference being I've already made the final selection."

"So you too," I whispered.

That made sense. No wonder his sudden rise in the 1990s had appeared to have come from nowhere. An average engineer who'd lost his job, got a divorce, then disappeared off the public radar, he'd reemerged several years later as a new financial mover and shaker.

"In fact, it took me a year," he corrected me as if reading my thoughts.

"So what do you want me to do? And what's gonna happen if I don't get selected?"

"Not much, I'm afraid. You'll be back to your drab old life, stripped of the benefits of your interface. Naturally, your memory of it will be wiped out."

"Well, I suppose it's better that being *annuled*. So what do I need to do in order to be selected?"

"You should-"

"Enough!" Khphor's voice rustled through my mind.

Valiadis and I looked at the alien in surprise.

"I have enough data now," he said, then turned to me. "You can go now, human."

I looked around me. The room had no exits. "Where do you want me to go?"

"But he still has tons of-" Valiadis began, then promptly shut up — apparently, on mental orders from Khphor.

Ilindi motioned me toward the far wall behind my back. "Don't be shy, human."

Cautiously I rose from the bed and stepped toward the girl. I wanted to take a better look at her. I took a couple more steps, then bumped into an invisible barrier.

Had she just called me *human*? Did that mean she was also one of *them*? I squinted, searching for something inhuman in her appearance.

Then I gasped. Her large rainbow-colored gaze was tinted with contempt. Her gorgeous head of glossy hair concealed two pointy ears.

"Phil, you'd better go now," Valiadis said.

"Ilindi's known for her temper."

I obeyed. The Tranquility she'd cast on me had already worn off. I couldn't wait to get out of that place and go see my parents. The bitter memory of Kira's death filled me with renewed grief.

I walked over to the wall which resembled the scaly hide of an albino crocodile. It gaped open before me, revealing a narrow bending passage.

As soon as I stepped into it, the opening closed, pushing me forward. I had no other choice than to keep going along the meandering tunnel.

After a brief while, I sensed a movement ahead. A large blob of gelatinous goo seemed to be creeping quickly toward me.

I hurried to ID it.

Acid Jelly
Level: 7

What, just its level? No social status, nothing?

The jelly filled the tunnel from wall to wall, reaching to my waist. There was no way I could walk around it. I couldn't leap over it, either. I might have, had I bothered to level Agility.

It was predatory.

I took a few steps back, looking for something — anything — I could use as a weapon. I ripped the shirt off my back, wrapped it around my hand and waited for the goo to approach.

It didn't take long. The jelly sort of tensed, then leapt toward me. Don't ask me how it did it.

Instinctively I closed my eyes, then punched it with my shirt-protected hand as hard as I could.

You've dealt 1 pt. damage to Acid Jelly (a punch)!

The creature's health bar hadn't even budged. Mine, however, plummeted as the jelly enveloped me, its heavy bulk pinning me to the floor. All I could feel was the unbearable agony of acid devouring me alive.

I screamed, choking on the gelatinous acid pouring down my throat.

I struggled for breath. The scalding pain in my chest soared way past my pain threshold.

My hands gnawed the floor as I struggled to get out, all the while realizing the futility of it all. My mind was going around in circles, thinking of the strange connection between my interface, the old Panikoff and today's convenient arrival of Valiadis.

I fainted...

... but I wasn't dead yet.

I could hear muffled voices reaching me though my slumber,

"Khphor, please! Why would he try to escape? And why the jelly, of all things? He had no idea of the elemental-"

"...premature contact with another candidate."

"Didn't he mention his grandfather?"

"Acid, yes."

"He what? With his *bare hands*? Can't you screen your candidates or something?"

"...just a surprise effect."

"... indicates the object's low levels of-"

The Augmented Reality interface has been uninstalled!

"HERE WE ARE!" Someone gave me a shove on the shoulder.

I opened my eyes.

"Here we are, son! Wake up!"

I was back in the cab. The mustachioed driver was holding on to my shirt collar, trying to shake me awake.

"Where are we?" I muttered, completely disoriented. "What's this place?"

"Where do you think?" the driver barked. "You wanted the Tsar's Grill, and that's where I've brought you! There it is, look!"

"The Tsar's Grill?" I stared in the window, confused. "How much do I owe you?"

"Six hundred[9]."

I paid, then scrambled out of the car, struggling with my numb body. The cab pulled away sharply and left.

The rain had stopped. I looked down, realizing I was standing in a puddle of water. I walked over to a drier place.

My pants' pocket vibrated. I pulled out the phone and stared at the strange number.

"Yes?" I said.

---

[9] Six hundred rubles is about $10 at the time of writing

"Where did you get lost to, time traveler?" Pavel's cheerful voice demanded. "We've been looking for you everywhere! The boss wants to see you! It's a good job Daria had your number marked down!"

"Is that you, sir? Sorry, but didn't you say I didn't need to come?"

"I said that? When? Why?"

He must have covered the receiver with his hand as I could hear his faint, muffled voice ask someone, "Are you all freakin' nuts? Which one of you told Panfilov not to come?"

Then his voice was back, loud and clear. "Never mind. Where are you now? You think you could get over?"

I looked at the restaurant's flickering neon sign and the open terrace packed with loud, happy people. There was something I had to think about... but I couldn't for the life of me remember what it was.

I paused. "I'm not far away. I won't be long."

"Please don't," Pavel said. "We'll be waiting."

The phone went dead.

With bated breath I dialed Kira's number. The phone kept ringing. I erupted in cold sweat and promptly received a system message warning me about my heart rate exceeding safe parameters.

Just as I accepted the fact she was dead, the phone clicked.

"Phil?" Kira's voice demanded. "Do you know what time it is? Are you okay?"

"I'm fine, thanks," I released a long sigh of relief. "Just missing you. How are you?"

"I'm fine *now*. Can you imagine, I was very nearly hit by a truck!"

"No! How did that happen?"

"I just left the car in the parking lot and was walking home. It was raining so I put my hood up and lowered my head. I didn't look around," she paused, apparently reliving the moment. I could hear her sob. "Then the phone went off in my pocket, so I stopped to answer it. And just as I did so, a godawful truck sped right past me!"

"Jesus. I had a feeling that might happen. Who was it who called you?"

"I've no idea," she replied. "The number didn't show. And they'd already hung up..."

Chapter Sixteen

A GLASS HALF FULL

"Right now, this is a job. If I advance any higher, this would be my career. And if this were my career, I'd have to throw myself in front of a train."

Jim Halpert, *The Office*

ALL THINGS CONSIDERED, IT HAD TAKEN ME MORE THAN an hour to rejoin them.

I lingered by the restaurant entrance, trying to unravel my stupid dream. I must have fallen asleep in the cab. I couldn't remember the whole thing, only the basics. My subconscious mind must have used my biggest fears, combining them into a perfect custom-made nightmare. It had shown me the things I dreaded the most — the loss of a loved one (because Kira was my closest family, probably closer than my parents even) and the call to save humanity (a real horror for an irresponsible loafer like myself). In my dream, they'd even stripped me of my interface which was my only fighting chance. And the wretched acid jelly? With my blennophobia[10], that was the most terrible mob I could think of!

What a weird dream. Really. Too many coincidences. The death of Kira who indeed had barely escaped with her life — saved by the bell, or should I say by the phone call? And this weird connection between Panikoff and Valiadis...

I had to make sure it had indeed been only a dream. I needed to know if I still had the interface. So I summoned Martha.

"Hi, Phil!"

She hadn't changed one bit. Same giggly smile, same skimpy dress, same bubble gum.

"Hi babe," I'd have loved to talk to her but I didn't have the time. "See you later!"

I walked into the restaurant nearly two hours after I'd left the Ultrapak office.

"Hi," the beaming hostess greeted me. "Do you have a reservation?"

"Actually, yes. You've got a group celebrating here tonight."

She raised a quizzical eyebrow.

I hurried to add, "Ultrapak office party?"

She nodded. "Please follow me."

She led me across the dimmed restaurant past the bar and all the tables. Soft music played; a songstress was crooning something on a small stage.

---

[10] Blennophobia: the fear of slime and mucus

We walked up a steep staircase — a challenge for a tipsy patron! — and arrived at their private room. I could see that the official part was already over. Mr. Ivanov, Pavel and a few of their deputies lounged in easy chairs around a low table apart from the rest, smoking cigars and sipping their cognacs.

The reps were crowded on a small balcony outside, laughing at Greg's tall stories. Someone guffawed, then immediately choked on their own laughter, exploding in a bout of coughing. That just had to be Cyril.

I never liked office parties. Ditto for seminars, training classes and other team building activities. An office party is an introvert's worst nightmare. Not a friendly after-work get-together with a few office buddies happily getting drunk but an organized outing scheduled and controlled by top management. Normally, its only purpose is to shape the workforce into an obedient, unthinking crowd, introducing them to the lemming mentality and corporate rat race. The said workforce would happily overdo on the free drinks, then the next morning it was back to the grindstone.

Each such "happening" tends to expose the worst in your fellow beings. It highlights things that are normally glossed over by the formalities of work etiquette, such as hypocrisy, vanity, backstabbing and shameless lewdness. Management praises company values, watching their workforce benignly from the height of their position, encouraging them to drink and be merry. It's not every day middle-class workers can afford to come to a place like this! The workers applaud their bosses' speeches until their hands are raw, then down their drinks and exchange whispered sarcasms about the speakers. At the height of the evening, company drivers are drinking with the IT experts, the advertising department is busy wooing the accountants while the boss' secretary — who feels as if she owns the party — accepts a drink from the chief analyst who'd already assessed her potential and is about to proceed to a more palpable analysis of her personal assets.

"Phil!" Pavel shouted over the music. He waved to me, inviting me over to their table.

Dammit. I couldn't expect a friendly work environment, not after the top brass had openly exposed me as their favorite.

I couldn't help it, anyway. I headed over to them.

"Look who's coming!" Mr. Ivanov roared. His face was crimson. He'd already removed both his jacket and tie and rolled up his shirt sleeves. "Phil, you bastard, come here to me! Come, I'll give you a big hug!"

His Mood bar was maxed out. Alcohol seemed to work as an emotion enhancer. I hadn't had the chance to check this theory yet, but it looked like I just might have to now.

I shook his hand, grudgingly allowing him to throw his arms around me. He gave me a bear hug and slapped my back. "Come sit with us!"

He motioned to one of his deputies who hurried to pull another easy chair up to the table.

"A cigar?" Pavel asked.

"No, thanks. I've just quit," I replied with just a

tad of guilt in my smile.

"Then you should drink with us," Mr. Ivanov announced.

The same deputy had already arranged for an extra glass to be fetched and filled it with some prohibitively expensive brew.

I glanced at its stats. *An 18-year-old whisky, market value: $313.65, chemical composition: 63.9% water, 36% ethanol, traces of various microelements.*

The reverence for expensive brands which had already taken a considerable knock during my last shopping session had now sunk to a new low.

As for the rest, I could see their sincere albeit mercenary interest in me. And although I knew very well I was nothing but a golden goose to them, still their attentions admittedly flattered me.

I needed to get a grip. I shouldn't let them fool me into submission. For me, Ultrapak was only a starting point. It would allow me to forget my financial worries and concentrate on personal growth.

Mr. Ivanov rose and delivered a lengthy speech, slightly staggering and constantly shifting his weight from his toes to his heels. Eventually everybody at our table rose, looking at him. My co-workers at the big table too stopped laughing and listened.

He kept speaking, nostalgically remembering the company's early days eight years ago. He told us how hard it had been to set up their own production line. Told us about the arrival of "our Pavel boy here who was just a snotnose then". His cigar dropped heavy clumps of ash as he poked it in the direction of the said

Pavel and his deputies, describing their own respective arrivals at the company.

My hand got tired holding the drink, so in the end I lowered it. This was going to take a while.

"So finally, today our company has entered a new era by closing a deal with J-Mart," he concluded. "All thanks to him!"

He nodded at me — thankfully without poking his cigar — and concluded, "Cheers everyone!"

Everyone screamed their approval of the toast and clinked their tumblers (or *"flat-bottomed beverage containers"*, as the system helpfully informed me).

I too touched my lips to my drink. It wasn't that I was a complete teetotaler but I knew better than to get drunk with people I barely knew, let alone in my bosses' presence.

I caught Mr. Ivanov's watchful stare. He shook a disapproving head at my unfinished drink, "What's wrong with you? Come on, bottoms up!"

"But I-"

"Drink, I tell you!"

The faces around me grew serious. I gave up, picked up the wretched whisky glass and downed it in one slug.

Mr. Ivanov's face softened. I received a minor two-hour debuff to Agility, Perception and Self-Control. By the same token, my Mood and Confidence had risen slightly.

"Aha! That's a good lad!" Mr. Ivanov commented, apparently pleased. "Move your chair over here so we can speak. I can't hear anything with this music."

I sat closer to him while Pavel and the others began discussing the Russian soccer team's chances at the approaching World Cup.

"They can't leave it alone, can they?" Mr. Ivanov commented, then changed the subject. "Where have you been?"

"I had to go home to let the dog out," I replied in all honesty. Sincerity had served me well until now. "He'd been on his own all day."

"Very good!" he replied. "The dog is man's best friend, as they say. One should never leave one's friends in trouble. So you live alone, then?"

"Technically, I'm still married, sir."

"What do you mean, 'technically'? Where's your wife, then?"

I wasn't too happy with his unceremonious interest but I saw no point in trying to avoid the subject. "We're getting a divorce. She's moved back in with her parents. It just wasn't meant to happen, I suppose."

"I'm so sorry," he shook his head. "But I'll tell you what: you two should try and make it work. Promise you'll do it! Promise me now!"

"I promise," I agreed with a smile. "There's nothing else we can do, is there?"

"That's my boy! Excellent! Give me five!" he slapped my hand. "Now tell me a bit more about yourself. What are your goals in life? What is it you'd like to do?"

"There's not much to tell, sir. I'm no spring chicken anymore. It took me all this time to realize I'd been just drifting along. So I decided to get my act together, finally. I started looking for a job — which I've almost found, I hope, — I've been jogging every morning, I started reading good books..."

"What kind of books?" Pavel interfered. He must have been listening to our conversation all along.

"Just sales-related. I've almost finished *No B.S. Sales Success.*"

"Dan Kennedy?"

"That's right."

"Did you read *Agile Selling*? Great book!"

Mr. Ivanov shook his head. "What if you discuss your to-read list some other time?"

"We're all done here!" Pavel leaned back in his chair and took a deep draw on his cigar.

"You said you'd almost found a job," Mr. Ivanov chuckled. "Well, let me tell you you've found one. Tomorrow morning get back to HR and tell them you've been hired. Your trial period is annulled. Pavel, did you hear me?"

Pavel nodded.

"You've already shown us your worth," the CEO concluded. "Now go and have fun with the boys," he motioned me toward the big table. "We have things to discuss."

He gestured to his deputy to fill up their glasses.

I was just about to ask him about my bonus when a new system message flooded my body with a wave of pleasure.

Quest alert: One-Day Chance. Quest

completed!

You've successfully closed a sales deal for packaging products produced by Ultrapak, Ltd.

XP received: 1500

Additional XP received: 500 (for thinking out of the box)

+20% to Satisfaction

Very soon I'd make a new level!

A pleasant shiver ran over my body. It took me great effort not to betray myself to anyone. My Satisfaction was close to 100%. In order to achieve Happiness again, all I had to do was have a meal and a good night's sleep.

The next message came as another pleasant bonus,

Your Reputation with Pavel Gorelov has improved!

Current Reputation: Amicability 5/60

I pulled myself together and turned to Mr. Ivanov, "Excuse me, sir..."

"What is it?" he seemed unhappy I was still sitting with them.

"One last question. The bonus for today's deal, are you going-"

"The bonus? Pavel, did you hear that? The bonus!" Mr. Ivanov laughed. "Isn't that typical! That's the young generation for you! They don't give a damn about ideals! All they care about is money!"

Pavel nodded and smiled without actually laughing.

My pulse was racing. I felt I would lose it any minute. I was dangerously close to getting up and telling them all to stuff their business where the sun didn't shine. The bonus of a fraction of their multi-million deal would have covered my daily needs and then some. I could manage quite happily on it without the need to close any more sales.

I awaited their answer with a smile frozen on my face. If he thought this was funny, so did I.

Having finished laughing, Mr. Ivanov finally said, "This, I'm afraid, is up to your immediate superiors. Pavel? What do you think?"

"Well, formally, it's out of the question. We're already being accommodating as it is, accepting you without the obligatory trial period. But! As a one-off incentive compensation, why not? Tomorrow Hermann is wiring us the down payment. We could, I suppose, use that money to pay him a bonus of, say," he paused, making mental calculations, "twenty grand[11]?"

Twenty thousand *rubles*? Were they taking the piss? I'd spent ten thousand just on buying the swimming trunks and that stupid three-visit gym membership!

And that's when my Reputation with them had already improved. Had it indeed been even slightly lower, they would have ripped me off, that's for sure.

"You're not happy, are you?" Pavel seemed to be

---

[11] 20,000 rubles is about $350 at the time of writing

enjoying it. "Very well, let's make it twenty-five. Enough said!"

"You can go now," Mr. Ivanov ordered.

You can go now, human, echoed in my mind

I was about to explode. I stood up, about to tell them to get lost, but reconsidered. I wanted these bloodsuckers to pay me my money first. Until then, I had to keep up appearances and play by their rules.

"Thanks," I said and headed across the entire length of the room for the exit.

I had no intention of staying. Pointless striking up friendships with people if you weren't going to become their workmate. I was already busy thinking how I could make money with my abilities.

Halfway across the room, I noticed Marina's slim outline on the balcony outside. Next to her stood one of Pavel's toadies, a guy called Dennis, waving his hands as he explained something to her.

I slowed down. It looked as if the girl could use my help. Her Mood was still deep in the red. A large exclamation mark of a quest giver flashed above her head.

I decided to wait till they finished talking and walked over to the big table, taking a place next to Greg's.

"Hi guys," I said.

"Aha, here's the hero of the day!" Cyril exclaimed. "Phil the J-Mart Slayer!"

"So, have they been sufficiently grateful?" an accountant girl nodded at the bosses' table. She was faking indifference — but according to her stats, her name was Vicky and she was dying of curiosity.

"You could say that," I joked darkly. "I don't even know what to do with all their gratitude. Should I reserve a table at McDonald's to celebrate? Or should I buy a vacation at my Granddad's country shack?"

"Have they blanked you?" Greg asked.

"Well, technically I'm still not on the payroll. So they offered me a one-off compensation. Which is the equivalent of one of their whisky bottles."

Wham! I'd never been a good judge of character. All of a sudden I was showered with messages reporting my improved Reputation with everyone within earshot. Indeed, sympathizing with losers is a signature Russian trait. Or was it simply that they'd had their Jealousy debuffs lifted?

As the news of my misfortune spread, new messages kept coming in. For a while, everyone fell silent. Then everybody began talking at once.

"Did you tell them it wasn't fair?" Vicky the accountant girl demanded. "You've brought them half as much again of what we sell now!"

"You should have waited till you were officially hired before closing the deal," a strange voice came from somewhere at the center of the table.

"What would you like to drink?" Greg fussed around me. "Vodka? Ah, no, you can't, you've been drinking whisky[12]. I'll go get some from the ITs."

---

[12] Russian drinking customs prescribe to stick to only one type of alcoholic drink throughout a party. Doing so prevents a reveller from getting drunk prematurely. Together with another Russian custom of always chasing a drink down

"Don't just sit here, have something to eat! Let me help you," Vicky took a clean plate and piled it up with some mixed salad, a generous dose of Olivier[13] and a big helping of roast chicken. "Max, go tell the servers to bring him the main course!"

"Did they at least put you on the payroll?" Cyril asked, picking at a chicken bone.

I nodded gratefully to Vicky and turned to Cyril, "The chief said, I'm hired as of tomorrow."

"In which case, welcome to the club!" he shouted. "Everyone has a drink? Here's to our Philip..."

"I'd rather you call me Phil."

"Good! Here's to Phil!" he announced, absent-mindedly raising his chicken leg in the air.

My tipsy colleagues happily joined in. By now, they were in such a state they'd drink to anything at all[14].

I attacked the chicken and the salads. The others left me to enjoy my food in silence.

"Better now?" Cyril finally asked.

I nodded.

He motioned me out onto the balcony. He

---

with some food, this is the "secret" behind the Russians' alleged ability to drink a lot without getting drunk.

[13] Olivier: a Russian potato salad

[14] Another Russian drinking habit prescribes to always accompany every drink with an appropriate toast. It's considered bad manners in Russia to sip one's drink alone when in company: you're supposed to only drink in unison with everybody else after a toast has been pronounced.

needed a smoke.

Greg followed us uninvited. Marina was still outside. Cyril and Greg lit up.

"Can I have one?" the girl asked.

Greg offered her a cigarette and a light.

"Phil, if you'll excuse my impudence," Cyril began. "How did you find Valiadis?"

"I have a nephew who's also Cyril," I replied off-key.

"That's my little brother's name too," Marina said thoughtfully.

"I got it," Cyril grinned. "You don't want to say!"

"It's not that," I said, trying to come up with a half-truth. "You know Valiadis is on Facebook, don't you?"

"So what?"

"His check-in is sometimes turned on. Not always."

"What the hell is check-in? Can't you two speak normally?"

"It's a feature on Facebook," Marina explained, "allowing everyone to see your location. And Facebook, just so that you know, is the American analog of our VK[15]. It means that Phil could use it to follow Valiadis' movements."

"Yeah, sort of," I agreed. "He was in a gym."

"No, wait a sec," Cyril insisted. "Surely you don't want to say that one of Russia's richest people reveals

---

[15] VK: VKontakte.ru, a Russian social media network similar to Facebook. Marina is being sarcastic, mocking Cyril's ignorance of social media.

his movements on Facebook? What, just for his enemies' convenience? How stupid is that? So you just stumbled across his actual location, went there and spoke to him, is that it?"

"Not really," I said, faking honesty, while in fact I was simply unable to keep up with all the lies. "I know a girl who works there. She pinged me when he arrived. So I just went there and pretended it was a coincidence. I was just lucky, that's all."

"Hah!" Greg said, visibly relieved. "You should have said so! Checking in, yeah right! That calls for a drink! Where's that bottle?"

"You go and get it," Cyril told him. "I need to take a leak... oops, sorry, Marina, I forgot you were here!"

Both of them left. Marina and I stayed alone on the balcony.

"So how was your first day at work?" I asked.

"Awful," she lit up another cigarette.

"Want to tell me about it?"

She paused, unsure. Then she took in a deep breath and blurted it all out, hurrying to finish before the other two returned,

"There's nothing to tell. They paired me with Den — Dennis. Apparently, he's married — yeah right! He was all over me. He invited me to have dinner with him. And I don't have time for dating at the moment, I need to prepare for my term exams. So I said, sorry, I can't. He took it very personally and stopped helping me at all. Then he said I was wasting my time. Said I wasn't going to make it, anyway. And here at the restaurant he started up again. He openly asked me to have sex with him. He said he'd help me with sales then and might even put in a word for me with Pavel."

"What a prick, excuse my French!"

She smiled. "It's okay. Nothing I haven't heard already on campus!"

"Just tell him to get stuffed. I'm gonna help you myself."

She gave me a wary look.

I laughed. "I don't need anything from you. Don't worry. Go do some reading for your exams. Deal?"

With a smile, she shook my hand on it. My Reputation with her had grown. Soon it would reach Amicability.

A new quest window opened.

Help a Struggling Student
Help your fellow trainee Marina Tischenko to close a sales deal for packaging products produced by Ultrapak, Ltd.
Deadline: the end of Marina's trial period

Rewards:
XP: 900 pt.
Reputation with Marina Tischenko: 30 pt.
Current Reputation: Indifference (25/30).

Penalties:
Reputation with Marina Tischenko: -30 pt.
Current Reputation: Indifference (25/30).

Quest accepted

I was surprised at myself. Before, I'd never really bothered to do anything even if I needed it myself. And now I was going all out trying to help absolute strangers. Not to earn more Reputation or XP points, mind you. It just felt good doing it.

I double-checked my own decision. I had no doubt I should do it. I was all for it.

"How long does it take to fetch a bottle of booze?" I mumbled, just to break the uneasy silence.

I took a peek into the restaurant. Greg had already forgotten all about us, busy drinking with someone else. Good. Time to make myself scarce.

"I'll be off, then," I said. "I've got to get up really early tomorrow."

"Me too," she said.

"Do you need a lift?" I asked. I didn't mean anything untoward, I just wanted to be helpful.

"What are you two doing here?" Vicky's shrill voice came from behind my back. "Hope I'm not intruding?"

"Of course you're not," I said. "We're waiting for Greg and Cyril to come back. One is gone to fetch some booze. And the other is at the gents'.'"

"Mind if I stay? Or are you two-"

"No, we're not."

It looked like I might have to stay for a while. Leaving now would confirm her worst suspicions.

Victoria "Vicky" Koval
Age: 29
Divorced

Children: a daughter.

Compared to Marina, she was slightly worse for wear. Still, she was taller, perfectly groomed and seemed to have a very high opinion of her charms. In the dimmed gloom of the restaurant, she looked just as attractive as Marina — and her eyes sparkled with promise.

"Would you like a glass of wine?" Marina offered.

"What a great idea, sweetie!" Vicky readily agreed. "We might as well paint the town red! What do you think, Phil?"

"Absolutely," I chimed in.

Not tonight, my little friend, I told my darker side. *Not with her. Not in this situation.*

You didn't have to have an alien interface installed in your brain to know she had the hots for me. Her Interest indicator showed as much.

The balcony doors swung open, letting in Greg and Cyril carrying an open vodka bottle, some glasses and some snacks on plates. Greg got busy distributing the plates and pouring out the vodka.

Marina arrived next, holding a wine glass for Vicky. She kept nursing it in her hands, not knowing what to do with it because Vicky was already holding a glass of vodka.

Cyril lit up another cigarette. "Well! They say that life has to be lived so that you have something to remember. And I propose we drink to the things that tomorrow we might be ashamed to remember!"

Vicky and Greg laughed. Yawning, I clinked my

glass on theirs, took a symbolic sip and set the glass down on the window sill. I couldn't stand straight anymore. It had been a very, very long day.

"Actually," Greg took a hearty bite of his food, "the top brass have already gone. They're going to play some normal music in a minute so we can dance. Girls, you fancy dancing?"

"I *luve* dancing," Vicky said.

"I don't," Cyril grinned. "But I can stand and watch. Phil, what about you?"

"Sorry guys, I really need to get back home," I said. "I'm so tired I might just drop dead any moment. No offense."

"That's all right," he assured me. "The party was all thanks to you, anyway!"

"I don't feel too special, either," Vicky hurried to add as she kicked off her stilettoes and changed into some street shoes. "Phil? Mind if we share a cab?"

"Not at all, but we need to drop Marina off first. She needs to go too."

"It's okay, I can manage," Marina protested.

"Marina? Are you going too?" Greg sounded lost. "Please stay! It's gonna be fun!"

"Sorry but I really can't."

"Greg, how about you drive Marina home?" Vicky asked.

I looked at Marina. She gave a barely perceptible shake of her head. No.

"Right," I said. "Greg, it's up to you whether you want to stay or go home. Your wife is pregnant at home, isn't she? I'm gonna take care of the girls."

Greg looked askance at Marina.

"He's right," she said. "You can stay. Or go back home to your girlfriend, whatever you prefer. I'll go with the guys," she walked back into the restaurant.

"I'm gonna call a cab," Vicky said, following her.

Greg heaved a sigh. "I'd better see you two off, then."

I turned to Cyril, "Well! Enjoy what's left of the party! It's been a pleasure meeting you."

"Wish I could say the same," he slurred. "I really didn't like you at first. I'm sorry to say that but it's true. But you seem to be okay after all..."

"Are you staying?"

"Absolutely. There's nothing for me at home, anyway. The place is empty; no one's waiting for me there..."

He doubled up in another bout of coughing. Unable to stop, he waved his hand at me, motioning for me to leave.

I headed back into the restaurant. As I walked past all the gyrating dancers, I met Dennis' unfriendly gaze. The company guy Marina had been paired with.

Ignoring him, I walked down the stairs toward the girls who were waving their hands at me from the entrance. Vicky was dancing on the spot. Marina stood hunched up like a ruffled bird. Greg was shifting from one foot to the other next to them, looking utterly pissed.

We walked out of the restaurant. The cab had just arrived. The two girls climbed into the back. I took the passenger seat next to the driver. Greg mumbled his goodbyes and scurried back in. A great big Envy debuff dominated his stats.

"Where to?" the driver asked.

The girls waited for me to reply.

I still had a few more difficult decisions to make tonight.

CHAPTER

SEVENTEEN

DOUBLE-POINTED SPEARS

I hate myself when I get feet so cold
That I can watch how innocents are hit;
I hate it when they break into my soul,
And hate it when into my soul they spit.

Vladimir Vysotsky, *The Things I Hate*
Translated from Rusian by George
Tokarev and Robert Titterton

THE DRIVER PATIENTLY WAITED FOR ME TO GIVE HIM AN
address.

I replied unhesitantly, "Marina? Where're you
going?"

That was the right thing to do. Had we dropped

Vicky off first, the entire office would be buzzing tomorrow, discussing Marina's easy virtues. Vicky would never have believed the contrary. This kind of notoriety was the last thing Marina needed. She was only a child, after all.

The two girls in the back seat got busy discussing some latest Instagram sensation while I closed my eyes and drifted off, losing my battle with sleep.

I must have really needed it. When Vicky opened the door and began to shake me awake, I struggled to find my bearings.

"Phil? Phil! Wake up! We're home!"

"Vick? Is that you? Where's Marina?"

"She's back on campus, don't worry."

I looked around. The cab was parked next to some high-rise building. The driver tapped his fingers on the steering wheel. Vicky looked at me expectantly.

"Well..." I said, "see you tomorrow? Or would you like me to take you home?"

She laughed. "That would be very nice of you! Come on, I've already paid."

She'd paid! Unwilling to embarrass her in front of the driver, I climbed out of the cab. It looked like I'd have to play it by ear.

In a perfectly natural motion, Vicky's hand reached for mine. Her fingers interlaced with mine. She led me toward the building.

Her Interest in me remained high. Her motives were pretty clear. My Sexual Frustration debuff was clocking up its last minutes. Liberal amounts of oxytocin coursed through my blood. The only thing that still stopped me was my married status and the wedding ring on my finger.

She paused by the building's front door and dialed the entry code. The lock clicked open.

Without stepping inside, I swung it open for her, letting her in.

"Phil?"

I showed her the ring.

She shrugged. "Please. Is it so serious?"

"Not really. We're getting a divorce."

"So? Don't you like me?"

"I do," I replied in all honesty. "But-"

She was a pretty girl. She liked me. She was free and so was I — well, almost. The night was still young. Had I had one extra shot of vodka back at the restaurant, we'd have already been all over each other.

No idea what was stopping me. Still, I hesitated. I'd never cheated on Yanna before. With this ring on my finger, I didn't feel free. It just wasn't the right thing to do.

She peered me in the eye, apparently weighing up her chances.

"Well, whatever," she finally said, unable to conceal her disappointment. She swung round and sashayed away, her back straight and proud, her head high.

My blood boiled. I couldn't take it any longer. With the tips of my fingers, I pried the almost-shut heavy door open again.

I took the ring off my finger and slid it into my

pocket. I caught up with her by the elevators and draped my arm around her waist as we stepped inside. Smiling, she pressed the button and turned to face me.

I kissed her.

With a weak groan, she greedily answered my kiss. Her hands brushed over my hair, my neck, my face... until we gave in to the impulse.

About an hour later, my Sexual Frustration debuff was successfully lifted.

Task Status: Remove the Sexual Frustration debuff
Task completed!
XP received: 50 pt.
+15% to Satisfaction

The system message had appeared at the least opportune moment. Still, its arrival added to the climax, their synergy showering me with some out-of-this-world sensations. This called for a second go, slow and unhurried.

Later, a new skill message appeared in my view,

Congratulations! You've received a new skill level!
Skill name: Seduction
Current level: 4
XP received: 500

We never got any sleep that night, sharing with each other the excess of our sexual energy. As Vicky took a smoke break, I checked my stats. My Stamina had grown a few percent.

With the first rays of sunshine, she dragged me into the shower with her to wash off the tangy aroma of our nightly exploits. From there she brought me to the kitchen. Despite the lack of sleep, we were both wide awake. She sat me down at the table and began cooking breakfast.

The only thing she had on was a misshapen black Armin van Buuren T-shirt. That morning, I saw her in a different light: not the office *femme fatale* but a rather plain girl, tall and fit. She had the broad shoulders of a swimmer which suited her a lot, adding to her posture and offering a great landing point for her long dark-blond hair.

The rising sun highlighted the smattering of freckles on her face. As she paused thoughtfully in front of the fridge, she wrinkled her nose in the cutest way. Without all the makeup, she looked at least ten years younger.

She dashed around the kitchen, slicing ham, cheese, bread and tomatoes, making coffee and pouring out the orange juice. Before I could protest, she'd grabbed the iron and pressed my office shirt.

"I have a daughter," she informed me. "She's at my parents at the moment."

"Cool. If she's anything like you, she must be a very pretty girl."

"She's pretty, yes, but in a different way. She took after her father," she must have noticed my uneasiness because she added, "He left us on her first birthday. He just didn't come back home."

"Why?"

"Well, I suppose it's about me. I had an awful character back then. He just couldn't take it any longer. We were too young and unwilling to compromise. Both of us. Come on, eat your breakfast now."

"I am eating it," I mumbled through a mouthful of food.

"What's on your agenda for today? I could give you a lift to work," she said jokingly.

"I still need to get back home, feed the animals and walk the dog."

"Do you have a dog and a cat? How cool! I wish I could have a dog! I love German Shepherds."

"That's exactly what I have. His name is Richie. He's not my dog, actually," I told her Richie's story.

I liked the fact that she wasn't fishing into all the details of my failed marital life and upcoming divorce. She hadn't even asked me about my wife's name. Strangely enough, I felt perfectly at ease with her which normally isn't the case after a spontaneous one-night stand like this. I felt at home at her place.

She was still interested in me. She kept casting glances at me. Her Interest bar stayed at 100%. Also, my Reputation with her had jumped directly to Amicability, bypassing Indifference altogether. Between this and my improved Seduction, I only had 700 pt. till the next level.

Having finished my breakfast, I received a Caffeine buff and an improved Happiness buff.

Happiness II
Your Satisfaction levels have exceeded 120%
+75% to Vigor
+2 to all main characteristics
Duration: as long as Satisfaction levels exceed
100%

I really should go back to the gym while the buff was still active, just to see whether I'd indeed become 2 pt. stronger.

Vicky saw me to the door. No idea what was going on in her head. Still, I could see that her Mood had plummeted.

I really didn't want to see her sad. I gave her a hug. She clung to me. I kissed her neck, then whispered into her little ear,

"Would you like to go to the movies?"

Her Mood rapidly improved. She beamed. "Why not? When? Today?"

"How about tomorrow? Tonight I have dinner at my parents'. Also, we could use some sleep, don't you think?"

"Okay," she released her embrace. "Now go. See you at work."

I barely made it home. Both Richie and Boris told me everything they'd been thinking about me, then demanded their food. While the cat head-butted my legs, Richie reared up, laid his front paws onto my chest and barked in my face, "Whassup, boss?"

"Sorry, guys," I said. I didn't promise it wouldn't happen again, though. I laid out their food and topped up their water bowls.

This time, I had even less time to walk Richie than the night before. "Sorry Rich, no time for ceremonies. Just do it, quick quick!"

He understood. He headed for the first suitable spot without sniffing around in search of that one unique place good enough to do the deed.

What a shame I didn't have the time even for the briefest of runs. Still, in my current state — twenty-four hours of rushing around with barely any sleep — any physical exercise might do me more harm than good. Strangely enough, I hadn't received a Lack of Sleep debuff yet. If I remembered rightly from my college years, it might probably appear closer to lunchtime.

I wasn't at all surprised, glimpsing Alik walking toward me from a distance. I already had a few ideas regarding his quest. Now was the perfect moment to check them while he was still on his way.

I opened the interface. Where was that map now?

I highlighted all the supermarket chains I'd studied the day before, then added a new search filter: "stock worker wanted".

Almost all of the stores remained on the map. Excellent.

"Oh Phil, hi man," Alik said, about to give me another bear hug.

"Hi, wait a sec."

I entered another search parameter, "90% probability of hiring Romuald "Alik" Zhukov."

Bummer. All of the stores had disappeared from the map.

"You all right, man?"

"Yes, wait!"

I brought it down to 80%. Nothing. 70%: still nothing. I dropped it down to 50%.

A lone marker lit up: a large wholesale store in the industrial zone.

"I think I've just found you a job," I said. "Stacking shelves in a store, would you mind doing that?"

"I wouldn't mind doing anything at the moment. I'd be happy just cleaning toilets."

"Have you even been to the North industrial zone?"

He scratched the back of his head. "Sure. Is that what you mean?"

"Why not?"

"Is there anything closer to home?"

"You've got a cheek, you! Which home? You don't have one, do you? You might just as well rent something for yourself in that area."

"All right, all right, keep your hair on."

"There's a supermarket there that needs a stock man. The name is Underground. Think you're gonna try for it?"

"Absolutely."

I gave him a critical once-over. Misshapen track bottoms, an old T-shirt and a pair of old socks in his sandals. Still, he looked fit and strong, that was the most important thing. "Did you drink anything today?"

"Only last night."

"What did you drink?"

"Just a beer," he said.

Still, I could feel his embarrassment. "What, for a starter? And then what, a couple of vodkas? I suggest you keep a lid on it for the time being or you might not last. You'd better put some decent clothes on, too. How about your identity papers?"

"I've got my ID and a proof of address. No driver's license. What do you want me to wear?"

"I don't know. Haven't you got any jeans or something? And a decent shirt."

"Eh," he faltered. "I think I've got a shirt but it needs some mending. I've got a pair of jeans though."

"Come with me," I said.

By then, Richie had already done all his business. Alik and I took the elevator to my apartment.

I rummaged through my stuff until I found a blue dress shirt two sizes too big for me, a birthday present from one of Yanna's numerous family still in its transparent packaging.

"Try this on," I told Alik. "The sleeves are a bit too short... never mind, you can roll them up later. Actually, it's not so bad."

"I'll bring it back," Alik said without taking his eyes from the mirror. He looked a different person.

"Just keep it. It's brand new."

"Thanks. Who do I need to speak to?"

"Just go there and ask to see the manager. Tell them that you know they need a stock worker and that's why you've come."

"Should I mention you?"

"No. Just say you want to do it. That's it, I must be off. You too, smarten yourself up and off you go!"

As I walked to the office, I couldn't stop thinking about Vicky. It wasn't love, of course, but still. She gave me this good feeling. My heart warmed when I thought of seeing her. Would I be able to invite her to my place? Would she run in horror on seeing my bachelor's den?

Finding a new place was getting a bit imperative.

OUR OFFICE RESEMBLED the film set of The Walking Dead.

My groaning co-workers stumbled about, weakly pretending they were busy. The water cooler was in overload as everyone hurried to quench their hangover thirst. Max, our system administrator, gulped beer from a large coffee mug. At least I thought it was beer, judging by the badly-concealed open can stashed away behind his server cables.

Greg arrived, lugging a large suitcase. He looked grim and decidedly misanthropic.

On seeing me, he cheered up a little. "Hi Phil. Remember how good it was last night? That's exactly how I feel now... *not.*"

"Is it so bad? Did you drink too much?"

"I wish. I stayed in the restaurant with the guys for a while, then we all went to that karaoke place. I came home and the door was locked from the inside. Alina refused to let me in. I crashed out right there on the stairs. When my alarm went off I couldn't work out where I was and what I was doing there. I had a filthy taste in my mouth. My whole body was aching. I was thirsty as hell. And then I discovered this suitcase on the steps next to me. What could I do? I tried to knock some more. As if! Alina just wouldn't answer the door. I have no family in town. I thought I might pop in at a friend's, to clean myself up and leave my stuff there but he'd already gone to work."

I wasn't used to seeing him so lost. "That's tough. You should make it up to her somehow. Just to wash away the guilt, you know."

"Don't," Cyril's sleepy voice butted into our conversation from a nearby desk. "She's probably not worth it."

"But that wasn't even my fault!" Greg protested. "What's there to make up for?"

"There's no guilt to wash away," Cyril summed up with a yawn and a stretch. He was wide awake now. "But I know somebody else who might do with a wash... you stink like a polecat, you."

Greg raised his arm and took a sniff. "You think? Anyway, what about you, Phil? Did you take the girls home?"

"Depends what you mean."

"No way! Don't tell me you all ended up in bed together!"

"Yeah right. I slept through the entire journey. So in the end it was them who took me home, not the other way round. At least I got some sleep."

Greg's face betrayed relief. I knew it. He was after Marina himself, jealous bastard.

I still had some time before the briefing to pop

into the HR and fill in my job application. Because, all things considered, I'd decided to stay here for a while.

A rep's job didn't require staying in the office which meant I could spend some time doing my own things. I really should help Marina find some clients, land a few for myself, receive my J-Mart bonus and keep an eye on Greg while I was here. Cyril too seemed to be okay. Not sure if I could become friends with them all but I quite liked spending time with them. It wasn't often I enjoyed talking to someone IRL.

The thought of losing my old online friends still smarted. What a shame I'd lost contact with them. I really should get in touch with them and invite them somewhere.

As I submitted my job application to Vicky, she was all businesslike. I couldn't agree more. I did like the girl. If things didn't work out between us, that wasn't the reason to ruin her reputation. Also, I still didn't know what company policy was regarding corporate affairs.

"Phil, welcome to Ultrapak! I'll send you your name badge as soon as it's ready. Please leave your contact information with Daria our office manager so she can order your business cards."

"Thank you very much, Victoria."

As I walked out of the room and out of sight of her workmates, I gave her a wink. She flashed a smile back.

During the briefing, I managed to offer a couple of useful suggestions. Afterward, a new message popped up,

Congratulations! You've received a new skill level!

Skill name: Communication Skills
Current level: 5
XP received: 500

I had mere 150 XP left till level 7. That was peanuts. Such rapid progress in less than a week made me regret the years I'd wasted playing WoW.

During the briefing, I also arranged it with Pavel to become Marina's mentor. Dennis didn't like it at all. He flared his nostrils out of spite but didn't object.

"You think you can do it?" Pavel's voice rang with doubt. "You've only been working here since yesterday yourself."

"Your product is easy to sell," I said. "It's just as good as everywhere else but its costs make it very interesting for the buyer. Plus you have an impressive client list. Yes, I think we can do it."

Pavel nodded and moved to the next subject on the agenda. Greg's eye twitched. Still, judging by Marina's stats, her Mood was now close to Happiness.

We spent the rest of the morning meeting with clients, lugging around bagfuls of samples, stacks of price lists and reams of business proposals with our contacts on them. I used my interface to calculate the optimal route between hundreds of small and middle-sized businesses in need of packaging deliveries. Bakeries, delicatessen shops, online takeaway joints, small restaurants... at the moment, they were all buying their packaging materials at prices much higher

I'll walk the dog and then I can come."

"Excellent. I'll be at your place in an hour and a half."

As I walked toward my house, I noticed some drunken merriment going on in the pavilion. I took a better look. There they were, Yagoza and Co, complete with the beaming Alik still wearing my shirt.

I headed toward them. Alik walked over to greet me.

"Phil!" I could see he was sincerely happy to see me. "They've hired me! Imagine! I start Monday!"

"Congratulations! Well done!"

"Thank *you*!" Alik said, then added guiltily, "I had to buy the guys a drink to celebrate."

I hadn't received any quest messages though. Apparently, he had to be officially hired for the quest to close.

He stank of booze. I knew of course that he was celebrating with the money I'd given him.

"Well, listen, you're a grownup man and can take care of yourself," I said. "You do what you want but-"

"There!" someone shouted behind me, then slapped my ears quite hard with both his hands. "Scared, ain't you? So you should be!"

I swung round. The guy gave me a chop under the chin. My eyes watered with the pain. I received a debuff to Perception.

Covering my ringing ears, I looked around me in search of the guy who'd done it.

I didn't have to look far. A filthy drunken

character was standing in front of me, guffawing at his own "joke". His eyes were mere slits in his fat face.

The entire pavilion guffawed with him.

Their stupid "joke" had become the last straw in the recent succession of dirty tricks others had played on me. I went into Enrage mode.

Clumsily I attempted to punch him, investing all my strength into the blow. My badly-aimed fist barely grazed his cheekbone. Immediately he punched me in the liver, knocking the wind out of me. I doubled up and dropped to the ground.

Alik stopped him before he could kick my head, "Rus, are you nuts? This is Phil!"

"I don't care if he's your grandmother!" the alcoholic growled.

"Leave it, Alik," Yagoza wheezed. "Your nerd isn't worth it. Come on, don't spoil the party. We've plenty of drinking still to do."

"Did you hear?" the fat drunkard said to Alik, slurring. "We have a good thing going, don't ruin it! Let's celebrate!"

I focused on his stats. *Ruslan, age: 36, unemployed.*

I remembered the two swindlers who'd tried to buy my computer off me. That one was also called Rus — a Rustam or something. I didn't seem to have much luck with the name.

The pain in my gut was excruciating. I waited for it to subside.

Alik left me and rejoined his buddies.

Rus for short. He's a good plumber, by the way, only he can't keep a job because he drinks too much. The one eating the sandwich is Sprat, also known as Alexey. Oops, he's choking. Give him a slap on the back, someone. This guy here is Vasily. Such a shame his wife Catherine had to divorce him. And that one over there is Muhammad Abu Talimov."

"No way!" the fat guy guffawed. "Did you hear that?"

"Jesus," Alik said. "That's right, he knew my name when I first met him! How did you do that?"

"Well, I might have guessed," Yagoza said heavily. "Or maybe you're buddies with our local cops?"

"Neither. It's irrelevant, anyway. What do you want?"

Yagoza rubbed his hands. "Pour him a drink! Let's give our guest a proper welcome!"

I had no idea what he was up to and I wasn't going to play along. "You've already greeted me, I believe. Can't say I enjoyed it very much though. Just tell me what you want and I'll be off."

"Who do you think you are?" the fat guy began.

"Shut your mouth," Yagoza said. "Were you born so stupid? I want you to apologize to mister... what's your name again?"

"It's Phil. Phil Panfilov."

"I'm very sorry, Mr. Panfilov. He's sorry too, aren't you, Rus?"

The fat guy shrank under his stare. "I am... It was a joke. Sorry about that."

I touched my still-smarting flank and winced.

Pointless going to the police. Not worth it. It had been me who'd attacked him first, anyway. Or that's what they'd say. In their eyes, it was only a joke.

"Apology accepted," I said and turned to leave.

"Phil!" Alik called behind my back. "Good luck, man!"

"You too," I swallowed the rest of the sentence.

I just hoped he could rise over his current environment. I didn't want him to go back to his habitual drunken lifestyle. He was still young, you know. He had a life to live.

At home, I peeled my shirt off and studied the bruise under my ribs. Nothing too serious. Still, this had sounded like a second warning. The first one had been when that fake Gypsy had attacked me. Combat skills weren't limited to a computer game. You never knew when you might need them IRL. Some people managed to live their entire lives without picking a fight once, but I'd somehow managed to do it twice in the past week.

For the moment, it was all academic, anyway. Time to get ready to see my parents.

I called my two pets into the kitchen. As they ate, I sent Richie's picture to his owner. Sveta immediately replied with a voice message,

"Thank you so much! I'm counting the days till I can see him again! I'll be back in five days. Please give him a hug from me."

Five more days. Which meant I could forget house-hunting for the time being. Not with a cat and dog in tow. I had to wait for Sveta to come back and collect him.

Kira called to let me know she was stuck in a traffic jam. I checked the map. She was still a long way away and might stay there for a while. So I took Richie out to the park, hoping for a quick run just to keep myself awake.

I didn't manage much running. My Happiness buff had long since disappeared. Between my aching ribs, the Lack of Sleep debuff and the weakness of hunger, I'd only managed some quarter of an hour of jogging at the most. Still, even that had been enough to build up a good sweat. My Stamina had grown another percent, bringing me very close to its next level.

By the time Kira finally arrived, I was already quite awake after a shower and a cup of coffee. Still, she was bound to start asking questions. I looked a sight. The black circles around my eyes spoke for themselves.

As she drove me to our parents', she showered me with questions. I gave her an edited version of my last few days' escapades, avoiding any unusual or uncomfortable details.

"Phil, come on. I think your new boss is okay. I would have done the same. The agreement was they'd hire you, and so they did. They even paid you a bonus. Which isn't that small, by the way. Some people have to work a whole month for that kind of money."

"I know, but-"

"But what? Had they given you a percentage on that deal, you know what would have happened? You'd have relaxed and lost momentum. At least this way they gave you enough incentive to keep selling, plus they did pay you something just to keep you happy. Besides, how can they be sure you weren't just plain lucky that day? And if you weren't, then your future earnings are pretty much guaranteed, aren't they? Trust me, that's the way they look at it."

"No good arguing with Mom," Cyril's voice came from the back seat.

I smiled. There seemed to be a whole bunch of Cyrils around me just lately, starting with my nephew. Then there was my new workmate Cyril Cyrilenko, the one with the coughing problem.

From Cyril, I logically thought about Vicky. Smiling, I sent her a quick text asking if Saturday's movie outing was still valid.

She replied within a minute,

Sure. Cant wait

I wished her a nice Friday night and added, *See you tomorrow.*

Kira's words had convinced me that Ultrapak wasn't such a bad option, after all. So should I really quit the moment my one-month notice period was over? Just imagine how it would look on my CV. Bet my future employers would have a few questions to ask me!

As we drove, Mom called, berating us for being late and saying that the food was already cold and Dad was hungry but waiting for us. Typical. Dad had always treated family get-togethers as big events — to the point of which he'd lose all appetite.

Kira and I spent the rest of the way talking about her son's academic successes. He was already quite proficient in the three Rs — and he still had another year until he started school.

Finally, we arrived. Kira parked up by the building. I got out of the car and looked over the courtyard where I'd spent my childhood years.

The place filled me with fuzzy nostalgia. The sandbox where I used to play with my friends, building sand cities complete with streets and apartment blocks; a peeling old slide I must have used thousands of times; a small garden where we'd tried to catch grasshoppers with a rare wing color. What a blissfully carefree time it had been, where unfinished homework or the call to go home were my biggest problems!

My parents lived in a quiet quarter in the city's historical suburb. Here the apartment blocks were squat and small, the narrow streets lined with tall, ancient oaks, chestnuts and maple trees which towered over the small front yard of my parents' house.

Dad stood on the small apartment balcony smoking, watching for us to arrive.

"Grandad!" Cyril screamed.

Dad beamed. "There they are!"

Once inside, I gave him a big hug. My heart clenched. This was my Dad, once so strong and powerful — and now he felt so small and frail in my arms. Both he and Mom had grown so old. His favorite checkered shirt hung loose on him, its hem bunched up inside his trousers. The only thing that hadn't changed was his smell: the strong aroma of tobacco and a classic Russian aftershave he'd stayed true to since Soviet times.

Groaning and complaining about her back, Mom supervised Kira who got busy laying the table in our small sitting room. My sister rushed between the kitchen and the table, all the while regaling Mom with the latest gossip about some mutual friends.

As usual, the TV was blaring out, showing the finals of the Wheel of Fortune[16]. The ticker tape below announcing the upcoming newscast. Old habits die hard: no amount of Internet could change my parents' Soviet-era trust in the television as the only source of the latest news.

The table stood next to the old sunken couch. My heart clenched again. That's where Yanna had sat only two months ago when we'd come here for my Mom's birthday. That day, Yanna had joined Kira and Mom early in the morning. Together they'd cooked, cleaned and polished the place while I was sleeping it off after a raid.

That had been the last time we'd visited my parents. And that was how I wanted to remember her. We'd been through so many good things together...

Dad and I decided to give our ladies some space and walked out onto the balcony. He struck a match and lit up a cigarette. When I'd been a kid, I used to love that smell.

He offered me the cigarette pack.

---

[16] The Russian adaptation of the American game show

"No, thanks. I quit," I said.

"Did you really? For how long have you been battling with that?"

"Just over a week. And it hasn't really been a battle."

"What, you don't even feel the urge?" he asked.

"Oh yes, I do. But I just grin and bear it for a couple of minutes. Then it gets easier. And how about you? How's Mom?"

"We're fine, thanks. Don't listen to her complaining all the time, it's just a habit she's adopted from those old hags next door. They say that complaining of poor health makes your children visit you more often. Attention seekers, that's what they are."

I believed him. I'd already checked Mom's stats first thing as I'd entered the house. She was fine, and so was Dad — for their age, of course. Their Old Age debuff kept ticking.

My Reputation with both of them was identical: Love, 1/1. Their social status levels were also impressively high: 30-plus each. That must have been due to Mom's decades of teaching experience and Dad's job as a fireman. As long as I'd known them, they'd always been ready to help anyone in need and kept a large circle of friends — the two factors which too must have contributed to their excellent stats.

"And how about you?" Dad asked. "Is it true what Kira said? Have you found a job?"

"Yeah. It all happened quickly. I went for an interview on Monday and by Thursday they'd already hired me."

"Oh. Are you sure about them? What kind of place is that?"

"Just a production company making plastic packaging. They seem okay. I can always reconsider if I want."

"At your age, son, you shouldn't be doing too much reconsidering. You'd better stick with them now and stop fooling around. Your CV is a joke," he gave me a long look which made me uncomfortable. "And this book of yours seems to take forever. Have you finished it yet? No? That's what I thought. And all those games... such a waste of time. And now you've lost Yanna too. Happy now?"

As I stood there listening to him, I was finally able to relate to his pain. Having lost my wife, for the first time in years I couldn't just dismiss his words as the ramblings of a clueless old man.

"Dad, it's gonna be all right. I assure you."

He turned away, wiping his glistening eyes with his fist. "Smoke got in my eyes, I think. Never mind, son. You're a big boy now. You don't need babysitters. Your life is yours to live."

I seemed to be having a déjà vu. This was what I'd told Alik earlier that day. Logical, really: I must have heard it from Dad hundreds of times.

"Dad? You two okay?" Kira asked, peeking onto the balcony.

"I'll just finish my cigarette and we're coming," he said. "Don't worry."

"I don't," she said doubtfully with a studying

look at each of us. Then she stepped back and disappeared.

Dad chuckled and put out his cigarette. We walked back into the apartment.

We had a nice family dinner. A few tactful questions about Yanna gradually evolved into a discussion about my plans for the future. Mom's cooking was predictably delicious even if unhealthy: according to her old-school Soviet cooking standards, there was no such thing as too much mayonnaise. Mayo salads for starters, followed by mayo chicken and — our festive staple — wild mushroom soup. Mom was rightfully proud of her mushroom soup which had never failed her — neither in the empty-shelved Soviet times nor in the penniless 1990s or later in the prosperous 2000s. That was Dad's favorite dish which by default made it everybody's favorite.

Little Cyril was yawning his head off. Mom and Kira began cleaning the table. Dad walked out for another smoke[17]. I tried to watch some TV as Cyril cheerfully zapped through the channels.

"Wait a sec," I took the remote from him.

A local news channel showed a picture of a missing girl. A voice off screen was reading her description.

I grabbed my phone and took a picture of the screen.

---

[17] Although smoking is still widespread in Russia, it's considered rude to smoke at home, especially in households with children. Family smokers usually go outside in order to have a smoke.

A girl named Oksana Vorontsova, fourteen years old, went missing about 8 p.m. on May 12 2018 and hasn't returned home since.

Oksana is five foot eight. She looks about 16 years old, slim with long dark hair, dark eyes, thick eyebrows and an upturned nose.

At the time of her disappearance, Oksana was wearing a pink cardigan over a white T-shirt, denim shorts and a pair of white sneakers.

We encourage everyone who might have any information regarding Oksana's whereabouts to step forward by calling the number below...

A long line of phone numbers followed: the police and the girl's parents as well as some volunteers.

I memorized them all, peering closely at the face of the missing girl, trying to remember her eyes, her smile, her chipped upper tooth...

Then I opened the map and sent a search request.

Nothing. Apparently, I didn't have enough KIDD points to access the data. I needed five units and I only had four: her picture, her name, her age and the name of the town — which probably doubled as her birth place. Not enough.

I cussed, then bit my lip and looked around me to check if Dad had heard me. He was still out on the balcony smoking. Cyril was fast asleep. Kira and Mom were talking in the kitchen.

I rose, carried Cyril into my parents' bedroom

and lay him on the bed. Then I returned to the sitting room and opened my interface.

On impulse I went to the skill tab and tried to invest the available skill point into Insight. Fingers crossed.

Sorry. You can't improve a system skill.

What kind of crazy game system was that? I'd activated this skill by investing an available level point in it, and now I couldn't improve it further? Did that mean I could only level Optimization through repeated use?

With a 30-day cooldown, yeah right.

Or maybe you couldn't improve it at all. As it was, it was already a cheat to end all cheats.

Oh. That wasn't what I should be thinking of. I tried to concentrate on the missing girl.

Dad had already walked back into the room and switched the TV to some crime series. He was watching it now while stroking me on the head.

"Sorry, Dad. There's something I need to do for my new job."

I sat closer to him, opened a popular social media network and entered the girl's name into the search.

Jesus. There were hundreds of them.

I continued narrowing the search results: first by age, then by country and finally, by town.

Six girls left. Two of the accounts had no pictures. Another one sported a photo of a teenage girl staring at you with that contemptuous pouted-lip look which teenage girls worldwide tend to assume for their selfies.

That was the missing Oksana.

"What kind of job is that?" Dad asked me. "Grooming underage girls?"

"Dad," I said, slightly offended. "Look at this."

I showed him the girl's picture on the TV screen, then her social media profile. "You see it's the same girl, isn't it? I think I've seen her somewhere before. So now I'm trying to decide whether it was her or not."

"And?"

"Give me one moment."

Her profile didn't contain anything useful, just the usual teenage array of memes, quotations and cute pictures. Relationship status: *"In active search"*.

Oh well. It looked like the active search stage was now over.

I clicked on "More" and saw the name of her school. Excellent. I memorized it, then reopened the map.

And what if she was already dead? How would the map react? Would it show me the location of the body? And in any case, if I failed to garner enough information, I'd have to call her parents anyway and try to come up with a believable excuse in order to help them find their daughter.

This time, however, I had enough KIDD points. A mark appeared on the map showing the girl's current location about forty miles outside the city limits.

I zoomed in. It was a small village. I could make

out the squat one-story houses and narrow side lanes. Despite the late hour, the light was on in the house where she was supposed to be. I couldn't see the details in the dark but the house's number and the name of the street were marked on the map.

"Dad, I think it's her."

He jumped off the couch. "Give her parents a ring, now."

I hesitated. Using my phone to call them probably wasn't such a good idea. They were bound to have questions. The police, too. *How did you know about it, sir? Why didn't you contact us straight away? You saw it on television? Are you some kind of an ESP guy or something? Or are you one of the kidnappers?*

"Come on, call them!" Dad spat, furious at my indecision. "You have any idea what her parents are going through right now?"

All right, but how was I supposed to disable the caller ID function in my phone? Then again, what was the point? The police could always get my number from the parents' cell provider.

Feeling doomed, I dialed the girl's parents' number.

An anxious female voice replied straight away, "Yes?!"

"Hi," I said, not knowing where to start. "Are you Oksana's mom?"

"Yes, yes! Do you know where she is?"

"She's out of town. You have a pen? It's Leafy Hollow, Kulikova St. 19."

Dad gave me an incredulous look. I waved him

away and repeated the address. "Yes, that's right. She's there now."

"Is she..." the woman's voice trailed away, unable to utter what could have become her own life sentence. "Is she alive?"

"Yes, she is," I said, praying I was right. Surely the system had a way of marking a dead body?

I listened to the woman's relieved sobbing. Then her husband took the phone from her.

"Hi, I'm Oksana's father. Call me Mikhail. I appreciate the information very much but could you please tell me where you got it from?"

"Just go and check the address I gave you. Don't waste your time. Call the police now."

"What's your name?"

"I'm Phil. If you have any questions you can call this num-"

He hung up. I just prayed he hadn't taken me for some stupid phone prankster. Doubtless they'd had their fair share of them already.

The conversation had knocked the wind out of me. I was absolutely drained. Avoiding Dad's inquiring stare, I checked my stats.

My Spirit was at zero. Wonder if it was some kind of mana analog required to use the system abilities? Or could it be related to fatigue levels? I needed to ask Martha tomorrow morning once I'd had some sleep and calmed down a bit.

"Where — did you — see her?" Dad demanded.

"But that's what I'm trying to tell you! I saw her there!"

CHAPTER

NINETEEN

RED, THE COLOR OF

DANGER

"Of course I'm dangerous. I'm police. I could do terrible things to people... with impunity."

Rust Cohle (Matthew McConaughey), *True Detective*

THIS WAS SURREAL. I'D JUST HELPED TO BRING A daughter back home to her inconsolable parents. I might have even saved her life for all I knew. Still, as I waited for the police car to arrive, I felt so anxious as if

I'd single-handedly planned and executed her abduction.

This irrational fear did have some grounds, though. It's true that we Russians have an arguably bigger fear of our police — or of uniforms in general, if the truth were known — than of actual criminals.

We have an affinity with criminals. We grow up together and go to the same schools. All of us know someone connected to criminal circles in some way or other. We too commit occasional offenses by trying to avoid taxes or breaking traffic laws. The semi-legal allure of tough-guy crime TV series has added to the criminal's somewhat romantic image. Just try and enter the Russian word for a "cop" in the Google image search. All you'll get is dozens of cartoons of bribe-taking traffic cops, corrupt police inspectors and overworked, drunken investigating officers.

This explains why I didn't expect anything good from meeting Major Igorevsky. As I made myself a cup of coffee, I scrolled through a number of Internet articles with advice on how to behave in this situation. They all boiled down to two things: if you're officially a suspect you should keep your mouth shut and deny everything. If they apply pressure, just suffer (hopefully not literally) in silence. And if you've been summoned as a witness, just answer their questions as honestly as you can (if you can), otherwise you might be charged with false testimony. And in any circumstance, demand to see your lawyer.

I didn't have a lawyer. And as for telling the truth... where should I even begin? Should I tell them about that last breakfast with Yanna? Or a piece of wetware in my head courtesy of the First Martian Company?

Please. They weren't born yesterday.

Dawn was already breaking. Even though I hadn't had enough sleep, the Lack of Sleep debuff had already worn off. I had no idea whether they were going to question me here or take me to the station, so I decided to get dressed and have breakfast just in case. I poured a generous helping of pet food into my beasts' respective bowls and fried myself a couple of eggs.

I'd almost finished them when Rich began barking his head off.

The doorbell rang.

I answered the door. Two young guys in plain clothes stood outside on the landing. Both had crewcuts. One was taller with a sharp face, the other squat and stocky.

Neither of them attempted to step inside. Somehow I didn't think they were afraid of the dog.

"Philip Panfilov?" the taller one asked.

He had a piercing, watchful stare. Very unpleasant. I didn't like it at all.

"That's me," I said. "Did you just call?"

"Police investigator Golovko," he showed me his card, then handed me a summons. "The person who called you was Major Igorevsky, the chief investigator. He has a few questions to ask you regarding your involvement in the Vorontsova abduction. We've come to take you to the station."

I studied the summons. ...Hereby summoned to

---

give evidence as a witness...

"Have you found the girl?" I asked.

"We have no authority to answer your questions."

"Should I pack a bag?"

"No. Just bring your ID papers."

They took me to the station in a shabby unmarked Korean car, its insides reeking of tobacco smoke.

The squat detective took the driver's seat. He never identified himself. I sat in the back next to Golovko who appeared perfectly relaxed but was watching me out of the corner of his eye. The squat guy mouthed a cigarette without actually lighting it.

My heart was racing. I just couldn't pull myself together. Trying to calm down, I began studying the two detectives' stats. Both were under thirty, married with children. Their social status levels were quite high. Ditto for their Intellect and Charisma. Their Perception, Communication Skills and Deception were even higher. Those were the kinds of skills you needed to successfully worm yourself into a person's confidence.

I also noticed a very high Composure on their respective skill lists. I didn't even have that.

These weren't fat cartoon cops, the butt of Internet memes. Despite their age, these guys were old guns who commanded respect.

By the time we'd arrived, the sun had already risen. I got out of the car.

This glorious Saturday morning was the best publicity for the upcoming summer. The chirping of birds filled the early-hour silence. The streets were devoid of rush-hour traffic. No crowds of grumpy pedestrians hurrying to their respective workplaces. The air was cool and fresh, the trees' foliage still wet from last-night shower.

I took a deep breath. I really didn't feel like going to the station. I'd rather have picked up Richie and taken him for a run in the park. Followed by a nice breakfast made from scratch and a good book to accompany it. Afterward, I could have spent a couple hours doing some work provided I'd received new orders, gone to the gym for an hour, then continued sorting out my interface, optimizing my skills and improving characteristics. In the evening, I could have invited Vicky to a restaurant before taking her to the movies.

It would have been a perfect Saturday, had I not ruined it for myself by answering some TV announcement.

"Follow me," Golovko said.

I walked after him, with the squat guy bringing up the rear. They took me past the front office to the second floor. We walked along a drab corridor painted with flaking blue paint until we came to the chief investigator's office.

I stayed outside watched over by the squat guy while Golovko walked in and reported, "Comrade Major, the witness is here."

"You mean Panfilov?"

"Yes, sir."

"Bring him in."

My Composure definitely left a lot to be desired. I shoved my shaking hands in the pockets of the light jacket I'd put on before leaving.

Major Igorevsky was forty years old. A bald patch was forming on his head. He was in his shirt sleeves. A tie hung on the back of his chair. He appeared exhausted, his eyes bloodshot. Doubtful he'd gotten any sleep last night.

"Good morning," I said.

"Morning, Mr. Panfilov. Please take a seat," the Major rose from his chair and proffered me his hand. He was courtesy incarnate. "I'm Chief Investigator Major Igorevsky. It was me who called you."

I couldn't in all honesty have said "nice to meet you" so I didn't. I just nodded and shook his hand.

"I've asked you to come here to give evidence as a witness. Thanks to your phone call, we were able to find the missing girl, Oksana Vorontsova," he paused, studying my reaction.

"Is she all right?" I asked.

"She's fine. That's all I can tell you at the moment. On behalf of all those that were on the case I would like to thank you for your cooperation."

I watched his status bars. His Mood was high, and so was his Interest in me.

I didn't reply. What did he want me to say? That I'd only done my duty?

The Major paused, then continued, "Now I'd like you to answer a few questions..."

For the next hour, he continued to ask me every possible kind of question about myself. My place of birth, my school, my work history, the names of my employers. He kept unraveling the chronology of my life thread by long-forgotten thread until finally he arrived at the point.

"Last night you called the missing girl's parents and gave them the exact address where we later found her. Where did you make that call from?"

"From my parents' house."

"Can anyone confirm this?"

"My parents and my elder sister."

"What's your parents' address?"

"Verbitsky St. 76, apartment 15."

"Have you ever been to Leafy Hollow before?"

"No, never."

"Where were you on Saturday night May the twelfth of this year?"

"I was at home playing a computer game."

"Can anyone confirm this?"

"My wife," I faltered. "We're going through a divorce. She doesn't live with me at the moment."

"Her contact information?"

I gave him Yanna's parents address and their phone number. It looked like I was deep in it.

"How do you know Sergei Losev?"

"First time I hear about him. Who is he?"

"Think again."

"I don't know him."

"Very well," the Major murmured, writing down my statement. "*The witness denies all knowledge of Losev...* How did you meet Oksana Vorontsova?"

"I've never met her."

"In that case, how did you know her exact location?"

"That's difficult. You might find it hard to believe."

"Believing isn't part of our job. Our job is to check the facts. How did you know where she was?"

"I saw it."

"How exactly did you see it?"

"I saw the announcement on TV. And then... then I just sensed I knew where she was."

The Major yawned. "You *sensed* it."

"I did. I was at a family dinner with my parents. After dinner, my nephew started channel-surfing. I saw the picture of the missing girl. And then I just knew where she was."

"Did you really?" the Major asked in dead seriousness.

He sounded so sincere that I would have believed him had I not seen his stats. His Deception skill was maxed out all the way up to "Divine".

"You have a remarkable talent," the Major continued.

"No, I don't. That was the first time it had ever happened to me."

"It's okay. No need getting so worked up about it. Here, have a drink of water."

"I'm all right, thanks."

"In that case, with your permission," he took a few swigs of water and set the cup aside. "But still, do you have any explanation of what happened to you at that moment?"

indeed detain me for seventy-two hours.

Oh. Like a stupid child, I put my finger in the gears of this heartless machine which was now sucking me into its works and was about to grind me into a lump of bloodied goo.

I tried to focus as my thoughts rushed around my skull in search of something I could grasp at in order to pull myself out of this situation. Finally, I had an idea.

I relaxed a little. "Excuse me, Comrade Major. What if you just show me to the girl? I'm pretty sure she'll say she's never seen me before."

"What's the point? You think she remembers what you look like? She's fourteen years old, for crissakes! I have a daughter her age! You plied her with vodka! You think she can remember anything?"

He didn't have a daughter. He had a son. The guy was a born actor. What did he want to achieve?

Now that I knew he was lying, I relaxed even more. If he'd lied to me on just that one thing, he could well have lied about everything else. Losev might have acted alone, in which case what was the point of this theater performance?

Now I was angry rather than scared. "Very well. Show me to Losev, then. Contact my wife. She can tell you where I was that night."

He cracked a sarcastic smile.

I heaved a sigh. "Or would you like me to find some of your other missing cases? Would you fancy that?"

"Go ahead, then," he agreed with surprising

ease.

He pulled out a file and began leafing through it. Finally, he offered me a few sheets of paper. All children and teenagers.

I studied the first one. A seven-year-old boy. Name: Nikita[20].

I looked up at the Major. He froze like a bloodhound sensing a trail.

The document contained enough information to start a search. I closed my eyes, unwilling to betray myself, and immediately saw a mark next to an apartment block on the map.

The mark was gray. As I focused on it, a box appeared above it saying, *Corpse.*

I checked the next few cases. Yegor, age: nine. *Corpse.* Christina, age: sixteen. This one was alive in Dubai[21]. Another teenage boy's corpse showed up in two different cities. Had he been a victim of illegal organ harvesting?

I'd have loved to have helped the Major out by sharing with him all the information I had. Still, this wasn't the right way to do it. They'd dragged me out of bed at night and threatened me, applying liberal amounts of pressure.

I was going to help them, sure. Still, I was going to do it on my terms. I'd help them all, not just this Major, but not today. Not now. At the moment, he could very easily pin all these poor children on me if he really

---

[20] In Russia, Nikita is an exclusively male name

[21] Dubai is known in Russia as a center of child trafficking

explanations first. Even as it was, if someone had decided to look into my life now, they'd be bound to discover some pretty inexplicable situations. Like my "prophesizing" session in the clinic. Or knowing the biographies of our local drunks. Or my "accidental" encounter with Valiadis. Even that wretched computer sale when I'd surprised the guy by knowing his life's details.

I finally made it to a coffee shop and ordered a large espresso. When the waiter brought it to me, I reached for the sugar bowl, then reconsidered. I really needed to lose some weight. I was pretty sure it was hindering my Agility numbers. I was surprised I hadn't yet received an Obesity debuff or something. Dr. Shvedova had warned me about it, hadn't she?

I took my time over my coffee, studying my updated task list,

- *visit parents;*
- *level up Insight;*
- *get accepted for the Ultrapak job;*
- *meet up with Yanna and file for divorce;*
- *take Vicky to the movies;*
- *send Major Igorevsky an anonymous message reporting the whereabouts of the missing children;*
- *choose a martial art to level up combat skills;*
- *choose the skills and main characteristics to level up;*
- *find out how to improve Agility;*
- *downsize;*
- *finish reading the marketing book;*

- buy some decent work clothes;
- return Richie to his owner Ms. Svetlana "Sveta"
Messerschmitt;
- contact some of my old friends and ask them out
to catch up on things

That done, I checked my quest list,

Help Alik Find a Job
Help a Struggling Student

These two tasks wouldn't take too long to complete. On Monday, Alik had to be officially hired. As for the "struggling student", a.k.a. Marina, that wasn't too difficult, either. Sooner or later, she was bound to close her first deal.

The task list itself was pretty self-explanatory — but not its order. Apparently, the system had its own prioritizing guidelines. My relationships with both Yanna and Vicky were at the top of the list even though I didn't consider them all that important. Or could the system have tuned in to one of my subconscious desires?

On Tuesday Yanna and I were going to file for divorce. I just hoped last night's phone call from her wasn't going to affect it. I should probably call her just to ask if everything was okay and if our appointment was still on. I really hoped she was doing fine regardless of how we'd parted. Had I gotten my act together a year earlier, we'd have probably lived happily ever after till death did us part.

with her. Trying to save my breath, I contacted her mentally.

"Hi Phil."

"Hi Marth. Are you all right jogging in that dress? Don't worry. You can wear what the hell you want. You'd better tell me what Spirit does."

"Spirit symbolizes your ability to take action, mentally as well as physically. The higher your Spirit, the higher heights you can reach in your lifetime."

"How does it affect system skills and stuff?"

"It doesn't affect them. It powers them. Without high Spirit numbers, you can't use system skills at all. Remember you asked me about something I couldn't reply to straight away?" she paused, waiting for me to remember.

I nodded.

She went on, *"I need to warn you about your current low Spirit reading. My visual appearance requires it, as well. I can disappear any moment now, I'm afraid. I could lower its energy consumption, but the result might not be to your liking."*

"Never mind. Just do it."

Martha's body disappeared, leaving only a very basic animated head. It always looked directly at me regardless of its position and used standard emotionless turns of phrase which were repeated in subtitles below.

"Would you like to set up your current virtual assistant settings as default?" the head asked without moving its lips.

"Yes, please. So how fast can Spirit levels restore?"

"That depends on your hidden Spirit regeneration ability."

"Can I speed it up?"

"You can, through sleep and meditation. Some users also use prayer."

"Only some? Can it help in my case?"

"Access denied. Insufficient faith levels."

She couldn't be serious, surely? "Which faith? You mean, religion?"

"Not necessarily. Still, a certain belief in a higher being of your choice is required."

Jesus. Really? I knew of course that faith could work miracles. Like, statues of saints weeping real tears, church officials opening offshore bank accounts, airplanes exploding at the sound of God's name. Surely making my Spirit regenerate double quick was peanuts for a force like that.

Still, I was curious why Martha had mentioned a "higher being of my choice" instead of just saying 'God' or 'Allah'. "Could you give me a list of higher beings who could boost Spirit regeneration?"

"Access denied. Insufficient authorization levels."

"Yeah right. Is it my personal-use license again? Or what now?"

What new mystery was this? Were religions illegal in the next century or something? In any case, this old format of contacting Martha felt like déjà vu. I almost missed her gum-chewing sarcasms.

I finally stopped and collapsed onto the nearest park bench. Today I'd covered a bigger distance. Overall, running felt easier and faster.

Richie was tired too. He slumped onto the ground next to me and began panting with his tongue hanging. I reached out to stroke him. He lowered his ears and wagged his tail.

A new system message appeared in front of me, obstructing the dog.

Your Stamina has improved!
+1 to Stamina
Current Stamina: 5
You've received 1000 pt. XP for successfully leveling up a main characteristic!

My already good mood soared even higher. Yes, I might still be a wuss who didn't dare wear glasses in public. My Stamina might still be half that of an average person — but by the same token, I was now almost twice as enduring as a week and a half ago.

Overcome with excitement, I grabbed Richie's head and gave him a hearty smacker on the nose. He licked my face with abandon.

"Get away, Rich! You stink!" I said, wiping my face.

Martha's pixelated head watched us impassively.

Talking about which, I still had this Spirit thing to sort out. And what if higher levels of system skills required more resources than I could ever amass?

I asked Martha about it. "Does Spirit grow numerically? All I can see now is percentage, a bit like Satisfaction. Does it have a set maximum value?"

"No, it doesn't. Spirit development isn't static. You can develop it through self-analysis, awareness, bringing harmony to your thoughts and perfecting your body."

"Which is what exactly?"

"You should try to look at yourself through another's eyes in every situation, sir. You need to observe yourself."

This switch to "sir" was a bit unexpected. It reminded me of the Major earlier that morning who'd done exactly the opposite. Still, in her case it was probably just the result of lowering her energy consumption levels which must have disabled her personalization module.

"Whenever you disapprove of your behavior, thoughts or emotions," she went on, "you need to reflect upon it, try to pinpoint the reason for it and decide what you can do to prevent it from happening again. You should try to think only of really important things. Things that do make the difference. You should also perfect your body."

"Yes, yes. *A sound mind in a sound body*, I know. Still, how would you level up Stamina?" I asked, remembering my own clumsiness and the task I'd added to the list only an hour ago.

"You need to do special workouts aiming to improve your balance and coordination. You should also do some weight training to strengthen your muscles and tendons."

Was it my imagination or was this version of Martha an absolute bureaucrat? She was talking in vague clichés without actually telling me anything. Could it be why the task hadn't been closed yet? Very well. I might have to look up some balance and weight training workouts on the net.

"Martha, does the system improvement of Luck require any preliminary training?"

"No such training is necessary."

"Thanks a bunch, Marth," I still treated her like a human being out of habit. "See you later."

She disappeared.

I opened my characteristic tab. Time to invest the level point I'd received into something useful.

Main characteristics:
Strength: 7 (a Comfortable Track Suit: +1)
Agility: 4 (a Comfortable Track Suit: +1; a pair of Speedy Sneakers: +1)
Intellect: 18
Stamina: 5 (a Comfortable Track Suit: +1)
Perception: 7
Charisma: 13 (a Comfortable Track Suit: +1)
Luck: 7

The numbers in brackets weren't included into a characteristic's final reading. Which was good for me because it saved me the trouble of using a calculator just to see my real results without all the gear bonuses. In fact, they weren't even round numbers. For instance, my sneakers added 1.364 pt. to Agility but I'd changed the settings to round off numbers the night I'd been personalizing the interface.

In actual fact, those fractions of a point could make all the difference. After a moment's hesitation, I changed the settings back.

I focused on Luck. A little box opened,

You have 1 (one) available characteristic point. Accept/Decline

This time I unhesitantly pressed *Accept*.

Warning! We've detected an abnormal increase in your Luck characteristic: +1 pt.
Your brain will be restructured in keeping with the new reading (8) to comply with your current level of decision making.

The world blinked. I found myself at the center of a great void. I couldn't even feel it: I couldn't feel anything. Light, sound, smells, gravitation — everything was gone. The one remaining sense — that of touch — put its imaginary hands in the air, surrendering to the *great nothing*.

It only lasted a split second. Then I was back sitting on a bench in the park. Richie was busy scratching his ear like mad with his hind leg. The fierce blinding sun; the transparent blue sky; the perfumed abundance of tree blossoms; a bumblebee buzzing over my head...

For some reason, my ear started itching too, so badly that I wanted to bury my little finger deep enough in it to scratch my very brain.

I rose from the bench and looked around. Everything seemed to be okay. I didn't feel as if I'd changed. Still, according to the system, my Luck had grown. What a shame I didn't get any XP for leveling a system characteristic.

"Richie, come," I said, reattaching his leash. "Let's go now. Heel!"

We entered a local mini market and filled a trolley with a few days' worth of groceries: some veg, a packet of chicken breasts, some precooked hamburgers and fish cakes, ravioli, milk, tea, coffee, rye bread, cheese, ham, eggs and various condiments. Seeing as I was trying to drink a lot these days, I also picked up a few large plastic bottles of water and a six-pack of sparkling mineral water. After some thought, I headed for the butcher's and added a packet of cheap offcuts for Richie.

Dragging it all back home was quite something, I tell you. Still, I got all my groceries to my apartment door in one piece.

As I walked, I continued weighing up my options. Finally I decided that the best thing to do was probably to continue investing all available points in Luck until I raised it slightly above average. After that, I could switch to Perception which shouldn't be underestimated, either. The ability to notice little things was an important asset for anyone, not just writers. I could always level up physical stats by working out alone — at least until I hit my first plateau. Then I might consider boosting them with some system points too, but not necessarily, considering I still had Intellect to level up. Now that I'd witnessed the ease with which the system had reprogrammed my mind and body, I was reassured that such an Intellect boost was bound to make me smarter.

And as for the remaining skill point, I couldn't think of a better investment than using it to boost Learning Skills. Made sense, didn't it?

That decided my priorities for the time being. As soon as I was back home, I had to invest the system point into Optimization and set up Learning Skills as my primary skill. Then I'd mark the Playing World of Warcraft skill as secondary and convert its 8 points into 4 additional Learning Skill points.

Each Learning Skills point increased the Learning Rate. One point gave you +10% to Learning Rate at level 1 and 25% at level 2. And at level 3, you received +45% to Learning Rate with each new point you invested. If I wasn't mistaken, at level 7 your Learning Rate increased 175%!

And if you counted the stat booster's effects which tripled your XP gained from skill use, then added 50% to Learning Rate for having set it as primary skill... you could easily see that my new skill acquisition would be eight times faster than that of an average man. One year of nonstop practice could turn me into a big author or a brilliant salesman, a hacker, a multilanguage translator, a lawyer, a politician, an expert in any field, or even a poker champion. And how about chess or snooker? Or even, if I approached my physical training seriously, an MMA fighter!

Having said that, the latter was a bit of an overstatement. No amount of stat booster could make you an MMA fighter in one year. Eight years sounded more like it.

I now had only one thing left to decide: who I really wanted to become. And I had to make up my mind pretty soon, too.

Even though I wasn't yet sure what I should concentrate on, I received a new message,

Task Status: Choose the skills and main characteristics to level up
Task completed!
XP received: 200 pt.
+5% to Satisfaction

Apparently, when I'd entered the task on the list, my only objective had been to decide how to invest my available Optimization point.

As I cooked lunch, I finished reading my marketing book.

Task Status: Finish reading the marketing book
Task completed!
XP received: 300 pt.
+5% to Satisfaction

I also received 2% to my Reading Skill and another 5% to my Sales Skill. There was no system message informing me of it. I only found it out when checking the skills status bars. It might be peanuts but they all added up, bringing me closer to the next skill level.

After lunch, I Googled a list of best general-interest non-fiction books and added them to my online library subscription. Not all of them were available but those that were, provided me with enough reading matter for the next year. I also added a list of marketing literature recommended by Pavel. I might have to alternate the books from the two lists. That would allow me to level up three things at once, improving my Intellect and boosting my Sales and Reading skills.

Wistfully I thought about sci fi, my favorite reading matter of all times. I might actually read a page or two before bedtime, why not? After all, nothing broadens our horizons like a good sci fi book, which in turn was bound to positively affect my Intellect.

I felt very uncomfortable without my computer. Before, it used to be my main entertainment center as well as my sole window to the world. I'd wake up by lunchtime, have a quick wash and boot it up straight away. In the evening after dinner, I'd return to it, spending all day in the same position. Quite often I hadn't even bothered to go AFK at all, taking my meals right in front of the computer screen. Predictably, my muscles were flabby, my joints creaky and my belly too big for my waistline.

Dammit! Had it not been for this surprise interface, I'd have wasted my prime years just sitting on my backside. Thank you so much guys, Khphor or whoever you are, and First Martian Company, Ltd. Funny I hadn't even remembered that weird dream properly, only a few blurred images devoid of any details, but I'd somehow remembered the name of the giant alien demon.

In the absence of the computer, I now had plenty of spare time. Before, I'd never had it simply because... oh well, never mind. Before, I'd always been too busy. I had daily quests to do, my Reputation with various factions to improve, achievements to complete, a cool mount to obtain and once I had obtained it, I'd had to go and find another one even cooler than the one before it.

There had been raids to call up, tactics to study, and hundreds — thousands — of hours spent on collecting an epic gear set which in less than six months would become obsolete and I'd have had to start it all over again, from one update to the other and from one patch to the next.

What I had now was also a game. I was basically doing the same things. Only now I had to perform them in real life, the only difference being that here, my achievements would never become obsolete.

At first I wanted to leave my Optimization gig till bedtime. Then I remembered that I might not have to sleep in my bed the coming night. So I decided to do it before leaving for the gym. You never knew, my new improved Learning Skills might help me pump weights too.

I opened the skill list and scrolled it all the way down.

You've unblocked a new skill: Optimization I.

Allows you to select primary and secondary skills.

The development of primary skills will take 50% less time than average. The development of secondary skill will take 50% longer than average.

Allows you to convert secondary skill points to primary ones at a 2 to 1 ratio, with the consequent deletion of the secondary skill.

Cooldown: 3 days

Warning! In order to activate the skill, an undisturbed 12-hour period of sleep is required. Please ensure your location is safe. You are recommended to adopt a prone position.

Skill points available: 1

Accept/ Decline

Oh. I'd completely forgotten that unblocking the skill would render me comatose for hours. I glanced at the clock. It was almost 3 p.m. That meant I might have to reschedule my gym session, as well as my date with Vicky. Leveling took priority.

I dialed Vicky's number. "Hi there," I began subtly. "How's it goin'?"

"Hiiii!" Vicky's cheerful voice replied. "I'm fine, thank you! How was your dinner with your parents?"

I smiled. "It was okay. A family get-together, if you know what I mean. I'm calling you about tonight..."

"Have you chosen a movie yet?"

"Not really. Actually, I meant to tell you..."

I could hear her hold her breath.

This was all wrong. It just felt *wrong*.

"I haven't chosen a movie, no," I said. "Honestly, I don't care. Any movie will do as long as we watch it together."

"Likewise," she mouthed.

"I'll come pick you up at seven."

"Okay. I'll be ready."

I sat there staring at the phone. A great feeling of relief flooded over me. You should always keep your word. Especially when it concerns little children and those who fall for you. Any such disappointment is like a big black smudge tainting their colorful inner world. Who knows which unkept promises would become the last stroke which could color it black?

Also, I had to be honest with myself too. If I'd made a decision to go to the gym, I had to do it. Also, if there was one thing my jogging experience had taught me it was that starting was the hardest bit. Once you eventually did start, the rest was plain sailing. And then you'd be happy you'd done it.

I did a bit of mental calculation to see how long it would take me to pick up Vicky and take her to the nearest theater. I checked its showtimes and couldn't believe my eyes. They were running *Warcraft*, of all things! I'd missed it when it was first released as I'd been lying in bed with a serious case of fever. And later, I just hadn't had the heart to watch it on the computer screen: it felt like a sacrilege.

I suffered a chain of flashbacks. My first steps through Elwynn Forest. Me in Plaguelands, fighting Scourge. Our Illidan raids in Outland and the Northrend campaign. Azeroth, destroyed by Deathwing. The mysterious Pandaria and the Orcish Horde of Draenor. Battling demons in the Broken Isles...

Not the best choice for the first date, I know, but.. I couldn't just delete twelve years' worth of gaming experience from memory. I really wanted to see how they'd adapted it all for the screen.

I needed to talk to Vicky when we got to the theater. She might actually agree to see it.

I checked a few online articles and videos about how to improve Agility. Then I added those admittedly simple exercises (like standing on one foot) to my workout program. I had to do them daily, either at home or in the gym. Now that I'd upped my Stamina twice, Agility was my weakest point.

Task Status: Find out how to improve Agility
Task completed!
XP received: 20 pt.
+1% to Satisfaction

I still had some time left, so I started checking online articles about the best martial arts for street fighting. I didn't aspire to anything more than that. All I needed was some self-defense tips. Although opinions were divided, most experts seemed to be in favor of boxing, Muay Tai and combat SAMBO[22]. The pros of boxing lay in its extreme simplicity and efficiency. Muay Tai was characterized by the combined use of all body parts and its efficiency at both long and middle range as well as in a clinch. And the fortes of combat SAMBO were in the fact that it was a complex system which had borrowed the best techniques from a great variety of martial arts, from wrestling, punching and kicking to submission locks and chokeholds.

As a total dummy, I should probably start with boxing. It wasn't as esoteric or difficult to practice as the other two.

The moment I made that decision, I received another system message,

Task Status: Choose a martial art to level up combat skills
Task completed!
XP received: 30 pt.
+1% to Satisfaction

Excellent. I was now halfway through to my next level 8.

XP points left until the next social status level: 3410/8000

---

[22] SAMBO (a Russian acronym for "weaponless self-defense") is a Russian type of martial art developed in the early 1920s for the needs of Soviet police and NKVD officers.

Now I could finally go to the gym.

I packed my bag, left Boris in charge of the coop and walked to the gym.

The practice came as a pleasant surprise. The same weights I'd struggled with the week before seemed very light today. My coach Alexander added a couple of small ten-pound weights to my bench press. Easy! Hey, where're my Strength points?

"This is normal," Alexander smiled at my enthusiasm. "This is what happens when you start training. For the first six months to a year you can expect crazy improvement. It's quite possible to triple or even quadruple your initial results."

Once I was done with his routine, I remembered my own: the Agility training. I headed for the room next door, filled with girls busy doing yoga and stretching exercises. Slightly embarrassed under their surprised glances, I performed the entire routine, about twenty minutes in total.

It took me another twenty minutes to take a shower, get dressed and drink a protein shake, after which I hurried straight home. Time was running short, and I still had Richie to walk in case I didn't sleep at home tonight.

"Come on, Richie, get on with it! Chop chop!"

He wasn't in a hurry, though. The pooch took his time sniffing every tree trunk and blade of grass in the park. Just my luck. What difference did it make to him where to do his business?

I took a picture of him and sent it to Vicky with

a message,

If I'm late, it's all his fault.

Aww, he's so cute! she immediately texted back.
Don't hurry, we have plenty of time.

Her message was pleasantly devoid of all the
pretentious emojis which was a welcome change from
Yanna.

After another half-hour, having sniffed his fill of
all sorts of unsavory things, Richie finally did his dirty
business. I took him home, calling a taxi as I walked.
At home I stuffed a couple of 5,000 ruble notes[23] into
my wallet just in case and walked back downstairs.

Had I still smoked, I would have smoked a
cigarette, just to add an extra touch of indulgence to
this fine evening. My mood was.. how can I explain...
you know, it's like having butterflies in your stomach
in anticipation of seeing someone very special.

Yagoza's HQ pavilion was empty. I wondered
how Alik was doing at his new job. Would he be able to
stay in the rut of a daily working routine without
relapsing?

That's when he showed up.

Not Alik, no. The fat guy.

---

[23] 5,000 rubles is about $75 at the time of writing

Chapter

Twenty-One

Painting the Town Red

"Friday, Muslims don't work. Saturday, Jews don't work. Sunday, Christians have a day off. And on Monday, you have a revolution!"

Vladimir Zhirinovsky

FATSO DID INDEED LIVE UP TO HIS MONIKER. EVEN HIS tent-size T-shirt failed to conceal his flabby belly spilling over his shorts elastic.

I momentarily tensed up. The puffy slits that he had for eyes looked very serious. I had no doubt he was heading toward me.

A yellow exclamation mark hovered over his

head: he had a quest to give me.

Yeah, right. What might that be? *"Lend Fatso some money for a bottle of vodka or buy him some alcohol of your choice. Reward: 5 pt. Reputation with Fatso"*? Or what was it?

"Good morning, sir," he said.

I just loved it. They're always polite when they want something from you.

Still, tonight he didn't at all resemble the drunken bully I'd met the day before. He was clean shaven, his hair combed. I even caught a whiff of some cheap deodorant.

"Morning, Rus," I said.

"I'd like to talk to you," he faltered. "It's Alik... he told me where to find you."

"Oh," I checked my phone for the taxi I'd called. It was already nearing my house. "Why?"

"Sorry, man... I'd like to apologize. And have a few words."

"Actually, I'm just about to leave. I have an appointment."

"Sure," he hunched up, suddenly listless. He reminded me of a deflated balloon. "I'm sorry," he turned round and walked back, retracing his steps.

I watched him leave. Suddenly I felt terribly sorry for him. His Vitality was below 60%. Could my rejection become the last straw in his already miserable life?

Besides, I just didn't like having unsolved problems and unfinished situations.

"Hey," I called after him. "What did you want to

talk to me about?"

He hurried back, swinging his fat hips in a most ungainly way.

"I just wanted to apologize," he gasped, trying to catch his breath, "for what I said to you last night. I'm sorry. I didn't know what I was doing."

As he continued to explain, I realized what my own mistake had been last night. It had actually been my fault all along. When I'd approached Alik like an old friend, I'd made it clear to the rest I was one of them. Fatso had apparently thought I was one of Alik's buddies and decided to play a prank on me to "punish" me for being late to their "party". And when I'd punched him, he'd apparently "acted on reflex", he now explained.

The cab was already waiting for me.

"It's all right," I said. "No hard feelings. Anything else? Just spit it out, man, I really must be going."

"I'm looking for a job," he mouthed breathlessly, as if afraid that Yagoza might overhear him and condemn him for such a shameful desire. "Alik said you helped him. Could you help me too, by any chance? I have a family, you know.. I just don't know what to do anymore..."

"What can you do?"

"Anything! I'm good with my hands, you know. I can fix anything. I'm not sure if I can lift weights though. I've got a bad back," he cast me a guilty glance as if his back presented an insurmountable obstacle to his job hunt. "One thing I can do well is plumbing. That's something I'm really good at. I won't let you down, *here's a tooth[24]!*"

A new quest box appeared in my mental view.

In the Gutter

Help your offender Ruslan "Fatso" Rimsky to find permanent employment

Rewards:

XP: 200 pt.

Reputation with Ruslan "Fatso" Rimsky, unemployed: 50 pt.

Current Reputation: Indifference 0/30

Why did I receive more XP for him than for the identical quest issued by Alik? Should I open my own recruitment agency, maybe? That was something worth considering.

I clicked *Accept.*

Now what could I do for him? I could check all the plumbing vacancies in town, I suppose. I could collect KIDD points on all potential employers and run them through a quick search to see which one was more likely to hire him. That couldn't be too difficult.

"Come to see me tomorrow evening, okay?" I said. "I'll see what I can do. I'm in number 204."

He threw himself on me and gave me a big hug, pressing me to his soft, ample bosom. "Thank you so much, sir!"

"Nothing to thank me for yet," I wormed out of

---

[24] *Here's a tooth*: an old Russian criminal oath meaning "you can take my tooth out if I lie".

his embrace. "See you tomorrow. And please go easy on the booze. If they give you the boot, I won't help you again."

"Not a drop!" he flicked his front tooth[25].

Well, well. Famous last words. Never mind. The main thing was, I could and would help him. The rest was none of my business.

As I rode the cab, I tried to work out what was happening to me. Why did I respond so eagerly to any pleas for help these days? Was it about closing quests and earning more XP points? Or did I really want to help all those people who kept crawling out of the woodwork?

I didn't know what to say to that. What I did know was that I probably wouldn't have bothered to help the likes of Fatso or Alik in my old pre-interface days. Or even Marina, for that matter, despite all her cuteness, as long as I viewed her as my job competition.

Did that mean that this funny gaming system was gradually changing my very philosophy? Or was it simply my knee-jerk gaming habit of accepting each and every quest that came my way?

As the cab pulled up by Vicky's apartment block, I realized what a patent idiot I was. I'd arrived for our date empty-handed, without as little as a bunch of flowers.

I was about to make a dash for the nearest flower shop when she walked out of the front door and beamed on seeing me.

---

[25] Flicking a front tooth is a Russian gesture used by seasoned jailbirds instead of saying, "Here's a tooth!"

Too late. I walked toward her.

"Hi," I gave her a peck on the cheek.

She did the same. "Hi Phil."

"Please forgive me. I was in such a hurry I completely forgot to get you some flowers."

"Good!" she laughed. "Imagine how I'd have looked with them. Also, my hands would have been full."

I took a closer look at her. She was pretty in a very wholesome way. She was wearing a pair of jeans and a plain white T-shirt. No makeup. The faint shampoo scent on her long hair was the only sign she'd actually made an effort.

I needed to stop comparing her to Yanna. That wasn't going to take me anywhere.

"Are we off, then?" she said, pointing at the cab.

I nodded. She climbed in first, I followed.

We rode in silence. I loathed wasting time on small talk but didn't want to discuss any serious issues in front of the driver. Whatever happened between us had to stay between us. I was happy enough that she'd reached for my hand and clenched it hard. By the end of the ride, her hand was wet.

As we rode the mall escalator, we turned to each other and asked in unison,

"What would you like to watch?"

We both laughed.

"How about Warcraft?" I offered. "I used to play the game for a long time and couldn't wait for the movie to come out.."

I began telling her why I missed the film's release

---

when she interrupted me,

"Phil, please. I don't care what we watch. It's been ages since I went to the movies. And by the way, I used to play it too. Not the one you're telling me about but the one where you had to build houses and armies."

"You don't mean it! That's it, then! Let's go see Warcraft!"

We were lucky to buy the last two good seats, at the center of the fifth row. The only other available seats were those on the very edge and those in the front row. They weren't the best choice for either watching a movie nor having a romantic date.

We still had a couple of minutes left so we went to the bar and bought ourselves some coke and a large popcorn to share.

I might have to jog it off tomorrow. I had a funny feeling that my Agility would improve with some weight loss.

By the time we entered the theater, the lights were already dimmed. I walked to our seats feeling like an icebreaker, trying not to push anyone and stay on my feet without spilling any of the popcorn or coke. Vicky followed in my wake.

We'd very nearly made it to our seats when the film's credits started, white on a black background. The theater plunged into darkness. I was forced to stop. When finally the credits had finished and the bright beginning of the movie illuminated the theater, I saw that our seats had been taken by some guys drinking beer.

"Excuse me," I said. "I'm afraid you've got the wrong seats."

"Piss off," one of them said without looking at me. "I'm watching the movie. Plenty of empty seats around. Just go and sit there."

And who might you be? Aha. *Yuri Shamanov, age: 23, a system administrator.* According to his stats, his Mood was high and so was his Interest in me.

And what was that status bar over there?

"Excuse me," Vicky piped up. "These are our seats!"

People in the back rows began to hush indignantly. As we'd stopped in front of somebody else's seats, those people weren't too happy with the situation, either.

I turned to the screen and immediately recognized the most epic of the game's locations familiar to everyone who'd ever played it, the one with the giant orc battling the human.

"There has been a war between orcs and humans for as long as can be remembered," Durotan's voice said off screen.

I focused back on Yuri. The new status bar was in fact Fear. He seemed to be afraid of me.

I focused on his buddy. That one seemed to be frightened even more. They were obviously scared they'd have to vacate the seats.

All this had happened almost instantly. I heard the Yuri guy talking tipsily back at Vicky, saying something undoubtedly rude and insulting.

I activated all of my 15 Charisma points

(including the 2 pt. clothes bonus).

"Listen, you idiot," I forced myself in front of his seat, blocking the screen view. I was seething with righteous anger, for two reasons. Firstly, I had a lady to protect. And secondly, because I was missing the opening of the movie I'd been so looking forward to seeing. "Vacate our seats *now*! You too!"

No idea whether it was my tone, my words or my glare, but both of them rose silently and headed sheepishly for their own seats at the end of the row.

We took our places.

For the first time in my life, I saw the orc who'd given his name to the Horde's new home...

I liked the film a lot, mainly because I was still nostalgic. I missed Azeroth...

"Good film," Vicky said, as if answering my unasked question.

"Thank you so much," I said whole-heartedly.

"What's that for now?"

"For liking the film I liked too."

Then I remembered our dinner agreement. "Are you hungry? Or are you one of those girls who never eat after 6 p.m.?"

She laughed, then joyfully pulled up her T-shirt, revealing a very flat stomach. "You really think I need to lose some weight?"

"How about we grab something to eat, then?"

"Me wants food. Me hungry," she hooked her arm through mine. Together we headed toward one of the non-fast-food places.

Task Status: Take Vicky to the movies
Task completed!
XP received: 10 pt.
+1% to Satisfaction

Funny that the system had listed this as a task to begin with. Not that I minded, though. Or was it supposed to be some socially meaningful action?

Once in the restaurant, Vicky quickly leafed through the menu, then ordered a Greek salad, a medium rare steak and half a lager. I ordered the same minus the salad.

They brought our beers straight away. I took a large gulp. "Have you been working at Ultrapak for long?"

"Three years," Vicky took a sip of her own. "I started as office manager. Than they transferred me to HR. I had to learn lots of new things, of course, but I like it."

"Isn't it funny I know you longer than I've been with the company?" for some reason, I found the idea quite arousing.

"It is indeed."

"Aren't you sorry you hired me?"

"I liked you already during the interviews," she said pensively. "I tried to convince Pavel you were a good catch. But judging by how he treated you the first day, I hadn't been very successful. I'm so happy you made it."

I smiled. "Why, because I showed myself as a competent sales professional with a good gut feeling?"

"Also," she raised her glass. "To you!"

"To you too," I said.

We clinked our glasses and sipped our drinks.

Afterward, she told me a bit about herself. She'd married early; after she'd divorced, she'd had to juggle two full-time jobs to provide for her little daughter and pay for childcare. What I liked about her, her story was devoid of any drama. Like, she'd done what she'd had to do.

Her earnestness demanded a reciprocal gesture. So I told her about myself, not even trying to gloss over certain things. About most of my life spent playing computer games. About sponging off my wife which was the exact reason why we'd split up. About Yanna's lack of faith in my literary talent.

I also said that I still wasn't a hundred percent sure what I felt for my ex-wife these days. My love for her still seemed to be smoldering.

Vicky fell silent, staring at her empty glass and apparently trying to digest my confession. Both our glasses were empty. I made a sign to the waiter to refill them.

"Vicky? Are you all right?" I asked.

I was pretty sure she was. According to her stats, her Mood was still great and her Interest in me quite high. Still, I wasn't comfortable. For some reason, her opinion meant a lot to me.

"Can I be honest with you?" she said.

"Absolutely."

"I'm just afraid you might get back together again. But it's not gonna happen tonight, is it?" she said with a sly smile. "So tell me, orc slayer, will it be your place or mine?"

* * *

VICKY FELL ASLEEP AROUND 3 A.M., HER BODY WRAPPED around mine. Tonight we hadn't been in a hurry. We'd taken our time making love. Our bodies seemed to have realized that they were free to do this any time we wanted. Why should we rush and exhaust ourselves? It was entirely up to us what to do with our lives and our bodies.

I studied Vicky's face in the moonlight. I hadn't been so fond of anyone for a long time. Gingerly I retrieved my arm from behind her head and went to the kitchen to get a drink of water.

Then I remembered. I'd wanted to activate Optimization, hadn't I? This would be as good a moment as any. I didn't have my whole life to do it. My license would expire in a year.

I returned to the bedroom, lay in bed next to Vicky and activated the interface.

New unblocked skill available: Optimization I.
Allows you to select primary and secondary skills.

The development of primary skills will take 50% less time than average. The development of secondary skills will take 50% longer than average.

Allows you to convert secondary skill points to

primary ones at a 2 to 1 ratio, with the consequent deletion of the secondary skill.
Cooldown: 3 days

Warning! In order to activate the skill, an undisturbed 12-hour period of sleep is required. Please ensure your location is safe. You are recommended to adopt a prone position.
Skill points available: 1

Accept/Decline

I clicked *Accept.*

Warning! In order to reorganize your brain's neural networks, you will now be suspended in a deep sleep. Please ensure-

I fell asleep before I could finish reading the message.

THE NEXT MOMENT, I opened my eyes.
I was wide awake.
Behind the closed curtains, the sun stood high in the sky. Boris the cat was treading unhappily all over me. Richie was licking my hand.
I was alone in bed. Vicky was nowhere to be seen or heard.
My head was perfectly clear. I was at home. Vicky was already gone. It was Sunday afternoon. I'd activated Optimization.

Which was exactly what my interface was trying to tell me,

You've activated a new skill: Optimization I.
Primary skill points available: 1
Secondary skill points available: 1
In order to receive more primary and secondary skill points, you need to level up the skill.

Would you like to select a primary skill?

Yes, I would. *Learning Skills*, definitely.

The moment I thought so, I received a new system message.

Thank you! You've just selected Learning Skills as your primary skill. From now on, it will be listed at the top of your available skill list.
The development of your chosen primary skill will take 50% less time than average.

Please select a secondary skill.

I concentrated, focusing on *Playing World of Warcraft*.

The system accepted my choice without even asking me to confirm it.

Thank you! You've just chosen Playing World of Warcraft as a secondary skill associated with your current primary skill. From now on, it will be listed at the bottom of your available skill list.

The development of secondary skill will take 50% longer than average.

Would you like to convert the 8 pt. of your secondary skill (Playing World of Warcraft) into 4 pt. of the primary skill associated with it (Learning Skills)?

Yes / No

I felt slightly jittery like a poker player who'd just risked all his chips in an all-or-nothing at the final table. Even though he might know he's got a strong hand, he's still nervous about the potential outcome. What if I woke up a complete vegetable? Messing with your brain wasn't a healthy idea, as any stroke survivor would tell you.

Still, I clicked *Yes.*

The system offered another warning,

The optimization of your chosen skill requires time. It will take 30 days to reorganize your brain's neural networks. The reorganization process will be performed during your deep sleep phases during that period.

Warning! Your secondary skill will be deleted without recovery option.

Your memories of all the events associated with

the development of the deleted skill will be preserved.
Accept / Decline

I "clicked" *Accept.*

All the system windows closed, leaving only the skill tab. The *Playing World of Warcraft* skill turned gray and inactive. The *Learning Skills* was now highlighted blue. When I focused on it, a message appeared,

Primary skill
+50% to development rate
Pending optimization

Excellent. I'd just activated the biggest cheat in my freakin' life, and it had only taken me three minutes.

I felt a powerful urge to make a dash to the shop and get some cigarettes. I could use a couple. Instead, I got up and walked into the bathroom.

A note lay on the floor by the bed,

Hi, Orc Slayer. You slept so well I didn't want to wake you up. Thank you for being so gentle and for the wonderful evening overall. Give me a call when you wake up.
Yours, Vicky

My Vicky! I absolutely had to call her. I just couldn't help myself.

She sounded happy to hear me.

"Hi Vick. I've only just woken up, can you imagine?"

"Thanks for calling me," she breathed a sigh of relief. "I was getting worried. You must have had a hard week."

"You could say that! Thanks for not waking me up. And thank *you* for the wonderful evening. See you tomorrow?"

"Sure," she paused, "my love."

She hung up before I could reply. For a while I sat there grinning like an idiot until I very nearly received a Lovey Dovey debuff. Then I rose and headed for the shower.

Later, as I was making my very belated breakfast, I remembered Fatso's quest and the missing children task. Dammit! Half the day was already gone. I had very little time left to do everything I'd planned.

A guilty Richie cowered in the corner. He'd done his business — a very big one — on the open balcony, unable to hold it for much longer.

I rushed around the apartment like a headless chicken, cooking and then eating my breakfast on the run, feeding the pets, starting the laundry, cleaning the balcony mess, getting dressed for my jogging practice, studying the available plumber vacancies online, writing the companies' names down, marking their coordinates on the map, then establishing the missing children's locations. Five dead. One teenage girl still alive.

Fatso had promised to pop by in the evening. Which was only a couple of hours away. I grabbed the

Major's business card and ran out.

I ran through the park and jogged a few more blocks to the nearest bus stop. There I took a bus to the city's western suburbs.

The bus was near empty. As I rode, I studied the plumbing vacancies, collecting the KIDD of all potential employers. My Spirit was below 50% already. I just hoped it would be enough to land Fatso a job.

At the terminal, I got off the bus and headed for the nearest shop where I bought a small bottle of vodka and some paper napkins.

Then I used the location map to detect the nearest computer club and headed over there.

The club's room was packed — mainly with children and teenagers. The place reeked of stale sweat. Heavy-duty cussing hung in the air, which sounded admittedly funny when uttered by those thin puerile voices.

"I'm so *** salty!"

"GG!"

"Nice panic pick, man!"

"You piece of ***!" shouted Victor Snezhinsky, social status: fifth-grade student.

His mastery of obscene lingo was amazing. The kid was only eleven years old and he already had level 4 in Swearing Skills! The guy was an expert!

The club looked so shabby I doubted they had video surveillance there.

I went over to the desk and bought some computer time. They sent me to a computer at the far end of the room. Its keyboard was falling apart, the mouse sticky and unpleasant to touch. Still, I didn't mind. On the contrary.

I went to a proxy site and used it to register a temporary email account which would be deleted within ten minutes.

I used the address to send a letter to the Major's email. No greeting, no signature, just the list of the children's names and their respective locations.

I pressed "Send" and breathed a sigh of relief.

Done. The task was closed:

Task Status: send Major Igorevsky an anonymous message reporting the whereabouts of the missing children

Task completed!

XP received: 500 pt.

+10% to Satisfaction

They were generous with the XP this time, weren't they? I had very little left to make the next level. My Satisfaction was close to 100% — but no Happiness yet.

XP points left until the next social status level: 4220/8000

I struggled with the desire to start WoW just to see if I'd indeed lost my skill. Then I easily remembered the tactics I'd used against Archimonde, the last boss of Hellfire Citadel. Of course. The Optimization process hadn't begun yet. It would only start next time I went to bed.

I opened the vodka, poured some on a paper napkin and wiped the keyboard and the mouse clean from any fingerprints. I even wiped the mouse pad, the desk itself and, in an enthusiastic bout of cleanliness, the filthy computer screen.

Time to go back home. I didn't want to make Fatso wait on my doorstep. He must have done enough waiting in big guys' offices.

I flagged a cab. As I rode, I did an advanced search on all of the companies which had a plumber's vacancy. Much to my surprise, when I entered *"90% probability of hiring Ruslan Rimsky"*, there were only two marks left on the map. By the time I'd copied their names and contact numbers into my phone, the cab had arrived.

Halfway to my front door I remembered I'd meant to call Yanna and ask her if our Tuesday divorce appointment was still valid. I dialed her number. I waited for a long time but she didn't pick up, so I hung up.

She'd broken her phone, hadn't she? Still, the call seemed to have gone through. There'd been no "temporarily unavailable" message.

I checked the map just to see where she was. Yanna's location was marked in one of those new elite residential suburbs where the likes of me would never be admitted.

Never mind. If she didn't reply, I'd text her later.

Fatso was already hovering by the front door. "Hi, man. I thought I'd come earlier. Is that okay?"

"You did the right thing," I said. "Have you got a pen? Never mind, just mark it down in your phone."

I dictated to him the two companies' names and addresses.

"Should I tell them you sent me?" he repeated Alik's question almost verbatim.

"Just tell them you came by yourself," I too repeated myself. "Good luck!"

He shook my hand, showering me with ramblings of gratitude.

"Don't thank me yet! Go and get the job first," I forced my hand out of his shovel-like mitt, gave him a slap on the shoulder and hurried home.

The laundry had already been done. I hung it out to dry, trying to think of the things I still had to do. It looked like I'd done everything I'd planned, and I still had some time left before bedtime.

Then it dawned on me. I gave Kira a ring, then called my parents. I told Dad about the missing girl.

The news of her discovery made him ecstatic. "Well done!" he repeated several times.

Afterward, I took a leisurely walk with Richie, enjoying the fresh night air.

Once back home, I had dinner and started the next book on my list. About ten p.m. I climbed into bed and continued reading. I had to get up early in the morning in order to iron the laundry and pop into the gym for a bit of a workout. And then there was Richie, dammit! I just wished Sveta would return soon. I was pretty fed up with having to walk that dinosaur amongst canines.

Later that night, I was awoken by a phone call. This was quickly becoming a habit.

Yanna? That's right. That was her picture grinning at me from the phone screen. "Yanna? Good night to you too!"

"This isn't Yanna, you scumbag! It's Vladimir!"

"Who? Vladimir? Very well. What do you want, *Vladimir*? And who the hell are you?"

"I'm her boyfriend. What the hell do you keep calling her for?"

"Eh?" I asked, trying to put my sleepy brain in gear. What did he want from me?

"Give me your address, you useless moron! We need to talk. Man to man."

Then I finally remembered. This must have been the Vlad, Yanna's latest acquisition.

Chapter

Twenty-Two

Simple Feelings

"You stink of sin."

Harold Pinter, *The Birthday Party*

BACK WHEN WE'D FIRST MET, YANNA AND I HAD GOTTEN on like a house on fire. A pattern had started to form: we'd spend nights going on extended raids from the relative comfort of my place where she would then crash later in the morning.

After a couple of weeks it had become pretty clear we were living together. In the mornings, both of us would leave: she to work, me to college. In the evenings we'd grab a bit of sleep, then keep burning the midnight oil.

The only thing left for us to do was move her stuff to my place and legalize our relationship just to keep our parents off our case.

That was when her exes had started calling, as well as new aspiring suitors. At first she'd pick up the phone and patiently explain that she was now happily married to another. After a while, she stopped taking the phone. And some time after that, she asked me to answer their calls.

"They just won't listen, will they?" she complained. "Can't you speak to them? Like man to man? Just to make it clear? I'm so sick and tired of them all!"

So I started taking their calls. Not many of those guys were sober, either. They'd just demand to speak to Yanna. Some disappeared off the radars as soon as they found out they were talking to her husband. Others kept a respectable distance for a while, patiently awaiting a new chance. A marriage isn't set in stone, you know.

But even my existence had failed to discourage some of the more persistent alpha males. They demanded to know my address in order to, as Vlad had just so eloquently put it, "talk man to man".

Yanna had always been popular in all kinds of social circles, from old college friends to accidental encounters with spoiled rich brats.

Now, however, the tables had turned. In Vlad's eyes, he was now the boyfriend trying to get rid of an overeager admirer.

The situation was ridiculous. I needed some

sleep. I hadn't slept well for several nights in a row now.

"Listen, Vlad. How about you get lost? I'm trying to get some sleep. Call back in the morning and I'll give you the address."

Funny he had to ask. He'd come here to collect Yanna's stuff, hadn't he?

"What did you say?" he slurred, drunk as a skunk. "Who do you think you are? Where are you now? I want the address!"

I began to seethe with righteous anger. The Nicotine Withdrawal debuff must have played its role in this too, as I seemed to be going into spontaneous Enrage. I needed my sleep, too. And now there was this moron, thinking he had the right to order me around!

I was about to give him the address, then meet him with a sword. A proper real-life sword, a replica Frostmourne[26] which I'd had made to order by a top craftsman for top bucks.

I opened my mouth to give him my address. Still, it didn't feel right. I'd do it differently this time.

"I'm in Leafy Hollow. Kulikova St 256," I offered a fictitious street number. "You can come if you think you're brave enough."

A new system message popped up.

Congratulations! You've received a new skill level!

Skill name: Intuition

Current level: 5

---

[26] Frostmourne: in World of Warcraft, the legendary runeblade owned by the Lich King.

XP received: 500

"Who's brave enough? Me?"

As I studied the message trying to work out how my last words could have affected the development of my "sixth feeling", Vlad went on and on, promising to inflict all sorts of problems on me, including lots of pain and suffering.

"You wait there, you scumbag! I'm on my way," he hung up.

But seriously, what did you want me to do? Judging by my upped Intuition, the mysterious game system seemed to be happy with me.

Or was I supposed to apologize to him saying I was only a husband who wanted to talk to his wife and ask how she was doing? Should I try to appease an idiot who hadn't even bothered to ask her who'd called? I don't think so! He could go and stuff himself. Also, I wasn't quite ready yet for any physical confrontation. I couldn't expect Alik to arrive conveniently on the scene every time I needed some assistance.

So if the guy didn't learn his lesson and kept calling me, I might just remind him of my real address. Let him come. We had a few things to discuss "man to man".

As soon as I'd made this decision, I received another message,

Congratulations! You've received a new skill level!
Skill name: Decision Making

Current level: 5
XP received: 500

What was this, Christmas? I had a mere 2,000 XP left till level 8, courtesy of Vlad and his uncontrollable bouts of jealousy. Thank you very much, man. Great job.

But still he'd ruined such a great dream for me. I'd been dreaming of having a family picnic in the countryside: my parents, Kira and little Cyril, Vicky, her daughter and myself. We'd just started a nice BBQ and then... and then that bastard had called.

I tossed and turned for another half-hour, unable to sleep. I kept thinking about Vlad, wondering if he'd already left.

Finally, I couldn't stand it any longer so I opened the map.

Oh no. He was sitting in some Irish pub. Yanna wasn't even with him.

I checked her location. She was still at her parents'. In which case, how could he have used her phone? Had they had an argument? Had he taken her SIM card just to spite her? Talk about soap drama.

Thus thinking, I finally fell asleep, perfectly dreamless this time.

My mental alarm clock awoke me at 4.50 a.m. The room was very cold. The sheets didn't keep me warm. A leaden sky hung low behind the window, spitting chilly rain. The balcony door was open.

My entire body ached. The sheer thought of having to climb out of bed and get ready for the gym,

---

then walk there under the cold rain, walk the dog, press my business suit and go to work, then spend all day pitching to clients... Why was I doing all this? Did I really need it?

Without opening my eyes, I curled up in my comfy little hole under the sheets and started thinking. The only reason I'd had to get up so early was because I had a job to go to. Had it not been for that, I could have had as much sleep as I wanted. I could go to the gym at some other time more convenient for me. How about Richie? Well, if he got really desperate while I was asleep, there was always the balcony. He was going in three days' time, anyway.

What else? Ah yes, money. I actually didn't need that much. My freelancing gigs earned me enough to pay the bills and buy groceries. And now that I had my interface, I really should try and search for some treasure — like a missing object of art, for instance. Or start a missing-persons bureau. Or become a bounty hunter. I could even open a recruitment agency offering a 100% employment guarantee.

If push came to shove, I could always level up my poker playing and start winning millions in online competitions. True, bad luck could thwart any amount of skill. But in the long run, my expertise would play its part, allowing me to raise my stakes a few hundred at a time, methodically increasing my bank roll while living within my means.

Any of the above scenarios would allow me to spend much more time leveling up. It especially concerned vital skills such as Insight. You never knew what it might offer me once I'd made the next level. I might be able to locate new mineral deposits or even detect sunken treasure ships. Or I might open a dating service guaranteed to find you the perfect partner. All these things made up part of the universal information field, provided you knew how to look for them.

Thus daydreaming, I'd lost a precious quarter of a hour that morning and very nearly gone back to sleep.

No matter how logical my musings might have seemed to me, the fact remained I was lying to myself. To add to this, I was breaking my commitments, thus lowering my social status. In other words, I'd relapsed back into my old habit of coming up with larger-than-life excuses in order to justify my own laziness.

By signing a work contract with Ultrapak, I'd given them a promise to turn up. They weren't just an abstract name for me, either. They were all real people: Vicky, Pavel, Mr. Ivanov, Greg, Cyril and Marina among all the others. I'd promised them to be part of their team: one of the many cogs in the mechanism which ensured its reliable function in society.

I'd promised to help Marina, too. I still needed to know what was happening to Cyril healthwise. I'd promised to take care of the dog: he was my responsibility.

Also, it would be nice to move to a better apartment. Nothing too extravagant: all I needed was a clean place, well furnished and well maintained, preferably in one of those new builds.

I know it might sound petty like some sort of

middle-class suburban dream. But then again, why not? What was wrong with wanting a pretty place with an Italian shower, a large-screen TV on the wall, a cool coffee maker and a clean elevator with all the buttons working? Was it too much to ask our alcoholic neighbors not to relieve themselves in the lobby or stop drinking in the playground in front of the children? Having said that, seeing them drinking behind the shabby rows of dilapidated communal garages behind the apartment block didn't please the eye, either.

Thus thinking, I suddenly realized I was standing in front of my bathroom mirror, violently brushing my teeth. I was really pissed with myself for having lost these precious minutes. By now, I could have already had my coffee and been on my way to the gym.

Yes, I was in a hurry. I threw my gym equipment into the bag and rushed out into the rain. I pulled the hood over my head, slung the bag over my shoulder and ran, leaping over the rain puddles.

It had already become a habit for me to review all the pending quests and past events. The Optimization process should have already started, too. I tried to remember my last WoW boss tactic just to check it.

A boss. Which boss? Dammit! I'd forgotten everything about my last instance raid. Did that mean the Optimization process had already started?

I tried to recall my WoW class and abilities. They seemed to be all right. I still remembered their names as well as all the buttons and rotation. Very well. It was early days yet.

Once I got to the gym's locker room, I changed into my workout clothes and jumped on the scales.

How much? I couldn't believe it! According to the scales, I'd lost over 4 lb. since my last gym session.

My coach wasn't there, replaced by a colleague: a stocky Caucasian highlander[27] called Arslan. He asked me a few questions about what I used to do earlier, then sent me to do the warmup.

The session was over before I knew it. I felt good. I managed to add some more weights to my presses: from 5 to 8 pounds, depending on the type. Alexander had been right: my shriveled muscles, shrunk from years of disuse, were now greedily absorbing all the exercise I could throw at them, jumping at their chance to grow and expand.

The System seemed to have noticed it too:

You've received +1 to Strength!
Current strength: 8
You've received 1000 pt. XP for successfully leveling up a main characteristic!

The above message had found me in front of the locker room mirror as I dried my hair. I just couldn't help it: I stood up and struck a Schwarzenegger-type pose, flexing my non-existent muscles.

A bodybuilder who happened to walk past chuckled good-naturedly. Sorry, man. I might look

---

[27] A Caucasian highlander: a native of one of the many republics located in the Caucasus mountains.

puny next to the real Arnold — but compared to how I'd been two weeks previously, I looked slightly better already. No wonder my jeans belt was falling off me.

My Agility training seemed to have garnered some results too. I'd gained 6% since my last practice. The fact that I was losing weight must have had something to do with that too.

From the gym, I hurried straight home. I had fifteen minutes to walk Richie and I had no desire to stay in the rain any longer than necessary.

As I walked, my phone rang. It was Yanna's number again.

"Yes?" I answered it cautiously, not knowing who I might be speaking to.

"It's me," Yanna's voice said. "Did you call Saturday night?"

"I did. Is our meeting on Tuesday still on?"

"I don't think so. We seem to be having a conference which would last through Tuesday and Wednesday. So it's probably Thursday or Friday. Is that all right with you?"

"I suppose so," I replied, slightly disappointed that this divorce thing seemed to be dragging on and on.

"Good. Talk to you later."

"Yanna, wait. You sure you're okay?"

"I'm flippin' fine! Why would you ask?"

"Well, probably because it was *you* who called me Saturday night."

"Ah. Don't worry about that. That's nothing. I was hanging out with the girls. We'd had a few drinks and I remembered how I used to trust you all those years. The faith I'd had in you. I spent the best years of my life supporting you. It just felt so unfair."

"I understand," I wheezed as I tried to walk fast.

"You okay? Why are you out of breath?"

"Fine. I'm walking home from the gym. I need to go to work now. Are you having an affair with that Vlad person?"

"That's none of your flippin' business. Did you say the gym?"

"Well, if it's none of my business, then he'd better stop calling me drunk in the middle of the night. He wanted to know why I'd called you. Does he know we're still married? Which is my second question."

She didn't reply. There was a long pause on the phone.

"Yanna?"

"Don't worry. He won't call you again. I've just sent him packing. Bye."

She'd sent him packing! She was simply teaching him a lesson. She'd keep her distance for a couple of days, ignoring his texts and phone calls, then she'd kindly deign to forgive him. Been there, done it.

I walked Richie, then left my apartment again, followed by his indignant barking. I could understand him. He was lonely. I'd read somewhere that dogs didn't have a sense of time. And if so, Richie must have been really suffering from those extended periods of solitude. The company of Boris didn't count, even though Richie seemed to consider her a member of his new pack with me as top dog, he as beta and Boris, as a miserable omega misfit.

"Courage, Private!" I crouched and patted his chops. "Only three days left, then you'll be back with your family! Behave yourselves, you two. Boris, that especially applies to you. Keep your claws away from that couch before it falls apart!"

Boris theatrically turned away and began grooming herself free from my ungrounded accusations.

I took a minibus to work. I could read the book as I rode. Reading non-fiction is quite different from reading fiction. With non-fiction, you can't just skim the pages, impatient to find out what happens next. I forced myself to take my time over each paragraph. Although it slowed down the reading process itself, it allowed me to absorb much more information, thus leveling up Intellect. The last book had brought me 300 XP points which was an excellent motivation to spend every spare moment reading.

It was actually amazing how everything seemed to fit together. The process of reading improved your Intellect while every finished book brought you more XP which added to your existing numbers, bringing you closer to your next level. And every level gained gave you a stat point you could then invest into any characteristic of your choice — like Strength, etc.

If you followed this logic, a 22nd-century bookworm should be a mountainous bodybuilder.

"Just look at that beefcake!" old babushkas[28] would gossip on a park bench. "What a wardrobe of a man! He must be an avid reader!"

I made it to work almost on time, just as all the others were entering Pavel's office for a briefing. I couldn't see Cyril anywhere. I took a seat next to Greg.

"Where's Cyril?" I whispered to him.

"He went to the clinic to take some tests this morning," Greg replied. "He's probably still there. I told Pavel about him."

"Thanks. How was your weekend?"

"It was okay. I do miss Alina though," he admitted. "I tried to make up with her-" he promptly fell silent, realizing something was wrong.

Silence hung in the air. Dennis — Marina's ex-mentor — chuckled.

"Mind if I continue?" Pavel asked. "Or are you having your own briefing? Phil? Don't you think it's a bit too early to start ignoring discipline and subordination?"

"He's our new prima donna," Dennis added his two cents.

"No, I'm not," I replied. "I was asking about Cyril who seems to be seriously ill. I'm very sorry. It won't happen again."

"How mature," Pavel commented, then went on with the briefing.

An hour later, we set off to do our rounds. Marina had some good news. She'd been contacted by

---

[28] Babushka (Russian) — literally, "Grandma". Here, an old lady.

one of the companies we'd visited last Friday and offered an appointment. They seemed to be interested.

We decided to go directly there.

As I was about to leave the building, Daria the receptionist stopped me and told me to see the bookkeepers'. Did they want to pay me my bonus already?

They did indeed. A portly payroll accountant handed me a fat envelope containing twenty-five thousand rubles. No signature required.

I'd already forgotten the last time I'd been paid in cash. For the last year and a half, my freelance assignments had been my sole source of income, paid electronically or via bank transfers.

"Spoiled rotten," she grumbled in response to my thank-you. "You've only been working here for what, a few days? Are you Ivanov's relative or something?"

"Exactly," I replied, peering at the stats that hovered over her head. "I'm his tenth cousin fifteen times removed."

I was dying to play a prank on her but promptly reconsidered. Making fun of payroll accountants is never a healthy idea. "Are you related to him too?"

"I wish!" the equally portly chief bookkeeper grumbled without raising her eyes from the paperwork in front of her. "Then we might be able to finally pay all the wages on time."

"Enough of your nonsense!" the payroll lady waved me away. "First cousin to the devil, you are."

As Marina and I walked across the lobby, we

stumbled right into Cyril. Waving his hands in excitement, he began telling us all about his visit to the clinic.

"Phil, I owe you big time, man! You saved my life, you know that?"

"Why, did they find something?"

"Something! They say it's emphysema! One of the deadliest things around if it goes untreated! The things they did to me! They spun me around, kneaded me, listened to my insides and made me blow into a tube. Then they sent me for an X-ray which showed it up as clear as daylight. Another six months, and I might not have come out of this alive! Surgery isn't always successful, they said. They've prescribed me a whole bagful of stuff: pills, injections, the works. I've got to quit smoking, I'm afraid. The whole thing has cost me a fortune. But at least I'll live."

"Congratulations!" Marina and I repeated, sincerely happy for him.

"This had been the worst weekend of my life," he continued. "I was beside myself with worry. But at least now I can finally breathe. I'm gonna quit smoking and lose some weight. And I'm gonna take all their medications! I was just about to smoke my last cigarette. You wanna keep me company?"

"I'm afraid we have an appointment," I said. "We're already late as it is. Actually..." an idea started to form in my head. I really needed to become friends with these guys. And now I knew how to do it.

"I've just received my bonus," I said. "How about we go somewhere tonight and celebrate?"

"Count me in," Marina said.

Cyril grinned. "Me too. And Greg, if you don't mind. Both of us could use a proper meal. You can't survive on microwaved pizzas for much longer, if you know what I mean. Who else are you gonna ask?"

Vicky, definitely, but could I do it without drawing unnecessary attention to our relationship? Or should I leave her out? I really needed to discuss it with her. The decision had to be mutual.

"I really don't know," I said. "I can't afford to invite the entire department. My bonus just won't stretch that far. You guys are the only people I actually talk to."

"That's even better," Cyril nodded his approval. "Much more fun without that crowd. Ah! I nearly forgot to mention Lola's sending her respects. Your doctor, remember? She asked when you're gonna come to see her."

Marina's eyes narrowed into slits.

"Never, I hope," I said, trying to turn this into a joke. "So you've got my permission to chance your arm."

"I might," he said. "She's a fine woman. Intelligent and beautiful, and a doctor!"

"Come on, Phil," Marina interrupted us. "We've got an appointment to make. They must be waiting for us already."

"Good luck," Cyril replied. "You two coming back for lunch?"

"Maybe. There's one more thing I meant to tell you. About this last cigarette thing... please don't. It's better this way. You've quit already. You've got a life to live."

Cyril shrugged. He reached into his pocket and produced a lighter and a half-finished pack of cigarettes. He fumbled with them for a while, then crumpled the pack in his hand and lobbed both into a nearby trash can.

"That's right!" I said.

I was happy for him. The game system, however, seemed to be happy for me.

You've received 500 pt. XP for performing a socially meaningful action!

XP points left until the next social status level: 6720/8000

The game seemed to be training me like a dog. Whenever I did something good or took care of other people, I received a reward. Still, much to my surprise, the rise in my XP had left me completely unenthusiastic.

We didn't make it back in time for lunch. Right after our first appointment with a packaged foods factory director (which made pizzas among other things — with compliments to those two, Greg and Cyril), we had to email all the information to their lawyers who were drawing up the contract. Then we moved to the next interested client on our list. This time it was a pastry shop.

Marina got the first contract. In my opinion, that was only fair. After all, she'd been the one who'd pitched them. No idea how the "universal information field" was going to process this result — but I'd received a new system message even before we'd signed the contract,

Quest alert: Help a Struggling Student. Quest completed!
You've successfully helped your fellow trainee Marina Tischenko to close a sales deal for packaging products produced by Ultrapak, Ltd.
XP received: 900
+10% to Satisfaction

Your Reputation with Marina Tischenko has improved!
Current Reputation: Amicability 25/60

Soon after midday, I closed my first deal as an Ultrapak staff worker. The pastry shop owner — a stout lady with a sharp glare and a garish manicure — had immediately begun pressurizing me for more discounts, insisting they pay after delivery. Still, all her attempts had failed miserably in the face of my 15 pt. Charisma. By the end of our meeting, the pastry lady had thawed out to the point of giving me a hug, pressing my face to the expanse of her generous bosom.

I couldn't help smiling thinking about it. This place would have been Fatso's dream job. Marina too kept laughing on our way back, remembering the scene.

In fact, Marina's behavior worried me a little.

She was definitely flirting with me. She'd thread her arm through mine as we walked, and whenever we rode a cab, her thigh would "accidentally' brush against mine.

I won't lie to you: her advances flattered me. Still, I had no intention of capitalizing on them in any way.

She definitely felt at ease around me. She treated me like a peer and old friend. By lunchtime, we'd found ourselves in the opposite part of town, so we popped into a café and ordered the menu of the day. And — this was quickly turning into a pattern — as soon as I finished my meal, I received a new social status level message.

Alik's quest message had popped up first,

Quest alert: Help Alik Find a Job. Quest completed!
You've successfully helped your neighbor Romuald "Alik" Zhukov to find regular employment.
XP received: 400
+5% to Satisfaction

Your Reputation with Romuald "Alik" Zhukov has improved!
Current Reputation: Amicability 55/60

This jump in Satisfaction resulted in a level 1 Happiness buff. Add to this my ecstatic joy at having received a new level. The combination culminated in a spasm of pleasure so powerful that I doubled up, unable to stand on my rubbery legs.

Congratulations! You've received a new level!
Your current social status level: 8
Characteristic points available: 1
Skill points available: 1

My body careened out of control. Trying to keep my balance, I grabbed at the tablecloth and pulled it to the floor with me. There was nothing I could do. My vision darkened. I was literally exploding with ecstasy. To the casual observer it must have looked like an epileptic fit.

The bout of pleasure lasted longer this time. I felt like that idiot from the old joke: "Who are all these people?"

When I finally came round, Marina's anxious face hovered over me. "Phil? Are you okay? Someone, call an ambulance!" she kept shouting at the top of her voice.

"I don't need an ambulance," I said, scrambling back to my feet. "I'm fine."

I told her the truth. I felt better than ever before.

"Are you okay?" a woman asked me — apparently, the café manager.

"I'm fine, thank you. I'm sorry about the mess. Please add all the broken plates to the bill."

"Don't worry about that," she said. "Just take it easy. You sure you don't want to see the doctor?"

"I might," I said. "Thanks."

I paid the bill and added a generous tip. Holding

Marina's hand, I walked out of the café.

Once outside, she lit up a cigarette. Her hands were shaking. "Phil, I think you do need to see the doctor."

"I'm okay. Don't worry," I racked my brain for a believable explanation. If I had to lie to her, so be it. "I have a very rare brain condition. It's not life-threatening. But it does give me occasional fits like that one. Now you understand, don't you, why I can't drive?"

She shuddered as if imagining me behind the wheel. "Of course."

By the end of the workday we'd finally made it back to the office from where we sent the duly signed supply agreements to our new partners. Greg and Cyril hadn't arrived yet. As we waited for them, I told Marina to start cold-calling other potential clients from our list.

"Don't drag it out," I said. "Just tell them you're an Ultrapak representative offering them packaging materials at 30% less than they currently buy."

"Yes, sir!" she saluted before reaching for the phone.

I listened to her pitch, using the pauses between calls to offer some advice and corrections and congratulate her on her work.

That was how Dennis found us.

"I can see you're comfortable here," he said, addressing me. "Isn't it a bit too early setting your backside down in the boss' chair?"

"I'm very comfortable, thank you," I replied. "No, I'm not setting my backside in anything. You happy with my answers?"

"Maybe," he cracked a sarcastic smile, baring his teeth and even gums. I had a very bad feeling about his smile. "That's not what I heard."

"Phil, leave it," Marina said. "He's not worth it. The guy is a total nincompoop."

"That's a big word coming from such a tiny girl," Dennis announced out loud, attracting the others' attention.

"Leave her alone," I said. "I don't give a damn what you heard. Just piss off, will you?"

"In a moment," he said with the same nasty smile.

Judging by the silence, the entire department had stopped whatever they'd been doing and were now watching us.

"Just one last question," Dennis continued. "Has this slut already put out for you?"

"So what if I have?" Marina announced, wiping the smug smile off his face. "Are you jealous or something?"

Dennis turned pale. "Did you hear that?" he spat out, turning to all the others. "I'm gonna write a report about these two and their professional misconduct! You're all my witnesses!"

I jumped to my feet, fully intending to punch his lights out. My Self-Control still needed a lot of work.

"Phil, don't!" Vicky's voice sliced through the silence.

Seething, I swung round, searching for her in the room. A new system message dropped into my field of vision, blocking the view.

Your Reputation with Victoria "Vicky" Koval has decreased!
Current Reputation: Dislike 15/30

"What's going on in here?" Pavel's voice demanded.

I heard some disjointed explanations of what had just happened.

"Right," Pavel said. "You three, into my office. *Now.*"

By the time I'd finally closed the system message, Vicky was already gone.

CHAPTER TWENTY-THREE

THE GAME STARTS FOR REAL

"Come on, be honest with yourself. At some point in our lives we all wanna be a superhero."

Dave Lizewski, *Kickass*

ALTHOUGH ONLY ONE YEAR MY JUNIOR, PAVEL WASN'T Ultrapak's commercial director for nothing. His social status level was already 18 compared to my 8, with Charisma to match. Which probably explained why it hadn't taken him very long to get to the bottom of this ridiculous conflict.

"Very well," he said. "Let's start with Den as he's been with us for quite a while. Could you please give us your rendition of what's just happened?"

This may have been a polite request but to us it sounded like an order.

Pavel shut his computer down to make sure we couldn't see what he'd been working on. He leaned back in his chair and laid his feet in his perfectly polished shoes onto his huge lacquered hardwood desk.

The desk gave you some idea of Pavel's pedantic nature. Everything on it was in perfect order. All the papers were divided into several neat stacks — apparently, depending on their importance and priority. An expensive colorful globe was studded with little red flags which must have marked the places he'd already visited. I doubted they were business trips. Somehow I didn't think that Ultrapak had business connections with Argentina or New Zealand.

"Ahem," Dennis took his time clearing his throat. "Allow me to start from the beginning. We recruited Marina as a trainee sales rep-"

"Keep it short," Pavel interrupted him. "What was going on in there and what exactly are you accusing them of?"

Dennis' Fear levels soared. You didn't even need to read his stats to know that because his ears had turned a fiery red.

"I just want to inform you about their professional misconduct," his voice broke into a squeak.

"And what exactly are you accusing them of?" Pavel enunciated.

"Of sexual misconduct! Which can't be tolerated! We all signed the rules. It's written here in black and white. And these two did it."

Marina began laughing uncontrollably. "Sexual misconduct can't be tolerated! That's a bit rich coming from you, isn't it? What a hypocrite! Just think that-"

"Quiet!" Pavel exploded.

"Sorry," Marina covered her mouth with her hand. "It's only that this was the reason I asked to work with Phil in the first place. Because this sicko was after me like a dog on heat, threatening to fail me during my trial period if I refused!"

"Please mind you language," Pavel said. "You're not on campus."

"Sorry," she repeated. "It's just that his so-called accusations are so ridiculous that-"

"Thank you. Mr. Panfilov?" Pavel squinted at me.

I could see by his low Interest numbers that he'd already come to a decision. Still, he was obliged to listen to all the guilty parties.

"We were busy all day visiting new clients," I said. "As soon as we returned to the office, we started making more calls. I was supervising Marina's cold calling when Dennis came over to us and demanded to know if there was anything between us. I'll repeat once again, for his sake, that there was absolutely nothing going on. There couldn't have been. Not because of the company rules but for other reasons I'd rather not disclose."

As I spoke, I glimpsed Marina's plummeted Mood. Did she really like me? Not good. Very bad timing.

"Thank you," Pavel replied calmly. "You two can go. Dennis and I will have a few words. You sure you're all right, Den? You look a bit pale."

"No, thanks. I'm fine," he croaked, shaking his head.

As Marina and I filed toward the door, Pavel called to us again,

"And congratulations on your first sales!"

"Thank you, sir," we replied in unison. Then we returned to our places, smiling uncontrollably.

A new system message reported the drop in my Reputation with Dennis. Which was logical, really. What did come as an unpleasant surprise was the respective drop in my XP.

So that's how it worked, then. My stats could plummet just as easily as they could soar. In itself, that was neither good nor bad. Forewarned is forearmed, as they say. It stood to reason that an athlete who stopped training and gained so much weight that he could only see his balls in the mirror would experience a drop in both his Stamina and Agility. I too had a funny feeling that engaging in antisocial behavior might result in me losing my hard-earned social status levels. I really didn't feel like putting this theory to the test.

Greg walked over to me. "Phil?" he whispered. "Is it true what Cyril told me? He said you're celebrating your bonus tonight. I'm dying for a proper meal. I think

I could kill for a steak."

"You wait!" Cyril interrupted him, also in whisper, then turned to me. "You'd better tell us what happened. Why did Pavel want you two on the carpet? Is everything all right?"

"Everything's fine," Marina hurried to reply, casting me a cautioning look. "There's nothing to tell, really."

I shrugged. "They'll soon know, anyway. Thing is, Dennis was being a total jerk. First he kept picking on me and when that failed, he accused us of having an affair. Before you ask anything, no, we didn't. Not in a million years."

"You sure you didn't?" Greg asked anxiously.

"What's wrong with you, man?" Marina gave him a shove in the shoulder. "Are you really so stupid? Besides, you're married, aren't you? And just in case you forgot, your wife is pregnant. As in, p-r-e-g..."

"So what?" he asked, sincerely surprised. "Phil's married too. What's the problem?"

"It's all right, I'll tell you later," Cyril half-promised, half-threatened him.

"Never mind," I said. "Just clock off and get your asses over to Jared's. You know where it is, don't you? You can take a table and order some chow. I still have something to do here. Okay?"

"Sounds good," Cyril replied for all the others. "Let's move it!"

Marina cast me a quizzical look.

"That's all right," I told her. "You can go too. This isn't about work. Just a private matter I need to sort out."

She nodded. The other two grabbed her under both arms and steered her to the exit.

"Oh, sorry," she suddenly said. "I think I left the computer on. You go, I won't be a moment."

"That's all right," Greg said. "We can wait for you here. How long can it take?"

"Just go! Wait for me outside, I won't be long! Have a smoke or something... oh sorry, Cyril. I forgot you quit."

"Come on, Greg, let's go," Cyril said, nudging his trainee toward the elevators.

Marina lingered next to me, expectant.

"Let's go to the stairs over there," I told her. "We need to talk."

We walked out into the stairwell landing which reeked of stale tobacco smoke. The door clicked shut automatically behind us. In order to get back in, we'd have to use our magnetic pass cards to unlock it.

Nobody in the building ever used the stairwell as intended, even if they only had to go down to the next floor. We were alone.

Marina rummaged through her purse, producing two packs of cigarettes one after the other. She pulled out a slim menthol cigarette and lit up.

I waited for her to turn her attention to me, than began the speech I'd already prepared and rehearsed in my head. I tried to make it sound logical and not too offensive. "You're a very good girl, you know that?"

"Oh, do give it a break," she wheezed as she exhaled. She took another tug on her cigarette, fumbling with the top button on her blouse. "I'm not chasing you or anything. I'm a big girl, you know. I do like you, that's true. That's why I was a bit thrown when you said that there could be nothing between us. Am I really so ugly? Or is it the age difference?"

"Please. Don't put that on me. You know very well you're pretty. And as for our age difference, I actually feel, er, flattered by your attention. But firstly, I'm still married-"

"You're getting a divorce, right? That's what everybody says."

"No, we aren't. Not for the time being. We haven't even filed for divorce yet. That's one thing. And the other-" I faltered, unsure whether being sincere with her was a wise thing to do.

"And the other?" she flicked the ash off with a nervous finger. The cigarette broke in two.

"The thing is, I already have a girlfriend," I said, leaving out the details. "And I think I love her."

"You *think* you love her or you love her?" she insisted.

Neither of my arguments seemed to have convinced her. She probably thought I was overcomplicating things.

I lost my patience. "Marina, do you mind? You're not my shrink, are you?"

The wretched Nicotine Withdrawal kept giving me spontaneous Enrages. I just couldn't wait for the blasted thing to finally be over.

I struggled to calm down. "Honestly, I just don't know."

"Very well. Let's go back, then," she said, putting out her cigarette. "Actually, I have one more question. Do I know her?"

"You most definitely do. You can even come with me now and try to rectify the situation. She heard what you said to Dennis about us."

"Vicky!" she exclaimed. "Of course! I should've known! That's why you dropped me off first that night in the taxi! Because you two were going to... you were going to..." she dissolved in desperate, child-like sobbing, curving her mouth and wailing.

She *was* a child, really. I tried to suppress my desire to give her a hug but couldn't. I flung my arms around her, trying to soothe her.

She clung to my chest, sobbing. Her long chestnut hair tucked behind her ears emitted the flowery smell of some cheap shampoo. I stroked it, tensing up whenever I heard the sound of footsteps on the other side of the door, ready to shrink away from her at any moment. I wouldn't be surprised if Vicky walked through that door in true soap-opera fashion: this was a very possible turn of events, considering the whole office treated this landing as a smoking room.

Still, luck must have been on my side this time. On top of that, the mysterious game seemed to be pleased with me. Vicky hadn't surfaced; instead, I'd received a new system message,

You've received 100 pt. XP for performing a socially meaningful action!

XP points left until the next social status level:

It should have been 120 pt., actually. They'd removed 20 pt. for the drop in my Reputation with Dennis. Question was, what exactly did the system consider a socially meaningful action? Had I received it for trying to soothe Marina or for not trying to take advantage of her feelings for me?

Probably the latter.

"Why, what's wrong with Vicky? Is it because of what I said? You've just said so, haven't you?" she rummaged through her purse again and hurried to clean up the mascara streaks with a cotton disk. Without the makeup, she looked like a high school student. "Go get her. I'll wait for you here. I'm gonna explain everything to her. Whatcha starin' at? Go and get her. Don't worry, I'm not going to say anything you're gonna regret. Go!"

I nodded. I could tell she meant it. She really wanted to help.

As I walked back into the office, I bumped straight into Greg.

"Where are you two?" he demanded. "Where's Marina? We're fed up with waiting already!"

"Jesus, Greg. Didn't I tell you you should go on your own? I still have things to do here!"

"But where's Marina?"

"We'll come together later. Don't worry, you're not gonna miss her. Just go now, I have other things to do."

He blew a noisy breath. "My stomach thinks my

---

throat's been cut."

On that note, he finally left.

I walked over to Vicky's office and knocked on the door. "May I?"

"Come in, please," her voice replied from within.

I walked in, closed the door and looked around the room. We were alone. The mousy middle-aged lady who shared the office with Vicky had already left.

"Hi," I said.

"Hi," she replied without taking her eyes from the computer screen, scrolling the mouse wheel fiercely.

"Listen, sweetheart..."

"Let's cut the crap."

"Okay. All I'm asking for is the chance to explain myself. Can we go somewhere?"

"Why? You can speak here if you want. I'll listen to whatever you have to say. Then you can close the door behind you."

"Vicky.... Ms. Koval, please."

Without saying a word, she switched off the computer, collected the stuff from the table into her purse and rose. "Very well. Where do you want me to go?"

"Actually, I wanted to invite you to a small celebration. I received that bonus, remember? So I'm buying dinner for the guys. Cyril and Greg, you know them. I'd love you to join me on a night like this."

"That's all very well," she replied in a level impassive voice, "but I'm afraid I can't come. My daughter's arriving in an hour. I need to go and meet her now. Enjoy your bonus and your celebration."

"Would you like me to come with you?"

"Before, I might have said yes. But not anymore, sorry. What am I supposed to say to her? '*This is Uncle Phil, we work together, that's why he'll be staying with us tonight*'?"

"Why not?"

"I don't think so. She's a big girl, anyway. You can't fool her. Is that what you wanted to talk to me about?"

"No, not really. Can we go to the stairwell? I need a smoke," I lied.

We walked out of the office. She locked the door and we headed for the stairs.

On seeing Marina, Vicky recoiled, trying to leave, but I held her by the waist and pressed my back to the stairs door, blocking the way. "You promised you'd hear me out."

She heaved a weary sigh and lit a cigarette. "I'm listening."

"Ms. Koval, that wasn't what you think it was!" Marina spurted out.

"Okay. That wasn't what I thought it was. Anything else?"

"Ms. Koval... Vicky... Vicky, please listen to me."

Marina was a smart little girl. She'd managed to strike the right note. "They'd paired me with Dennis for the trial period. You know him, don't you?"

"I know everyone who works here. And?"

"And from the very first day, he just wouldn't leave me alone..."

Marina went on, telling the story of Dennis' harassment in an orderly, logical manner. She explained how I'd helped her by taking her under my own wing and supervising her first meetings with clients.

Cross-armed, Vicky kept smoking as she listened to her, her body language betraying her defensive position. Her Interest in the story fluctuated, hovering under 50% which meant she'd already crossed me out from her close friends' list. Still, her Mood was just above zero which meant that not all was lost.

"The rest you saw for yourself," Marina concluded. "I'm very sorry I said what I did. I just freaked out. I mean, when I said that I'd had it off with Phil — oh sorry, I mean that he and I were in a relationship. There's nothing between us at all, whatsoever."

With bated breath, I awaited a system message informing me of my improved Reputation with Vicky. Still, something was wrong there. Either she didn't believe Marina or the whole incident had left a bad taste in her mouth, but her Dislike status wasn't in a hurry to change.

"I can see now," she said. "Thanks for taking the time to explain. If I were you, I should report the incident to the boss. Sexual harassment can't be tolerated. Still, I can't see how it can possibly concern me. I work in HR. You could have sought my advice, I suppose, in which case you should have made an appointment to see me in my office. There's no need for all this cloak-and-dagger stuff."

I winced. She was getting bitchy now. "No need at all, I agree," I said dryly. "Sorry we had to trouble you on this insignificant matter, Ms. Koval."

"No trouble at all. Have a good day," she used her pass card to unlock the door and turned back, about to walk out. "You've got lipstick on your shirt, Phil."

She left, leaving me and Marina alone on the landing.

I felt drained. I hadn't gotten enough sleep last night, what with Vlad calling me in the middle of the night and my 5 a.m. reveille, followed by some quality iron-pumping in the gym, the unpleasant conversation with Yanna, and an exhausting day of contract closing. Among other things, I'd received a new level, had to confront yet another jealous freak in the shape of Dennis, ruined my relationship with a girl whom I liked a lot (which wasn't actually my fault), had been hauled across the carpet by the boss and had to comfort Marina.

And I still had lots of stuff to come. I had the dinner appointment with the guys and after that, I still had to distribute the points I'd just received. I also needed to have my hair cut (which would have to wait till tomorrow), call my parents, speak to Alik and Fatso to find out how it had gone with their new jobs, sign up for a boxing class and keep searching for a new place.

As for Vicky, I already knew from experience that she needed some space in order to calm down and think things over. It would probably be better to leave her alone for a few days. And then... time will tell.

Confounded, I kept mulling over it all as we walked to Jared's, completely oblivious of Marina trotting by my side. As we approached the bar, she timidly touched my elbow,

"Phil, you okay?"

"I'm fine," I replied, unwilling to ruin the night for her. "Let's party!"

The party didn't last very long, though. Having toasted my bonus and Marina's first sale, I ordered myself a mixed salad with a few bits of egg and tuna buried in a haystack of rocket lettuce. I needed to lose some weight if I wanted to improve Agility. I'd been obliged to get myself a beer but I'd managed to make it last all night.

At least Greg and Cyril didn't stand on ceremony. Their plates were heaped high with steak and French fries. Having finished his rare steak, Cyril timidly ordered a jumbo size burger taller than my beer glass.

Marina kept a low profile. She barely spoke, casting long piercing glances at me in expectation of my reaction — any reaction. I tried not to look at her.

After a couple of hours of unenthusiastic gossip and tepid discussion about Cyril's health and Greg's matrimonial problems, a crimson-faced Cyril cleared his throat,

"I think I'm gonna have a cigarette! Why not? Technically, I'm supposed to quit today. But today isn't over yet! Which means-"

"Which means what?" Greg asked, already a bit

slow on the uptake.

I shook my head. "Please. Don't. That's alcohol speaking, not you. It drops your guard."

"See if I care! We're celebrating, aren't we?" he waved to a waiter.

The waiter approached our table. "How can I-"

"What kind of cigarettes do you have?" Cyril interrupted him.

As the waiter recited all the available brands, I made up my mind. Time to go home.

"Excuse me," I interrupted the waiter, "Could you please repeat the beers except for me and make out the tab? Then you can get him his cigarettes. Sorry, Cyril, no offense. I can't stop you from killing yourself but I've no intention of financing it. I hope you understand."

The waiter nodded and disappeared, mumbling something about "one moment".

Cyril shrugged. Greg just sat there looking blank. Marina kept staring at me, trying to lock her gaze into mine and hopefully read something in it.

"What's gotten into you?" Cyril asked.

"To be honest with you, I'm dead on my feet. I can't keep my eyes open."

"That's normal," Cyril said. "Thanks for the party. I just thought we'd stay a bit longer. Was it the cigarettes?"

The waiter brought the beers and the tab in a box. I glanced at it and laid a few bills on top. "Keep the change."

He gratefully collected the money and left. I

shook the men's hands. "Thanks for keeping me company."

"Phil?" Cyril raised a quizzical eyebrow. "You sure you're okay?"

"Yes, I'm fine! I have no problem with you whatsoever. My only problem is, I'm falling off my feet. Marina, you stay with the guys. I'm sure they'll take care of you. See ya!"

She didn't reply. I could see she wasn't happy with me at all. Still, it was better that way. Had I offered to share a ride, she'd have jumped at the chance, and then tomorrow I wouldn't be able to prove anything to anyone. Either Greg would let it slip in a conversation or she'd come up with some stupid story simply out of spite. Cyril too could be trusted to say something stupid. Then I could forget all about Vicky. She wouldn't forgive me a second time round.

It didn't take me long to get back home. At this late hour, roads were virtually empty.

The moment I opened the door, Richie barged out, sweeping me out of his way as he rushed toward the elevator. Oh well. He was my friend and my responsibility. I locked the door and followed him.

As I walked Richie, I opened the interface. I still had to decide how best to invest my skill point. Leveling up Luck was more or less clear. But the skill point I hadn't decided what to do with yet.

Never mind. That would have to wait.

Just in case, I perched myself on the edge of a park bench still wet from the rain and added the point to Luck.

Warning! We've detected an abnormal increase in your Luck characteristic: +1 pt.

Your brain will be restructured in keeping with the new reading (9) to comply with your new decision-making choices.

The world blinked out of existence, then reappeared. I was already used to this phenomenon.

Oh well. Apparently, I'd just become luckier. Which was hard to believe, considering my ill luck earlier that day which had brought Vicky into the room just as Marina was snapping profanities at Dennis.

I opened my characteristic tab. Much better. Still not much to write home about but at least I showed some progress.

Philip "Phil" Panfilov
Age: 32
Current status: sales rep
Social status level: 9
Classes: Book Reader and Empath
Married
Wife: Yannina "Yanna" Orlova
Children: none

Main Characteristics:
Strength: 8
Agility: 4
Intellect: 18

Stamina: 5

Perception: 7

Charisma: 13 (+3 bonus from the Standard Business Suit)

Luck: 9

A *book reader*? And an *empath*? I opened my skill list.

That's right. Both skills were listed at the top. I had level 6 in both Empathy and Reading Skills.

I giggled, imagining myself weeping in empathy over some tear-jerking romance novel.

Oh well. It could have been worse, I suppose. I could have been classed as some Paranoid Lemming.

I tried to add the skill point to Learning Skills but failed,

Sorry. You're attempting to add a system point to a skill currently undergoing Optimization. Current progress: 3%.

Just on the off-chance, I tried to add it to Insight and received another message,

Sorry. You can't improve a system skill.

I tried again and again, "clicking" the Insight icon with my gaze and receiving the same message until finally the system lost patience with me,

How many times do we need to tell you? You

can't invest a system point in a system skill!

My inner wordsmith recoiled at the phrasing. They used "system" twice in the same sentence, useless hacks!

Whatever. My Vigor had already dropped below 20%. I needed some sleep. Still, Richie was taking his time.

"Come on Rich, get on with it, for Christ's sake," I mumbled with a jaw-wrenching yawn.

It probably wasn't such a good idea to make leveling decisions in this state. I decided to check my skill list instead. I scrolled through it until I came to Running. It was still level 1.

How come? Between the stat booster and all the bonuses, I would have expected it to be at least 2 or 3 by now. Something was definitely wrong here. Maybe my running technique wasn't good enough? I made a mental note to look into it once my head had cleared a bit.

I scrolled the list all the way down and — surprise! — discovered a new system skill, gray and inactive.

I summoned Martha and asked her — for purely esthetical reasons, you understand — to assume her old human form. "Is it possible to create a separate system skill list, pretty please? I've just found yet another system skill absolutely accidentally. I didn't even know it was there."

"Of course. Here you are. I would advise you to manually change the settings to receive new alerts every time a new system skill is added. At the moment,

---

they are displayed at the very edge of your field of vision. How are things, overall?"

"Fine," I grinned at her good old bubblegum-blowing self. "Did you really need to ask? You're sitting in my head 24/7, anyway!"

"Phil, Phil. You're still confusing me with the program. I'm not the program in your head. I'm only your virtual assistant. My memory only stores the logs of our meetings and conversations, as well as your queries. I thought you'd already returned the dog to its owner?"

"Not really, as you can see. Richie, you're really cheeky! You've had plenty of time to do your business!"

Richie stopped circling the grass in search of an arcane devil-may-know spot he found suitable for his needs. He sat down and looked at me quizzically, tilting his head.

I cast an angry glance at my watch. It was way past my bedtime. "Never mind. Thanks, Martha."

I reopened the skill window. It now contained two tabs: one for the main skills and the other for the system ones. The system tab only listed three skills. One was Insight II, followed by Optimization I.

And what was that? I peered at the end of the list.

Heroism

My suppressed WoW memories stirred in the depths of my subconscious.

Heroism? What, just like that? Would it improve

my main characteristics, maybe?

I studied the skill's description.

Oh, no. It was much much better. It was out-of-this-world freakin' awesome.

New unblocked system skill available: Heroism.

Skill type: Passive

Allows the user to unblock his or her heroic abilities.

Skill points available: 1

Accept / Decline

My drowsiness disappeared as if by the sweep of an ogre's paw. Yes, please! *Accept!*

CHAPTER TWENTY-FOUR

THE HERO

"No one in the world gets what they want and that is beautiful."

Ernest Cline, *Ready Player One*

NO, I DIDN'T AWAKE A SUPERHERO. NOT EVEN A NORMAL hero. But unlike the days before, this morning I unhesitantly sprang from my bed the moment I realized I was awake.

Because today I could become a Hero.

How did I know, might you ask?

Last night, the moment I'd pressed *Accept* I'd been granted access to the skill's full description,

You've activated a new skill: Heroism.

Skill type: Passive

Allows the user to unblock his or her heroic abilities.

There are ten abilities which humanity can bestow on its most worthy specimens. All of them were considered a myth during the Dark Era (the times preceding the discovery of the Universal Information Field). Their carriers were branded as "superheroes" whose names only belonged in songs and legends.

Humanity's progress has turned these achievements into reality.

Still, as the Law of Equilibrium requires, the Commonwealth of Sentient Races can only grant heroic abilities to a limited number of human beings whose social status levels are the highest. Each of them receives the title of Hero.

Warning! The restrictions and requirements for unblocking heroic abilities are calculated on an individual case-by-case basis, taking into consideration the current average social status levels in each particular segment of our Galaxy.

Warning! The user's successful leveling up of Heroism which has resulted in his or her outstanding services to humanity can be rewarded by the system. Similarly, criminal abuse of heroic abilities can result in its being blocked again.

Warning! As you level up Heroism, its requirements regarding the unblocking of heroic abilities

---

and the number of abilities which can be used simultaneously may vary.

Warning! In accordance with the Anti-Munchkin Act, a user can only unblock one heroic ability per every twenty social status levels gained.

I summoned Martha and buried myself in research. I had too many questions about this. A new tab appeared in my skill window, entitled Heroic Abilities. Just reading through it had plunged me into a dreamy wistful trance.

You'd think that by then, nothing could surprise me. Still, I was deeply shaken. Everything that had happened to me before could still be explained rationally (sort of), either by saying I was off my trolley or by suspecting I'd accidentally fallen prey to some classified military research. But this...

The entire list of superhero abilities was divided into several tiers. The more awesome the ability, the higher the requirements for its potential user.

Realistically, I could hope to acquire the first one of the two tier-one abilities:

Tier 1
Ability name: Lie Detection
Ability type: Passive, Heroic
Considerably increases the user's ability to detect a person's insincerity

Unblocking requirements:

- *Heroism: level 1+*
- *Social status: level 10+*
- *Empathy: level 5+*
- *Communication Skills: level 5+*
- *Perception: level 10+*
- *Charisma: level 10+*
- *Luck: level 10+*
- *Intellect: level 20+*

All I needed was to bring my Perception, Luck and Intellect up — and make level 10 in social status, of course. And that was it! No one would ever fool me again! Or at least as long as I had this interface in my head.

The second ability was something I knew intimately from my gaming experience. My rogue used to be an expert in it. Suddenly I was dying to acquire it.

Tier 1
Ability name: Stealth and Vanish
Ability type: Active, Heroic
Allows the user to activate the Stealth system module in order to become invisible to all creatures around him or herself for a minimum duration of 15 sec, depending on their Spirit numbers. Can be used in combat.

Unblocking requirements:
- *Heroism: level 1+*
- *Social Status: level 10+*

- Strength: level 10+
- Agility: level 10+
- Perception: level 10+
- Stamina: level 10+
- Luck: level 10+
Cooldown: 1 hr.

Stealth and Vanish rolled into one! This ability could do wonders in combat. Dammit! Just having to choose between the two was already giving me a headache. Knowing that I couldn't have both in the nearest future was a torture. Imagine what I felt when I finished studying the list.

I asked Martha whether it was normal that my first heroic abilities only required social status level 10. According to her, yes, it was perfectly normal. Firstly, because our society wasn't yet improvement-oriented. Unlike our descendants, we basically lived simply to satisfy our own consumerist needs. We wanted good food, lots of rest and quality entertainment. Which was why there weren't that many high-level individuals among us. Currently, the average social status level on the planet hovered just below 9. Which turned level 10 into some sort of litmus test pinpointing such a person as one of the best half of our society as opposed to at least four billion of his or her fellow Terrans.

Secondly, both first-tier skills appeared to have purely defensive functions. The first one was pretty self-explanatory. It allowed the user to detect any lie or insincerity in others, thus preventing him or her from suffering damage, moral or financial as well as physical.

And as for the second skill...

"Martha, in theory I could use Stealth just to sneak into a bank vault, couldn't I? Come to think of it, I could penetrate any kind of public function. Or peep at girls in the gym locker room. I could eavesdrop on all sorts of confidential conversations..."

I continued to shower her with examples of the skill's illegal use. I suppose it was understandable. Every one of us must have dreamt of being invisible at some point in their lives.

"Phil," she interrupted me, "judging by your logs, you've already performed a number of socially meaningful actions. So do you think the program can tell such an action from an illegal one?"

"I suppose so."

"Exactly. Only this time the penalties will be much much higher. The Commonwealth of Sentient Races can protect itself from any internal threat, trust me."

Okay. In any case, all I could do was drool impotently over it. There was no way I could meet the skill's requirements before the license expired.

The second tier of superskills turned its owner into a demigod. Not permanently, no. And still, wouldn't you have loved to have become a demigod, if only for a few brief seconds? Provided the timing was right, of course.

Tier 2
Ability name: Regeneration

Ability type: Active, Heroic

Removes all negative effects from the user, such as Disease, Curse, Poisoning, Bleeding or Exposure to Radiation. Accelerates Recovery and improves Confidence, Self-Control, Satisfaction, Vigor, Mood and Willpower. The acceleration rates depend on the user's Spirit numbers.

Unblocking requirements:
- Heroism: level 2+
- Social status: level 20+
- Meditation: level 5+
- All main characteristics: levels 20+.

Cooldown: 1 to 14 days depending on the gravity of the damage to the user's body.

Basically, this was absolute health. All you had to do was keep activating it every time the cooldown expired, and you could expect to live compos mentis until the ripe old age of 200 — or at least until the time when they learned how to make human beings truly immortal, by organ cloning or using some sort of rejuvenating elixir.

And just think of the possibilities it offered to all kinds of hazardous occupations!

Still, for someone like me it was truly irrelevant. I was going to lose all of my system skills and abilities in less than a year, anyway.

But still, as a seasoned damager, I loved the next superskill on the list:

Tier 2
Ability name: Sprint
Ability type: Active, Heroic
Ability class: Combat
Accelerates the user 100% by modifying his or her Metabolism and Perception for the duration of 5 seconds.

Unblocking requirements:
- Heroism: level 2+
- Social status: level 20+
- Agility: level 20+
- Strength: level 20+
- Stamina: level 20+
- Perception: level 20+
Cooldown: 30 min

Can you imagine? This wasn't just about being able to move twice as fast. This ability gave you a different perception of time. It would allow anyone — even me with my clumsy blows and the agility of a quadriplegic — to defeat a mixed martial arts champion in the ring. Okay, maybe not a champion and not in the ring even, but it would give you a fair chance in a street fight. That would leave Fatso no chance of winning, that's for sure.

Forget fighting: this ability could make me a valuable asset in any sport, soccer even. I could spend the entire game standing motionlessly on the opponent's half of the pitch until the moment was just right, then I'd activate it and score a perfect goal. Ten seconds were more than enough to thread my way past the frozen players. With only a thirty-minute cooldown, I was guaranteed to score at least three goals in each game. That was more than Ronaldo and Messi ever could!

The third second-tier ability was tailor-made for the Hunter class.

Tier 2
Ability name: Taming
Ability type: Active, Heroic
Greatly increases your chances of taming any non-sentient creature and turning it into your pet. The progressive leveling of the ability allows you to activate your pets' abilities and increase the number of commands. The number of the tamed creatures depends on your Spirit numbers.

Unblocking requirements:
- Heroism: level 2+
- Social status: level 20+
- Taming: level 5+
- Empathy: level 5+
- Stamina: level 20+
- Strength: level 20+
Cooldown: 24 hrs.

It would have been great to tame some cool creature like a shark, a lion or a giant python. Still, at the moment I had my hands full with Richie and Boris, thank you very much. This ability could have come in very handy in some RPG world where you could use a motley crew of pets to help you cleanse dungeons. But in real life? A zoo? A circus? I couldn't think of much else.

If Tier 2 still seemed remotely doable, Tier 3 required the kind of stats I couldn't ever hope to achieve. The descriptions of the abilities themselves appeared so fantastical I didn't even bother to try to apply them to myself. I just heaved a sigh after disappointed sigh as I imagined myself using them to help my family and the whole world.

Strangely enough, by the time I'd reached that tier, I'd somehow stopped thinking of how I could benefit from them. On the contrary: I kept asking myself how I could help other people by using them. Don't get me wrong: I wasn't going to obliterate all crime or bestow law and order on the entire country. All I wanted to do was to make the world a tiny bit better.

That got me thinking. In all those superhero movies, there's always an evil overlord bent on thwarting the hero's efforts. And who were the evil overlords of the real world?

Okay, so let's presume I'd become a new Superman. A flying legend who wears his underpants on the outside, invulnerable and almighty. So I'd go and make quick work of all the scum of this world, eliminating drug cartels, blowing up terrorists' dens and feeding all the dictators to the dogs. I'd bag all the pedophiles, murderers and corrupted officials and take them to a desert island in the middle of the ocean to play hunger games.

And then what? I mean, seriously? Would it make anyone happier? If we took actual human beings — like Vicky, Alik or Fatso, — would their lives become better for it?

At this point, an idea struck me. A really good one. I hurried to put it on my to-do list, then promptly put it out of my mind. Because the list of superskills kept unfolding. And what I saw on it would have made all those LitRPG-based "inner greedy pigs" drop to the floor and die with envy. Imagine how I was supposed to feel, a useless thirty-two-year-old who'd only very recently considered it the epitome of luck whenever he'd managed to lay his hands on a couple of purple pixels.

> *Tier 3*
> *Ability name: Foresight*
> *Ability type: Active, Heroic*
> *Allows you to transport yourself to a new reality model for the duration of 15 seconds, then return to the skill activation starting point.*
>
> *Unblocking requirements:*
> *- Heroism: level 3+*
> *- Social status: level 30+*
> *- Intuition: level 10+*
> *- Meditation: level 10+*
> *- Perception: level 30+*
> *- Intellect: level 30+*
> *Cooldown: 24 hrs.*

Never mind it was only fifteen seconds. True, you could only use it once every twenty-four hours — so what? This was a cheat to end all cheats. Other admittedly awesome things like Flight or Invisibility didn't even come near. Imagine being able to find out the exact outcome of your every word or action. Think of all the things I'd have done differently in the past had I had access to this highly useful skill.

I used to have this friend once. At the time, casinos were still legal in Russia, so we took full advantage of the fact. That day, he'd won a little. While me, I'd lost every penny. We'd drunk a lot. I was itching to either win all my money back and go home or just lose everything and also go home.

So I'd talked him into lending me all the money he'd had on him. It was early morning and that was the only money he had. I bet everything on red and it came up zero.

Later, I'd never managed to pay him back. He kept reminding me, and then one day he just struck me off his list of friends.

I knew I couldn't win his friendship back. The least I could do was pay him what I owed him. This too was now an item on my task list.

Some other time, we were driving back from a fishing trip. We were both drunk. I wasn't keeping my eyes on the road and managed to run over a kitten. We stopped to check on him.

What we saw came back to haunt me in my dreams for years afterwards. The kitten kept silently opening and closing his mouth. He was probably calling for his mom.

The next day, I brought Boris home.

I also used to cadge money off my old grandma (on Mom's side). She used to live in a small studio apartment. For as long as I remembered, she'd always given me little presents on her pension payment days. First it was sweets, replaced by children's books and toys as I grew older. By the end of high school, she usually gave me money.

That day, I needed some money in order to take a girl to the movies. Naturally, there were other costs, like buying her flowers and taking her to a café afterwards. Gran said she didn't have any. I didn't believe her. I yelled at her. I was full of spite. The next night, she died of a heart attack.

I wouldn't have even needed all of the fifteen seconds of the Foresight skill. Five seconds would have been plenty to notice her quivering mouth and a single tear rolling down her cheek. Five seconds, more than enough to regret my words and actions and to hate myself. My throat still seized every time I remembered I hadn't even bothered to apologize. I hadn't given her a hug — no, I was furious at the sight of her tears thinking she was putting up a good show. How could I? Great God, Phily, how could you?

Phily... That's where Kira had gotten the habit of calling me so.

I kept reminiscing, remembering other occasions when I should have stayed instead of leaving; when I should have spoken up instead of staying safely silent, as well as those when I should have bitten my tongue and shut up. All the times when I'd succumbed to my urge for instant gratification and equally instantly regretted it, as well as times when I should have followed my impulses rather than regretting my reluctance until this very day.

True, not all of those things could have been rectified with Foresight. Still, I could have righted quite a few wrongs.

A sympathetic Martha watched my self-flagellation session. Richie whined in confusion. Still, it brought me some sort of relief.

A new system message popped up,

Congratulations! Your Spirit has improved!
+100% to Spirit
You've received 1000 pt. XP for successfully leveling up a secondary characteristic!

After this, I finally forced myself to go back home where I continued going through the list, yawning and trying to keep my eyes open.

Tier 3
Ability name: Berserker
Ability type: Active, Heroic
***Triples** all your main characteristics for the duration of 15 seconds.*

Unblocking requirements:
- Heroism: level 3+
- Social status: level 30+

- All main characteristics: levels 25+
- Spirit: 300%+
Cooldown: 24 hrs.

This was basically God mode for a duration of fifteen seconds. With it, you could set new world records in any sport or make scientific breakthroughs. You could become a champion in virtually anything. No idea what could happen if you tripled your Luck, Perception or Charisma, but it wouldn't be too bad, that's for sure.

Judging by the emphasis placed on the first word — "***Triples***" — this factor could probably grow as you continued to level up. In which case, the skill's duration was likely to grow too.

Just out of curiosity, I asked Martha about it. She confirmed my conjectures.

And the next skill on the list... well, it could easily make anyone the next President of anything. Like President of planet Earth, for instance. It could turn you into either a powerful leader of an evil overlord.

Tier 3
Ability name: Persuasion
Ability type: Active, Heroic
The skill endows the user with a 100% power of persuasion, allowing him or her to win over all human beings whose social status level is lower than his or her own. The possibility of winning over those human beings whose social status level is equal or surpasses that of

the user wanes accordingly.

Warning! Any attempt to use the skill for anti-social purposes will result in it being permanently blocked.

> *Unblocking requirements:*
> *- Heroism: level 3+*
> *- Social status: level 30+*
> *- Communication Skills: level 20+*
> *- Leadership: level 20+*
> *- Public Speaking: level 20+*
> *- Perception: level 30+*
> *- Charisma: level 30+*
> *- Intellect: level 30+*
> *Cooldown: 24 hrs.*

Almost immediately, I could think of at least several ways of using the skill. The dumbest of them was to shoot a video of myself and upload it to YouTube. That was it. It didn't really matter what it was about. I could tell them to walk around naked from now on. Or send donations to my personal bank account. Or support Mr. Panikoff's favorite soccer team, Zenith. I could even tell them to kick the bucket — figuratively as well as literally.

The possibilities were limitless. And even if the video got blocked, I could always gatecrash a rock concert and address the audience.

The final skill in Tier three reminded me of a Paladin bubble.

Tier 3
Ability name: Invulnerability
Ability type: Active, Heroic
The skill creates a temporary nano film which envelops the user's entire body, making him impervious to any attacks or other aggressive acts. The skill can self-activate without the user's knowledge whenever there's a threat to his or her life or wellbeing.
Duration: 15 sec

Unblocking requirements:
- Heroism: level 3+
- Social status: level 30+
- All main characteristics: levels 25+
- Spirit: 300%+
Cooldown: 24 hrs.

This was a warrior's dream. Just think of all the heroic deeds you could perform if you knew you were invulnerable. Not in everyday life though... definitely no good for a couch potato like myself, but... just think about it. A self-activating Invulnerability skill! Once you had it, you didn't have to worry about a thing. You could walk under ladders and board planes without worrying they might not reach their destinations.

The last tier was uncategorized. It only contained one skill.

Ability name: Reload
Ability type: Passive, Heroic
Saving the life of the most valuable society

member is the ultimate peak of social protection. The skill allows the user to stop time and reload the world at the exact moment which caused his or her death. This is a very particular heroic ability which requires forceful Spirit withdrawal from all of the sentient beings located in the given segment.

Unblocking requirements:
- the "Segment's First Hero" achievement. Segment name: planet Earth.
Cooldown: no less than 1 astronomical year, depending on the segment's population numbers.

Reload the world? Was I really sane and reading this?

I immediately remembered my weird dream: the death of Kira, the monstrous Khphor, the alien girl called Ilindi, and Valiadis.

My dreams were never as detailed and colorful as they're usually described in books. Inevitably, I'd forgotten them as soon as I climbed out of bed. This time, however, it was different. Was the program playing games with me?

Martha failed to produce a clear answer. "Human dreams are just that, Phil: dreams. They have nothing to do with reality. They're caused by memory defragmentation."

"In this case, what's with this world reloading nonsense?"

"Oh, that's easy-" Martha's eyes glazed over. He avatar disappeared for a brief second, then froze motionless, then disappeared again.

"Sending request to server," the mechanical voice of the system assistant announced. "Please wait. Server connection timeout. Impossible to establish connection with the server."

And that was it. Martha was gone. I tried to summon her again but all I received was the dumb automated voice.

I'd have to look into it later. Time to go to bed.

Only when I was falling asleep did I realize I'd very nearly nullified my Spirit reserves.

... No, I didn't wake up a superman. I was still a regular Joe. But at least I was able to spring out of bed the moment I realized I was awake.

Because today I could become a Hero.

CHAPTER TWENTY-FIVE

THE STORY OF THE HERD OF SEALS

"Don't tell me what I can't do."
Lost

TUESDAY MAY 29 2018

IT HAD BEEN TWO WEEKS SINCE I'D FIRST NOTICED THE funny specks of dust floating in my vision. They'd later begun to take shape until finally they'd formed Alik's name floating over his head.

That day, Yanna had left me. And the same night, I'd received my first level in Stamina after completing my night run.

It may have been two weeks but it felt like six months. So much had happened in this brief time! So many new people I'd met! But the person I'd learned the most about was myself.

Today, just like two weeks ago, I stood in front of the bathroom mirror studying my reflection. I had no stubble: these days, I shaved every morning. My cheeks seemed to have sunken a little. I could almost recognize my own face under the melting layer of fat.

My hair almost touched my shoulders now which made me look admittedly ridiculous. So I decided to dedicate the day to my own needs. Once the morning meeting with Pavel was over, I needed to finally get a haircut, then start looking for a new place.

I was gradually coming to the conclusion that I might have to quit Ultrapak. This wasn't the right moment to tie myself down with office work. As long as I had this program still installed, no amount of money — much less a sales rep's earnings — were worth the missed opportunities.

Crazy, really. I'd only been working for them for three full days. Which was my personal record in this respect.

As I drank my morning coffee, I watched a few jogging videos, committing to memory their technique and breathing tips. I'd made every mistake in the book, hadn't I? Two weeks of running nowhere! At least I'd managed to improve my Stamina a bit but just think of all the XP I'd lost (500 per level, to be precise) by not leveling properly.

I finished my coffee and got on with my morning routine: a quick warmup followed by a run in the park in Richie's company. This time I kept checking the video on my phone to make sure I did it correctly. The results weren't long in coming: now I was gaining 1% for every 200 meters. By the end of my run, the status bar was already at 94%. Still, my previous running experience must have had something to do with it too. Wrong technique aside, I must have done something right. I was itching to make level 2 in Running straight away but it didn't look as if I was going to. I had to go to work. Even with this, my job was becoming a problem.

I took a hot and cold shower after which I received a new message,

Your Agility has improved!
+1 to Agility
Current Agility: 5
Experience points received for improving a main characteristic: 1000

What a shame I didn't have bathroom scales. Yanna used to have them, but she'd reclaimed them with all her other stuff. Still, I didn't need scales to know I'd lost weight. It looked like my theory had been correct. Once I'd lost another five pounds or so, my Agility might improve again. In any case, weight loss alone wouldn't do it. I definitely had to persevere with my coordination and balance exercises.

I had a funny feeling that by showing me the

superskill list, the program had been teasing me, trying to accelerate my progress. For some reason, it made me think of Russia just before the Second World War when they had been training all and sundry to become pilots and paratroopers. It was true that I'd had more progress in the last two weeks than I'd had in years but apparently, the program wasn't too happy with it.

Then it dawned on me. I'd been acting like a useless noob, spreading myself thin over all those reputations, leveling choices and whatnot. I'd been reactive instead of proactive and goal-oriented.

Like when Fatso had attacked me, I'd immediately decided to level Boxing. And I still hadn't even found a boxing club. Similarly, the moment Ultrapak had contacted me I'd decided to level Vending. The moment I'd seen that missing girl on TV, I'd had to call her parents simply because I couldn't bear seeing her grieving father. And once the Major had told me that the parents of many other missing children were in the same position, I'd hurried to send him the kids' coordinates.

So basically I'd been chasing too many tails instead of doing what any gamer should. I had to decide on my char's build, choose a strategy and follow it without getting distracted by every roadside bunny. If you took the missing children, for instance: why had I had to stop at the Major's list? Shouldn't I have begun by creating two databases: one of all wanted criminals nationwide and the other of all missing children? Then I could have worked my way through both and sent the results to the police and all interested parties. Logical, don't you think?

And how about the First Hero achievement? The one that was mentioned in the Reload description? There should be other achievements as well, but which ones?

As I waited for my ham and eggs to cook, I summoned Martha and asked her. Much to my relief, this was my old Martha, ripped denim shorts and all. Apparently, my Spirit had recovered over the course of the night. The only difference was, her chewing gum was now gone, replaced by an e-cigarette.

"All achievements are generated by the program," Martha breathed out a large puff of vapor which dissipated before it could reach the ceiling. "Ditto for rewards. That's not counting the great feats of valor which are generated annually by the Council."

"This is crazy. Feats of valor controlled by a Council? What kind of totalitarian society is that? You sure it wasn't created by some errant time traveler from Stalin's era?"

"Sorry, I don't understand the question. If you're implying that our social structure is similar to that of the Soviet Union, then my answer is an emphatic no. In actual fact, I would greatly appreciate it if you stopped posing questions which require connection with the server."

I unsummoned her and had my solitary breakfast (solitary if you disregarded the other two, Richie and Boris, eagerly awaiting their share of ham from my plate). In two days' time, Richie would be gone. Sad. Admittedly, I'd gotten quite attached to him. The

---

feeling seemed to be mutual, judging by his Reverence reading.

Strange I hadn't received any XP for it, though. Could it be because improving one's Reputation with a pet had no bearing on one's social status?

As I walked through the front door, I saw Fatso cross the courtyard. I could barely recognize him. His usually disheveled hair was slicked down. He was wearing a neat pair of summer pants and a pressed short-sleeved shirt. The only thing still left from his past was a new pair of grandpa socks peeking from his sandals. He looked like a poster-perfect image of an AA member on the mend.

"Morning, sir!" he waved, hurrying toward me.

"Morning, Fa- ahem, Ruslan."

"They've hired me!" he grinned, flashing a gap between his teeth. "Can you imagine? They really did!"

He gave me a bear hug, slapping my back.

Quest alert: In the Gutter. Quest completed!
You've successfully helped your attacker Ruslan "Fatso" Rimsky to find permanent employment.
XP received: 200 pt.
Additional XP received: 300 (for promptness)
+10% to Satisfaction

Your Reputation with Ruslan "Fatso" Rimsky has improved!
Current Reputation: Amicability 20/60

Now my quest log was completely empty.

"Congrats!" I said.

"Thanks! My wife's asking if you'd like to come round for dinner. I'm asking you too, of course. Would you like to come?"

"Absolutely," I said, unwilling to decline his heartfelt invitation. "Let's do it this way. When you receive your first paycheck, then we'll celebrate. Okay?"

"Yes, sir!"

"Please don't 'sir' me," I said. It felt really awkward when this middle-aged family man treated me with such reverence. "You know my name, don't you? It's Phil."

He looked closely into my eyes, then chuckled somewhat approvingly and shook my hand. "Very well, Phil. See ya!"

He headed for the bus stop. I got into the cab that had just arrived. I could have taken the bus too but in my new frame of mind, this was false economy. Time was a precious asset, and I'd rather have used it to make more money.

As I rode, I continued reading. This had already become a habit. At some point, I put the book aside for a moment to jot down a few interesting leveling scenarios which had just occurred to me. I opened the Notebook app on my phone and marked it all down,

XP points are awarded for quests, tasks, socially meaningful actions as well as new skill and reputation levels.

XP points received for new skill levels are

awarded regardless of the skill or its initial level.

Tracking wanted criminals: IMPORTANT!!!

Zero-level skills get leveled faster than all others.

How about money??? My own business???

Skill leveling... That got me thinking. I did a quick overview of everything I had at the moment. Some progress bars were almost 100% full, like those for my MS Word and Excel skills. My Cooking skills were actually at 99%. One more plate of ham and eggs, and I'd receive a new level.

Several other skill bars were equally full. Soccer, swimming, poetry, table tennis, weightlifting, DIY skills, poker and chess playing — another hour or two spent on each of them, and I'd progress to the next level. Easy XP points!

That decided it. I had to quit my new job. I could give my single sale to either Greg or Marina. In the meantime, I had to start thinking how to make some money. Ideas were aplenty, from a missing persons bureau to a recruitment agency. And that's not even counting some truly crazy possibilities like leveling up poker or competing in CS:GO tournaments which were held on an almost daily basis and boasted impressive cash prizes.

As I pondered over it all, the cab arrived at the office. I was so lost in thought I'd very nearly walked past Cyril and Greg who were lingering on the porch, huddling up against the morning chill. Both looked rather worse for wear.

Both were smoking. That last fact annoyed me quite a lot. Still, I pretended it was none of my business.

"Hi," I said.

"Hi," the two replied in rueful unison.

"How is it going?"

Greg waved my question away. "It isn't."

"Nah," Cyril mumbled.

"Why, what's up?" I glanced at my watch. Five minutes till the briefing.

"We went to see his wife last night," Cyril nodded at Greg. "He wanted to make up with her."

"And? How did it go?"

"It didn't," Greg shook his head. "She opened the door, saw me and closed it again."

Cyril chuckled. "He was drunk as a skunk!"

"And what time was that, may I ask?"

"Four, five a.m.?" Cyril said. "When you left, we took Marina home and decided to go to the club. That's where he got a bit emotional. He decided he needed to go and see her straight away. I did my best to talk him out of it! In the end, I went with him just to make sure he didn't get into trouble. Never mind. Let's go now before Pavel chews our ears again for being late."

When we entered Pavel's office, all were already present and correct. All but Dennis, that is. His chair was empty.

Marina ignored my nod and proudly looked the other way.

"Everybody here? Let's get this show on the road," Pavel announced. "Good morning! First things first, I have some good news for our trainees. As of today, Dennis is no longer with us. Which means we can keep two of you once the trial period is over. Now let's move to business. Cyril? What have you got on the Butchers Market?"

Faking enthusiasm and suppressing jaw-wrenching bouts of yawning, Cyril went on to report on his client.

That was decided, then. I was wasting my time here. I could almost physically sense it slipping through my fingers, dwindling with every passing moment.

After the briefing, I lingered in Pavel's office to break the news to him.

"Phil? What is it?"

"May I have a word with you?" I said.

He rubbed his hands. "I think I know where this is going! Another surprise sale? Something big? I just love it! Come on, spit it out!"

"I'm afraid I can't work here any longer," I said. "I quit. I haven't submitted my resignation yet. I don't even think it's worth it. I've only worked here for three days. You could just rip up my application as if I didn't even exist."

"Yeah right! How do you want us to file your bonus, then? What name should we put on it?"

"Just file it under representation expenses. You're the expert."

For a while, he studied me with a stony face as

---

if trying to work out what I was playing at. I looked back at him, perfectly relaxed. I wasn't asking for a rise, after all.

He gave up first. "What's up? Not happy with the bonus?"

"I'm afraid it's personal."

"Don't tell me Valiadis has poached you!"

"Please don't try to second-guess it. I've got nowhere to go. As I said, I have a lot of family responsibilities at the moment. I can't afford to work nine to five."

"Is that all?" he laughed. "That's not a problem. You can be as flexible as you want. I can run it past the boss now if you wish. The wage might not be the same but a bonus is a bonus, right? Tell you what, I'm gonna talk him into giving J-Mart to you. You'll be getting your monthly cut off their orders, what would you say to that? Come on, tell me!"

For a brief second, I hesitated. His offer was generous indeed.

Still... no. Dashing around town like a headless chicken, meeting people... no. Too time-consuming. I could use it more productively, that's for sure. And I couldn't pretend I was working while doing other things. That wasn't right. Somebody else needed this job more than I did. Marina, for instance.

"Tinker, Tailor, Soldier, Sailor," I began, tracing the desk top with my finger from left to right. "Wizard, Warrior, Rogue or Gambler..."

He raised a surprised eyebrow. "Excuse me?"

"I'm afraid I can't," I said. "I'm very sorry."

"Are you sure?"

"I am."

"Shame. So you did take offense."

"I swear to you I didn't. It was a joke. Just a joke," I rose, about to shake his hand and leave.

He rose too. "Can you at least finish this week? Whatever you make, you'll receive in your envelope as soon as the deal is closed. You don't need to come to briefings, either. I can tell the guys that you... eeeer... that you had to go to the doctor, for instance. Would you like that?"

"How about my J-Mart earnings for this month?"

He scratched his head: an innocent, very human gesture which tipped the scales in his favor.

Why not? I could agree to his offer and work for another week. That might pay for a new laptop, too.

"Ah, fuck it," Pavel said. "My karma could use a boost too. Very well!"

We shook on it.

"I have a few things to sort out today," I said. "Is it all right?"

He nodded. "You can be as flexible as you want."

As I left his office, a new message flashed before my eyes.

Congratulations! You've received a new skill level!

Skill name: Perseverance
Current level: 3
XP received: 500

I closed the message. That was nice of them.

From Pavel's office, I headed to Cyril. I had another skill to up.

"Cyril, man, can I borrow your laptop for an hour?"

"Do you know what you're asking for? It's like soliciting someone to spend an hour with their wife!"

"Okay, okay. I promise I won't go anywhere near your adult sites bookmarks. The history of your BDSM adventures is safe with me. I just need to write a Word document. May I?"

"The things I do for my friends! I was about to break my own record, you know that? And now I'll have to reopen it and start again! Come and take a seat. We have an appointment with a client, anyway."

He rose and shouted at the top of his booming voice, "Greg! Where are you? Let's go, man!"

"Thanks," I said.

Cyril headed for the exit with a very reluctant Greg trailing behind him like a listless shadow. His Mood was deep in the red. I just hoped he didn't do anything stupid.

I took Cyril's place at the desk and opened a new Word document. Someone kept sniffing heavily behind my back. Ignoring the noise, I started typing, impatient to jot down a short story I'd been thinking about for quite a while but never got around to actually writing.

The sniffing behind my back grew louder. Menacing, even.

However, I was dead to the world. The story's MC was quite young and also quite jealous, unsure whether his girlfriend was faithful to him. As the story unfolded, he received a gift: a supernatural ability to know the answer to any question. But the more important the question, the more life he would lose.

"You sure you have a heart?" Marina finally said.

I turned round. "Oh hi there!"

"Hi yourself," she grumbled.

"Why didn't you speak to me at the briefing?"

"Why, should I have?"

"Okay," I said, returning my attention to the text. Still, I didn't even get the chance to finish the next sentence.

"Phil!" she exploded.

I continued to type. "Speak up," I said without turning.

"What are you writing?"

"A short story."

"A *what*? Are you nuts? Do you realize what's gonna happen if Pavel sees you doing this?"

"Well, if you keep your voice down, he won't see anything."

"Oh. Sorry. Well... I just wanted to apologize I didn't reply to your greeting. I'm very mad at you."

"Apology accepted. Do you need help?"

"Yes, please," her voice shook, betraying whiney girly notes. "I need to draw up a base of all the clients I've already visited. And I've no idea how to make up those tables!"

"That's not a problem. I'll help you. You start making phone calls. I'll finish this and give you a hand."

After about an hour, I'd finally finished the three-page story which ended with the MC's untimely demise of old age. I spent some more time trying out all sorts of styles and page layouts and even studied the Help pages, until finally, I had the desired result.

Congratulations! You've received a new skill level!
Skill name: MS Word
Current level: 6
XP received: 500

This was a very useful skill... and the main kill candidate for the next Optimization.

Very well, but what was I supposed to do with this story now? I only had a couple of percent left till my next Creative Writing level. I edited the text, adding a couple of flashbacks and a few insights for my MC, and threw in a few detailed descriptions for a good measure.

Yes!

Congratulations! You've received a new skill level!
Skill name: Creative Writing
Current level: 4
XP received: 500

I opened the writers' portal where I'd once uploaded the first chapters of my unfinished book, and published the story there. I didn't give a damn about feedback. I was fully prepared to write my proverbial million words of crap before I could master the craft.

I logged out, closed the laptop and walked over to Marina. She was typing something, squinting shortsightedly at the screen.

I pulled up a chair and sat next to her. "Show me."

She pulled the laptop toward me. "Look. I keep moving it around but it just won't budge. I type in numbers but they change to something completely different."

"Jesus. You poor child of modern technologies! This isn't an Apple tablet, is it? Do you have it all on paper?"

"Yeah. I've got it all here. The clients' names, the contact persons, the approximate demand..."

"You wait a sec. I'm gonna make a chart now. All you need to do is enter the data."

I habitually threw together a quick table with all the entries she needed. It had taken me five minutes at most. I glanced at the skill bar. I had a mere 6% left till the next level.

"Marina? Go and take a smoke break. You're distracting me."

She took offense. "How am I distracting you?"

"It must be your pheromones. Sorry. Would you please?"

She pushed the chair away, sprang to her feet and sashayed off, indignantly swaying her hips.

Now that she wasn't looking over my shoulder, I opened a new document and created a new macro-based table, checking myself frequently against the Help pages. That took me another half-hour. Marina had been back twice, but I sent her off for another break and then to get us some coffee. By the time she was back with it, I'd got a new level. Easy XP!

Congratulations! You've received a new skill level!
Skill name: MS Excel
Current level: 5
XP received: 500

I checked my XP bar:

XP points left until the next social status level: 4650/9000

I couldn't help smiling. I'd made half a level in less than twenty-four hours.

"You're so handsome when you smile," Marina whispered. "Have you done it?"

"Oh, thank you. Yes, I have. Look," I pointed at the table. "You enter the client's name here and their contact person's name here. Now you add the dates and-"

As I explained, an idea struck me. Pavel really should have the trainees connected to their CRM[29] database. What was he afraid of? That they might sell

---

[29] CRM: Customer Relationship Management software which allows a company to monitor and control their clients' list.

the data to someone else? Possible.

"That's it, Marina, I must dash," I finally said.

"Why? How about me?"

"You, my dear, are perfectly ready to work on your own now. Powerful you have become, my young Padawan."

"Yeah right," she replied, looking lost. "Does that mean I can now use the Force?"

"You'd better use Charisma. You're totally good at it."

As I left the office, I ran a quick map search for the nearest men's salon. I had only one search criterion: "haircuts with a high chance of Charisma improvement". No idea whether my query had done anything because all of the town's salons remained on the map. It looked like any decent haircut could improve my Charisma.

I lingered next to the salon's door. I really had to discuss this with Martha. She might help me choose the right hair style.

I summoned her.

"Hi Phil! How's it hangin'?"

"Hi yourself. What kind of language is that? Where did you learn it?"

"Phil, Phil. I don't have a memory, do I? I only know what I learn from you. So how's it hangin'?"

"Straight down. Actually, I need your advice. I need to have my hair cut. What style would you suggest?"

"What do you want me to suggest?" she inquired, taking a languid pull on her fat e-cigarette.

"Can you choose a haircut with the most Charisma?"

"Do I need to? To me, you're charismatic enough as you are, my lord and master."

"Oh Martha, *please*! That's not funny anymore. You're wasting my Spirit!"

"Okay. Seriously, I can't help you with that."

"What *can* you do, then?"

"I can activate my virtual makeover tool featuring potential haircuts."

"Excellent! Let's do it!"

I worked my way though a good fifty images, from completely bald to a Mohawk, then picked the most neutral of the whole lot. Short back and sides and longer on top with slightly raised short bangs. Perfect for the summer weather.

Now that I knew exactly what I wanted, I bade goodbye to Martha and walked into the salon.

"Hi, my name's Katerina," the receptionist beamed. "How can I help you today?"

"I think I need a haircut. Could you do it now?"

"Just a moment. I'll go and check with the stylist."

She left her reception desk and disappeared into the salon, then promptly returned. Her beaming smile appeared perfectly sincere but I could see that the girl was in a foul mood. No idea what had happened to her but her composure was amazing.

"The stylist will be free in twenty minutes. You think you could wait?"

"Absolutely."

"Please take a seat. Would you like a tea or a coffee?"

"A black coffee, please."

As I sipped the piping-hot drink, I continued reading on my smartphone. With any luck, I could up my Reading skill already today. I also kept watching Katerina out of the corner of my eye. Now that she thought that no one was watching, she'd finally allowed her emotions to get the better of her. She sat cross-armed, frowning and staring at the floor in front of her.

I tried to tune in to her and feel what she was feeling. She was definitely upset but still it wasn't anything too serious. This wasn't grief but something rather mundane and annoying.

What could it be? Had she had an argument with a neighbor? Or her boyfriend? Or maybe one of the clients had been rude to her?

I set my phone down on the coffee table, rose and walked over to her.

Noticing that, she transformed immediately. She sat up, laid her hands on the desk and squinted her eyes in a smile, showing her readiness to hear me out. "Yes?"

"Katerina, I hope you'll excuse me.. I know it's none of my business but I just wanted to tell you... it's all gonna work out. I know it will."

"Really? Oh, I'm sorry!" her face turned crimson. "But how do you... Where did you..."

I looked her in the eye and repeated, "It's all gonna be fine."

As I walked back to my seat, I noticed that her

Mood had grown a notch. A couple percent, maybe, but she definitely felt better.

Congratulations! You've received a new skill level!
Skill name: Empathy
Current level: 7
XP received: 500

Oh. I hadn't done it for the XP! I'd known, of course, that I'd had very little left till next level but I'd had no idea how to advance Empathy.

And now I knew. You had to place yourself in another person's shoes and try to feel their pain.

The process of having my hair cut unfolded without any further ado. The stylist — a middle-aged woman with shaven temples — listened to my explanations and nodded her understanding, then switched on her trimmer.

I watched my transformation in the mirror as a long strand of hair dropped to the floor to my right. And another one... With every passing moment, I looked more like Gary Oldman's character in *The Fifth Element.*

The shampoo, cut and blow-dry resulted in a new system message,

Congratulations! You've received a new skill level!
Skill name: Charisma
Current level: 14

XP received: 1000

That's leveling strategy for you. I studied myself in the mirror, thanked the stylist, left her a tip and walked back to the receptionist's desk. As I paid, I gave her a wink,

"Chin up, Katerina!"

She smiled and nodded. "Thank you. See you next time!"

Having thus satisfied my tonsorial needs, I stepped into a coffee shop next door. Leveling strategy was all well and good, but I still needed to find a roof over my head. Time was an issue: I had less than a week until the landlady kicked me out.

I checked the available rental options, then sorted them by location. I wanted to move to the same neighborhood as my parents. They had a very good park there, ideal for jogging, and an excellent but affordable gym with its own swimming pool and boxing group. Sounded perfect. Also, they seemed to have a very nice office building which offered small office spaces for rent. I might need one later on when my budding business idea finally took shape.

I called several numbers but each was answered by a real estate rep. After speaking to one of them twice, I decided to ask him to help me. I described my needs to him and he immediately came up with a few offers, suggesting I started viewing them later in the afternoon. I made an appointment to see him.

I glanced at my watch. I still had about three hours left until our RV. What could I do? I really didn't feel like meeting new clients today. Should I go home for lunch? Another waste of time.

I gave my parents a ring, then called Kira to share all my latest news. Then I took one final swig of coffee and dialed Vicky.

It took her a while to reply. Finally, she did pick up, "Yes, Phil?"

"Hi. I wondered if you could give me Greg's address? You must have it in your database."

"Why?" her voice tensed. "Is he all right?"

"Well, you remember, the night when you and I..."

"Yes, I remember. You can skip it."

"That night, Greg came home drunk early in the morning but his wife wouldn't let him in. He's been crashing at Cyril's ever since. Last night they went to see her but she didn't want to know. He's pretty desperate. His wife is pregnant. The child needs a father!"

"This I understand very well," she said pensively. "What I don't understand is where you come into it."

"Well, I just thought I might go and speak with her. Why not?"

"Is your name Mother Teresa? Why is it you always need to interfere?"

"So is that how you see it? Really?"

Silence. I looked around the café and gestured to the waiter to bring me the tab.

Vicky cleared her throat. "Sorry. I wasn't thinking. Here's the address..."

The Uber driver — a stout highlander from the

Caucasus complete with a bushy moustache — kept talking about his grandchildren as we drove. I listened, inserting the right noises into his soliloquy.

What was I doing? Did I really have to meddle in other people's affairs? Or was I simply after more "socially meaningful actions"? If I managed to bring a family back together, I could expect a hefty XP reward.

Or was I trying to improve my Reputation with Greg? Even worse, did I think I had the right to control other people's lives for them?

I shook my head in disagreement.

I meant none of these things. All I wanted was to help a friend.

And I fully intended to do so.

Chapter
Twenty-Six

Against All Odds

"Once you've taken a few punches and realize you're not made of glass, you don't feel alive unless you're pushing yourself as far as you can go."

Green Street Hooligans

GREG'S WIFE LIVED IN A BRAND-NEW HOUSING COMPLEX, so new that its infrastructure was still in a sorry state. The evidence of barely-finished construction works was everywhere: gravel sidewalks and driveways awaiting a layer of tarmac, large heaps of sand and stacks of concrete slabs. The sad sight was somewhat compensated by the freshly-planted young trees and flowerbeds by the apartment towers' front doors.

The driver pulled up by the right entrance. The many steel buttons of the entry phone seemed to scowl at me. I dialed the apartment number.

"Who is it?" a young but listless female voice sounded in the speaker.

"Alina? Hi, this is Phil. I work with Greg-"

"Thank you! Bye!"

She hung up.

I dialed it again.

"What now?" her voice rang with bile.

"I'm sorry, could you let me in, please? I need to speak to you."

"You can tell Greg he shouldn't bother coming back, ever! Or sending his drinking buddies," she hung up again.

What could Greg have done to deserve this kind of treatment? It couldn't have been just that one drunken night. That alone wouldn't have merited this kind of castigation.

I tried again. No reply.

And again.

"What now?"

"Alina," I said, investing all my sympathy for both Greg and her into my tone. She was only a pregnant girl disillusioned with her husband. "Could I speak with you just for five minutes? Please."

The front door lock clicked open.

"Seventh floor," her voice came from the speaker.

The elevator wasn't working. I had to take the

stairs. I was fully prepared to combat the climb on rubbery legs, puffing and panting, but surprisingly I took the stairs two and three at a time and reached the seventh floor without even getting out of breath. I just loved this Stamina thing.

The doorbell didn't work. I tapped delicately on the door.

A shadow flitted past the eyehole. The door opened a crack.

I saw a pretty petite girl of about twenty years old with an already rather rounded belly. Her hair was pulled into a ponytail.

"Are you Alina?" I asked.

"Yes," she cast me a wary look without inviting me in.

"Allow me to introduce myself again. I'm Philip. I work with Greg. He's a good guy, really. After you kicked him out, he's been such a sorry sight. You know what I mean?"

"Did he send you?"

"He's no idea I'm here!" I pressed my hand to my heart and activated every available point of my charisma, empathy and communication skills, as well as seduction and deception. "I swear!"

She heaved an uneasy sigh and stepped away from the door.

This could be understood as an invitation to enter. Then again, it might not.

I entered slowly, giving her a chance to reconsider, then closed the door behind me. It felt like trying not to scare off a shy young deer. As I did so, I took the opportunity to check her profile,

Name: Alina Chernik

Age: 19

Current status: unemployed

Social status level: 3

Unclassified

Unmarried

Children: pregnant with a male child. Term: 148
days

Criminal record: yes

Her Mood was normal. It didn't look as if she was too upset about their breakup. Her Interest in me was quite high though.

"Take your shoes off and come in. There're some house slippers over there," she said before disappearing into what was probably the kitchen and leaving me alone in a tiny hall.

The apartment was an equally tiny one-bed. The house was new but the decoration left a lot to be desired. The ancient faded wallpaper was probably a Soviet-era leftover. The plinths were coming off the walls. One of the glazed room doors was split in two which was in fact a serious hazard. Apparently, Greg wasn't the handyman I'd thought he was.

I slid my feet into a pair of well-trodden slippers (probably, Greg's) and followed her.

The kitchen was equally shambolic. A tiny free space in between the gas stove, a cupboard, a dining table and a brand new Samsung fridge — which looked almost alien amid all the mess — was stuffed with garbage bags and a plastic washing horse. The dining table was heaped up with unwashed plates and food leftovers. A switched-on smartphone glowed next to an unfinished cup of tea, its screen showing some glitzy girly Instagram feed.

She must have noticed the expression on my face because she hurried to explain,

"The elevator doesn't work. You know, don't you? And I can't climb all those stairs. Not in my state. Would you like some tea? I've just made some."

"Yes, please."

She moved the heaps of plates aside, freeing up some space on the table. Reaching into the fridge, she produced a small bowl of homemade strawberry jam. I noticed with embarrassment that the only thing she wore was a flimsy silky dressing gown which didn't leave much to the imagination.

"It's my mom's jam," she said, struggling to squeeze her body through the narrow space formed by the table and a chair rubbing against the fridge. "How's Greg?"

I took a sip of tea. "Not good. Last night I invited him and some workmates to the restaurant to celebrate a bonus I'd received. Later, Cyril — he's another workmate of mine — told me that when I'd left, Greg was desperate to come and see you. He wanted to apologize."

"That's exactly what he did!" Alina's voice rang with emotion. "He arrived here in the middle of the night, drunk as usual! Nothing new there!"

"And what did you do?"

"What do you think? You really think I should have let him in?"

"Mind if I ask you something? Are you two officially married?"

"No. Why? What's that got to do with it?"

"Just wondered. Didn't Greg ask you to marry him?"

"Yeah, sort of," she grumbled. "He wanted us to have a registry office wedding. That's not what I want! I wanted a proper wedding with lots of guests, a limo and a honeymoon. Not just sign our names on some stupid piece of paper..."

As we spoke, I began to get a better view of the whole setup. A perfectly clear view, even. A young uni student from a one-horse backwater town who'd managed to land an older guy, also a stranger to the city but with prospects of a stable job and a place to live. She'd promptly got pregnant, fully expecting him to tie the knot. Although admittedly smitten, Greg had failed to handle the unexpected change to his status with enough enthusiasm. Still, he'd gone through the motions and proposed to her.

Now that she'd made it, she was supposed to be happy. Only she wasn't. Because the newly-baked father of her child wasn't really ready to marry anyone, was he? He kept on partying with his buddies every weekend; he wasn't even making preparations for the big day, just a boring registry office ceremony. Apparently, Greg believed lush weddings to be a waste of time and money. That wasn't how she used to envision the start of her marital life back in her small workers' town.

As I'd gathered from her rambling story, her own father was the henpecked type. His rare protests against her control-freak mother's rule usually manifested themselves as garage drinking sessions, sharing a bottle of beer or vodka — or both — in the company of a few friends. After each such session, her mother would turn him out, forcing him to sleep rough outside. In the morning, he'd arrive with a bouquet of flowers, beg her forgiveness and be on his best behavior for the next six months or so, catering to his wife's every whim.

That was apparently the marital scenario which had been imprinted in little Alina's young brain. So imagine her astonishment the first time she'd turned a drunk Greg from the door. He refused to come back at all and "spent a whole week groveling somewhere".

"You mean he didn't even call you?" I asked in surprise.

"Yeah, sure he did. I didn't pick up. Why should I?"

Good question. "Do you work?"

"I'm four months pregnant!"

"And this?" I pointed at the space around myself. "Is it him who pays the rent?"

"Yeah."

"Does he leave you enough money?"

She snorted. "If you call it money. *This* is money," she nonchalantly picked up the phone and scrolled through her Instagram feed, showing me the pictures of overdressed and overly madeup girls. "We can barely make ends meet."

This *"we"* was a good sign. It meant she still considered Greg and herself a family.

"You didn't answer my question. Does he provide for you?"

"Yeah. So what?"

This *"So what?"* of hers was the last straw. "What do you mean, *so what*? You're pregnant. You rely on him to provide for you and your future child. And you dare turn him away from the door as if he's a mangy dog. Could you please put your phone down for one moment? He loves you and does his best to provide for his family. He overdid it a couple of times with his workmates, I agree, but-"

She snorted. "Workmates! They're useless lowlifes just like himself."

I got the impression she was just repeating her mother's own words without even realizing what she was saying. "You do understand, don't you, that the more you call him an alcoholic and useless lowlife, the sooner he'll become one? It's you who keep bashing this idea into his head!"

"He drinks!"

"And the more you keep going on about it, the more he'll drink! Don't tell me you've never touched alcohol."

"*Alcohol?* I'm pregnant!"

"Excellent. Very commendable. And before that?"

"Well... maybe..."

"Do you love him?"

"I don't know. I suppose so."

"You do or you don't?"

"Yeah... I do."

"Then I'd like you to listen to me. He's not an alcoholic," I began, enunciating every word to make sure they embedded in her mind. "He works hard to provide for you and your baby. When you showed him the door, he didn't go rogue. He's currently crashing with our other workmate, Cyril. He loves you and has no intention of ever leaving you. But if he sees he can't sponsor your Instagram dreams, you might just push him over the edge. Then he *will* leave you. He might even find another woman, not as-"

Bang! A new system message crashed into my view,

You've dealt critical damage to Alina Chernik: verbal injury
   -30% to Spirit
   -30% to Confidence

Oh wow. How could that have happened? Apparently, the thought of Greg ever dumping her had never crossed her mind. That's how deeply she was invested in the false image of her own father.

Her eyelashes fluttered. Her lower lip began to shake. Had I driven her to tears? I must have done.

A tear slid down her cheek. "Does he have anyone?" she asked over suppressed sobs.

I paused. Let her ponder over it for a while. I took a sip of my tea, all the while monitoring her stats. Her

Mood had plummeted. Which was a good sign, I suppose.

I finished my tea and glanced at my watch. Time to move it.

"No, he doesn't," I said. "He loves you. He will change too, provided you stop nagging. Because that's the reason he drinks, not vice versa. He can't stand to see you unhappy. And you two could be very happy together."

Silence fell. Finally, she seemed to have calmed down a little. She wiped her tears and poured me another cup of tea.

Someone knocked on the door.

Alina jumped to her feet, accidentally pushing the table. Spilt tea flew everywhere. "That must be my neighbor. Don't worry, I'll answer it."

"I must be off, anyway," I said, rising. "Thanks a lot for the tea. Take my advice and let Greg back. You'll see how happy you two can be."

"Okay," she agreed, heading for the front door.

Congratulations! You've received a new skill level!

Skill name: Power of Persuasion
Current level: 2
XP received: 500

That was strange. Only level 2? With my profession? How on earth had I managed to sell anything at all, then? Or could it be that my selling only advanced Vending, and that the Power of Persuasion only concerned more haughty matters?

A male voice came from the hall, husky and distinctly Georgian,

"Here, Alina, light of my life, take a look at what I've got for you! Here're some salmon eggs so your baby can grow faster! And fruit, look: some oranges, apples and bananas, best quality, I hand-picked them myself! And the rump steak, not a trace of fat! You'll see when you cook it- Who the hell is that?"

He stared at me from under his large flat cap, uncomprehending.

Name: David Leonidze. Age: 48. He was short and stocky, a picture-perfect Georgian complete with a traditional mustache and flat cap.

"It's Greg's workmate," Alina hurried to explain. "He's already leaving. Mr. Leonidze, this is Phil. Phil, this is Mr. Leonidze, our upstairs neighbor."

"Phil?" Mr. Leonidze gave me a long scrutinizing look. "And what might he be doing here, I wonder?"

I smiled, noticing a wedding ring on his finger which only confirmed the "married" status in his data. "What *I'm* doing here? I could ask you the same question. Are you taking your chances with married women? Your wife have any idea where you spend your lunch break?"

Mr. Leonidze turned crimson. He set the shopping bags down by the coat rack and threw his hands in the air. "Who do you think you are? Why do you need to pry into other people's lives? I'm a neighbor! I'm here taking care of a pregnant girl whose husband has dumped her, and now I have to listen to your allegations! You've any idea who I am? I don't think you do! And you, who are you?"

"What if you get stuffed," I said slowly, unexpectedly for myself.

"Phil, you've got it all wrong," Alina said, suppressing laughter. "I gave some money to Mr. Leonidze and asked him to get me some groceries. He works at the farmers market. I can't lug the shopping up the stairs, I already told you."

Oops. It looked like this time I'd really put my foot in it. If only I'd had that Lie Detection ability! But even without it, I could feel I'd gotten the wrong end of the stick.

Then again, you couldn't be too sure. This Mr. Leonidze might have had his own agenda. Otherwise why had he reacted so aggressively to seeing me? Had he taken me for a rival?

"I see," I said. "Sorry, Mr. Leonidze. Greg is an old friend of mine. That's why I jumped to conclusions."

He reluctantly shook my proffered hand. "I though the same about you," he admitted. "So what about Greg, is he planning on coming back? He's chosen the wrong time to chase skirts. Or did he expect me to take care of his pregnant wife?"

Aha. It looked like Alina had spun him a different version of the story.

"He's coming back tonight," I said confidently, looking at the girl. "Isn't he?"

"Well, if he apologizes properly and-" she began listing the conditions on which she might have him back.

"Alina, light of my life, what are you talking about?" Mr. Leonidze interrupted her. "This is the father of your child, sweetheart! You two promised to be together in good times and in bad, in sickness and in health!" he thundered ceremoniously like an MC at a wedding. "He's part of you!"

Was it my imagination or had she just blushed? Had we managed to get through to her? Dear Mr. Leonidze. His words couldn't have been more timely. They'd fallen on soil already prepared by me.

Alina nodded. "Okay. He can come."

"Wait a second, sweetheart!" Leonidze, that seasoned old wolf, kept instructing the girl. "What do you mean, *'He can come'*? Philip isn't a radio transmitter! Here, take your phone and give him a ring right now! Tell him you love him! Tell him you miss him!"

Wow. He must have critted her verbally too because Aline turned round and went into the kitchen to get her phone. We heard her speak,

"Hi, Greg? Will you come home... please?"

Leonidze and I exchanged satisfied nods. Trying not to make a noise, we both left the apartment. Leonidze wished me luck and headed upstairs. I walked down the steps, feeling so happy for Greg.

As I stepped outside, I received a system message awarding me 2,000 XP for a socially meaningful action. Now I had only 350 pt. left till level 9. I could easily make that by upping any skill of my choice.

I called Greg just to see if he was all right.

Judging by the excitement in his voice, he was.

"Hi, Greg... No way! You don't mean it! Excellent! Well done! Don't forget to bring some flowers! Exactly! And you know what? I have a funny feeling it's a boy. Just a premonition. Oh come on, what celebration are you talking about? It can wait! Go and see her *now!* Surely Cyril can cover for you? Good! See you tomorrow, man!"

Once that out of the way, I called the real estate woman — her name was Galina — and double-checked our viewing appointment. It was still valid, so I headed straight there.

A short plump woman was waiting for me by the house. I looked around and quite liked it. The courtyard was neat and green. The apartment block was relatively new and appeared to be in good condition.

I peered at the woman. One look at her stats was enough to tell me I had to be doubly careful.

Name: Galina Pakhomenko
Age: 39
Current status: real estate agent
Social status level: 4
Class: Fraudster. Level: 4
Unmarried
Children: Andrei, son
Age: 22
Criminal record: yes

A fraudster? Very well. I might need to double-check all the paperwork. I made a mental note to watch how I paid the deposit.

"Are you Phil?"

"That's right. Nice to meet you. Are we going to see the landlord?"

"That's not necessary. I have the keys and a power of attorney. Follow me. I'll show you everything. Are you planning to live on your own? What do you do for a living? The apartment is a dream, I tell you!"

She went on and on, showering me with information about the apartment as well as herself, her vast experience and her happy clients, interlacing her story with questions about myself. She used her magnet key to unlock the front door and shepherded me toward the elevator.

"You can't wish for better neighbors! They're nice and quiet. The apartment opposite belongs to an old lady, she's very sick so she never leaves the building. And her children have moved town and they don't even visit her."

"Excuse me," I interrupted her soliloquy, "who does the apartment belong to?"

"Er... didn't I say? It's my grandma's. Or her cousin's, rather."

"How about the paperwork? The deeds? The maintenance certificate?"

We entered the elevator. The moment the doors closed, Galina switched on the offensive. "You shouldn't be like that with me! The paperwork's fine! Do you take me for a swindler or something? You've any idea what kind of people my clients are? They rent three-story mansions! And you're grilling me over some shabby little one-bed! If you don't want to rent it, just say so! Don't go wasting my time!"

This was getting a bit theatrical. What was she playing at? Did she intend to shame me into submission? Did she think I would feel so embarrassed by my own lack of trust that I'd apologize and ignore the paperwork?

Very well. Two could play this game.

"I'm very sorry," I said. "I really didn't mean to upset you. It's just that these days you can't trust anyone, you know. My dad's a lawyer. He told me to always double-check all the paperwork in serious matters like this one."

No, my Dad wasn't a lawyer. But somehow I doubted that Galina would ever get the chance to find that out.

"Okay, okay," she grumbled. "You'll see the paperwork in due time. What kind of lawyer is your dad? Does he work for the police?" she visibly tensed.

"Oh no! Nothing of the kind," I hurried to add, watching her relax with relief. "Just a corporate advisor. Not any more though. He's retired now."

The elevator stopped.

"Here we are," she said dryly, stating the obvious. "Follow me."

Fourteenth floor! Imagine the views!

"Take your shoes off," she said. "The apartment gets cleaned but still. I have a few more viewers today. We'd better keep it tidy."

I liked the place the moment I saw it. The

kitchen wall had been torn down, turning the lounge into a single living space. The apartment must have been recently redecorated; everything was shiny and brand-new. It wasn't cluttered with furniture, either; in fact, perfect for a bachelor like myself. A small dining table for four, a few chairs and a couch facing a large flat screen on the opposite wall.

In the kitchen area, there was an electric stove with an extractor, a few kitchen units and a wonderful new fridge with a filtered water dispenser. There was even a small utility room with a washing machine waiting to be loaded.

This apartment was worth every penny of what she wanted for it.

"Cable TV included in the rent," she said, noticing my interest in the television. "Over two hundred channels! And fiber optics."

I gasped. "Awesome."

We moved to the bedroom. Apart from the bed and a large wardrobe, it also housed a small computer desk unit complete with bookshelves.

"You pay every three months," she said. "That's one hundred thousand rubles plus the utility bills.[30] Plus the deposit of one month's rent, thirty-five thousand. You'll get it back if you return the apartment in the same state as you found it. So?"

"Yes, absolutely," I said unhesitantly. "But I'll

---

[30] One hundred thousand rubles equals $1600 as of time of writing which means that the monthly rent for this apartment was about $530 plus the utility bills.

need until tomorrow. I need to think about it."

Everything sounded so perfect there had to be a catch here somewhere. Her high level of Fraud worried me quite a bit.

She shrugged. "As you wish. You can leave the deposit now and take as much time to think as you want. Otherwise, it'll go today. I've loads of takers."

"How many?"

"Loads. If you pay a ten-grand deposit, I'll wait till tomorrow," she kept glancing at her watch. "It's up to you. The next viewer is coming in a quarter of an hour."

"In that case, could you show me the paperwork?"

"Of course," she said with ease. "If you wish. Here."

She laid a plastic folder on the table and began leafing through the papers, showing them to me. "This is my passport[31]. My name's Galina Pakhomenko, as you can see. Here's the power of attorney from my grandma, here, read it well.. *'I do hereby nominate, constitute and appoint... to enter into binding contracts on my behalf for the renting or leasing of my real estate property situated at... shall have full powers and authority to rent, sell and alienate...'* And here're the deeds in her name..."

I pretended I was studying the papers. Instead, I opened the map and ran a quick check for her

---

[31] In Russia, a person's passport is the most common type of ID document. There're no plastic ID cards; a driver's license isn't accepted for identification purposes, either.

"grandma", copying her name and other particulars from the papers.

My back erupted in cold sweat. According to the map, her remains were currently rotting at the city dump.

"And where is she now?" I asked matter-of-factly.

"Where do you think? Back in her country cottage, of course. She was so fed up with the city, you can't imagine. She kept criticizing everything: the air, the people... If you listened to her, everything was wrong here! So she said she wanted to go home to die."

"She was probably right," I agreed, rummaging my brain for what to do next. "But I'm afraid I don't have ten grand on me."

"How much do you have?"

"A couple of grand? I just wasn't prepared to rent it straight away."

"Very well. I can see you're an honest young man. Two grand will have to do, then! I'll wait till tomorrow. But if you don't pay tomorrow, I'll rent the place out and keep the deposit."

Now I could see right through her little scheme. If she managed to rent the place out today, she'd just pay me the two grand back. And if she didn't, she could always count on me to come back. And even if I changed my mind, she'd keep my two grand.

I reached for my wallet and gave her two one-thousand notes without exposing its contents. "Can you give me a receipt?"

She heaved a sigh. "What is it with young people

these days?"

She wrote a receipt for me, anyway. "Would you like to see something else?"

"I don't think so. This place is perfect. I'm just not sure if I can raise a hundred grand at such a short notice. Depends on whether I receive any bonuses."

She seemed perfectly happy with my explanation. "I'll be waiting for your call. Tomorrow."

"Very well," I said as I put my shoes back on in the hall. "See you tomorrow!"

"Yes, yes. See you tomorrow," she hustled me out and locked the door behind me.

I dialed for an Uber. I hadn't yet decided where to go next. Should I report her to the police? Yeah right. I had nothing to tell them, really.

Pointless going to work now. It was too late, anyway. Should I go home, then? But what was I supposed to do with this apartment? And the fraudster's old grandma who hadn't even received a proper burial?

Finally, I came to a decision. I knew only one person who could help me. And judging by the map, he was currently available.

I walked outside and headed for the dedicated Uber stand.

The driver took me to our local police station. I dialed Major Igorevsky whose business card was still in my wallet.

"Speaking," his voice replied.

"Major Igorevsky?"

"Yes. Who is it?"

"It's Phil. Phil Panfilov. You questioned me about that missing girl, Oksana, remember?"

"Oh yes. I was just about to call you myself."

Was he really? How interesting.

"Where are you?" he asked.

"I'm outside the station. Do you think you could come and see me? We need to talk."

"In five minutes," he hung up.

A system alert informed me of my heart rate exceeding safe parameters. You bet. I was restless. It would have been a perfect moment for a cigarette, had I not quit.

I remembered all the details of the night I'd spent in his office. I wasn't sure anymore whether I'd done the right thing calling him.

The Major didn't take long. He looked tired but just as polite.

"Nice to see you, Mr. Phil," he lit up a cigarette. "Did you have another *vision*?"

"Not exactly. Just something I'd like to clear up."

He nodded at the street. "Fancy a walk?"

"Sure."

We headed toward a small boulevard next to the station.

As we walked, the Major finished his cigarette in a few deep, powerful tugs and reached for another. He turned it in his fingers, reluctant to light up. "Spit it out."

I gave him a concise run-down of my apartment hunt and Galina's offer of my dream place.

"What did you say her grandma's name was?" he

asked. "I'll have it checked straight away. If you're right and she's indeed dead, I find it strange they rent her place out. The most logical thing would have been to sell it."

"What if they decided to rent it out while they're looking for buyers? To make a quick buck on the side, you know."

"Possible. Everything's possible. Any more intel you wanna share?"

"What intel?"

"Please. Why do you have to play hard to get? If you have a tip for us, it'll be strictly between us two. Upon my word."

I activated the map and maxed out the zoom. "The city dump," I said. "The south west sector. The closest reference mark is a deformed blue pushbike without wheels, barely seen under the mountain of trash."

"Got it. We'll look into it. And the real estate agent, what did you say her name was?"

"Galina Pakhomenko. Here's her cell number. I also have a receipt with the apartment's address."

"Well done!" the Major copied all the data into his notebook, then pulled out his smartphone and took a picture of the receipt. Having done that, he put the phone and the notebook back into his pocket and lit up his cigarette. "This gives us some evidence against her. Would you be prepared to testify?"

"Not really."

"Okay, okay, don't sweat it. Thanks anyway."

"Nothing to thank me for yet. Will you let me

know how it went?"

"Depends on how it goes," he proffered his hand. "I'll see you around."

"Likewise," I shook his hand.

His grip stayed firm. "Oh, and by the way," he locked his gaze with mine, "I received a very interesting email the other day. From some anonymous well-wisher. It listed the locations of some of the missing children I'd been looking for."

"You don't mean it!" my surprise sounded sufficiently sincere. "And? Did you find them?"

"We most certainly did. Each and every one of them. One of the girls was still alive. We found her in forced slavery in Dubai. They freed her today and brought her to our consulate. She should fly home tonight."

"Did you find those who'd done it to her?"

The Major's face darkened. He lobbed the cigarette butt into a trash can. "Not yet. We have a few leads but the investigation is still ongoing."

"Shame."

"Don't worry. I'll get those scumbags if it's the last thing I do. You'd better tell me if you think you could look for some more."

"Sorry, Major. It doesn't work like that."

"Oh please, grow a pair! It's strictly between you and me. Just check out the Missing Persons page on our site, okay? You never know, you might have another... *vision*," he said without releasing my hand.

"I'll see what I can do," I said.

"You're a very good guy, you know that?" the

Major suddenly concluded.

He let go of my hand, turned round and walked back to the station without saying good-bye.

It was a good job he couldn't see me. A debilitating wave of pleasure flooded over me. I collapsed onto the nearest park bench.

You've received 10,000 pt. XP for performing a socially meaningful action!

Congratulations! You've received a new level!
Your current social status level: 9
Characteristic points available: 1
Skill points available: 1

XP points left until the next social status level: 9650/ 10,000

WHEN I FINALLY came round, I was bursting with energy and enthusiasm. I was so happy that things had worked out with the Major the way they had; that he, for reasons admittedly somewhat selfish, hadn't disclosed the source of the tip. I might be stupid or naïve even, but I was so happy I hadn't chickened out that night. Hearing Oksana's mother's "God bless you!" on the phone that night had been reward enough.

True, I wasn't crafty or streetwise enough to meddle in this sort of business. If tomorrow the powers that be got me by the short and curlies, I'd have only myself to blame. Still, for the first time in thirty years I finally felt like I was doing something that had purpose and meaning.

In this boisterously euphoric frame of mind I went home, picked up Richie and took him to the park. I needed to finally up my Running. That might give me the points needed to make my next level.

Another thirty minutes, an hour max, and my social status might hit level 10.

I entered the park and set off running. My body felt light. Richie trotted along, frolicking among the trees.

"Hey dude," three dark silhouettes stepped in my path. "Got a smoke?"

"Sorry, I don't smoke," I replied without slowing down as I tried to thread my way past them.

The next moment I stumbled over somebody's outstretched foot and tumbled to the ground. I struggled to tuck myself up and landed on the flats of my hands, grazing them raw on the tarmac.

CHAPTER TWENTY-SEVEN

DROP ME OFF BY THE ROADSIDE

"When plunder becomes a way of life for a group of men in a society, over the course of time they create for themselves a legal system that authorizes it and a moral code that glorifies it."

Frédéric Bastiat

I HURT MY KNEE AS I FELL. A CHAIN OF LOG ENTRIES flashed through my view, reporting the damage taken. Nothing serious, but still not very pleasant.

As long as I could remember, from my first

kindergarten days till my reluctant college fighting experiences — and a few times later in life — I'd never been good at facing aggression. Whenever I'd crossed paths with a street goon or a college bully, I'd break out in a cold sweat and stand shaking on rubbery legs as a panicky, clammy fear flooded over me. Any such encounter had left a long, unpleasant aftertaste as I'd tried to suppress the memory of my fear — of both pain and humiliation — and the anger with myself for being such a wuss.

This time, however, I felt annoyed with them. The pain in my knee meant I might have to skip tomorrow's running practice and gym session. I might even have to take a week off or more.

And just to please, Richie wasn't around, either, apparently otherwise distracted. Had he been next to me, these goons might have thought twice before accosting me. What was even more annoying, I'd never gotten around to practice street fighting — which, considering the stat booster which came with my Premium account, was a real shame.

All these musings had flashed through my head in a matter of seconds. The goons guffawed. They must have taken my reluctance to jump aggressively back to my feet as a sign that I was a wimp and therefore fair game.

Where was Richie, dammit?

Clutching at my injured knee, I scrambled back to my feet and peered at my attackers, weighing up my chances. I wasn't going to fight back, no, although admittedly I was itching to finally learn to stand up for myself. I was just trying to work out how to get out of this unscathed. I didn't give a damn about any injuries to my pride. Pretty soon I might be able to pay back in kind as long as I took physical leveling seriously and learned to stand up for myself.

There were three of them, and they *could* fight. There was only one of me: a recent noob far removed from the imbaness I aspired to. I didn't have a snowball's chance in hell.

Two of them were eighteen. Their leader, a burly guy with a crew cut, was twenty-one and went by the moniker of Tarzan. All of them wore shorts; the two younger ones had T-shirts on while their leader boasted a bicep-revealing wife-beater. Their social-status levels weren't much to write home about: 3 and 4 respectively. What a shame. So much life wasted.

They grinned at me expectantly. Tarzan bared his teeth in a smirk, took a deep tug on his cigarette and spat at my feet. "What, no smokes, bro?"

In the dim light of the park lamps, his teeth seemed to illuminate the space around us. His minions began flanking me inconspicuously. It looked like I couldn't just swallow my pride and part with them nicely. These guys meant business.

I spat on the ground. My saliva was tinted with blood as I'd bitten my tongue in my fall. "I don't smoke."

I drew in a lungful of air and called at the top of my voice, "Richie, come! *Come!*"

The goons looked around themselves, peering into the darkness as they tried to work out who I was calling to.

"That's it, guys," I said calmly. "You've had it."

"No way!" Tarzan said, faking surprise. "You screwing with us? Are you stupid or something?"

"Richie, *come!*" I yelled. I had no hope in hell of running away from them: just standing on my injured leg was a challenge.

My field of vision shifted momentarily, edged with a fiery crimson. Time slowed down. I could see a fist hover in the air about a foot away from the back of my head. Martha's voice read out the message that appeared in my view.

Warning! Potentially lethal aggression detected!

Danger of illegal activity targeting a user whose social status level is at least threefold more than that of his attackers.

Forceful activation of heroic ability: Sprint.

Ability class: Combat

+100% to the user's Speed

Requires changes to the user's metabolism and perception of time

Awaiting activation confirmation...

Still hearing Martha's voice, I ducked, trying to dodge the knuckle duster on the youngest goon's fist. It shot past within inches of my head.

I stood up. Without even realizing what I was doing, I mechanically clenched my hand and punched him in the stomach.

For some reason, he squeezed his eyes shut and screwed his face into a grimace of agony. The guy slowly doubled up as he rose into the air in a gravity-defying ascent, then traced an arc over the ground as if mimicking a B-movie slow-motion stunt.

Awaiting activation confirmation...

Sending request to server. Please wait. Server connection timeout. Impossible to establish connection with the server.

Forceful activation of heroic ability: Sprint is canceled.

Time sprang back to normal. My attacker zoomed through the air, then landed a dozen feet away from me where he lay motionless. I stepped back, turning so that I could keep an eye on the remaining two. The leader's other minion had already taken a swing with a large, heavy monkey wrench. Now his hand stopped halfway through the air as he stared open-mouthed at his buddy crouched in the fetal position on the ground.

"What did I just say?" I spat at their feet and cracked a grin. I'd leveled up Spirit just in time, hadn't I? "Come on, punk!"

Slowly the "punk" stepped back, casting wary glances at his two friends.

I was bluffing, sure, but that seemed to be the only solution. To run off would be to expose my weakness to them. Also, I wasn't going to run fast, not with this leg of mine. And this way there'd still be hope that Richie would find me.

Indeed, he came running. I could hear his

barking and the snapping of branches as he charged through the bushes toward me. No idea how dogs know it, but he immediately took his place at my side in an aggressive crouch, growling. The fur stood up on his hackles, his ears flattened — my pet was at his best, spreading an Aura of Fear for many feet around.

I grabbed hold of his collar as if trying to restrain him, while in fact I was sponging off his confidence and courage.

"You'd better watch your back now, Mr. Bolt," the leader said threateningly, then turned to his minion, "Just leave him and let's get outta here."

"And how about him?" the younger one pointed at his friend still lying on the ground.

"He'll live. He'll come round and get back to us," the leader replied, then left the scene with the proud posture of a bodybuilder, his back straight and shoulders spread.

Without lowering his monkey wrench, the other one gave me a wary look and stepped toward his buddy lying on the ground.

"Don't be afraid," I encouraged him. "I won't hurt you. What's up with him?"

"He seems to be breathing," he replied.

"Take him away before I-" I began.

The sounds of shouting and stomping of feet came from the direction in which the leader had just left.

The goon peered into the darkness, then announced, "Now run like hell! We've got help coming! Run!"

With my plummeted Perception and bad eyesight, I finally recognized their leader running back toward us followed by a burly dude.

"There he is!" the leader lunged at me. Before I could dodge, I received an almighty stomp in the ribs. Choking on my own wind, I collapsed hearing a chaos of voices and the growling of Richie who'd sunk his teeth into my attacker's arm.

"Don't move!" I heard Alik scream. It was he who'd apparently hurried to their aid.

Wailing like a Banshee, Tarzan tried to beat off Richie. Richie was shaking his head with the unfortunate attacker still in his jaws.

"Down! Down!" the other goon yelled at the dog. "Get off!"

"Phil, get the dog off!" Alik shouted in my ear as he helped me up to my feet.

Ignoring him without even trying to grasp his role in the situation, I suddenly became enraged beyond pain and fear, which was immediately confirmed by a system message informing me of my excessive adrenaline and noradrenaline levels. I received a "Fury and Valor" buff with bonuses to strength, agility and stamina which also offered a heightened pain threshold, metabolism and confidence.

"You son of a bitch!" the goon groaned. "Get your dog away from me!"

"Phil, would you please take Richie away?" Alik asked, then ventured hopefully, "Richie, come on, boy!"

Richie squinted at me. Clever dog. With a heavy

gait I headed toward Tarzan, fully intending to wipe the grin off his face.

"Phil, please," Alik held me back by my shoulder. I brushed him off.

"Phil!"

"Shut up," I took a wild swing, about to bash the bastard's brains in.

"Stop, for Christ's sake!" Alik yelled, yanking my arm back.

"What now?" I exploded. "Are you defending this piece of crap?"

"Just cool it, man," Alik kept urging. "It's all right! Everything's okay now!"

I peered into his eyes framed by long eyelashes. His pock-marked face breathed peace. Slowly I came back to my senses.

"Richie, off!" I said. "Alik, whassup, man? Did they tell you how they'd jumped me?"

"Not yet," he said. "We'll get to that bit now."

Richie relaxed his jaws, releasing Tarzan's hand. Still growling, he stood next to me.

Soon we had everything sorted out. The three thugs — who were a couple of rungs below Alik in their unspoken street hierarchy — apologized and even paid me a "penalty". Tarzan emptied his pockets, scooping out all the bank notes and small change he had on him, a half-empty pack of cigarettes, a lighter and an open packet of chewing gum, and handed everything to me.

"What's this for?" I asked.

"For the trouble," he wheezed. "We're sorry. We shoulda known better."

By then, the other guy had already come round. He frowned blankly, trying to grasp the situation, then promptly joined in,

"We're very sorry, sir. We didn't recognize you. We've heard some good things about you already but we've never seen you before. So it's our fault."

"I don't need your money," I said. "Tarzan has already paid enough for my single bruise. You'd better get him to the first-aid station now. Let them see to his wound. The dog might have rabies, you never know."

"Alik, please don't mention this to Yagoza, man," Tarzan asked. "Please?"

"I won't. You'd better ask Mr. Panfilov," Alik nodded at me.

Was he trying to level up my Reputation with street thugs for me?

Tarzan switched his gaze to me, awaiting my decision.

"I won't, either," I replied, promptly receiving a Reputation upgrade with all three of them.

Alik gave each of them a brotherly hug. The goons left, two of them supporting their staggering friend.

"Listen, man, I'm sorry," Alik said. "They're my hoodies, I've grown them from scratch. They didn't recognize you, that's all."

"It's me who has to be sorry, man," I said, mimicking his tone. "But don't you think it's a bit sick? Had it been some strange guy, they would've just taken his money and his phone, gave him a good thrashing and just left him here. D'you think it's correct?"

He didn't reply. We walked along the park lane, me still limping, him pensively tousling Richie's haunches, until we came to a brightly lit busy street. The sight seemed to jerk us back to reality.

"You know, Phil," Alik finally said, "They're just kids. Red-blooded youngsters high on adrenaline. They need money. They're prepared to work for it. But no matter how hard they try, they're getting nowhere. They've got no jobs. They've got nothing! How do you want them to earn their way in life? You tell me!"

"You want me to tell you?" I asked as an idea began to form in my head. "Very well. Listen up..."

WHEN WE LEFT THE PARK, ALIK FORCED ME DOWN ON A bench and was about to dash off to the nearest drugstore for some medication. By then, my knee had swollen. I'd struggled to walk. The Fury and Valor buff had already expired, and its cooldown had rewarded me with agonizing pain in my whole leg.

"You need to put your leg up on the bench," he told me before leaving, "That way it might slow the swelling down."

"Wait a sec. These hoodies of yours, are they always so crazy? They very nearly killed me!"

"Oh, no. Not at all. Normally they'd just put the fear of God into someone and that's it. But today they decided to go for it. They wanted to find a guy, knock him out straight away and check his pockets. Tarzan's got a baby daughter, you see. They share a one-bedroom place with his parents. His father is a paraplegic. His disability benefits are a joke. They have no food in the house, you understand?"

"I'm trying to. He's a fit, healthy guy. He's been in the army, hasn't he? He could have easily found a menial job, like unloading cargo trains at the station. Or he could have offered his services as a night guard..."

"And you think he didn't? He gets up before five a.m. every morning to join the other bunch of guys who're waiting to be picked by casual employers. He accepts every job he's offered!"

"I still don't understand. Sooner or later, he'll get himself arrested. And then what? Who's gonna put food on the table?"

"You don't have children, do you?" Alik replied. "I don't. And his baby girl is real sick. She needs surgery or she might kick the bucket pretty soon. His dad needs his medications... Never mind. Wait for me here. I won't be long."

After a quarter of an hour, he emerged from the 24/7 drugstore with a pot of some ointment he'd bought with his own money. I applied it and leaned my elbows on the bench as I waited for the medication to work. Alik hovered around, sighing at his own thoughts, then admitted he had nowhere to spend the night.

"How's that?" I asked.

"I used to crash with this guy and now he's got himself a woman. I spent last night in the park. I woke up in the middle of the night because I was frozen solid!

I had to jog around for a bit just to get warm. So this morning the boss caught me sleeping on the job. And then I had to unload fish and stack it in the freezer and that's when I got frozen stiff!" he emitted a jaw-wrenching yawn which ended in what sounded like a groan. "And I'm starving."

"Food isn't a problem," I said. "Let's go to my place and cook something now. And as for a place to stay... can't you rent something?"

"I could, I suppose... only I used your money to pay off a loan and all the overdues. And the new boss won't give me an advance. Which is logical really, I've only been working there for two days. But I've already found a place just next to my new job..."

"Listen," I said, " I have an idea. I'm gonna move to a new place in a couple of days. And my apartment has been paid for at least another week in advance. You could stay there if you want."

"Really?"

"Why not?"

He didn't reply. A new system message answered my question instead,

Your Reputation with Romuald "Alik" Zhukov has improved!
Current Reputation: Respect 40/120

As I blinked the message shut, I felt strangely touched. This was the first jailbird in my life who'd had respect for me. Someone might say this wasn't much to be proud of. Still, I beg to differ. In the eerie neon light of a nearby publicity billboard Alik looked a lot like a blue troll. Not that idiot from the movie but the proper WoW one: clumsy but burly and tall with muscular arms hanging to his knees. That's why his streetwise respect for me, a wussy nerd, was akin to the respect felt by an aggressive Horde troll to an Alliance player.

"Let's go, then," I said, scrambling to my feet.

"Let me help," he stood next to me, threading his arm under my shoulders.

"Richie, heel," I said, feeling a sudden bout of sadness. Svetlana, the dog's owner, was bound to collect him the next day.

We reached my apartment without any further innuendos. Shame I'd failed to improve Running, though. I'd missed the opportunity to make a new level.

"Come in and get comfortable," I said. "Richie, let's clean your paws first."

As I'd walked home, I'd had plenty of time to work out what must have happened in the park. The so-called "heroic ability" — and not even the most impressive one at that — had allowed me to literally step into Neo's shoes, albeit for a few seconds. The incredible sensation of my superiority was multiplied by self-righteousness (because I'd known I was doing the right thing, otherwise the program wouldn't have activated the ability to begin with) which had been far beyond everything I'd ever experienced before. That was one hell of a powerful ability which allowed you to be in control of any situation, almost like a turn-based combat in Fallout. Normally, I should have received it at level 20 or so.

Now I knew what to look forward to.

"Phil, mind if I take a shower, man?" Alik asked, sniffing himself. "I can't stand myself for much longer."

"Absolutely. Clean towels are in the bathroom cupboard."

He took his time. Judging by the sounds coming from the bathroom, he must have thrown his clothes in the wash.

In the meantime, I got the dinner going. I really should spend the next morning closing more deals. I had some good ideas — and I really wanted to pay Pavel back with some nice sales numbers without disappointing him. I also had to go to the gym, walk Richie — which would probably be our last walk together — and think what to do about moving to a new place. I needed to look into the legality of Galina's apartment. If it was bad news, I'd have to shop around some more: this time I might use my interface search function.

I also needed to contact Yanna and find out whether our Friday divorce appointment was still valid. We should have done it today but that was something I couldn't help.

I opened my task list and made it smaller, leaving it hovering in my view. I had to decide on the tasks' order and priority.

- *meet up with Yanna and file for divorce;*
- *pay my casino debt back to my friend Gleb Kolosov*

- work out a wanted criminals search strategy

- downsize

- having moved to a new place, leave the old apartment keys with Romuald "Alik" Zhukov

- return Richie to his owner Ms. Svetlana "Sveta" Messerschmitt;

- contact some of my old friends and ask them out to catch up on things

The last two petty tasks on the list — to level up Running and to get a haircut — hadn't earned me any XP at all, not even a measly 5 pt. I got a funny feeling that the program kept making it harder for me to proceed. These days, it didn't offer rewards for every petty task just to make sure I completed it.

I studied the task's priority order. Apparently, the *Augmented Reality! Platform* still believed my divorce to be my prime objective.

Why so? How would it change if, for some reason, I reconsidered and reconciled with Yanna? You'd think that saving a family was a more socially meaningful action compared to splitting one?

Also, why would the program consider my ancient casino debt to Gleb — I remembered his name now, thanks to the mention on the list — more important than my search for wanted criminals? What if the very fact of paying him back didn't really matter? What did matter, however, was restoring his faith in friendship and fellow men?

Without hesitation, I opened my smartphone and searched through social media until I'd located his profile. After that accident, he'd removed me from his friends list. Luckily, he hadn't blocked me. I wrote him a long message telling him how ashamed I was of what I'd done and offering to pay him back at any time convenient to him. I also added that it would be nice to meet up with a few of our old friends — say, this coming Friday — and catch up on things.

I wrote similar messages — leaving out the debt-paying part, of course — to all my old college friends, guys and gals, the contact with whom I'd lost when I'd stopped answering their invitations, completely consumed by a new WoW content update.

A content update... What was its name again? I couldn't remember. This Optimization thing seemed to have had its effect on me.

Thus musing, I returned to my potato-peeling, onion-chopping duties. I decided not to bother with any complex dishes. Chicken legs and French fries, good enough.

I might have failed leveling up Running earlier that night, but my half-baked attempt at cooking had brought me the few XP points I so badly needed.

The chicken legs were still far from done when I received a new message,

Congratulations! You've received a new skill level!
Skill name: Cooking
Current level: 4
XP received: 500

That was enough to receive a new level, the second one for today. I'd made level ten!

Heroism, here I come!

Congratulations! You've received a new level!
Your current social status level: 10
Characteristic points available: 1
Skill points available: 1

Now I had two skill points and two characteristic points available. One of which I absolutely had to invest into Luck to make level 10. That way it would finally reach the worldwide average. Also, that was the number required for all level-1 Heroic skills.

I was dying to invest another point into either Intellect or Agility. Still, I decided to take it easy for the time being. My acquisition of Heroic abilities might force me to alter my initial leveling strategy.

I opened the skill descriptions,

Tier 1
Ability name: Lie Detection
Ability type: Passive, Heroic
Considerably enhances the user's ability to tell if someone's being insincere
Unblocking requirements:
- Heroism: level 1+
- Social status: level 10+
- Empathy: level 5+
- Communication Skills: level 5+
- Perception: level 10+

- Charisma: level 10+
- Luck: level 10+
- Intellect: level 20+

Tier 1
Ability name: Stealth and Vanish
Ability type: Active, Heroic
Allows the user to activate the Stealth system module in order to become invisible to all creatures around him or herself for a minimum duration of 15 sec, depending on their Spirit numbers. Can be used in combat.
Unblocking requirements:
- Heroism: level 1+
- Social Status: level 10+
- Strength: level 10+
- Agility: level 10+
- Perception: level 10+
- Stamina: level 10+
- Luck: level 10+
Cooldown: 1 hr

My current social status level answered both skills' requirements. Still, I could only choose one. My stats were closer to Lie Detection, provided I made level 20 in Intellect and level 10 in Perception. At the moment, I had 18 and 7 respectively. Also, both characteristics kept growing organically. According to the slowly filling progress bar, my Intellect improved with every book I read. As for Perception, now that I'd quit smoking, it kept expanding naturally with every day. If I finished reading Stephen Hawking's *A Brief History of Time* tonight before bedtime, that might be enough to receive a new Intellect level. Then I could expect a new level in Perception the day after tomorrow after the expiry of the Nicotine Withdrawal debuff.

If I invested one point into Intellect now, I could reach the level 20 that was required. That way I could later invest the points awarded for the next two social status levels into Perception, and then... bingo!

How did it feel, being able to always tell when someone was lying? Truth isn't always a good thing, you know. How many married couples live happily ever after with a few well-concealed skeletons in their respective closets? Would it undermine my faith in humanity?

True, as soon as my license expired, so would this double-edged ability — but sometimes even a few months of knowing where you're standing with a certain person can drive you up the wall.

In which case, how about Stealth and Vanish? Having said that, what was I supposed to do with it? Offer my services to an intelligence bureau? Get enlisted and go to hot spots? Become a bounty hunter? In this case, the skill requirements weren't just as easy to fulfil but were still doable.

I really had to give it a good think. Which leveling strategy should I choose? What did I want to become? What was my vision of helping the world? How would it affect me? Or my family? Did I want money and fame? Or would I rather become some kind of picture-perfect Marty Sue who could achieve everything, making even the wildest of my dreams come true?

I got so carried away I'd completely forgotten about dinner. What was that smoke in the kitchen?

It was the chicken legs, dammit.

LATER AT DINNER, we discussed my idea while demolishing the food.

"So that's what we're gonna do, help people?" Alik asked.

"We're gonna help everyone who needs our help," I said, finishing off everything still left on my plate. "It can be people, or dogs, or cats..." I rose and began putting the kettle on.

"*Cats?*" Alik gulped a big mouthful of his dinner without even chewing. "How do you want us to help *them*? And why?"

"We could find new homes for abandoned kitties. Find good jobs for those who need them. Or suitable accommodation for those looking for a new place. Basically, we'll be a broker's agency bringing people together. We'll be matching vendors with buyers, landlords with tenants, athletes with coaches, singles with those looking for a partner... Why, might you ask? Firstly, they'll all pay us a fee. Secondly, we'll also be doing lots of non-profit stuff. We'll try to spread the word about it on social media which should improve our agency's visibility...."

"Sorry, didn't get that last bit," Alik interrupted me. "Improve what, did you say?"

"Well, for instance, we could create our group on Facebook. Are you on Facebook?"

"Of course I am!" he sounded offended. "Here, let me show you…"

I wanted to ignore the offer but he'd already opened his ancient smartphone and was shoving his Facebook profile in my face. I glimpsed his last post, a snippet of street wisdom:

"I have been fighting since I was a child. I'm not a survivor, I'm a warrior."

His profile photo featured Alik crouching with a cigarette, blowing smoke at the camera. You could tell at once he was a tough streetwise cookie. And this was the man I was discussing my future business with?

"Excellent! You know what I mean, then," I steered the conversation back on course. "The more people know about us, the more clients we're gonna get."

The kettle began to boil. Alik jumped from his stool, "I'll make it. What do you drink, tea?"

"Yes, please."

We drank our tea in silence. Alik pensively scrolled through his Instagram feed. Finally, he asked,

"Phil? Why do you need me and my guys in all this? Seriously?"

"Firstly, there's too much work for me alone," I said. "I'd have to hire some assistants, anyway. Secondly, your guys are tough. Their skills might come in handy one day, you never know. And finally, can't I do it just to help you? To support your progress in life, what's wrong with that?"

"I see," he replied, his voice suddenly hoarse.

"But that's not all," I said. "Tell your guys they'll be basically our combat section. Which means they have to clean their act up. No drinking or smoking. We'll go to the gym, all of us, and train together."

I knew full well this sounded like the pipe dream of a naïve wuss. These were seasoned muggers with God only knows how many victims to their names — possibly, even murders. As soon as I had Lie Detection activated, I might need to run "Alik's guys" through it. If I found something major, I might even need to take justice into my own hands.

But then again, if I didn't, who would? If I failed to provide them with an opportunity to do something with their lives, they might continue their perilous slide down the wrong path.

"Consider it done," Alik thumped his chest with a fist. "Should I quit my new job?"

"No, you'd better stick with it for a while. We might not start for another month. I still have my own job to sort out and lots of other things. I've got to get a divorce first.. plenty of things to do. Then I'll have to make a plan and see what exactly we should be doing and how to go about it."

He nodded. "Mind if I smoke? I can go out onto the balcony."

"Sure. You can sleep on the couch. The bedclothes are in the closet, help yourself. I need to get some sleep. I've got to get up early tomorrow."

"Me too. The commute to my new job is a nightmare. I'll have a smoke, clean the plates and go to bed."

"Excellent. Good night!" I said.

"Same to you," he headed for the balcony.

I climbed into bed, opened a book and only then remembered I'd forgotten to distribute the available skill points. I spent some quality time pondering over this. I couldn't improve Learning Skills because Optimization was still in process. Should I invest in something else, maybe?

In the end, I decided it wasn't worth it in the long run. Once Optimization was complete, I'd receive my 4 points and add them to the current 2 which would allow me to bring the skill up to 9. That would give me +270% to Learning Rate in less than a month! That's not even counting the stat booster and the skill's priority status. Which in turn would allow me to level up Reading much faster, thus accelerating my Intellect too.

This sounded like the right decision. Especially considering the fact that the more advanced a skill was, the harder it was to level. That's when the extra system points would come in handy.

I finished reading the book on my smartphone. In the lounge, the couch creaked its rusty springs as Alik kept tossing and turning, heaving an occasional sigh in synch with his own thoughts. Finally, he fell silent, then began snoring.

Just as I finished reading the last page, my Reading skill predictably upped.

Congratulations! You've received a new skill

level!

> *Skill name: Reading*
> *Current level: 7*
> *XP received: 500*

Right. But where was my new Intellect level?

I checked its progress bar and heaved a disappointed sigh. Only 99% full. Never mind. I'd have to leave it till tomorrow. I had to stop reading for the night. I couldn't keep my eyes open. They itched as if full of sand.

So I invested a system point in Luck.

Warning! We've detected an abnormal increase in your Luck characteristic: +1 pt.

Your brain will be restructured in keeping with the new reading (10) to comply with your current level of decision making.

The world must have blinked — not that I would have noticed it in the darkness of my bedroom. I did feel a new embrace of the great void, though.

Now the second point... I really should invest it in Perception. Intellect could wait. At the moment, Perception took priority.

It was the first time I was trying to upgrade it, so I expected to experience something extraordinary, like when I'd first upgraded Strength.

Warning! We've detected an abnormal increase in your Perception characteristic: +1 pt.

Your sensory organs responsible for the reception of visual, auditory, olfactory, tactile and gustatory stimuli, as well as those responsible for your balance and spatial orientation, will be restructured in keeping with the new reading (8) to comply with your current level of Perception.

Changes required: new adjustments made to your eyes, ears, nose, skin, tongue, vestibular system and nerve endings.

Warning! In order to activate the skill, an undisturbed 3-hour period of sleep is required. Please ensure your location is safe. You are recommended to adopt a prone position.

Accept / Decline

I pressed *Accept* and immediately was forced into an obligatory sleep.

I awoke in the middle of the night from the insistent vibration of my phone under the pillow. It looked like this Perception thing did improve my senses. Before, a paltry thing like this would never have awoken me.

I pulled out the phone and stared at the screen. WTF? Was I seeing things? Or was it indeed my almost-ex mother-in-law?

Their whole family must have been on a mission to strip me of my sleep! Were they on a schedule? First it was Yanna, then her new beau, and now it was her mother in the flesh, as large as life and twice as ugly!

"What is it?" I snapped in the receiver.

"Phil, sweetheart, it's me, your mom-in-law," her voice echoed. "Is Yanna there?"

"My mom-in-law? I thought you made it pretty clear during our last meeting you were no 'mom' to me any longer? No, Yanna isn't here. She hasn't been here since the day you came here to collect her stuff."

"Phil," she broke down, bursting into tears, "Yanna's gone!"

Another sleepless night, dammit.

Chapter Twenty-Eight

Caught in the Eye of the Storm

"It takes three to divorce."

Aleksander Kumar

"PHIL, WHERE'RE YOU GOING?" ALIK'S VOICE ASKED ME from the lounge.

"Go back to sleep. I won't be long."

Cussing, I laced up my sneakers. That stupid, careless girl! Not to mention her control freak mother!

I was angry with myself more than anything else. As it had just transpired from my brief but rather mournful discourse with Mrs. Orlova, Yanna hadn't been seen for a while. At first, her mother had thought she must have moved back in with me but when she'd heard I hadn't seen her either she'd dissolved into panic. I wasn't even sure what exactly she feared the most: the fact that her girl had gone missing or the probability of our reunion.

Apparently, my father-in-law had been invited to the funeral of some ex co-worker who lived at the other end of the country somewhere. In the meantime, Yanna had returned home from Vlad. Not for long though because, as you can well imagine, two snakes sharing one nest is a recipe for disaster. Even if they lie curled up together, nice and snug, it doesn't mean they're enjoying a hug. They're simply competing for the best spot in the cage.

So Yanna, being younger and less experienced in the fine art of Chinese water torture, had left home and hadn't been heard from since. At first, my mother-in-law had rejoiced thinking she'd finally managed to nag some sense into her daughter.

"Because Vlad is such a respectable young man with lots of potential," she explained.

I'd heard enough. I mentally told her to kindly return to whichever dark corner of Inferno she'd crept out of, then hung up.

Five minutes later, the landline in the kitchen began buzzing. I was too sleepy and disoriented to simply unplug it, so I hurried to answer it, afraid of waking Alik up.

"We've been disconnected," Mrs. Orlova sobbed, then continued with her story.

Cursing my good manners and respect for old people, I didn't dare hang up on her twice. Also, I was admittedly curious to find out whatever could have happened to Yanna.

So basically, she'd been missing for three days now. She'd left her parents' home just before the weekend. Mrs. Orlova had assumed she'd simply returned to Vlad. Since then, there'd been no trace of her anywhere. Her telephone was switched off. She hadn't showed up at work, either. Vlad had assured them he hadn't seen her at all. Mrs. Orlova had called all of Yanna's friends, with zero results.

"You sure you didn't upset her?" I asked.

Because if she had, then Yanna might have told her friends to lie to her mother, offering her a cooked-up story. I wouldn't have put it past her.

"God no, I didn't!" Mrs. Orlova exclaimed. "All I ever did, I tried to convince her to get back with Vlad."

This time I hadn't batted an eyelid. No point in hanging up on her. Even though formally Yanna and I were still married, in my ex-mother-in-law's eyes I was a finished case, a has-been with whom she could be perfectly open. In her naïvely tactless simplicity, she had no consideration for my own feelings.

By the end of our conversation, I'd already located Yanna on my mental map. Now I had to decide what to do about it.

I couldn't just ignore Mrs. Orlova's call. We were still family, after all. Her motherly concern for her daughter's wellbeing was perfectly understandable. And in her old-fashioned vanity, she wouldn't go to the police, afraid for her family's good name. Just the way her brain worked.

Judging by the map, Yanna was perfectly fine. But simply giving her address to her mother would trigger another tidal wave of questions and suspicions, and I really wasn't in the mood to deal with them.

So I did my best to calm my "mom-in-law" down, then called a cab and got ready to pay my ex a visit.

"Phil, wait," Alik emerged out of the lounge, wrapped in a sheet. "Problems, man?"

"It was my mother-in-law. Apparently, my wife's gone missing. I'm gonna check out a couple of places where she might be. Go back to sleep now."

"No way," he declared. "I'm coming with you. One sec."

It was pointless trying to argue with him so I just waited for the cab as Alik got dressed. A couple of minutes later, we left and headed for some hotel in the suburbs where, according to the program, Yanna now was. Its name — Red Rose Inn — said nothing to me, but judging by its location, it wasn't the Hilton, that's for sure.

Alik took the passenger seat next to the driver[32]. As we drove across the deserted night city, he engaged the man in a passionate discussion about our soccer team's chances at the home World Cup. The road before us glistened, reflecting the golden glow of streetlamps.

---

[32] In Russian cabs, the seat next to the driver's is available for passengers.

"We're gonna do 'em all!" Alik ranted. "We're playing on our own turf, aren't we? At the very least we're gonna get out of the group stage!"

"I don't think so! Our team is at its absolute worst in years-" the driver began.

I didn't listen any further. I really felt like asking him to turn round and take us back home. My brain was boiling. What the hell was I doing? This was the most stupid, pointless and irrational thing I'd ever done in my life.

My heart was silent. No prompts coming from that department. Ditto for the interface which hadn't issued me any tasks nor quests. Why on earth was I going there, then?

Was it because I wanted to see Yanna? Not really.

Did I believe she was in need of my help? Hardly. She wasn't in some deserted out-of-town location. She was staying in a hotel. And I had this confident feeling that she was perfectly fine.

Was I trying to appease my indefatigable mother-in-law? Yeah right. Part of me was currently on a protest rally, shaking banners in the air and demanding she be granted a personal cauldron in hell.

What was it, then? Was it my desire to help her simply because I could? I concentrated, focusing on my feelings. Nope. Not that, either. Even though this alien software seemed to be breeding altruism in me, uprooting my inbred selfishness, this particular task had too many cons. It was going way too far, compromising my private life and my own goals; it even messed with my sleep.

As we approached the hotel, I finally had an epiphany. I was going there to bring closure to the whole thing. To officially finalize my relationship with Yanna and her family. I still couldn't forget the morning when I'd been crumbling under the pressure of my freshly-acquired Strength. How they'd arrived without warning and begun rummaging through the place, throwing my own possessions on the floor. I remembered Vlad yelling at me for no reason whatsoever and then leaving as I stood outside like an idiot watching his Jeep whisk Yanna away.

That had been our parting scenario.

I'd thought I'd never see her again barring a brief divorce appointment.

Now I had the chance to bring this to a different kind of closure.

"Here we are," the driver said. "Red Rose Inn."

"Could you wait for us, please? We won't be long."

"It's ten rubles a minute," he warned us.

"That's all right. Alik, mind waiting for me in the car, please?"

"Yes, but are you sure-"

"Sure I'm sure. I won't be long."

I climbed out of the cab. The driver pulled off in search of a parking space.

You wouldn't know this was a hotel. Its sign wasn't even lit. The single streetlamp cast its dull light on a crude wrought-iron depiction of a rose mounted on the wall.

I walked in and looked around, searching for the reception desk. A guard was quietly snoring on a couch at the far end of a small lobby.

I walked closer. A young guy was slumped in his chair behind the reception desk, his head hanging to one side. He too was asleep.

I pressed the bell. With a startle, the guy jumped from his seat and stretched his lips in a smile. "Good evening... eh, good night... how can I help you?"

"Good evening. Could you please give me the room number of Ms. Yanna Orlova?"

Much to my chagrin, my mental map had denied me access to that kind of information. Most likely, I didn't have enough Insight.

The guy pulled out a large guest book from under the desk and paused, thinking.

"I'm afraid, this is confidential information," he said, setting the book aside.

"Listen, Dmitry," I said, reading the name tag pinned to his chest. "She's my wife."

By then, the guy was fully awake and professionally vigilant. "I'm afraid we can't provide that kind of information. It's a question of our guests' privacy."

"Then could you please give her a call? Ask her if she could come down or receive me in her room."

"I'd rather not disturb her. Do you know what time it is?"

He was good. Nothing to say there. I had to try a different approach.

I pulled out a wallet and laid one of the bank

notes on the desk in front of him.

He gave it a disinterested glance and pushed it back to me. "Thank you. I don't need that. If you have no other questions, I'll have to ask you to leave the building. Otherwise I'll be forced to call security."

"Don't bother," a voice said behind me. "Security's never too far away."

I turned round. A heavy-set goon in a crumpled business suit towered behind me, sporting a gold crown in his grin.

"Come on, don't play too hard to get," he addressed the receptionist. "We have spare rooms, don't we? Because it's a room you want, sir, right?"

"Absolutely," I said. "How much did you say it was?"

"Same as you have here," he whispered cordially, nodding at the money on the desk. "We'll keep it off the books, won't we?"

The receptionist stared at him, mesmerized by his nerve. He finally switched his gaze to me, looked at the money, then turned toward the key rack behind him. He took off a key on a fat barrel-like keyring marked "23".

Before I could reach for it, the guard took the key from the receptionist's hand. "Allow me to show you to your room. Follow me."

He leaned across the desk and whispered something into the receptionist's ear. The young man nodded and slipped the money into his pocket.

I followed the security guard upstairs to the third floor, then along a narrow corridor reeking of stale dust until we reached room 33.

"Your lady's here," he whispered conspiratorially. "I didn't tell you anything! I'll take a nap in your room while you two are talking."

The sounds of his footsteps faded down the stairs. I heaved a sigh and knocked on the door.

I didn't have to knock twice. The door swung open as if Yanna had been waiting for someone to arrive. She didn't appear sleepy even though her hair was in disarray and her house coat, so familiar to me, hung almost open without concealing much.

"You?" she sounded surprised. "What are you doing here?"

Unwilling to disturb the other guests' sleep behind the flimsy plasterboard walls of their rooms, I shouldered Yanna out of my way, walked in and closed the door behind me. "Let's keep it quiet. Anybody else here with you?"

"That's none of your flippin' business," she replied even though I could see perfectly well she was alone.

The room was quite small. A droning TV was casting uneven light on its walls. An open suitcase sat on the floor, heaped with her stuff. A half-empty whisky bottle stood by the bed.

"Well, come in, then," she turned round and walked back to the bed in a purposefully hip-swaying catwalk-style gait.

I slumped into an easy chair opposite. "I won't be long. Your mother called me. She's worried sick about you."

"That'll teach her! First she ruined Dad's life and now she's doing the same with me! She just can't keep her nose out of my business, can she? Cigarette?"

I shook my head.

"Oh come on now! What's wrong with you? Come here and let's have a smoke together. Just like we used to."

"I don't smoke anymore, sorry. Just give her a ring now and tell her you're okay, and I'll be on my way."

"Oh really? So you're bossing me around now?"

"I'm not. And you shouldn't be drinking."

"That's my business!" she announced with drunken panache. "Want some?"

"No, thanks."

I rose from the chair and walked around the room in search of her phone, intending to dial my mother-in-law's number, switch it to conference mode and leave it there. I'd done all I could here. Alik and the cabbie were probably already fast asleep waiting for me.

"You've lost weight," she noticed. "You look almost like the guy I fell in love with all those years back. Your haircut suits you."

She reclined on the bed, blowing smoke rings up to the ceiling as she sarcastically watched me searching through the room.

I finally located her phone behind the mini bar. The screen and the phone itself were cracked but it didn't look too serious. I pressed the button, and the screen lit up, displaying the bitten apple logo.

"Put it down *now*!" she snapped.

I walked closer to the bed. "What's the pin number?" I asked her calmly.

"Anything else you wanna know?" her voice rang with the familiar theatrical notes of indignation. "Just leave it alone!"

I typed in her birth date. The phone obligingly unblocked. Very smart of my clever ex-wife.

Realizing what I'd just done, Yanna shot off the bed and grabbed the phone. Her nails sank into the flat of my hand as she tried to prize it free. "Give it to me *now*!"

"Oh, take it! Now go to hell and take your mother with you!"

I was thoroughly fed up. Let them sort it out between themselves. If she didn't call her mother, I could always do it myself later.

I let go of the phone and walked toward the exit, licking blood off my hand.

"Call your mother," I repeated. "I'm off now."

I strode toward the door.

"Hey..." I heard behind me. "Phil?"

I absolutely should not react to this, I thought. I had to open the door, leave the hotel and go back home to get some sleep so that in the morning I could start implementing my plan which brought me closer to my goal.

I'd had enough of all those love innuendos. First Yanna, then Vicky, Marina... not again.

I opened the door. Mechanically, I turned round — then couldn't turn away again.

Yanna stood at the center of the room. The house coat lay in a heap by her feet.

I peered at her dainty profile. I knew I hadn't received any system messages. Which was weird because my Reputation with her had inexplicably grown from Animosity to Amicability. Her Interest in me was nearing 100%. Her Mood bar was going off the scale, soaring then plummeting non-stop. I didn't know she was capable of that. She must have been possessed: either by a demon or by some psychotic time traveler.

Strange I hadn't received any Reputation messages, though. Earlier in the clinic, I'd received quite a few such messages about people I didn't even know, even though they'd been a considerable distance away from me. I'd received no XP points for befriending her again, either.

And what was that? A small buff (or debuff?) icon had appeared in my interface, with a brief prompt next to it. I focused on it.

Aha. That was the Intoxication II debuff. It decreased all the characteristics and also lowered Self-Criticism and Self-Control while raising Sexual Arousal which in turn improved the likability of all objects of the opposite sex.

"Phil, quit stalling. Come here to me," her languid voice rang with the familiar commandeering notes.

"You're just as beautiful," I said with a sigh, pulling myself together. "Thanks, but no thanks."

"What?" confused, she grabbed a sheet from the

bed and covered herself with it. "What did you say?"

"When you feel better, send me a message and give me the divorce appointment date."

I walked out, then added before closing the door, "And you really should call your mother."

The sound of the door closing shut coincided with a new system message reporting a new drop in my Reputation, followed by a furious torrent of f-words. Something smashed the door hard. Probably the phone.

Your Reputation with Yannina "Yanna" Orlova has decreased!
Current Reputation: Hatred 30/360

That was okay, then. I'd been afraid that the program was getting glitchy. Or the local info field segment was. Or both.

They were probably right saying that love and hate were just one step apart. I took that step as I'd crossed the doorway of her cheap and nasty hotel room.

Half an hour later, Alik and I walked back into my apartment and collapsed onto our respective beds, intent on getting some much-needed sleep. Whatever was left of it.

* * *

AFTER I'D AWOKEN IN THE MORNING, I HURRIED to check my physical state. Despite last night's trip across town,

I felt well rested. My knee didn't' hurt at all. That ointment Alik had gotten from the drugstore must have been really good. Either that, or the program had been glitchy after all and its booster must have affected Recovery as well as leveling rate.

In any case, the swelling had gone down. I bent the knee several times and felt nothing. Then I climbed out of bed. My body seemed to be in perfect condition. I could pack my gym bag, after all.

Alik was still asleep, sprawled on his back like a child across the unfolded couch. He was still wearing his jeans and T-shirt. The sheets lay in a corner in a heap. It didn't look as if he'd used them. Boris was standing on his broad chest, pawing it and purring like a tractor.

Richie whined, desperate for his walk. I shook Alik awake. He sprang off the bed straight away — apparently a habit he'd developed while sleeping on park benches.

"Morning," I said. "Mind walking Rich for me? I'm gonna make us some breakfast."

"Yeah... Wait, let me wake up..." he mumbled, stretching and grunting. "Is it the 30th today?"

"Yeah. In a day's time, summer's officially starting!"

"That's cool, man! They promised to pay me on the 1st for the days I worked in May!"

Alik headed for the bathroom. Richie and Boris followed him and froze like guardsmen outside.

"Come on, you freeloaders, breakfast's served!" I called them.

This wasn't their usual command but they understood. Both rushed into the kitchen, shoving each other out of the way, Boris desperately voicing his protest at the silent but equally determined Richie. The mutt checked Boris' bowl first, received a hearty slap on his cheeky black snout from the indignant puss, and turned to his own.

While Alik was making himself presentable, I boiled a good dozen eggs, sliced some bread, cheese and ham and poured out the coffee.

"Where's the leash?" he asked.

"It's over there by the front door somewhere. Can you find it?"

"I've got it! Rich, where are you?"

"He only understands commands. Tell him 'Come!' or 'Walkies!'," I said.

Richie pricked up his ears. Alik walked into the kitchen with the leash, hooked it up to the dog's collar, grabbed a sandwich from the plate, then took the dog out, muttering, "Come, Rich, come, heel, good boy!"

By the time they were back I'd had a light breakfast. No good stuffing my face now as I still had some exercise to do.

As they walked back in, I was already lacing up my sneakers. Richie was panting. He stank to high heaven. Had they gone for a run or something?

"Alik, the apartment keys are on a hook by the front door. I'm off to the gym."

"D'you pump iron?" he sounded surprised.

"Sort of. I'm off now. See you in the evening! Don't forget to lock the door, please."

The gym was uncrowded. Either everyone had already left on vacation or they'd all reached their weight loss goals. My coach Alexander was there, ready to work with me.

No idea why, but this time I had a much better awareness of my own body. It could have had something to do with my improved Perception. As I performed deadlifts, I could literally sense every muscle involved in the exercise. That helped me a lot to perform it correctly.

"Excellent, Phil. Well done! Your technique is much better now," Alexander commended me. "Let me add a few more weights."

Virtually all of the weights were at least five pounds heavier than what I'd used the last time but they felt almost the same. I had to work hard, sure, but I could still do it. I'd already noticed that leveling Strength came easier to me than any other characteristic. Its progress bar was already 50% full and growing. Another couple of gym sessions, and I might be able to bring Strength up to 9. And after another couple of weeks, I could finally reach level 10 that I so desperately needed.

I finished my weight training with a brief cooldown to keep my blood pumping. I spent five minutes on a maxed-out treadmill until I ran out of steam and was forced to slow down.

Now, Agility. Even though I'd received a new level the previous morning, the progress bar was already almost full. And I hadn't even noticed! That must have had something to do with the fact that I'd lost some weight.

I jumped on the scales. Compared to the previous morning, I'd lost another two pounds. It could have been my active lifestyle and regular meals — this was a far cry from my WoW years when I'd constantly stuffed my face with chips and candy bars, washing them down with sugar-loaded drinks. Or could it also be my new improved Perception kicking in? Hadn't Martha said something about the characteristics affecting each other?

I finished off my training session with a few sets of agility exercises and headed for the shower.

As I left the locker room, I reached for a towel off the rack. My foot slipped on the wet floor. My stomach churned. My heart dropped. I waved a desperate arm in the air and managed to restore my balance.

The program must have deliberated on this for a while until it came to the conclusion I deserved a new level. Just like that!

Your Agility has improved!
+1 to Agility
Current Agility: 6
Experience points received for improving a main characteristic: 1000

I drank another protein shake, refueling my body with everything necessary for its growth, said goodbye to the friendly receptionist and hurried home. I had big plans for today. No time to loaf around.

Alik had already left. I changed into my business

clothes and headed for work.

As I approached the office building, I saw Greg hovering on the steps smoking. He was dressed to the nines, his white shirt starched, his shoes polished, the pressed creases on his slacks perfectly straight and razor-sharp.

"There he is!" he announced on seeing me. "I've got something to tell you! My wife and I, we've made up! Can you imagine?"

"Judging by the way you look, yes," I replied. "I'm very happy for you. Did you bring her flowers?"

"Flowers! You should have seen the bouquet I bought her! So heavy I could barely carry it! And then we didn't leave bed for *hours*!"

"Excellent. Well done. So how did it happen?"

"I've no idea!" he frowned, wrinkling his brow in thought. "Wonder if she just missed me?"

"I'm sure she did. Where's Cyril?"

"He's upstairs already. He's quit smoking for good now. The other night in the bar he'd smoked so much he spent all night puking."

"I see. Let's go in, then?"

Once Pavel's briefing was over, the CEO wanted to see me. It was Pavel who broke the news to me. He waited for all the others to vacate his office, then said,

"Phil, please wait. The boss wants to see you. He needs to discuss something with you."

Mr. Ivanov was enjoying a cup of coffee and a cigarillo in his office, flicking the ash off into a massive bronze tortoise ashtray.

"Ah, Phil. Come in and take a seat, boy."

"Good morning, sir," I pulled up one of the heavy soft chairs lining the conference table and sat down.

The CEO took a deep tug on his cigar. "So you're leaving us, are you?" he squinted at me. I know, I know. Pavel couldn't talk you out of it. So I'm not even going to try. I just want to tell you that you're always welcome back. On Friday you can go to the bookkeepers and get your back pay. We added your J-Mart and a few other bits and pieces to the final tally. Pavel gave me all the numbers. If you close something else before the week's over, we'll add that to your pay as well. We never short-change our workers."

"Thank you, sir."

"Nothing to thank me for yet. One more thing. What are you up to? Tell me. What are you going to do?"

I paused, contemplating his question. It wouldn't be a bad idea to open up to him, at least a little. "Not much really. I have a few ideas though. I seem to be pretty good at bringing people together. So I thought, why not open some sort of recruitment agency?"

He drew on his cigarillo, waiting for me to go on, but I fell silent. He chuckled. He must have been relieved that I wasn't leaving them to join the competition because he began showering me with encouragement,

"I think it's a brilliant idea! Well done! And what's more, if you find someone really good, send them here first, okay? And I'll tell Vicky — you know her, don't you, the girl who works at HR — to send you our vacancies. Agreed?"

He rose and proffered his hand, making it clear the meeting was over.

"Agreed," I said, answering his handshake.

His grip on my hand tightened. "And if it doesn't work out, just come back to us," he said, locking my gaze with his. "We'll find you a vacancy. You might even take Pavel's place, you never know."

"I'll keep that in mind, sir."

"Very well. Now go."

On my way out, I popped into Vicky's office just to check up on her. She wasn't there.

"She called in sick," her workmate told me.

I suppressed my impulse to phone her. It could be a gut feeling. Or it could be that I was just afraid of having another dry conversation with her.

I did check her location on the map, though. Vicky was at home.

Cyril and Greg had a meeting with a client, so I got the use of his laptop again. I needed it to collect as much data as possible on all potential buyers within our city limits. Using a smartphone would have taken me much longer.

I studied the market, pinpointing those who might be interested, then ran several searches narrowing the results first by their packaging suppliers, then by price. That brought the list down to several eligible options. That done, I sat down to study their top management lists.

Today was Wednesday. I had three days to work my way through the list. I decided against doing anything about the other list, the one I'd made for Marina and myself. It's better that she had it, that way at least she had some work. I actually hadn't even spoken to her yet. Pavel's praise seemed to have given her wings, so much so that she'd dashed off to meet her clients immediately after the briefing.

I'd better not waste time, either. I still had some house hunting to do in the afternoon. I'd already researched some hot real estate offers. After I'd broadened my search by raising my rent ceiling, I ran the city map through the search and came up with a perfect option directly from the landlord.

Before contacting him, I called the Major just to find out whether I could still count on the apartment offered by Galina.

"Comrade Major? This is Panfilov..."

"Oh hi, Phil! Are you calling me about the old lady? Yes, we've checked it. Unfortunately, there's nothing we can charge her granddaughter with," he sounded well-rested, cheerful and even sincere, strangely enough. "Apparently, she was the only surviving relative of the deceased. She said she hadn't bothered with the funeral expenses. According to her, she'd just had the old lady's body taken to the dump, end of story. Sounds hideous, I know, but we can't charge her with that. And as for the apartment, it's not so simple. I shouldn't bother if I were you. Formally, it belongs to no one at the moment as the direct heirs haven't yet received the title deeds. My guys are looking into it now. The power of attorney, however, is a forgery. At least that allows us to charge *her*."

"I see. Thanks a lot, Comrade Major."

"Thanks don't pay bills," he joked, laughing. "And stop calling me Comrade Major. I'm a Lieutenant Colonel now!"

"Congratulations, Comrade Lieutenant Colonel!"

"Thank you, sir," he replied in the same military vein, then continued in dead seriousness, "Have you looked at our site lately?"

"I'm afraid not. I didn't have the time."

"Shame. Well, just keep me posted. All the best," he hung up.

I dialed the new apartment's owner straight away. His place had come up at the top of my search results. Everything fitted, from "90% probability of renting the place to the account user" to "criminality levels lower than elsewhere in the city".

The landlord was a man in his early 60s. He agreed to show me the place at any time, adding simple-heartedly,

"I posted the ad last night but received no takers. It's funny. I've just had it redecorated. It's never been rented out before. Could it be the price? I'm sure we could come to an agreement."

"What if I have a look at the apartment first?" I suggested. "I'm working at the moment. How about 3 p.m.?"

"Yes, of course. Here's the address..."

I didn't need the address. Still, I pretended I was writing it down.

I hung up and looked around. The office was quiet. Most of the workers were already out working. I was about to shut the laptop down when I remembered about my short story. I might just as well go and check if it had received any reviews.

It had indeed.

CHAPTER

TWENTY-NINE

I CAN DO IT!

"Float like a butterfly, sting like a bee!"

Muhammad Ali

I STILL REMEMBER MY VERY FIRST SHORT STORY. WHEN I was in middle school, our Russian literature teacher asked us to write an essay. She offered a variety of topics, from "My future profession" to "The works of Leo Tolstoy". We also had the option of writing about anything at all. I think I was the only one who'd picked it. I wrote a short story about a little boy who had this particular superpower of always knowing the best places to fish. At the time, I was crazy about fishing. My Dad and Granddad always used to take me on their fishing trips. Whenever they returned home empty-handed, I was disconsolate because it had taken us a lot of preparation and a very early rise, often at three a.m., to make it to the river in time for the fish rising in the morning.

The boy in my story whose name was Alexander (I'd told you I'd always hated my own name, hadn't I?) always knew the exact places where to cast for the hugest fish possible. Thanks to his superpower, his Dad and Granddad never came home empty-handed.

In the story, my little MC promptly lost his ability the moment he told a lie. That had been the condition set by the wizard who'd bestowed the superpower on him. The moment he lied, the wizard had said, he'd lose his magic powers. That was the extent of this rather controversial story which even had a bit of a moral lesson in the end.

Our teacher gave me a D, then read the story to the class. As I now understand, her voice rang with some sort of sadistic enjoyment as my classmates rolled on the floor with laughter. You probably all know how it happens. We've all been to school at some point. I said red-faced wishing the earth could swallow me whole, counting seconds until she'd finished reading.

"Absolutely and totally devoid of any writing talent," she finally said. "What kind of mediocre reverie is this? What's with the wizard? We can't change our lives by waiting for miracles to fall into our lap! What were you thinking when you wrote this?" she demanded, shaking my notebook in front of me.

Then there was my famed book and me

publishing the first chapters on the writers' portal. Nothing good had come out of that, either.

So you can imagine my anxiety as I opened my story page on the site.

The reviews were few but they very nearly made me reach for a non-existent pack of cigarettes.

A very heartwarming story, thanks a lot.

That sent goosebumps up my spine! You have a real talent.

Excellent writing and storytelling.

As I kept reading them over and over again, I struggled with the temptation to invest the remaining two system points into Creative Writing. It took all of my willpower not to do so. I had a better plan. When I got my Ultrapak money, I'd buy myself a very plain laptop and continue writing for at least half an hour a day, practicing the skill.

The moment I thought so, the idea added to my task list. Excellent.

I closed the page, cleaned my browser history, shut down the laptop and set off for my meetings with clients. I had three of them scheduled for today and I fully intended to close all three.

The first meeting at a small local grocery chain was textbook-perfect. By cleverly employing all the relevant skills, I managed to successfully talk my way past all the bureaucratic watchdogs and got seen by the director himself.

My high Empathy levels now allowed me to tune into his mood and choose an appropriate approach. By seeing his Interest bar, I could promptly change the subject and speak about other things, raising his curiosity. My advanced Communication Skills made it easy for me to find common ground with anyone regardless of their social standing. My decent Seduction skills permeated all secretarial barriers with just a hint of flirt, doubling the effects of my Vending and Communication skills.

The chain's director knew what I meant the moment I spoke to him. He invited the company buyer in, discussed all the finer details with her and made the decision to sign up with Ultrapak in less than a quarter of an hour of me entering his office. After an exchange of handshakes, I pitted our lawyers against theirs and left them to work on a contract.

My next meeting was in fact a bonus. The grocery chain's director simply called his friend the butcher and insisted he see me.

That happened even quicker. The butcher, a grim and swarthy Dagestani highlander, compared the prices, tut-tutted, checked the samples, spat through his teeth (we'd met on the street outside his business) and immediately gave orders to his people to drop their current supplier and sign us up instead.

I continued going through my list. The third meeting didn't go as smoothly. It had nothing to do with me though: according to their vice director, all their decision-makers were apparently on vacation. I didn't have enough KIDD to double-check it; I did my best to convince her but she wasn't prepared to accept the responsibility of such an important decision. All I could do was mark the date of her bosses' return in my calendar and make a mental note to hand the client over to either Greg or Marina.

The last meeting, however, was downright unsuccessful. The company owner didn't take part in any internal decisions, delegating everything to his management team — who weren't at all motivated to change anything at all. After some pointless looking around, I managed to find a guy who seemed interested enough. He listened to my spiel for a few minutes, looking utterly bored, then ripped a page out of his pocket notebook, wrote a large number "15" on it and moved it across the desk toward me.

"Is this your cut?" I asked. "On top of our price?"

He nodded.

"I'll speak to the director," I said, then bade my goodbyes.

I had big doubts whether Pavel would agree — but in this case, all I had to do was communicate the information to him.

Not a bad result for half a workday! In the past, each successful sale had cost me hundreds of wasted calls and dozens of unproductive meetings. I used to close a couple of percent of my client base if I'd been lucky.

In actual fact, should I stop spreading myself too thin, maybe? Why not concentrate on vending instead? By the end of this year, I could make it big trading in

---

real estate, oil fields and crypto currencies. By the time my license expired, I could have made enough never to have to work again and live for the rest of my life on passive income.

Still, something told me I didn't need alien software to achieve all this. I had to take a different route. There must be more to life than joining the ranks of movers and shakers.

It was about 3 p.m.: time for my apartment viewing. I didn't have time for lunch so I just bought a carton of yogurt and drank it in the cab on my way.

The apartment owner met me by the front door, visibly happy to see me. No matter how hard I'd tried, I was about five minutes late.

"I'd lost all hope," he said. "It happened to me before that someone phoned and said they would come and then they didn't turn up. Can you imagine?"

"Sure I can. Sorry I was late. I was busy at work."

"Of course. I understand," he started nodding so vigorously that I feared his gray head would drop off.

I liked the place the moment I saw it. The lawns and freshly-surfaced tarmac in the gentrified little courtyard, the playground and the fondly whitewashed tree trunks. The good-looking front door complete with code lock. The lobby was light and spacious like that of a theater. I even liked the apartment owner, mild-mannered and slightly naïve.

I could see that the house was new and quite expensive. Not exactly posh but not far from it, either.

The landlord explained that they'd bought the

apartment for themselves but that circumstances had forced them to move to the capital. Things were going really well for their only son so they wanted to be close to him to help with their grandchildren. As far as I understood, they didn't want to sell the apartment, for two reasons: firstly, because they believed that real estate prices were still on the rise and secondly, because they just didn't have the heart to sell something they'd invested so much effort and TLC in.

The apartment was excellent, very light with high ceilings and two spacious rooms. Even though the place was absolutely packed with new furniture and electronics, it didn't look cramped. I could see they'd put a lot of time and money in it. Bathroom taps were glistening as if they'd just arrived from the shop. Or maybe they had. More important, the apartment came with its own shower cubicle[33] which I'd missed in my old flat with its tiny flaking bathtub and leaky shower hose.

The final touch was his bright red-and-chrome electric kettle. I'd seen one of those on TV, and the water had boiled almost instantly. Its futuristic design resembled a space rocket ready to take off.

I walked around the apartment pensively. I could already imagine myself setting my books on the shelves and putting away my things. I already saw myself making food on their comfortable electric stove and drinking coffee on their covered terrace

---

[33] In Russia, all apartments come with a bathtub but not with a separate shower cubicle.

LEVEL UP BOOK ONE

surrounded by potted flowers.

The landlord must have interpreted my silence as indecision. "We could drop the rent a little if you're not too sure," he said. "It's getting a bit urgent. We have a plane to catch the day after tomorrow."

"That's not necessary," I said. "The price is fair for this kind of place. I'd love to live here."

He couldn't contain his happiness. His lips stretched into a smile. "Excellent! Mind if I give my wife a ring? She's quite anxious."

"Please do. And please tell her not to worry about the plants. I promise I'll water them."

Having spoken with his wife, he reached into his old briefcase and produced a rental agreement. Squinting shortsightedly, he entered my particulars into it.

"Oh," I remembered, "before we sign, I have a cat."

"You don't mean it!" he said happily instead of tensing up and worrying about his furniture. "We have two, Coco and Bagheera. My wife dotes on them. Cats are great! What d'you call your cat?"

"Boris," I said, slightly taken aback by his reaction. "Only it's a she."

"Nice!" he grinned. "She's gonna love it here. You can keep her toilet on the balcony. We planned on doing the same."

I signed the agreement, paid him for the first month and promised to transfer two more monthly payments into his account the following week. He handed me the keys to the apartment and the lobby.

He finished by imploring me to pay the utility bills on time, then left, leaving me in my new apartment.

It was so clean I could simply move in and start living. I didn't even have to buy anything. The place had everything, from modern micro-fiber mops to a full set of crockery. They had at least five skillets for every possible occasion.

The thought of skillets reminded me of Yanna and of my promise to phone my mother-in-law. Without further ado, I checked her location on the map and realized I didn't have to bother. She was already back at her parents'. I might have to call Yanna anyway, but I could do it tomorrow. I just wished this divorce thing was over already. We didn't have kids or property to share so hopefully we could get it done quite quickly.

I saw no point in delaying my departure. I searched online for a removal company; they were quite happy to come, pack everything up in boxes, load them, take them to my new place and unload everything. We agreed on the next day as soon as I returned Richie to his owners.

I left my new apartment and walked to the nearest gym.

This one was twice as expensive but it was worth it. It had a large swimming pool, a much broader choice of workout equipment and, most importantly, it had a boxing group.

When I inquired about it, the gym manager asked the coach to come over.

He was forty-five and a multiple champion — not

just in boxing but also in kickboxing, SAMBO and mixed martial arts. He gave me a critical once-over and suggested I concentrated on my physical shape first.

"We train fast," he explained. "And don't forget your age. You're starting a bit too late in life. You might find it tough. Very."

"I can do it."

"I don't think so, er..."

"I'm Phil."

"Very well, Phil. This isn't a weight loss group. All the boys have been training for a long time. Many of them compete professionally. If we take you, it means that we'll have to lower the tempo. Which we can't afford."

"Very well. How about one-on-one sessions, then?"

"That's possible. It'll cost you two grand an hour[34]."

I did some mental math. I should have enough. And if Mr. Ivanov lived up to his promises, I'd have even more.

"Can we start straight away? Can I buy my training gear here?"

"What, *now*?"

It looked like I'd managed to surprise him. He dropped all formality. "What's the haste? Ae you in a hurry to get even with someone? Or is it about a girl?"

"It's about me. Let's get it on, then!"

With a surprised whistle, he glanced at his watch, paused for a couple of seconds and pointed

---

[34] 2,000 rubles is about $35 at the time of writing

towards the sports shop, "Go get your gear and get changed. Did you take a subscription? You have ten minutes — okay, fifteen — to get your ass in gear."

"What should I buy?"

"A helmet, gloves, bandages, shoes, skipping ropes... you won't need any of that now," he said confidently. "You might never need them, in fact. Go get yourself some sneakers, a pair of shorts and a T-shirt. Time's running."

I barely made it. He took me to a small room about twenty by thirty feet where we started straight away. A pile of mats was heaped up in one corner; two more were occupied by punch bags.

The ten-minute warmup completely did me in.

"I told you," the coach snickered. "And we haven't even started yet."

By the end of the training session my jaw was aching. My arms were dropping off. And all that I'd done was learn to keep my stance and practice left-right combinations. I liked the fact that instead of just ordering me around, my coach had taken the time to explain things to me, peppering them with funny and enlightening stories from his rich sporting past.

The session ended with countless exhausting pushups on my fists and some twists from the waist which made me feel like throwing up. Licking my grazed knuckles, I listened to all the instructions that he was trying to drum into my head,

"Start your morning with a proper workout, not just a wake-up. I want to see you sweat. Do you run? That's good. No elevators. You should take stairs

---

everywhere. No smoking. No overeating. Lots of sleep. I want you to drink a lot of water, preferably a glass every hour. Buy yourself a rope and do some skipping every time you reach for the TV remote or your telephone. Always look into the eyes of those you're talking to. You'll use that in the ring. Absolutely no drinking! And then you might have an almost negligible chance of getting somewhere. Got it?"

"Yes, sir!"

"Good lad. Go get showered. Come back the same time the day after tomorrow."

"Can I come tomorrow, please?"

"No way," he snapped. "You won't have enough time to recuperate."

"I will!"

"I've seen stubborn guys like you," he said sarcastically. "None of them lasted more than a month. But it's up to you. It' your money. In that case, I'll be waiting for you tomorrow at 8 a.m. If you're even one minute late, you don't need to come."

"Affirmative! See you tomorrow!"

I left the gym feeling excited. I'd just started leveling a very important development branch; I'd enjoyed the training; I'd liked my new coach, and...

And I'd also got a new system message,

Your Stamina has improved!
+1 to Stamina
Current Stamina: 6
You've received 1000 pt. XP for successfully leveling up a main characteristic!

Level 6! It was double the level I'd had three weeks ago! Of course this was only a piece of alien software; of course it was due to its booster which had accelerated my development threefold — but what it did mean was that I could have done the same on my own without any alien help and it would have only taken me two months.

I bade my goodbye to the coach but didn't go to the shower. They had this wonderful air-conditioned treadmill room at my disposal. Why not use it to bring my Running level up?

No sooner said than done. Earlier that morning in the gym, I'd only fallen a fraction short of my goal, and I fully intended to make up for it now.

After eight minutes of running, I received a new message,

Congratulations! You've received a new skill level!
Skill name: Running
Current level: 2
XP received: 500

Finally! This had proved the hardest skill to level up. How many miles had I clocked up on my internal meter! How much sweat and pain in my bursting lungs! How much gunk had I brought up! I'd gotten the impression that the leveling up of this particular skill had been cursed as if there'd been some nasty debuff cast on me. A bit like in Fallout where a perk can give you an advantage while aggravating something equally important just to balance it out.

When I got back home, Alik was already busy in the kitchen.

"I've walked your mutt," he informed me, casting angry glances at Richie. "I had to run around the block after him. He chased after some bitch and I only just managed to catch him."

"Thanks! What're you making?"

"Just some stew. I bought some meat in the shop. Not much, just five pounds or so."

"How much? You think you can eat all that?"

"Hey, you don't know me. I love a good stew," he said, sniffing the aroma in the kitchen. "Everything all right?"

"Yeah. I can barely stand on my feet. Call me when it's ready, I need to pack up. I'm moving out tomorrow. Oh, and would you please feed the cat?"

"No problem. D'you have any onions?"

"Yeah, in the grocery shop."

"I got it. I won't be a moment," he said, stirring the pot.

I looked at an empty packet of pepper on the table. He didn't like his food bland, that's for sure.

I spent the rest of the evening packing, eating, talking to my homeless roommate and reading Robert Cialdini's *Psychology of Persuasion.*

I kept reading until I finally achieved my reading goal for today:

Your Intellect has improved!

+1 to Intellect
Current Intellect: 19
You've received 1000 pt. XP for successfully leveling up a main characteristic!

I went to bed early because all of my reserves — bodily and spiritual as well as willpower — had been absolutely drained.

When I was already lying in bed, I remembered the Major's request and opened the Wanted Criminals page of our local police site.

It only listed nine names. Murderers, terrorists, drugs and arms dealers, rapists... Nobody had made me a judge but it was in my powers to bring them to justice.

I immediately initiated a search which produced zero results.

The program kindly informed me that I had 1 KIDD point missing. I had their pictures and names, as well as dates and places of birth. I needed another piece of data. And to get it, I needed to either go through the Major completely exposing myself to him, or search for it myself hoping that the criminals were on social media.

I just wasn't up to it at the moment. My hand holding the phone fell listlessly onto the bed. I flaked out.

As I awoke the next morning, my internal clock was nearing 6 a.m. I felt totally broken. The physical exhaustion I could understand: after all, I'd had two workouts the night before, weightlifting as well as the boxing session.

But I also felt strangely apathetic. I had absolutely no desire to get up. I didn't even feel capable of walking the dog — or do anything at all, come to think of it.

I stayed in bed and tried to go back to sleep but I couldn't. I just didn't want to get up, as simple as that.

I opened my interface hoping that the sight of my stats might cheer me up a little.

Philip "Phil" Panfilov
Age: 32
Current status: sales rep
Social status level: 10
Classes: Book Reader and Empath. Level: 7
Married
Wife: Yannina "Yanna" Orlova
Children: none

Main Characteristics:
Strength: 8
Agility: 6
Intellect: 19
Stamina: 6
Perception: 8
Charisma: 14
Luck: 10

Secondary Characteristics:
Vitality: 89%
Satisfaction: 78%

Vigor: 61%
Metabolism: 72%

My low Vigor and Metabolism could be explained by the fact that I'd just woken up. Ditto for Satisfaction: I was hungry and thirsty, not to even mention the fact that I'd received no quest rewards for quite a while. As for Vitality, it had grown 20% over the last three weeks. Just think it used to be 69%!

So everything seemed to be fine. What was wrong with me, then?

I opened my profile and began scrolling through it.

Found it.

I couldn't have noticed it earlier because the list was too long to have fitted into my mental view in its entirety.

Self-Confidence: 59%
Self-Control: 70%
Spirit: 21%
Mood: 34%

Why? I'd just had a good night's sleep. Why was my mood so low?

I summoned Martha and asked her.

"Good morning to you too," she said, sounding slightly offended.

"Are you being funny?"

"I'm not. Your Nicotine Withdrawal debuff is about to expire. The program is mirroring the real-life consequences of quitting smoking. That requires a lot of energy so I'd better switch off."

She disappeared.

"I see. Thanks," I said into empty space, unable to take my eyes off a faded icon of the Nicotine Withdrawal debuff. It was flashing with the tiny little numbers of a countdown.

Nicotine Withdrawal
Duration: 14 days
Your body is deprived of nicotine!
Nicotine takes part in your body's metabolism. -5% to Metabolism
Warning! High probability of a spontaneous Enrage!
Warning! Your aggro radius has increased!
-3% to Satisfaction every 12 hours

5... 4... 3... 2... 1...
Bang!
Bang!
Bang!

The Nicotine Withdrawal debuff has expired!
+30% to Satisfaction

Happiness I
Your Satisfaction levels have exceeded 100%
+50% to Vigor
+1 to all main characteristics
Duration: as long as Satisfaction levels exceed 100%

Your Perception has improved!
+1 to Perception
Current Perception: 9
You've received 1000 pt. XP for successfully leveling up a main characteristic!

Your Stamina has improved!
+1 to Stamina
Current Stamina: 7
You've received 1000 pt. XP for successfully leveling up a main characteristic!

The relief at the debuff's expiry felt as refreshing as a cold shower after a hot sauna. A tidal wave of relief flooded over me. It was as if I'd finally let go of a heavy boulder which I'd been lugging around all this time.

I had a momentary anticipation that something important would happen over the next two or three days, something that would bring a close to my past life and open up a new phase.

Also, I really wanted to see Vicky. As soon as I cleared up a few chores — like moving, getting divorced and quitting my job — I'd have to speak to her straight away.

It must be Happiness working its magic.

Chapter Thirty

DROP LIKE A STONE, RISE LIKE A PHOENIX

"Don't ever get angry at a man for stating the truth."

Ayn Rand, *Atlas Shrugged*

AT 8 A.M., I HAD MY BOXING SESSION. I NEEDED TO GET my butt in gear. I scooped up all the workout clothes from the dryer and shoved them in a sports bag, adding a pair of gym shoes I'd bought last night at my new fitness center.

Then I dressed in my business clothes as I wouldn't have the time to go back home and change.

I crept into the kitchen trying not to awaken Alik. I made myself some coffee, fed the critters, added a Caffeine buff bonus to my Vigor, then took Rich for a walk.

When we came back home, I gave him a long

hug. Richie laid his head on my shoulder and waited patiently for me to let go of him. Then I left.

At 8 a.m., I was already at the gym. The coach seemed a bit surprised by my arrival. He yawned and we started training. He kept both of us awake with his jokes and snappy commands.

Now I was convinced that on top of accelerating my development, the leveling booster also improved recovery. That could be the only explanation why today's session had felt even easier than yesterday's. It was as if I hadn't spent another hour pumping iron followed by a running practice and a murderous boxing session with my martial-arts champion coach. To train every day had been the right decision, after all.

As I was doing a series of pushups to finalize my training for the day, I received a new system message,

New unblocked skill available: Boxing
Current skill level: 1
XP received: 200 (for learning the skill)

Then I received another confirmation of the fact that all skills were interconnected,

Congratulations! You've received a new skill level!
Skill name: Hand-to-Hand Fighting
Current level: 2
XP received: 500

That made sense. Still, as I leveled up, the gap

between skills might grow resulting in the weakening of the connectivity between them.

After the gym, I started doing my rounds, visiting more clients from my list. Prior to every meeting, I checked the map to make sure that the persons I needed to see were available. Soon after the second meeting, I received a new level in Vending, and after the third one, in Communication Skills. Those two skills seemed to be interconnected too because both seemed to require establishing friendly contact with potential buyers. Now I had level 6 in both which qualified them as professional.

Soon after midday, just as I graced the doorstep of my third client, I received a phone call from Svetlana Messerschmitt, Richie's fourteen-year-old owner.

"Hello? Is that Phil? This is Sveta. How are things?"

"Hi Sveta! Are you back already?"

"We've just arrived now. We're at the passport control in the airport. What time can I come and pick Richie up?"

"How about four p.m.?" I asked, trying to work out what time I might have to see the removal guys and go to my new apartment.

"Absolutely! Can I have your address, then?"

The meeting with my third client wasn't a success. No matter how hard I tried, their director refused to see me point blank. His secretary insisted he was "out on business". My map told me otherwise. I did my best to convince her but just couldn't get past that unyielding woman who must have followed her boss' instructions to the letter. If he didn't want to see someone, he expected her to fall on her sword rather than let someone through.

By lunchtime, I was ravenous. It wasn't just the training but also the fact that I'd skipped breakfast. I decided to treat myself to a quick set menu in a nearby restaurant. One portion wasn't enough for me; I ordered another one, getting the feeling I was stocking up on fuel. My Spirit, Satisfaction and Vigor all began to restore, building me a new body molecule by molecule as they grew new muscle tissue, tendons and ligaments.

Back in the office, I didn't see any of my friends so I went straight to Pavel and reported to him the results of my meetings from the last two days. I made a special point of describing the meeting with the guy who'd asked me for a cut of our price. I derived great satisfaction from the cringe on his face.

"Screw them," he said. "As for yesterday's other clients — the butcher and the supermarket chain — we've already signed the contracts. The first deliveries will be on their way tomorrow."

"Excellent. That's all, then," I glanced at the watch. It was time for me to go. Sveta would arrive any moment. "I need to be on my way. I'm moving apartment today."

He nodded his understanding. "That's not a problem. A man's got to do what a man's got to do."

I shoved my chair aside and climbed from behind the desk.

Without looking at me, he continued, "Shit, I'm

already toying with the idea of firing everyone and giving you their salaries."

"Pavel, please..."

"I'm only joking," he said. "Or maybe not. Come on, piss off."

On my way home I called Kira to tell her the news and invite her to my housewarming.

"Phily," she said sternly, "You really should get a decree nisi first, then start partying. Or have you changed your mind? Are you two back in your love nest already?"

"I don't think I love her. I thought I did when I was in fact only jealous. But that wasn't love. It was a habit, more of an attachment really. Or my wounded pride, maybe. Whatever, but it certainly wasn't love."

Kira pricked up her ears. "Jealous? Of whom? Did she give you a reason?"

"I didn't need it. And when I did get it... I already told you that she'd found someone when she'd left me. When I had a reason to be jealous, I didn't feel like it. Can you imagine? I'd even imagined all sorts of adult scenes in my mind but nothing stirred inside me."

She sighed. "It's normal. It's very often that people confuse love with other things. Are you angry with her?" she asked, arriving at an unexpected conclusion.

"Oh no! Everything was all right with her, as you well know. It was my fault, I have nothing more to say about it. What do you think?"

That was a pretty self-explanatory question. Still, she replied,

"It wasn't only your fault. At last I don't think so. It takes two to tango. When a couple splits up, the fault lies with both even though one can be less guilty than the other. Don't even argue with me. You know very well how much hassle I had with my own man. But did I do something to help him change? I argued with him, I moaned and bitched, I refused to talk to him, I tried to mold him after my own taste while not realizing you can't change anyone by force. You need another approach."

Her confession surprised me. "What kind of approach do you mean?"

"Just a different one. You can't be a prison guard to the one you love. You can inspire them. Alternatively, you can deprive them of everything that could help them grow and..." she paused, searching for the right words, "and make their own decisions to be responsible for themselves and their loved ones. But what could you expect from a twenty-year-old girl just out of college?"

"True."

"So I'm sorry but it's all your fault, Phily."

Oh. That was quite a turn-around. So typical of my big sister.

"If you'd come to your senses a couple of years earlier, everything would have been fine now," she said. "Which means you're a dickhead."

"I know."

"It's probably a good thing that you didn't have a kid," she continued pensively. "Children shouldn't suffer for their parents' mistakes."

"You might be right. Listen, how about dropping in on our parents, say, on Saturday?"

She laughed. "Can't see why not! But let's do something useful for them. I suggest we bring them some deli and some decent groceries."

We spent some more time discussing the details and then parted friends. I decided against telling her that I'd quit my job. She wouldn't have understood.

Alik wasn't at home. I moved freely around the place, stacking up all my things by the wall in the lounge. A faint smell of tobacco seemed to linger in the kitchen. He must have smoked in the morning on the sly, letting the smoke out of the window while he'd had his morning coffee.

As I waited for Sveta, I sat in the kitchen and read while I drank my coffee. Richie was lying comfortably by my feet. Boris lay spread out on the chair opposite.

Time flew as I read. The doorbell rang. Richie barked and ran out into the corridor.

"Richie!" a girl's voice called from behind the door.

I answered it. A tall lanky sun-tanned girl stood in the doorway next to a bespectacled man — apparently, her father. He was a bit older and taller than myself.

Richie groaned his excitement. He launched himself at the girl and laid his paws on her shoulders trying to lick her face. The girl was emitting the cutest of squeaking noises.

"Hello," her father said. "Are you Phil?"

"In person. Come in, please."

The man stepped inside. "I'm Andrei. Sveta, take Richie and come in the house."

Both entered and closed the door behind them.

"Go through to the lounge," I invited them just in case they wanted to talk to me. "You don't need to take your shoes off. I'm leaving this place in half an hour."

The man just couldn't help himself anymore. He eased his daughter away, grabbed the dog's head and started stroking it, repeating, "Richie, good boy, you're back with us now... good boy, clever boy!"

Sveta looked up at me. Her eyes welled with tears. Unable to restrain herself, she flung her arms around me. I very nearly hugged her back but stopped myself just in time. I didn't want her father to misconstrue anything. So I just stood there stock still with my arms pressed to my hips.

"Thank you so much for finding him and for looking after him!"

Something wet brushed my neck. The girl was almost as tall as myself.

"Well, that's enough! Sveta, let Phil go!" her father commanded in a mockingly stern voice, then turned to me. "We've had him since he was a puppy, you know. Sveta used to bottle-feed him. He was so funny — clumsy and awkward..."

According to my interface, both were perfectly happy. I was happy for them too. And for Richie, of course. Still, I felt so sad. For me, the dog was firmly associated with a particular stage in my development.

He'd come into my life just when I'd needed him the most, alleviating my solitude and keeping me company on my jogs in the park. He'd helped me quite a few times, too: once when I'd tried to sell my computer to that idiot and again the other day when I met up with those hoodies.

"You promised me a puppy, remember?" I asked.

"Of course. We're going to do something about it pretty soon, too," Sveta's father said. "We're about to put him out to stud. We already have a suitable bitch for him."

As if sensing he was about to leave me, Richie laid his head on my knee and licked my hand by way of good-bye.

Immediately, I received a message about my improved Reputation with both father and daughter. Interestingly, I'd received the same exceptionally high number of points with both — 60 pt., no less — jumping straight to Amicability and earning me 120 XP.

Still, that was something I only realized later when they'd bidden their goodbyes and left, promising me to regularly share Richie's photos and videos.

The bitterness of parting with him was slightly sweetened by yet another message,

You've received 1000 pt. XP for performing a socially meaningful action!

XP points left until the next social status level: 8970/11000

Soon the removals men came. They expertly packed all my stuff into boxes, sealed them and loaded them into their minivan.

I asked them to wait downstairs while I made one last round of the apartment where Yanna and I had spent the biggest part of our marital life. I thought about all our happy moments together — because we'd had quite a few — and our arguments even though I couldn't remember any of them properly. That's just the way our brains work. We tend to forget the bad stuff.

I left a note for Alik in case I couldn't get through to him on the phone,

Hi man,

I'm gone. Make yourself at home and don't deny yourself anything.

The food is in the fridge. The rent expires on June 12.

Call me when you want,
Phil

I spent the rest of the day unpacking in my new place. As I was hanging my clothes in the wardrobe, I tried them on. It looked like I might need to have a complete makeover. My pants were falling off me. Even with a belt they looked baggy. My shirts were already too tight across the chest, threatening to rip all the buttons off the moment I spread my shoulders.

Still, that could wait, especially because I was planning to embark on a prolonged weight training marathon starting next week when I wouldn't have to work for Ultrapak any longer. The possibility of a complete Regeneration or Foresight wasn't something you could pass up in favor of a career, no matter how smooth or brilliant.

And once that out of the way, I would embark on my ultimate idea. I had to start a socially meaningful business. You can't take on every skill under the sun which was why I couldn't count on them for any extended leveling. I'd have to engross myself in social work with those who needed it, performing more quests and raising my Reputation with as many people as possible.

But that was next week. Now I had three days to sort out any unfinished chores.

The tasks I'd already performed today had earned me another 900 XP:

- leave the old apartment keys with Romuald "Alik" Zhukov;
- return Richie to his owner Ms. Svetlana "Sveta" Messerschmitt;
- downsize

Interestingly, "Downsize" had been updated to just "Move to my new apartment".

Yanna called in the evening. She didn't bother to say hello. "I'll come straight to the point," she said. "Tomorrow ten o'clock at the registry office."

"I'll be there," I said.

She hung up. I stood there listening to the

dialing tone.

Before, I might have given her a piece of my mind. Like, I didn't want to be talked down to and all that. Now, however, I saw no point in it. I said I'd come, that was well enough. The tone doesn't mean anything; the message conveyed is what matters. The speaker might be tired or sick; they might not have time for protracted conversations. So the tone they use doesn't really mater. Only the message itself.

After my conversation with Yanna, I got ready for a run. This part of the city was new to me. Rich wasn't with me anymore. If the truth were known, that made me a little anxious. I also wanted to explore the neighborhood and do a bit of shopping.

I ran out of the back yard onto the street and around the block. I couldn't help thinking about my first jogging session the night Yanna had left. Just like now, I'd run along unknown streets and side lanes rediscovering places I never knew existed in all of my thirty-two years here. And I'd been born here! So unlike the virtual Azeroth where I used to know every nook and cranny.

While I was running, Alik called me to ask how I was settling in. Once again he thanked me for the lodgings.

"It wasn't a moment too soon," he said. "You understand that, don't you? You've really helped me out. I owe you one."

I went back home, cooked and ate dinner, then went to bed.

Tomorrow was going to be a busy day. The first

day of summer. The first sunrise in my new apartment. The boxing session. The divorce. My last day at Ultrapak. My first day without the Nicotine Withdrawal. And finally, meeting some old friends. I might have to give my weightlifting session a miss. There was simply no way I could fit it in.

I slept like a log. For the first time, no one disturbed me.

* * *

THE MORNING PROVED TO BE A BIT HECTIC. TO KICK IT off, the program hadn't woken me up until almost 7 a.m.. Apparently, it had something to do with the proverbial sleep phases.

I hurried to get ready. Even so, I was a couple of minutes late for my boxing practice. Luckily, the coach was late too, so my tardiness went unnoticed.

My third practice gave me 5% to my hand-to-hand skill and 25% to my Boxing skill. My Stamina, Agility and Strength had also grown a little. And maybe that wasn't everything. I simply didn't have the time to monitor every possible improvement.

"You're a quick learner," the coach said almost grudgingly. "If it goes like this, I might send you to the district championship early this fall. Provided you keep this momentum up."

Who, me? In the district championship? That was something totally new to me. It sounded admittedly cool.

From the gym I went directly to the registry

office. Yanna wasn't there yet, so I waited for her outside. After a ten minute wait I decided to call her.

"Oh, give it break! I'm coming now!" she snapped and hung up.

After another twenty minutes, Vlad's Jeep pulled up at the opposite curb. Yanna climbed out of the passenger's seat and crossed the road, heading for me. Vlad stayed in the car.

"Good morning," I said.

"Yeah yeah. Good or bad, it makes no difference. Let's get on with it. I've already spoken to all the right people and greased all the right palms. They'll give us a simplified divorce. All the paperwork has been filled in already. All you need to do is sign it. Come on, then."

She didn't look so special. A bruised cheekbone was camouflaged with a thick layer of foundation. Her eyelids were swollen as if she'd spent the better part of the morning crying till her makeup had run, then hurried to reapply it and hadn't made a good job of it. The lightweight scarf that covered her neck barely concealed some marks which looked as if someone had tried to strangle her.

"Yanna? You sure you're all right?"

She cast a quick glance at the Jeep. "Let's go now."

Confidently she led me in the right direction and peeped into an office. "Can we come in?"

"One moment," a female voice said from behind the door.

Yanna closed the door and leaned against the wall. She looked up at the ceiling and blew a loud breath. She looked sick and tired of everything.

I was a bit worried about her stats. She had several debuffs like Depression and Lack of Sleep. Her Mood was deep in the red.

I looked at her face, drawn and aged, the same face I'd loved to kiss. I felt sorry — not for her but for everything that hadn't worked out between us. But then for her too. I had no idea what was going on in her life but whatever it was, it wasn't good.

"Yanna, listen," I tried to reason with her.

She visibly tensed up.

"Firstly, please forgive me," I said. "I haven't lived up to your expectations. I behaved like a lazy pig. I had no ambitions. All I could think of was the game."

Her Interest seemed to stir a little. I didn't need an internal interface to know that. You can't just live with somebody for several years without learning to pick up on their vibes. Before we'd begun to draw apart, we used to be as one.

"No, I'll never forgive you," she said. "But carry on."

"Secondly, I'm very sorry we have to part ways like this. There were many good things between us, especially during the first couple of years. Remember how cool it was? Do you remember our nights on the balcony when we'd open a bottle of wine with a knife and fork until we finally bought that stupid bottle opener? Remember?"

"Oh, give me a break," she said, unable to conceal a smile. "What kind of family man were you if you couldn't even afford a bottle opener?"

"At least I was one hell of a rogue, no? Do you remember how we used to shine in the arena? We were *the* gladiators! Remember how we screamed and yelled when we finally got a title?"

Her drawn face softened.

"Remember our first kiss?" I said. "You winked at me at our first clan meeting. And then you allowed me to take you to my place."

"I was so stupid! You used your high position in the clan to seduce a gullible young girl!"

"And remember when we had nowhere to go so we went to your place for the night?" I said. "That was when we'd already started talking about the wedding. And your mom walked in on us in a particularly inopportune moment. Remember?"

"I remember everything better than you do if you absolutely need to know!" she snapped. "We had some good moments, you're right. But what next? Don't you understand you're going downhill? At least you've finally found someone to employ you. At thirty years old, you're still like a child. All you can think about is eating, sleeping and playing your wretched games! You have no ambitions whatsoever. For you, life is one big joke."

"I understand you very well," I said. "And that's the third thing I wanted to tell you. I know where you're coming from. I don't hold any grudges. I suggest we stay friends. Or at least buddies. If one day you need my help, I promise I'll be there for you. You only have to say the word."

I decided not to tell her about any of my recent

achievements. It might have looked like empty bragging in an attempt to fix things. Especially because my so-called achievements weren't so much to brag about, really. All I'd done is managed to attain the levels of an average human being, and even that with the help of the mysterious program.

Yanna's large eyes welled with tears. She stepped toward me and clumsily tried to give me a hug but stopped and proffered her hand.

Ignoring her handshake, I scooped her up and pulled her toward me. "Everything's gonna be all right. Don't cry. Things will work themselves out."

We just stood there, locked in an embrace.

The office door opened, letting out a woman with a child. The female voice called,

"Next, please!"

Reluctantly Yanna eased herself away from me and wiped her tears. She hooked her arm through mine and led me into the office.

Less than an hour later, we left the building as former partners. Even though I'd been expecting this to happen, my heart still hung heavy, no matter how hard I'd been trying to assure myself and all the others that I didn't love my ex-wife anymore.

"Bye," Yanna dropped, hurrying to Vlad's Jeep.

"Good luck, girl," I whispered.

My logs opened on the Divorce task, updating it:

Task Status: meet up with Yanna and file for divorce
Task completed!

XP received: 500 pt.
+15% to Satisfaction

I paused, waiting for the bout of Satisfaction to subside, then went to Ultrapak. I wanted to end my last day with them on a really good note. I spent all afternoon visiting new clients and selling their products until I'd worked my way through my entire list. In total, I'd closed seven contracts that week not counting the unfinished one which I handed over to Marina as soon as I got back to the office.

Pavel was out. As I waited for him, I shot the breeze with Cyril, Greg and Marina, promising them to stay in touch and take part in Cyril's birthday party soon.

Then I remembered my resolution to write for at least half an hour every day. I appropriated Cyril's laptop, opened a new Word document and jotted down a quick vignette, filling a couple of pages with my thoughts on marriage and divorce. I saved what I'd written and paused thinking whether I had something else to add to the subject. I didn't, so I published it in my blog. After a few minutes, comments and likes started flooding in.

Just then, Pavel entered the office. I deleted my work and closed the laptop.

He listened to my report. He must have already scratched me off his list of workmates because he was quite curt when he wished me good luck and sent me to the bookkeepers for my dues.

They paid me almost 300,000 rubles[35] for the days I'd worked, including bonuses. That should have been more than enough to last me a while. Now I could afford another month of boxing training, pay the rest of my rent for the first trimester, buy a new laptop and still have enough money to live for a month or two. I'd already given some thought to what I was going to do later. Whatever it was, it wasn't worth worrying about. As long as I had my health, I'd find some way to make money.

Having finished with that, I checked on Vickie but she was still sick.

So stupid of me! Old habits die hard. I could have simply checked her position on the map.

I bade my last farewells to my friends. Marina didn't even try to conceal her sorrow. She urged me to call her whenever I felt like it. I then said good-bye to all the others, paid my respects to Daria — our Instagram-inspired receptionist — and left the building to see my old friends.

I popped into the bank on my way and put the money on my account. It would have been stupid to arrive at a potential drunken party with so much cash in my pocket. I only kept a few notes as well as the twenty grand I owed to my old friend Gleb.

The bar was busy and loud as it always was on a Friday night. Gleb was already sitting at the table I'd reserved, drinking a dark unfiltered beer.

He looked depressed. His hair was disheveled, his clothes unkempt. He'd never been a sharp dresser

---

[35] 300,000 rubles is about $5,000 at the time of writing

but he'd always taken good care of himself. His hair had always been slickly parted. Judging by his stats, his Mood left a lot to be desired. Even the bar's inadequate lighting couldn't conceal the gray strands in his hair. His temples were completely white.

"Gleb!" I said, approaching him. "It's been a while!"

"Phil! Great to see you, man!" he gave me a bear hug.

His joy seemed sincere. No amount of game playing could replace real-life contact. Physical hugs seemed to charge you up with something warm and positive. Because we're social animals. We need it.

For a while, we maintained a rather formal conversation, asking each other about the usual aspects of our lives: families, children, etc. etc.

We'd been friends since junior high. That was when he'd first appeared at our school. He'd been rather average in everything. A B-student with no particular talents, he wasn't funny or popular, neither a nerd nor a hooligan. Still, at the time he'd given me the impression of being solid and reliable. It just so happened that we shared a desk[36]. Then we went to the same college. Our friendship continued — right until the moment I'd let him down.

"Oh, I nearly forgot," I said. "Here you are."

I laid the money on the table in front of him. "This includes all the inflation and late payment

---

[36] In Russian schools, all the desks are double which seat two students.

charges."

Grinding his teeth, he stared at the money without touching it. "Too late," he whispered. "Way too late. I needed it for my mother's surgery. Don't you understand? We sold everything! Everything we had, you understand? We scraped together just enough to take her to Israel for treatment. She needed a bone marrow transplant. We found a matched donor for her. That was incredibly lucky. She had a very rare blood group."

"I'm so sorry... I didn't know. Why didn't you say?"

"I didn't want any fake sympathy. From you or anyone else. That money wouldn't have saved her, anyway. It was peanuts compared to the bill we got from the clinic. It was just that everything seemed to happen at the same time. I was so desperate for that money and you just took it and blew it in that wretched casino. I didn't want to give it to you, you remember that, don't you? A year later, our father left us. My brother got married and fled the nest. And I..."

He was getting drunk before my very eyes. No idea how much he'd already drunk before I'd arrived but his speech was already slurred. Finally, he spilled some beer over the money and took it. He blotted the notes with a napkin and put them neatly away in his tattered old wallet.

Task Status: Pay my casino debt back to my friend Gleb Kolosov
Task completed!

XP received: 500 pt.
+10% to Satisfaction

After an hour, I realized it was time for me to call it a day. Gleb was already drunk as a skunk.

Much to my disappointment, nobody else had turned up. Not even Sergei Rezvei, one of my best friends who'd agreed to see me without ado. That was so not like him. Still, the program had closed the task and even rewarded me with some XP. I had 630 pt. until my next level.

I put Gleb in a taxi. First I tried to get his address out of him, intending to send him off alone. Then I realized it wasn't such a good idea. He was drunk and he had money on him.

So I jumped in the taxi with him and took him home myself. It took me quite some effort to haul him up to the fifth floor where I handed him over to his wife: grim, plain and old before her time. I told her I was happy to meet her and explained that Gleb and I were school friends.

I really should meet up with him again sometime and find out what his problems were.

The next morning I pumped myself full with energy drinks and had a double gym session. My boxing coach handed me a pair of gloves and made me punch the bag, encouraging me with his constant "That's good! Good! Again! Faster! Harder! Harder! Faster!" which sounded almost like the soundtrack from an adult movie. Having finished with him, I headed for the weights room.

I didn't need a coach there. I'd already jotted down a workout schedule and marked down the weights I'd planned to use. And seeing as I had nowhere to hurry to, I spent another half-hour on the treadmill.

Totally spent, I basked under a hot and cold shower for a while, got dressed, had a protein shake and walked home.

I gave my sister a ring to find out when we were going to see our parents. She was all hyped up as usual. She started by threatening me with a gastronomical apocalypse, then told me to buy some fruit and a cream cake. By the end of our conversation, she was already doubting my ability to choose the right cake or fruit so she just told me she'd buy everything herself. All I had to do was turn up on time on my own accord because she "had better things to do than driving every young dickhead around town".

Already when I was approaching my house, I got a funny feeling I'd missed something. I turned around and saw a familiar figure sitting on the bench. How the hell?

"Mr. Panikoff?" I called to my first quest giver in disbelief.

"That's me!" the old man grinned. "Phil, if I remember rightly?"

"Exactly! May I ask you what brings you here?"

"I live here. We moved not long ago. Everything's all right with you? You look tired."

"That's because I've just been training. If the truth were known, I can barely move. Does that mean we're neighbors now?"

"It certainly looks that way," he feigned surprise. "Oh well. It's been nice to see you again."

"Likewise," I said.

"Oh, and by the way," his voice changed ever so slightly. He stopped lisping. His words had a metallic ring to them. "You don't think you spend too much time helping your new friends, do you? All those Aliks, Fatsoes and Glebs? They're the true dregs of society. When are you going to start leveling up properly, may I ask? Or are you waiting for Khphor to come whistling round the mountain?"

He must have verbally critted me because his words had a shocking effect on me. I was floored. Flabbergasted even. It felt as if he'd whacked me with a baseball bat.

"Answer my question!" he demanded.

"How do you know?" my voice failed me.

"*We*," he stressed the word, "we know everything about you. So just answer the question. What's you current Insight level?"

"Two."

"So Valiadis was right about you, then. You still have the program. Shame. Very well. Now I know everything I need to know. You can go now."

"So what's gonna happen next?"

"In what respect?" he asked me.

"With me and with the program."

"Sorry, I don't understand what you're talking about," the old man replied in the his old shaky and lispy voice. "You sure you all right? You look worn out."

"I'm fine," I said. "Thanks for asking."

He picked up the newspaper which was lying in his lap, opened it and began reading, shielding himself with it.

For a while, I stood next to him studying his stats. There was nothing unusual about them. He was still the same 83-year-old pensioner with a social level of 27.

"Mr. Panikoff," I made another attempt.

He put his paper down. "Yes, Phil? What is it?"

"What number apartment are you at? Seeing as we're neighbors now..."

"Oh yes, of course! At number thirty-seven. Please drop in sometime."

"With pleasure," I said, heading for the door.

Back home, I finished reading yet another book. I still had about an hour left until meeting with my parents.

That's when I made another decision.

It had nothing to do with Valiadis or my leveling, not even with the weird Mr. Panikoff, my dear old-age pensioner. You didn't find this type of task in the logs. There was no quest in the world which could issue it.

That was something I desired with all my heart.

I looked at the map. She was at home. I left the house and went to see her.

I had to ring the bell several times before the door finally opened.

Vicky stood in the doorway wrapped in a towel. Her wet hair hung loose. A drop of water made its way down her face.

She stared at me in surprise. Without saying a word, she let me in. I shut the door and took a long look at her. And she, at me. She appeared so vulnerable — young even — that my heart clenched.

"My daughter is with my parents again," she finally broke the silence. "Hi."

"Hi," I replied, forcing the sounds out of my dry throat. "And I'm about to go and see my own parents now. Would you like to come with me?"

"Actually, I would."

END OF BOOK ONE

Want to be the first to know about our latest LitRPG, sci fi and fantasy titles from your favorite authors?

Subscribe to our NEW RELEASES newsletter:
http://eepurl.com/b7niIL

Thank you for reading *Level Up!*
If you like what you've read, check out other LitRPG novels
published by Magic Dome Books:

Level Up LitRPG series by Dan Sugralinov:
Re-Start
Hero
The Final Trial
Level Up: The Knockout (with Max Lagno)
Level Up. The Knockout: Update (with Max Lagno)

Disgardium LitRPG series by Dan Sugralinov:
Class-A Threat
Apostle of the Sleeping Gods
The Destroying Plague

World 99 LitRPG Series by Dan Sugralinov:
Blood of Fate

Adam Online LitRPG Leries by Max Lagno:
Absolute Zero
City of Freedom

Reality Benders LitRPG series by Michael Atamanov:
Countdown
External Threat
Game Changer
Web of Worlds
A Jump into the Unknown

**The Dark Herbalist LitRPG series
by Michael Atamanov:**
Video Game Plotline Tester
Stay on the Wing
A Trap for the Potentate
Finding a Body

Perimeter Defense LitRPG series by Michael Atamanov:
Sector Eight
Beyond Death
New Contract
A Game with No Rules

Point Apocalypse *(a near-future action thriller)*
by Alex Bobl

Captive of the Shadows *(The Fairy Code Book #1)*
by Kaitlyn Weiss

The Game Master **series by A. Bobl and A. Levitsky:**
The Lag

You're in Game!
(LitRPG Stories from Bestselling Authors)

You're in Game-2!
(More LitRPG stories set in your favorite worlds)

Moskau **by G. Zotov**
(a dystopian thriller)

El Diablo **by G.Zotov**
(a supernatural thriller)

More books and series are coming out soon!

In order to have new books of the series translated faster, we need your help and support! Please consider leaving a review or spread the word by recommending *Level Up* to your friends and posting the link on social media. The more people buy the book, the sooner we'll be able to make new translations available.

Thank you!

Till next time!